P9-DNY-458

Twilight

Also by Nancy Pickard

Generous Death
Say No to Murder
No Body
Marriage Is Murder
Dead Crazy
Bum Steer
I.O.U.
But I Wouldn't Want to Die There
Confession

Published by POCKET BOOKS

NANCY PICKARD

Twilight

A JENNY CAIN MYSTERY

POCKET BOOKS
New York London Toronto Sydney Tokyo Singapore

This book is a work of fiction. Names, characters, places and incidents are products of the author's imagination or are used fictitiously. Any resemblance to actual events or locales or persons, living or dead, is entirely coincidental.

POCKET BOOKS, a division of Simon & Schuster Inc.
1230 Avenue of the Americas, New York, NY 10020

Copyright © 1995 by Nancy J. Pickard Trust

All rights reserved, including the right to reproduce this book or portions thereof in any form whatsoever. For information address Pocket Books, 1230 Avenue of the Americas, New York, NY 10020

ISBN: 0-671-78271-1 (hc)

POCKET and colophon are registered trademarks of Simon & Schuster Inc.

Printed in the U.S.A.

Dedicated to my Friday friends,
without whom no week is complete:
Janice, Randy, Sally, Kevin, and Fran.

I offer heartfelt thanks to Cuky Choquette Harvey, who dreamed one night of Jenny Cain, a fortune-teller, a fair, and a theft, and who generously gave her dream to me.

I am indebted to the following books and their authors for information and inspiration: *The Woman's Encyclopedia of Myths and Secrets* by Barbara G. Walker; *The I Ching* in the Richard Wilhelm translation rendered into English by Cary F. Baynes; *A Guide to the I Ching* and *The Philosophy of the I Ching* by Carol K. Anthony; *The Book of Runes* by Ralph H. Blum; *First Steps in Starting a Foundation* by John A. Eadie; and *The Festival Hopper's Guide to New England* by Darrin and Julie Craig.

There really is an old-fashioned "Dime Store" in my hometown. Its wonderful atmosphere and its hilly old wooden floor inspired its namesake in this novel. All of the characters and events I have created are imaginary, however. "God's Highway" follows its haunted path only in my fantasies.

As always, there would be no book without the perception, patience, and skill of my editor in shining armor, Linda Marrow, and my friend and agent, Meredith Bernstein.

Prologue

There was a strange night last winter when my husband and I were coming home from a party at the other edge of town. Geof was driving the Jeep, his car. I was beside him, in the passenger seat. We were both awake, we were sober, but it seemed for a moment like a dream or a hallucination, all the same.

It was after midnight, closer to one o'clock.

We weren't talking, and the radio wasn't on, but it wasn't exactly quiet in the car. There was engine noise, and the blast of the heater—it was hovering around freezing outside—and the moan of the tires over the pavement. I guess there may have been a whining of the wind, too, but I don't think I was consciously aware of it. There wasn't time to notice it, or to label it: "wind." It's only there in my memory, or my imagination. I do vaguely remember the sound of something slapping rhythmically against the car body, maybe one of the mud flaps.

My ankles were cold, I recall that, for sure.

And I was tasting onion, from a potato chip dip at the party. It's funny, really, how the taste of onion dip and the memory of cold ankles are the sensory cement that glue together my memory fragments of that uncanny night.

I recall that Geof had his gloves off, both big hands on the wheel, his handsome forty-year-old face looking relaxed, but tired. He is a cop, a lieutenant in the Port Frederick, Massachusetts, police department, who gets periodically and thoroughly sick of people. Although he has a gregarious nature, it was unusual for him to agree to go out with friends on a weekend night when the truth was that he'd rather be home watching a movie with me.

I was leaning my head back against the seat, staring out of the windshield at the yellow lines in our headlights. Every now and then I glanced at my husband, feeling a warm and quiet pleasure in his company. I was deeply aware of how much more safe and secure I felt traveling down the highway with him at one o'clock in the morning than I would have felt by myself. And I was thinking that it was good of him to have gone with me to the party—I would not have insisted; we are enormously close, but we are not clones, after all. I could have respected his desire to burrow in at home, and I would still have had fun at the party, on my own. But I didn't have to. And so, I found myself savoring the delicious feeling of being encapsulated in a cozy, moving island with him as we traveled toward home.

Suddenly, I sat up and looked back down the highway.

"Was that *snow* on that truck?"

"What, Jenny?"

That's all I had time to say—and he to respond—when it hit.

Wham. Snow dumped on us from above, as if the gods had suddenly opened their fists. Big, gloppy flakes immediately pasted themselves to our windshield. Our headlights were full of swirling white. The air, the highway, the sides of the road, the sky—everything changed color. One minute, there was black sky above us; the next minute, there was blowing white. When I turned around in the passenger seat of our Jeep, I was amazed that I could still see dry black pavement and brown grass at the sides of the highway behind us. And then even that vision of safety was gone, and we were in the middle of an honest-to-God, slick and dangerous snowstorm.

"Damn it!" was my husband's response.

He shifted to a lower, slower gear, cautiously using the clutch, avoiding the brakes. Then he switched on the windshield wipers. I fiddled with the defroster in an attempt to blow more hot air on the windshield, which was rapidly crusting over. We were in the Jeep, so I wasn't really worried, but I didn't like it, either. Suddenly, I wanted nothing more than to be *home.*

And then again, just like that, things got worse.

A lot of red brake lights up ahead warned us to slow . . . slow . . . slow . . . until we found ourselves stopped dead in the right-hand, westbound lane of the highway. Suddenly there was nobody going the other way. And there were cars cautiously forming a line behind us.

Geof released a string of expletives.

"I don't fucking *believe* this."

I knew what was coming next.

There was a police-band radio and even a cellular telephone in the Jeep, so he could have turned to either of those to find out what was going on up the road ahead of us—an accident, probably—but I knew he wouldn't settle for that. He'd have to get out of the Jeep. Walk down the side of the road, until he disappeared from my view in the snow, and satisfy himself with a firsthand view of the situation. He'd want to find out if they needed help, a hand from a fellow cop, a little traffic control . . . or worse . . . picking up bodies, helping paramedics, taking names.

He started pulling on his gloves.

"What do you want me to do?" I asked him.

He looked around, through the windows at the swirling white, as if seeking an answer for my question. There was a red stop sign at an intersection about ten yards ahead of us, and we could just barely make out the end of a gravel driveway a few feet beyond the sign. Past the driveway, all was black and white, because the highway dropped off down a hill, and then rounded a bend that straightened out onto a little bridge.

"When the traffic starts to move again," Geof said to me, "why don't you pull into that driveway and wait for me, Jenny? Don't come looking for me, because there may not be any safe place for you to stop the car down there. I'll walk back and find you." He glanced at me for assent. "All right?"

"Yes."

Always prepared, Geof had heavy black rubber boots in the back, which he located and began to pull over his good brown loafers. From the floor behind us, he also pulled out a ski mask that covered everything but his eyes and his mouth, and he put a battered old winter cap on over that. He'd worn a long, stylish black overcoat to the party, so that was sufficient to keep the rest of him protected. When he was fully ready, he opened his door, letting a whirl of cold air and snow into the car.

"You know where we are?" he asked me.

He appeared weird and sinister in his stocking cap—which was navy blue with knitted red circles around the holes for his eyes and mouth—and slightly ridiculous, when I considered the whole ensemble.

I nodded. "Crowley Creek's just over the hill down there," I said. "You know who lives at the end of that driveway, Geof. It's the Kennedys, Ardyth's folks, the people who own the Dime Store." He and I both had gone through the Port Frederick, Mass., public schools with their daughter, though I knew her better, since she and I were the same age. Ardyth Kennedy and I had never been friends, exactly, but at least her parents would recognize me, if I had to ring their bell, seeking refuge. "If I start to freeze to death, I'll go knock on their door."

He leaned over to kiss me through the red hole for his mouth, so that I felt as if I were being kissed by four lips. Then he was gone, a large black shadow bent into the wind at the right side of the road, quickly disappearing from my view.

It took forty minutes for the traffic to begin to move again.

And still, I didn't know what had actually halted us. I could have turned on the police radio, or placed a phone call and found out. I still don't know why I didn't do either of those logical and natural things, but I didn't. I simply sat alone in the silent car and passively waited to find out. Maybe I didn't want to hear the sense of crackling urgency that would have pelted me from the radio, not while I knew that my husband was down there.

I just wanted to wait, calmly. And then to see him.

When the car ahead of me inched forward, I did, too. I merely paused at the stop sign, however, because I didn't want to take the chance of sliding or stalling. Then I cautiously turned into the gravel driveway, bumping over a stripped Christmas tree that lay across it. I assumed that the Kennedys had put it out for the trash men to pick up the next day. This was only ten days past Christmas, mind you, only four days—or nights—into January.

I pulled out of the way of the traffic and turned off the engine.

After another ten minutes passed and Geof still didn't reappear, I decided that the Kennedy's house looked warm and cozy and well-lighted at the end of the drive, and that maybe Nellie and Bill Kennedy might provide a cup of coffee for a weary traveler.

And that's where Geof found me a half hour later.

I was holding a cup of hot cider in my hands, while Nellie anxiously paced her kitchen, stopping frequently to pull back her curtains and stare into the storm, both of us wondering what had happened . . . and if anybody was hurt or killed . . . and whether we knew any of them. Bill was asleep upstairs, but Nellie had been awakened by the terrible sound of vehicles crashing together, she told me. It was she who'd called 911.

"Three-car pileup," Geof told us, as he stamped his boots on Nellie's welcome mat. "And a pickup truck. Two people pretty seriously injured, the others banged up, but nobody's dead. They got off lucky. One of those damn fools ran the stop sign and skidded down the hill into the other lane and hit the pickup truck, and then everybody else piled into them. It was a damned mess. Thank you, Mrs. Kennedy."

She was coming toward him with a cup of cider.

It had involved nobody that any of us knew.

"I'm so relieved," Nellie said.

We left her kitchen a half hour later—when it was nearly three o'clock in the morning—and made it safely home an hour after that. The next day, when we found out that one of the accident victims had died, we took it kind of personally, having been there. But then it was over, apparently, and that was all there was to it.

Except that things connect—winter snow, spring rains, autumn leaves—in ways we never suspect and nature never intended. And now I think that it may have been some unconscious connection with me . . . and that night . . . that caused Nellie Kennedy to break down in front of me, ten forgetful months later. After that—after Nellie cried—it seemed as if *everything* started to crash together, like vehicles sliding horribly out of control on a slick highway . . .

1

TEN MONTHS LATER, THE MONTH WAS OCTOBER.

This time, Nellie and I were holding cups of hot coffee, not cider, and we were seated in her office at the back of the Dime Store, not in the kitchen in her home. And this time, it was all business for *me,* instead of for my husband.

My business is foundations, not the undergarments, but the charitable kind, like the Ford Foundation or the Carnegie, only smaller. At the time of this meeting with Nellie Kennedy on a cool Thursday morning in October, my history was that I had been employed for years as the director of the old-line foundation in town, the Port Frederick Civic Foundation, but I'd left them a couple of years before, in order to "explore my options." One of those options turned out to be starting my own foundation, with the passionate help of some of my best friends.

Because of that, something wonderfully serendipitous had evolved between Nellie Kennedy and me after that strange, sad, and snowy night in January. She and I had made a connection that night that was turning out to serve both of us profitably and well. To me, she was no longer Mrs. Kennedy who lived out near Crowley Creek, nor was she merely the mother of a girl I'd gone to school with, or even just the owner of a locally famous emporium.

She was "Nellie" now, instead of "Mrs. Kennedy."

"Nellie, I owe you," I said to her, that day, ten months later, without the slightest idea of what was about to come barreling down on me. I only knew it was a beautiful morning, and I liked and respected this woman enormously, and I was happy to be in her company. Smiling, half teasing, I added, "I won't go so far as to say that anything I have is yours . . ."

The tense, tired face of the plump woman seated beside me relaxed slightly into a faint smile.

". . . but I will say—no, I will swear it, vow it, pledge it—that if there's anything I can do for you, any favor, all you ever have to do is ask."

Nellie Kennedy stared at me for a moment, absorbing my heartfelt promise. Then, suddenly, this woman who had only previously touched me to shake my hand to close a sale, grabbed my wrist. At fifty-six she was nearly twenty years older than me, but her grip was as strong as a farmhand's.

"Do you mean that, Jenny? Because there is somebody you could help, as a favor to me."

She stared intensely into my face, her deep, intelligent, Irish-green eyes compelling my attention, my assent.

Lord! I'd fully meant my pledge of indebtedness. In the last few months this woman had saved my bacon more times than if I were a pig at a slaughterhouse. She'd saved me thousands of dollars, she'd saved me time. As the director of my own private foundation, I was also in charge of the first annual Port Frederick Autumn Festival, which we were sponsoring. For her part, Nellie was the owner of the one store in town that would let me order vast quantities of supplies at nearly wholesale. Without Nellie Kennedy and the Dime Store, ten days from now we might be raking leaves on the town common instead of hosting a spectacular festival there. *That* was the connection we'd made that night in her kitchen over cider: I'd buy thousands of dollars' worth of supplies from her; she'd cut me the best deals.

Nellie had more than kept her end of our ten-month bargain.

And now, I would honor my I.O.U. to her, any way, any time—which looked like it would be . . . right now.

I just hadn't anticipated such a dramatic response on her part, not from this brisk and efficient woman who wasn't ordinarily given to emotional outbursts. To tell the truth, neither had I expected Nellie to cash in my I.O.U. quite so soon! But I placed my free hand over my heart and smiled as I pledged her my mock-solemn troth:

"Whatever it is, by God, I'll do it."

"Oh, Jenny." Her hand relaxed and slipped away from mine as if she were embarrassed to have gotten so personal as to touch me. She really was quite a businesslike person, pleasantly brisk and even rather formal at times. But her eyes filled with apparent tears, and I was startled to see her lips briefly tremble. What floodgates had I breached here with my easy gift of gratitude? She said, "There's a young woman that I want you to help. Melissa Barney. Do you know her?"

"I don't think so."

"You recognize her name though, don't you? It was in the paper last month when her husband died. Benjamin Barney. Do you remember now?"

I squinted, thinking.

"Kind of, yes, but tell me about it."

"He got killed on God's Highway, out by our house. At the crossing where the hiking path intersects with the road. A woman ran the stop sign at the top of the hill by our house, and she struck him and killed him. He left Melissa and their two little boys."

"Oh . . . ," I said, regretfully remembering. "That was so sad."

By "God's Highway" she meant a famous bicycle and hiking trail that wound over hill and dale through several Massachusetts counties on its popular way from Boston to the sea. It was actually right where our winter traffic pileup had occurred, though of course there hadn't been anybody walking on the trail at the time, not at one o'clock in the morning in a snowstorm. The trail hadn't had anything to do with it. But I knew of the nature trail, better and more personally, I suspected, than most people did. The foundation I had worked for, the Port Frederick Civic Foundation, had funded the local stretch of that controversial project ten years before.

Oh, yes, although I didn't say so to Nellie, I knew God's Highway very well.

Just a reference to it a whole decade later could still send an uneasy quiver snaking through my gut, and it was even now inspiring tears from Nellie.

It was oddly shocking to see those tears streak her makeup.

I wouldn't have expected tears, not from Nellie.

Never *over*-made up, she was nevertheless always powdered whenever I saw her. A buxom, top-heavy woman, she had a preference for dark dresses with shoulder pads and loose waists and for neat, wide-heeled pumps in dark colors; her beautician-blackened hair always looked curled, waved, and sprayed into permanent place. Nellie Kennedy was attractive in a dated sort of way that perfectly suited her personality and her life. In her appearance on this particular morning, it was only her tears that looked out of place.

"Melissa says it wasn't an accident," Nellie said, to my surprise. "Melissa says it was murder," she told me, intensely emotional, her mouth quivering on the last word.

"Murder?"

I frowned over the word.

When you're married to a cop, it's not a word you're inclined to take lightly, or to use indiscriminately. It has definite and precise legal meaning, and I couldn't see how that applied here.

"Well, vehicular homicide, I guess she means," Nellie amended, "or something like that, but it seems like murder to her. She feels like Ben got murdered by this criminally negligent woman." With visible effort, Nellie continued. "Melissa says that woman was homicidally careless, that she ran our stop sign, and she was speeding down the hill when she hit poor Ben. And that was no accident, Melissa says, because accidents imply innocence, and she says that woman is guilty as sin, because of how she killed Ben."

And then she surprised me again.

"I was there, Jenny."

I felt a welling feeling of sympathy, not only for the victim and his family, but for Nellie, as well.

"It was on a Sunday, and I was home starting supper, and I heard the brakes squealing, and then I heard a crash, and I went running down the hill, and I saw it all. I'm the one who called 911."

"Poor Nellie!" I exclaimed, and I reached out to pat her hands. "Not again!"

"Again?" Amidst her tears, she looked startled.

"You called them the night we were there. You know . . ."

"Oh." Her lips trembled, as she remembered that night, too. "Yes, it was like that. Only this time, when Ben got hit, I ran down with a blanket from our living room, and I covered him with it, and I held his hands while we waited for the ambulance and the police. I just couldn't leave him! And that woman, the driver who hit him, she was too hysterical to be of any help to anybody. I made them let me ride with him in the ambulance, and I was in the emergency room when his wife came in—Melissa—and I sat with her while they operated on him. He had terrible injuries. And I was with her when the doctor came in and said Ben had died."

"Nellie, how awful."

She looked down at her manicured hands, the short fingernails painted with clear polish. "You can get to know people awfully well at a time like that."

"I'd imagine so," I said softly.

"I went to Ben's funeral. I met the children. I stayed in touch."

Nellie looked up at me, her eyes dark and wet.

I'd had not a hint of this tale from her at any time before this. If she had been upset, around that time, she hadn't let it show at work. But then, one thing I'd learned about Nellie Kennedy while I was her customer at the Dime Store was that her family and their business—which supported her and her husband, Bill, and probably still contributed to the upkeep of their only child—came before any other personal considerations. If I hadn't ambushed her with my offer of a favor, Nellie might never have broken stride to tell me her story of being thrown shockingly among strangers in the hours of their most desperate need.

"Did you know these people, the Barneys, before, Nellie?"

"No, no, but now I know Melissa as well as I know my own daughter, and I know she needs help, Jenny."

"Okay," I encouraged her, "hit me with it."

Here it came, my word made deed.

"She's frantic to do something to keep anybody else from ever being injured or killed at that trail crossing," Nellie told me. "There was that other death, too, you know—"

The traffic fatality, I supposed she meant, but that was due to the road conditions, not to the trail . . .

"But she doesn't know how to do it." The words were spilling out of Nellie. "And I don't know how to advise her. It would help so much if you would talk to her. She needs to accomplish this one thing so that she won't have to feel that Ben's death was entirely in vain." Nellie's face, never particularly expressive until now, pleaded with me. "Will you?"

"See her? Talk to her? Of course."

"May I have her call you?"

"Anytime. I don't know what I can do—"

"But you'll try," she commanded me.

"Yes."

Nellie grabbed a tissue from a box on top of her desk and blew her nose. "You can listen to her, Jenny, you're good at listening. Help her figure out a plan. If she needs money, your foundation can give it to her. You know everybody in town—you can direct her to the right people. You're like me, you're used to running things. She's an artist, a sculptor, she doesn't know anything about being in charge of anything but kids. You can get her organized, so she feels as if she's *doing* something. It'll make her feel better, at least."

A little grief therapy?

But Nellie! I run a foundation, I'm not a psychologist!

I didn't say it. I'd plunked myself into this, and I owed her. I would gladly pay her back in the denomination of her choice. Who knew? Maybe I'd dig a worthwhile project out of this situation, maybe there'd be some way for me—or for my brand-new private foundation—to help out. We were scouting for causes to fund, people to assist. This might turn out to be such a case. I tried to cheer myself with that idea, but it didn't alleviate my uneasy feeling about Nellie's request. A grieving widow. A dead husband. Two fatherless kids. A sympathetic friend who wanted to help the family. Those were the emotional ingredients of a heart-tugging story in *People* magazine. They were not necessarily the ingredients of any problem that my foundation could solve, and they sounded altogether like people I could too easily disappoint.

I didn't want to disappoint Nellie Kennedy.

"I wouldn't be able to stand for something like this to happen again," Nellie said, in a near whisper. Her voice broke, and she began to cry again. "I just wouldn't be able to bear it. Not again."

I was surprised by the strength of her reaction.

But then, I thought, it must have been terribly traumatic for her, the trip to the hospital with the dying man in the ambulance, and all that came after. I would have guessed that Nellie Kennedy could handle nearly any situation coolly, but even she, it appeared, could be strained beyond endurance. In a way, that fact made it easier for me to accede to her plea; I'd be happy to do this little thing, for her sake.

I decided not even to think about the aphorism: *No good deed goes unpunished.* This was Nellie. And I'd volunteered my promise, she hadn't wrested it out of me. And the decision was made. Done deal. Period.

As she worked at getting her emotions back under control, I sat in sympathetic, respectful silence and gazed beyond her to the commercial bustle out on the sales floor of the Dime Store.

I loved coming here, most everybody in Port Frederick did.

It was a wonderful old-fashioned emporium, nearly an institution. The Kennedy family—although a good Irish bunch by way of Boston, they weren't related to *those* Kennedys—maintained the original wooden floors, now grooved and smooth from generations of Port Frederick feet. The floors actually rose and dipped, like hills, so that walking on them was like taking a little hike indoors. The Kennedys had also saved the high wooden shelves that cast the narrow aisles into nineteenth-century shadows, and the vast wooden sales counter against a side wall. Just about the only blatant concessions to this century were the lights overhead, the plateglass windows in front, and the computerized cash registers. And some of the merchandise, of course, which ranged from sewing machine bobbins to artificial flowers.

On this day, ten days before Halloween, it was a black and orange world in the Dime Store. Ghosts and goblins hung cheek by jowl with jack-o'-lanterns, and the candy bins had to be refilled nearly every day with licorice whips and candy corn, Gummy Bears and jawbreakers.

The other proprietor of the Dime Store, Nellie's husband, Bill, shuffled into the doorway of her office where we sat in back, filling it with his tall, raw-boned New England frame. If he noticed the evidence of his wife's dismay, the big, quiet man didn't say so in my presence.

"Hello," was his greeting to both of us.

"Bill, you know Jenny Cain," his wife said.

"Well, of course I know her."

As well he should, seeing as how I'd been a regular, buying customer for many weeks. Nellie was my business agent, though, not Bill.

To me, he said, "Getting your Christmas shopping done?"

It was a familiar jest. Every time, Bill Kennedy asked me that, with such an earnest expression on his long face that you'd hardly have known he was fooling. By now, the joke was tiresome to me.

"Just about," I said.

"What are you doing, Bill?" Nellie demanded of him, her voice so sharp that I felt embarrassed to be there. This often happened, and I never liked it, though it didn't appear to faze Bill much. Maybe that's why she did it, I sometimes thought, to provoke a response from him after all their years of marriage. Bill was about Nellie's age, fifty-six or fifty-seven. Looking at him, I could still see the high school basketball player he used to be. There was a hoop affixed high on the back wall of Nellie's office; Bill was always standing in the doorway and tossing things at it. And missing. The floor beneath the hoop was often a littered mess, which he left for Nellie, or their cleaning crew, to pick up. This morning, it was an orange nylon jacket that he held in his big hands.

He bunched the fabric into a loose ball.

With a high overhand, he tossed it at the hoop.

"Bill! What are you thinking!"

The jacket touched the rim, then fell in a heap.

He looked puzzled, as if he couldn't understand why he'd missed.

"I'm ready to go home when you are," he said, looking at his wife hopefully. It was another one of Bill's little witticisms; no matter how early the hour, he was always "ready to go home."

"Home!" Nellie's response was an indignant snort of sarcasm. She might not manage to poke him into fighting back, but he was adept, though it seemed unintentionally so, at provoking her. "I'll be ready for that in about twelve hours, Bill!"

It was 10:30 on Thursday morning.

A frosty, crisp October morning, of the sort that always made me feel electrically alive the moment I awoke. Looking at Bill Kennedy's shambling form, I wondered if he'd ever felt that way about anything, or anybody. His daughter, maybe. His wife, I hoped. At the very least, basketball?

Ten days from now would dawn, not only Halloween, but also the weekend of the Autumn Festival, created and sponsored by the Judy Foundation, which was founded, directed, and to some extent funded by: me. On that date, less than two weeks hence, the festival, the foundation, and I would either launch ourselves as a civic force to be reckoned with, or we would sink ignominiously in full sight of half of New England. I could only pray those two days in October would be as perfect in weather and temperature as this one.

"Catch the Patriots-Chiefs game, Bill?" I asked him.

Football was about the only actual conversational gambit I ever managed with him, and even that was a stretch, given my sketchy knowledge of the sport.

"Pitiful."

By that he meant the New England Patriots had lost badly the previous Sunday to the Kansas City Chiefs.

Somehow, his responses always sounded like dead ends to me. They didn't give me much more to say in reply than "yup," or "nope," or "sure thing." But I tried. Hauling hard at my fleeting memories of the little bits of the game I had watched, I pulled up the first fish that popped to the surface. "I'm impressed with that new young running back of theirs, that Dawson, aren't you?"

Bill nodded. "It's amazing he can still play the game after all these years."

I blinked in confusion, as I often did with him. *Huh?* I thought Lake Dawson was a young guy, not long out of Notre Dame. Somehow, it just didn't seem worth the effort to pursue the question.

"Sure is," I said, giving up the conversational ball.

"Well, back to the salt mines," Bill announced by way of farewell. It was his usual *adieu.* When he was gone, the office now lightened by the absence of his large frame in the doorway, I avoided looking at Nellie. It was embarrassing, how ineffectual her husband was. Nellie was the business, it appeared to me, and Bill was in the way.

"I don't know how you do it all, Nellie."

I thought I was being tactful, while acknowledging her burdens.

She read perfectly the message underlying my words.

"Bill's fine," she said, using on me the same sharp tone she'd lashed him with. "I'm not good with people, not like Bill is. He's our PR man, he loves the kids, and that makes their mamas happy. Bill's wonderful."

It was a stout defense. I felt ashamed of myself. I'd read the situation all wrong. She loved the big, useless, gentle lout, and I had offended, and I was sorry for that. But I didn't want to make it worse by saying so.

"If he has a fault," Nellie added grudgingly, "it is only that he spoiled our daughter."

Somebody sure did, I thought sourly. This time, however, I safely kept my disparaging thoughts about her family to myself. The offspring herself could be seen through the plateglass windows, even as we spoke of her, which is probably what had inspired Nellie to refer to her at all. It looked to me from where I sat as if Ardyth Kennedy, thirty-seven-year-old town council member and GOP candidate for mayor, was glad-handing the Dime Store customers out there in the innocent autumn air.

Smart Ardyth.

Almost everybody stopped by the Dime Store at one time or another, for most every little thing. And right now, before Halloween, was an especially ripe time for Ardyth to pluck the registered voters from the vine.

Canny Ardyth.

How I dislike her! Every bit as much as I admired her mother. My feelings toward the only Kennedy child went way back to grade school, where her ambitions first sprouted. Or maybe that happened originally in the womb. It wasn't possible to be too cynical about this. President of this, chairman of that, it seemed that Ardyth had always been running for something in Port Frederick. Her only goal ever seemed to be to get elected—never to lead, to change things, or implement ideas. I'd never heard Ardyth voice an actual idea, only opposition to unpopular causes and support for the popular ones. Partly as a result of that, she was a very successful politician.

And now she was pitted in the upcoming November general election against the Democratic incumbent, who just happened to be my good friend Mary Eberhardt. Who also just happened to sit on the board of directors of my new foundation. None of which biased me against Ardyth, of course. No, I was pure in my antipathy toward dear Ardyth; it predated such adult concerns, going straight back to kindergarten.

Clearly, Nellie was not entirely blind to her daughter's character.

"Excuse me, Jenny," she said, getting up. "I'd better get out there. She knows she's not supposed to mix her business with ours. They don't complain, but it offends some of our customers, and it annoys or intimidates a lot of the others." Nellie's voice had a defeated sound that I never heard except in the context of her daughter. "That girl has never listened to anything I say, but she still thinks her dad walks on water. If he'd tell her, she'd stop it."

"Nellie?"

She glanced at me.

I held up her tissue box next to me, and she took the hint.

Her face was a mess from crying, and she wouldn't have thanked me if I had allowed her to go outside looking like that.

While she sat back down to repair herself, I borrowed her telephone.

As I punched in the numbers, I glimpsed myself behind Nellie's reflection in her mirror: pale complexion, thin nose, Swedish-blonde hair currently worn longish and straight, tucked behind my ears, with bangs. I wasn't sure I liked the look, but Geof, my policeman husband, did. He said it gave me a virginal appearance that vastly amused him, the cad. I saw the gleam of one gold ball earring. Two blue eyes looked away from the mirror, as the phone rang a third time at my office.

Then I heard the voice of a festival volunteer.

"The Judy Foundation," she chirruped.

Oh, God, how sweet the sound of that!

"Hi, it's Jenny. I'm running late this morning, so if anybody comes looking for me, would you please tell them I'm on my way?"

"Sure thing, boss."

"Whatcha workin' on?" I asked her.

"The witches' costumes for the tax collectors."

Made perfect sense to me.

Based on attendance figures I had gathered from similar weekend festivals in New England, I had projected a "gate" of anywhere from five thousand to fifteen thousand people over the two days of our big event. It was an estimate that both exhilarated and terrified me. With our Halloween theme, the volunteers selling admittance tickets were to be costumed as witches. This being Massachusetts, we had dubbed them our "tax collectors."

I asked her, trying not to whine: "Does that have to be done there at the office?" Our new headquarters was already packed with festival paraphernalia. As much as possible, I encouraged my precious, beloved volunteer workers to take their projects away with them. But she said they were only holding a design meeting this morning, and they'd do the actual sewing in their homes.

"Bless you," I said to her before hanging up.

I was leaving anyway, so I followed Nellie as she threaded her way through the crowded aisles of her store to the front. Already, she looked defeated—like a general who knows he's going to lose the battle but who feels he has to make the fatal charge anyway.

2

Outside, the mayoral candidate had transferred her attention to a flock of protestors in an empty parking lot across the street where my beloved little white Miata convertible was parked with its top up against the chill. There were three men, seven women, all of them neatly and conservatively dressed—the women in dresses, the men in suits—all of them marching raggedly in a wide circle, and all of them carrying signs protesting the celebration of the pagan ritual of All Hallow's Eve.

Halloween, girls and boys.

They were fundamentalist Christians exercising their rights of free speech, but they were nothing like their more aggressive kin—the anti-abortion pickets. This crew had been around for years, variously protesting at schools and at stores that sold Halloween items. It made sense for them to picket the Dime Store. I had nothing against them; they never accosted anybody, they were always quiet, never yelling or obnoxious, always rather sweetly polite.

This year's crop of protest signs read:

Celebrate Christ, not Satan!
Boycott pagan rites!
Hex on Halloween!

There was also a drawing of an evil-looking jack-o'lantern with an *X* through it, and underneath that, one of those Christian freeform fish symbols that you see on cars a lot. I wondered if any of them knew that the fish was originally a pagan symbol for the vulva. Whenever I saw one on a Volvo, I always thought: Volvos for Vulvas. Perhaps not what the drivers had in mind.

"Mother!"

The klaxon call reached us on the sidewalk.

We watched Ardyth march across the street toward us, dragging two of the male protestors with her. She had hold of the edges of their signs; they had to grip their poles to retain ownership. And thus did she steer her following tugboats into safe harbour in front of us.

In appearance, she was a younger version of her blackhaired, sturdily built mother. They even dressed similarly—big shoulders, simple, draped, waistless dresses, practical pumps. But in demeanor, Ardyth was her mother multiplied by a factor of at least ten. And only her blue eyes proved that Bill had sired her.

"Mother," she began, "I asked you to show more respect to these people! Didn't I say to take the Halloween displays out of the windows? Not everybody thinks it's so innocent, you know. Some very fine people—" Ardyth gestured backward, nearly knocking the wind out of one of the men. Wisely, he stepped back out of her range. "—believe the opposite, and it is their God-given, constitutional right to say so, and it is our democratic obligation to—"

Her stentorious speaker's voice rose, her finger pointed high.

I had always suspected that this might have been what it was like to live with Patrick Henry.

"—invite them peaceably to assemble—"

"Ardyth!" Her mother snapped it firmly, grimly. "May I speak to you a moment in private?"

"Mother, you know I do not support the concept of closed meetings. There is nothing we could possibly say to one another in secret that I would not willingly utter in the presence of these—"

"Ardyth!" Nellie grasped one of her daughter's wrists and jerked the twit toward her. I was struggling to keep from laughing. Ardie was such a shallow pond you could have waded in her without getting your ankles wet. You could see clear to the bottom of her without half trying. Still, she was good for a laugh, so long as she wasn't picking a fight with you. What she wasn't good for was the higher development of my own character; Ardie drew pettiness out of me as if I were base metal and she were the magnet. When Nellie had got her daughter within a few inches of her own face, she whispered so that only the three of us could hear the words: "Dear, most registered voters love Halloween."

Ardyth blinked.

I laughed. Bad move. Never laugh at a politician.

She smiled briefly at her mother and even at me.

Then she turned that smile on the minority voters behind her and said expansively, "My family will always support your right to demonstrate peaceably for the sake of your sincerely held beliefs. When I am elected mayor, I will see that your rights are protected. Do carry on."

Looking relieved and—did I detect it?—amused, the two men nodded at us and started to make their escape, clutching their signposts.

"Wait, wait!" Ardyth commanded.

With every sign of reluctance, they faced us again.

Ardyth's busy forefinger jabbed through the air—at me.

"I'd like you to meet Jenny Cain," she announced. "This is the woman who thought up the idea for the Halloween Festival—"

"Autumn Festival," I corrected her diplomatically.

"Ardyth, please," her mother begged, too weakly to have any effect.

I smiled at the protestors. They stared at me appraisingly. I thought: *If Ardyth Kennedy provokes these people into picketing my festival, I will boil her in oil.*

"Jenny heads that new foundation, the Judy Foundation—what kind of name is that anyway, Jenny?—that's heavy into feminist causes—"

I will grind her eyeballs to powder.

"And she's in charge of the whole shebang. The Halloween Festival was her idea, hers and the mayor's. When our city should be thinking about large and important issues connecting our interests with those of other municipalities—"

That was a favorite political theme of hers: "connections," whatever that meant.

"—our mayor thinks only about Halloween."

I will pulverize her bones and burn them to ashes.

"Ardyth's coming to the festival," I cheerily informed them, "as the Wicked Witch of the West."

"Very funny, Jenny."

And yet I saw it in her eyes, a sparkle of pleasure. There was nothing Ardyth Kennedy liked better than a good fight, except winning it. She argued only to triumph, never to compromise, or even to communicate. It unnerved me to realize that she had an uncanny instinct for picking the winning sides. What did that bode for my festival?

"Some of us," she was saying, "hold our sacred beliefs more devoutly in our hearts than others do, Jenny."

"Do you have beliefs, Ardie?" I asked her, feigning sweet surprise. "The same ones, I mean, from one week to the next? From morning to night? Of the same day?"

"I've been talking to Peter Falwell," she said.

It was not such a non sequitur as you might think.

My ex-boss, she meant, the president of the old Port Frederick Civic Foundation, and my archenemy, not to put too melodramatic a point on it. She and he had allied themselves against Mayor Eberhardt. Ardyth's political savvy. Pete's access to money and power. They were a team made in election hell. Demon spawn. These good folks should have been picketing the two of *them.*

"Pete wonders whether you can handle such a big job, Jenny—"

I will feed their livers to the crows!

"—considering you were fired from your last one."

"I was not fired. I quit."

It rang hollow, as such defenses always do, regardless of how true. As she had known before she voiced her purposeful lie. It wasn't the first time that she had lied about me; that first time lay back in the mists of our personal history. Now the appraising stare of the two protestors took on degrees of doubt and—was it?—pity.

Her mother was clucking like a distressed hen.

"Oh, Ardyth, baby! Please! Jenny's our best customer!"

Thanks a lot, Nellie.

"Calm down, Mother, I'm only pointing out to Jenny that the entire image of our city rides on her ambitious schemes—"

"Thank you," I said, cutting her off at that pass before she got into a full gallop again. "It's so good of you to put things in perspective. I have to go. Good-bye, Ardie. Nellie, I'll see your friend Melissa whenever she wishes." Another bad move. I should have known better, should have been satisfied with "good-bye." But Nellie was obviously upset about her daughter's obnoxious behavior toward me, and I just wanted to make her feel better.

Indeed, she said, "Jenny, thank you," softly, meaningfully.

The strong businesswoman appeared overwhelmed by her daughter. Nellie must have wondered sadly sometimes: "How did my child turn out to be like this?" Or, maybe she had already pinned down the answer: a father—ineffectual, undisciplined, doting—who had irretrievably spoiled the girl.

Really, someday I've got to follow my own rules and stop trying to save people who haven't hollered for help. One day I will take the hint that when people want to be rescued they will, dammit, say so.

I hadn't learned that yet.

The proof arrived immediately.

"Melissa?" said Ardyth, with a rising inflection. "Not Mrs. Barney again? Mother, I don't want you involved with that woman. We can feel sympathy without getting sucked into other people's personal lives, you know. Heavens, I am the first to feel deeply her tragedy, but the woman is unbalanced, she's gone quite overboard about the whole thing. Even though I sympathize, of course. And while we're at it, let me repeat that I don't want anyone in this family involved with God's Highway, either—"

I threw an apologetic glance toward Nellie as I turned away.

"It's a blasphemous name, anyway . . ."

Ardyth's voice trailed off.

I turned my head and saw why.

Her hypocritical politicking had been wasted, because the two men had finally made their escape. As they recrossed the street, dragging their signs behind them, one of them cast a glance over his shoulder at me. I was following them to the parking lot, but keeping my distance down the length and width of the street. The other man—short, dumpy, fiftyish, ordinary-looking in a brown suit—wasn't looking at me. But his companion, younger by maybe ten years, paused for a brief moment to stare. He was scarecrow tall and thin, and he wore a blue suit and a burr haircut that disguised what I suspected was balding, graying brown hair. It gave his face a lean, rather surprisingly attractive ascetic look—the look of long-distance runners, saints, martyrs, and fanatics, the kind of elongated, soulful face that El Greco painted so hauntingly. I'd been struck by its odd and melancholy beauty as they stood silent and grave behind silly, ambitious, dangerous Ardyth.

I gave him a little wave, since he was looking my way.

His gaze remained sober, speculative, as he turned his long, handsome, dour face away from me.

Damn. Now I had funamentalist anti-Halloween fanatics to worry about . . . in addition to everything else. At least, they'd never been known to cause real trouble. Although, the more I thought about the kind of people who would picket Halloween near grade schools—as these folks were known to do—the less I liked them. People who would frighten children with the specter of a devil and a flaming hell were people who might do anything, no matter their peaceful history.

Feeling a little awkward—and annoyed—after his rebuff, I kept going on toward my car, wanting nothing more than to make a wide enough circle around them that I could completely avoid any further contact.

But when I was in the driver's seat with the engine on, I heard a soft knocking at my window. It was the El Greco man, standing there with the post of his sign tucked under one armpit, obviously wanting me to roll down my window so he could say something to me.

"Yes?" I said, with a polite smile.

"I hope you'll pardon me for accosting you like this," he said, unexpectedly courteous. He still didn't smile, but there was a politely hesitant note to his bass voice, and a depth of some sort of feeling, even warmth, in his dark blue eyes that made me soften a bit toward him. Maybe his vision was poor, maybe he just hadn't seen my wave, and that's why he hadn't returned it. "I just wonder if I might say something to you?"

"That's all right," I said. "What is it?"

"You look like a sensitive sort of person. I thought you honestly might not be aware that the celebration that today we call Halloween really does derive from a pagan ritual in honor of the Lord of Death. I thought you might not know, and that you might wish to be aware, that in honoring this holiday, you—although inadvertently, I'm sure—honor Satan, and that you are also paying sinful homage to the forces of dreadful pain, terrible evil, destruction, annihilation, and eternal damnation."

I stared up into his terribly sincere blue eyes, but my attention was caught by a silver cross pinned to his lapel, a heavy piece of jewelry that pulled down the fabric of his suit. The cross was about two inches wide by four inches long and about a quarter inch thick, and plain as glass. I could, in fact, see a bit of my face reflected, distorted like a troll.

Jerking my gaze away from the cross, I looked back up into those somber blue eyes, and I said, "You know, the truth is I think I can understand your concern, in a funny sort of way . . ."

He cocked his long skull to one side, interested, hopeful of my conversion, I supposed. And it was true that I found I had a feeling in common with him.

"Between you and me," I told him, surprising myself a little with my confession, "I feel rather that way about New Year's Eve. I look at all of the parties, the wining and dining, the festivities, and I get a sinking feeling, because I know that it was originally a rite intended to bury all the old goddess myths and religions. I understand that it was an essentially antifemale celebration, in which the patriarchy of the new male religions symbolically—and sometimes actually—put to death the ancient female power. And it makes me feel sad and angry, for all those centuries of ignorance and suffering."

His face hadn't gone blank. He didn't look outraged. But he was observing me soberly again, as he had when we were both crossing the street, with those blue eyes that seemed to burn out of an old Spanish painting.

Plunging on, I said, "But then I realize nobody's doing that on purpose now. It long ago lost all those meanings. Now it's a symbol of hope for a new year, and people have a right to celebrate it any way they want to. So, I don't mean to offend you, really I don't—" I looked right into his eyes, hoping I could reach him, so that we could briefly meet on some plane where we had detente, if nothing more. "—but I'm afraid I feel that way about Halloween, too. I look at it, and I see only the faces of the children, having as great a time with their candy as I did. Do you see what I mean? I sympathize with your feelings, but I can't possibly agree with you."

He inclined his head slightly, almost a bow.

"God bless you," he said.

Pleased that he had taken my little speech so graciously, I said, "Well, thank you."

But it appeared I had only interrupted his benediction.

"And keep you from your devilish ways. Fire waits for those who serve the Black Master. You will burn eternally, torn limb from limb by the horses of the Apocalypse, tortured by everlasting blisters and boils, with no one to save you, and no angel of mercy even to tend to your dreadful wounds." He looked worried, even grieved, as if he could actually see the awful future he was predicting for me, and it broke his heart. "I will not bother you again. I have issued the warning of the Lord." He shook his head, sincerity and concern for me burning in his eyes. "Go very carefully, because the path you have chosen, the way of death, is the most dangerous one in all this wicked world."

Perhaps I should have felt annoyance, or even anger, at his presumption, but he just looked so damned unhappy for my sake that it was all I could do to keep myself from comforting him. I wanted to say, "Hey, really, I'll be all right, don't worry about me." Instead, I just nodded in farewell and then gently prodded the Miata's gas pedal to start inching away from him.

As I moved away, he did, too.

But in turning, the long wooden pole to which his sign was affixed grazed my arm, which was, bent at my elbow, protruding from my driver's side window. "Ow!" I said, but didn't look and kept on moving, because I wanted to get completely away from the man. It was only when I turned my head to peek back at him in my side mirror after I pulled into the street that I noticed there was blood on top of my forearm. I was wearing a business suit that day, but I'd taken off the jacket before I went into Nellie's store and had laid it across my passenger side seat. And I'd rolled up the sleeves of my silk blouse, leaving my forearms bear. Now the blood from a long scratch was running into the loose cuff of peach silk above my elbow.

"Dammit!"

My tolerant understanding proved shallow, as I burst out aloud,

"That idiot scratched my arm with his signpost! How am I ever going to get blood out of silk?"

Furiously, at the first stoplight I dug into my glove compartment for tissue, with which I temporarily staunched the light flow of red beads. It was only a superficial scratch, maybe four inches long, but not deep. The blouse was ruined, though, and I was incensed.

Leave me with a mark of the devil, would he?

"I ought to send you my cleaning bill!"

Or the charge for a new blouse.

As the light changed, I brought my arm into the car, to keep the tissue from blowing off. It stuck nicely to the blood, an effective emergency bandage.

I told myself to calm down, that it was only an accident.

But was it? One thing the scratch had revealed was that I wasn't quite as sweetly transcendent about his little Satan lecture as I had acted. I'd had experience with religious fanatics before—who hadn't, in one form or another, even if it was just somebody coming to your door to preach to you? But this guy, I had to admit in retrospect, had been downright spooky in the power of his dreadful sincerity.

I said out loud, "Well, I powerfully and sincerely advise you to stay away from my festival!" Then I smiled, even laughed a little. "Or I'll sic the Goddesses on you." My board of directors, I meant. They'd decided that it was too boring to be called "directors," or "trustees," and they'd rather be known as the "Goddesses." Privately, of course.

Personally, I didn't have much truck with goddesses.

I'd been doing a lot of reading about myths and rituals lately—because of our Halloween theme for the festival. I'd learned, for instance, that Halloween was originally a Celtic feast of the dead; the Celts believed it opened a crack in time when the living might commune with the ghosts of their ancestors. Besides fascinating me, the research had effectively killed any sentimental notions I might ever have had about matriarchies or goddess religions as opposed to patriarchies and gods. They all sounded like bad ideas. Unbalanced, unjust, arrogant and savage and frequently horribly avenging, and just plain out of whack with my idea of natural relationships between grown-up men and women. I didn't want either a patriarchy or a matriarchy, thank you very much. I thought it was high time for everybody to grow up, without anybody needing to lord—or lady—it over anybody else.

And speaking of growing up . . .

As the scratch stopped stinging and I calmed down, I thought about a certain underlying message for me that had been unconsciously hidden beneath Ardyth's jibes:

Welcome to the big leagues, Jenny.

She was right about that: There was a lot more riding on the festival than I had ever risked before. However it turned out, success or failure, I'd be pulling other people's fortunes up or down with me. Never in my years in foundation work had I ever attempted anything of this scale and importance. I'd never had so much of other people's money riding on anything. Been responsible for so much. Had so many people depending on me. Put so much at risk for myself and my friends and my town.

I put the Halloween protestor out of my mind. I would buy a new peach blouse. My skin would heal. But my foundation might be mortally wounded, might even die an early and untimely death, if the festival didn't go off as planned.

I almost—but not quite—looked forward to talking to Melissa Barney. A small favor. How nice. How . . . manageable. And, at a time when I felt like the hub of a giant speeding wheel, it was downright refreshing to know there was no connection between the death of her husband and the birth of my foundation.

For a smart girl, I can sure be dead wrong sometimes.

3

It was nearly eleven-thirty by the time I pulled into Abigail Adams Lane, which is one of our downtown side streets. Although the narrow cobblestone street was lined with picturesque stores and offices, I only had eyes for the modest brown two-story saltbox house at the end.

What a little beauty!

New roof. Fresh white trim paint. Neat little front yard. Orange and yellow mums. Newly repaired driveway leading to a parking lot in back. All accomplished with donated supplies and volunteer labor. Topped off by the generous gift of a discreet brass plate beside the doorbell, engraved: THE JUDY FOUNDATION, EST. 1995.

Now it was increasingly known as "Judy's House."

I parked across the street from it (all other places being taken by volunteers' cars) and would have lingered to enjoy the view, except that it was spoiled by the presence of a wine red Jaguar convertible with a tan top. The sleek and gorgeous Jag was parked in front of a white Dodge van with an empty bicycle rack on its top.

The Jag's driver, golf-tanned, elderly, elegantly white-haired, looked over at me. He was waiting imperially for me to come to him. The mountain. Mohammed. There was a boy beside him.

Oh, well, I had to get out of my car sometime.

And I couldn't behave like a child and pretend he wasn't there.

I strolled casually across the worn-down cobblestones to his car.

"Good morning, Pete." I peered in, saw that the boy looked eleven or twelve. "Hi," I said.

"Hi," he said.

"My grandson." Peter Falwell, ex-employer, nemesis, enemy of my family, couldn't keep the pride and affection out of his gravelly voice, not even in front of me. He'd stolen my family's third-generation canning business, this pirate had, many years before. And gotten clean away with it. I truly hated only one person on earth. This man. By comparison, for someone like Ardie Kennedy I felt the mere irritation of the cat toward the flea. Pete was looking annoyingly dapper this morning, wearing one of the large railroad insignia tie tacks that had lately become a trademark of his appearance. I'd heard he had a fabulous model train setup in his basement, and now I wondered if the child beside him might not be the reason why.

"Chapman, this is Ms. Cain."

The boy—stocky, handsome, sandy-haired—stared at me out of wary brown eyes. Damn. Was it fair of Pete to turn the next generation of his family against me? He'd been talking about me, I could see, prejudicing this child with one-sided stories. Which, to be honest, is exactly what I might have done if it were my grandkid. This was war between Peter and me, and fair didn't enter into it. The only problem was it was a war in which my own family had disarmed me.

I stood weaponless before him.

"I hear you're involving yourself with God's Highway again, Jenny."

Involve. I thought I recognized one of Ardie Kennedy's favorite words, to go along with *connections.*

"Do you, Pete?"

"Don't. Not that you ever take wise advice. But I'm giving you fair warning. Don't."

"Why?"

"Because it is sacrosanct. A national treasure. You nearly scuttled it at the beginning. Don't meddle with it now. It doesn't need fixing, and certainly not by you."

I could easily guess the source of his instant information: a phone call from his hyperventilating political puppet, Ardyth. What I couldn't guess—and never had understood—was the reason for Pete's devotion, from the inception, to the cause of a nature trail so beloved by conservationists. They called it "God's Highway" because all the little squirrels and rabbits, deer and foxes loved it, and wildlife was protected there. Usually, Pete Falwell had about as much environmentalist in him as did his favorite ex-President, Ronald Reagan. I could have told him I wasn't "involved" . . . yet. But that wasn't any of his business, one way or the other.

"You coming to the festival, Pete?"

A wicked question.

But he surprised me. "In fact, I'm coming, and I'm bringing Chappie and some of his little pals."

I smiled at the boy.

Tentatively, his mouth crooked upward. He looked like a nice kid. He just wasn't sure whether it was okay to be friendly to me.

"Come early on Saturday," I advised the boy, "for apple fritters and hot apple cider. And stay all day and come back on Sunday. Kids get in free. I promise you'll see everybody you know, and you'll have a great time. There will be carnival rides and games and lots of crafts, if you like that kind of thing—" He had grimaced at the mention of "crafts," which made me smile. "And more food than a dozen twelve-year-olds could ever eat."

"I'm ten," he said shyly.

"Oh, well, then we'd better order *more* food."

That made him laugh. He and I could be friends, I thought, if it weren't for the poisonous toad in the driver's seat.

"There will also be," interjected Pete, "thousands of strangers tromping over our town common. If any harm comes to the common or to any of the structures the foundation helped to restore, you will be held responsible, Jennifer."

By "the foundation," he meant the one he headed—my old source of employment—not my new one. In Pete's view, made clearly and repeatedly known to anybody who'd listen over the past two years, this town wasn't big enough for the both of us—the Port Frederick Civic Foundation and the Judy Foundation. I knew it was. They did great work—Pete, notwithstanding—but they couldn't do it all, and there were many projects they wouldn't touch that I couldn't wait to get my radical hands on.

"That's what insurance is for, Pete."

The words came out of my mouth before I could catch them, too impulsive to censor them. I waited for his inevitable verbal jab on the sensitive subject of insurance and was surprised when he didn't grab the chance to take a poke at me.

He merely hurrumphed and turned his key in the ignition. That meant that the only cliché left for the old fart to say to me was, "You mark my words . . ."

The idea of that made me smile again, which caused him to stare at me with renewed suspicion and dislike.

"What are you thinking?" he demanded.

"Why don't you put the top down on this baby, Pete?" I patted the roof of the Jaguar. "Nice fall day like this? Your grandson would love it."

"Oh, yeah, Grandpa! Can we, can we?"

Pete's right hand moved to the gearshift. "Now, Chappie, it's much too cool for that today . . ."

Pete laid his right arm along the top of the boy's seat and looked behind him. I saw him put the car in reverse to get a better angle at pulling out into the street.

And so, having sowed a single small seed of familial dissension, I started to happily walk around the front of the Jag.

The next thing I knew, I was sprawled in the street, on my face on the rough cobblestones. I heard voices yelling. A car door slam. And a second slam. Footsteps running. I opened my eyes and saw concrete curbing less than an inch from the top of my head. And suddenly I was aware of hurting in a whole lot of places.

"Grandpa, Grandpa!"

"Jennifer, for heaven's sake, why did you walk in front of me? Here, get up, you're all right! I barely tapped you. Here—"

"Wait, wait!" A female voice, sounding familiar. "Leave her there, wait until we find out if she's okay to move—"

"Grandpa, she's bleeding, oh, I'm gonna be sick!"

"Chappie, get back in the car. Now!"

I placed my left palm down on a cobblestone and used its hard, gritty, old roundness to push myself over onto my side. I might hurt, but lying on those damned stones wasn't making me feel any better. I looked up, saw Pete's face—looking more angry than concerned—hovering over me, and also the much kinder, younger, and more upset-looking face of the woman who made our festival supply deliveries for us. She was down on both knees in the brown grass between the curb and the sidewalk, her face upside down. A long silver pendant on a silver chain had dropped out of her blouse and now swung just above my eyes. To her, I said, "I'm okay. Honestly." I hated looking stupid in front of Pete. "I didn't even hit my head. Help me up, will you . . ." For a moment, I couldn't remember her name, and I wondered about brain damage. "Uh. Cleo?"

"Are you sure, Jenny?" One of her strong arms came around my shoulders, the other reached for my left arm. "Oh! You've scraped yourself!"

"No, no, that was earlier." I laughed a little as I looked up at her. "Is today Friday the thirteenth?"

"You scared me to death," she said, as she got me to my feet, totally without any help from the elderly gentleman, I noticed. She tucked the silver pendant back out of sight, into her blouse. "I thought you'd bonked your head smack into the curb. Are you really sure you're all right?"

"Of course, she's all right."

Thoroughly put out by his cavalier attitude to my safety, I glared at Pete and was surprised to find a glint of a smile in his cold blue eyes.

"Jenny's tougher than she looks," Pete informed the delivery woman. Then he glared right back at me. "Don't you even think about suing me, Jenny Cain. You stupidly walked right out in front of my car. It was entirely your fault, not mine."

"You had your car in reverse, Pete," I retorted.

"I did not."

"Did too," I snapped, and then I giggled, we sounded so much like children quarreling. He heard me and looked at me as if I must be concussed. "And thank you so much," I added sarcastically, "for your kind sympathy."

"Oh, you're all right," he said dismissively.

Pete swiveled on the heel of one of his well-polished shoes, and strode back to his waiting car and grandson. The boy, I saw, still looked huge-eyed. I smiled at him, to reassure him.

"Let's go in the house, Cleo," I said, "before the heartless old bastard runs me down again. He *had* that car in reverse, I know he did. I saw him do it."

"I believe you," she said, like a nurse to a sick patient.

She probably didn't, I thought ruefully, because who would think that Pete would change his mind, throw his car into forward gear, and bang his bumper smack into the side of me, sending me sprawling? Even I couldn't believe he had done it on purpose. I just thought he'd done it without looking first, and now he refused to accept responsibility for my injuries.

I did hurt, no matter my disclaimers.

The side of my right knee hurt like hell where he'd hit me, and my entire left side felt bruised, because it had taken the force of my fall. On top of that, the cobblestones had sandpapered me and my clothes from stem to stern. I looked forlornly down at myself. New blouse. New skirt. New hose. I could salvage the shoes.

"I'm a mess," I said to Cleo.

"Yeah, but you're alive," she pointed out, as she held open for me the front door of Judy's House.

It appeared that nobody else had witnessed my accident.

Not wanting to make anything more out of it than it really was—which was essentially nothing at all—I excused myself and limped to the bathroom at the back of the house to clean myself up. I always kept a change of clothes at work, and they certainly came in handy that morning, as I quickly stripped to my underwear, sponged my bare skin down to remove pebbles and blood, and then pulled on fresh outer clothing. This time, it was a bulky, comfortable, and comforting Irish fisherman's sweater over a short black suede skirt. Of course, I had spare stockings, and my flats were okay to put back on. A quick brush through my tousled—and grit-filled—hair, a dab of new makeup here and there, and I was a new woman.

She felt like banged-up goods.

My right knee was starting to swell, along with a place high on my left thigh and another one at the top of my left shoulders. My back felt a bit wrenched, as did my neck, and, oh hell, every single vertabra in my spine, if I told the truth.

I popped three over-the-counter painkillers before I left the bathroom, washing them down with cool water cupped in my hand. Given the way I was feeling, I hoped they worked soon.

Should I surrender and go home?

No way. Too much to do.

I figured I could limp well enough through the day to get most of my work done, and then I would scurry home for a long soak in a hot and healing bathtub.

I came back out into the foyer to thank Cleo.

Cleo was the regular delivery woman from our local express company, Post Haste. By now, ten days before the festival, and dozens of packages and express letters later, she and I were on a first-name basis, even though I had temporarily forgotten it out there in the street.

At the moment, she was coming through the front door with a cardboard box.

If you looked only at Cleo's face and her height, she appeared too slight for many of the loads she carried. But over several weeks of watching her tote and carry, I had learned she had the strength of ten. Of me. I'd felt some of that comforting strength when she helped me up.

"I'm really grateful you were there when it happened, Cleo. Thanks so much. Pete probably would have backed up his car and run over me again." She laughed, thinking I was joking. Hah. I stepped closer, trying to get a look at the package in her hands. "What do you have for us this morning, Cleo? Something from Portsmouth, I hope, I hope?"

She grimaced in apology. "Sorry, still no, not yet."

I drew a calming breath to quell the panic that threatened to rise in me every time I drew that negative response from her. Or from the postman, or from anybody else delivering mail to us. *Damnation!* When would it arrive? I called them every day, the people in Portsmouth, every day! And they swore, "Tomorrow, Ms. Cain." Forget the mail, I pleaded desperately with them, "just fax it. Please." And still our fax machine refused to burp up the all-important document from Portsmouth.

Without the packet from Portsmouth, no festival.

That was a thought so painful it put my physical complaints clean out of my mind. Or maybe the pills were starting to work.

"It's another shipment from the Dime Store," Cleo announced, setting it down with a soft thump and a sigh. "It's got a spiderweb stenciled on the return address." She put a gloved hand to the small of her back and smiled at me. "You guys get the most interesting mail of anybody on my route."

I wasn't really listening. Partly, I was distracted by my worries about the missing package. But mostly, I was distracted by the simple fact of being in the house again. Even then, several months after its opening, I could hardly believe it was real. We'd done it. I'd done it. Started a private foundation of our own. Renovated a rundown property to call our office. And with our festival, we'd splashed onto the philanthropic scene like kids doing cannonballs off the high dive.

At the moment, happy chaos reigned inside. At least, I hoped it was happy. I heard female laughter from upstairs. Good sign. We like to keep our volunteers happy, we do.

Cleo and I were standing in the entryway.

"I'll bet," I surmised from her description of the spiderweb, "that these are the plastic spiders for the bag toss."

"I won't even ask what that means," Cleo said with a laugh.

"Prizes for the kids," I told her. Carefully, leery especially of my right knee, I bent down to where she had placed the box on the floor, squatted there, and started to rip into it, to check. Immediately, I slowed down, because a shaft of pain in my left wrist let me know of yet another place I had thrown my weight down in the street. Moving ever more carefully, I said, "Let's see if it is."

"Want a knife?" She pulled a utility blade out of a scabbard on her belt and offered it to me, handle first. I took it and used it to slice wrapping tape and to pry staples loose.

I didn't know her last name, even though I probably saw her more often, at least by a strictly numerical tally of encounters, than I saw my own husband. As she hovered there above me as I knelt in the foyer, I was aware of her odd presence: and unusual combination of youth and maturity, of fey and physical. Kinky, flyaway light brown hair sprang from her head like a soft halo, and she had pale skin, a ready smile, and a high, light voice, but she also boasted pretty damned impressive biceps and her thighs strained at her uniform shorts in warmer months. She had large, rather melancholy-looking blue eyes. With those eyes that sometimes didn't seem as if they belonged in the same face with that quick smile—and in her utilitarian brown uniform of pants and shirt—Cleo looked like a sweet-faced fairy who happened to have stumbled into a temporary job driving trucks. I guessed she was only in her late twenties, maybe early thirties at most, but I didn't know anything personal about her.

I flipped back the last flap, hurrying now because it hurt to squat.

Started pulling out wads of crumpled newspaper.

And then screamed and jerked back up, adding a bit more noise to my scream because of what the sudden movement did to my body.

"Holy shit!" I said, and again and again.

"Oh my God, oh my God, oh my God," Cleo was screeching, as both of us jumped back from the package, she with more alacrity than I. "Is it alive? Is it alive?"

When nothing inside the package moved, I braved a closer look.

The massive black hairy creature—a tarantula—that had scared me to death when I unveiled it, hadn't moved a single evil-looking hair.

It couldn't.

I started to laugh, nervously.

"Look, Cleo."

It was enclosed in glass, one of those paperweights.

She edged slightly nearer to it, until she could see it, too. In a disbelieving, shocked voice, she said, "You're giving those away to little kids as prizes?"

"No!" I really did laugh then. "I was expecting those little black plastic spider rings, you know? This is a mistake. Somebody just sent the wrong thing."

"I've been driving around with that?"

"Some people love spiders," I said, in fairness.

"Yeah, but we don't have to know them."

I laughed again and felt the cementing of a stronger connection with her than we'd had before. Accidents will do that. And shared laughter. Suddenly, for no reason, my aches and pains felt a little eased.

Our shocked and petrified screeches had drawn an audience: Volunteers from upstairs were thundering down the stairs wondering what was the matter. Several of them repeated our screams when they glimpsed the contents of the package. But there was one woman volunteer who said in disgust—at us, not at the spider—"Oh, you guys. You'll give girls a bad name. It's dead, for heaven's sake. And it was gorgeous when it was alive. Back off, you sissies, I'll take the poor baby away before you hurt his feelings."

"Send him *back*, will you?" I asked her.

But when she picked up the paperweight—ugh—and then the box it came in, she looked at it and said, "Can't. No return address."

I glanced at Cleo. "I thought—"

"Just this spiderweb that looks stenciled." The volunteer looked all over the box, then rummaged through the wadded newspaper, even turned the paperweight over to examine the bottom of it, saying humorously as she did so, "Let's ask Mr. Tarantula." But she shook her head. "Nothing here, either."

"Didn't you say he came from the Dime Store?" I asked Cleo.

"Yeah, but sometimes they don't unpack what comes in for you from the wholesalers, if the whole shipment's for you. They just forward it on here."

I knew that; it was one of the economies that allowed Nellie to charge us so little. I didn't ask her to check shipments against invoices; we assumed that load of labor and time, and we did the work of sending back anything that required returning, as well. She was our contact for availability and price, that was all, and it was generously more than enough. There wasn't any other local firm that handled so much of the merchandise we needed and that was willing to work as hard for us as Nellie was. I was adamant about spending our money locally, so I couldn't go out of town to approach wholesalers on my own. But I also really did have to pinch every penny until it snarled at me. The Dime Store was the perfect answer, and at the end of it all, Nellie knew she would still have enough profit for her store to make it all worthwhile. Not to mention the fact that she'd made customers for life out of every one of our volunteers, which sometimes seemed like half the town.

The volunteer holding the paperweight asked me, "What should I do with this handsome fellow?"

I thought I saw a hopeful look in her eyes.

"You want it?"

"Really?" She actually looked eager; I couldn't believe it.

"He's yours, unless somebody claims him." I said wryly, "Give him a good home."

With a great deal of laughter and pretend shivers, the volunteers began to wander back upstairs. I turned to Cleo, whose blue eyes looked even wider than usual, and said, "I hope that's not what's in all of the other boxes."

"You and me both," she said passionately. "I'll check for that stencil on every damned one of them." She visibly shivered. "I told you, you get the most interesting mail." She glanced at her big-faced wristwatch. "Geez, I've got to get moving, or I'll never make our guaranteed deadline. Some of our customers, if they don't get their packages by noon, they hang the nearest delivery person." Her gaze was direct and efficient now. "Where do you want me to put all the rest of the boxes, Jen?"

"How many?"

"Fifty. Well, forty-nine, minus the spider."

"Please stack them here in the hall for now, Cleo. We'll figure out what to do with them after we inventory them."

"Jenny?"

"Hmm?"

"Where does all this stuff go that I bring you?"

"The heads of our committees fetch most of it," I explained, "and disburse it to their members. By now, we've got supplies stashed all over this town. Next Friday, we'll all converge on the common like locusts on a wheat field."

"And set it all up?"

"A miracle will occur from dawn to dusk," I said, nodding. I'd thought she was in a rush to leave, but since she asked . . . "We won't do it all that day. Our construction volunteers will start building the temporary structures this weekend."

"I'd be scared of so much responsibility."

"Not me," I confessed. Tarantulas notwithstanding, I knew I had to appear steady as a schooner captain to my crew, but I wasn't acting when I said to the delivery woman, "I eat it up. Give me something to run, and I'm happy as a witch on a broomstick."

What I didn't add was there were a few people in town, like Pete Falwell, who would dearly love to see me tumble off that broomstick and fall ingloriously on my bum. In their opinion, the women in charge of Judy's House and the Port Frederick Autumn Festival were uppity witches who had challenged the patriarchal status quo, and burning was too good for us. Call me paranoid, but I figuratively and frequently sniffed the air, to see if I smelled the sulfur of matches being lit.

As Cleo trotted off to her van, I called out to her, "Thank you!"

She turned around and made both of her hands into five-legged spiders, spreading her fingers wide, and then she grinned. Taken aback, it took me a second to catch her grin and lob it back. Trotting backward, she called to me, "You know what spiders mean in mythology, don't you? Fate!"

"What? Fade?"

"Fate!" she repeated, and wiggled spiderly fingers at me again.

What a surprising sort of delivery person you are, Cleo, I thought, as she turned away, the sun lighting her halo of hair. Was she the sort whose idea of a joke for All Hallow's Eve was to deliver tarantulas-under-glass? Nah, surely not. She'd jumped back as far as I had, on first sight, and squealed just as loud. No, I would call Nellie, myself, to track the provenance of our anonymous arachnid. She would either know—or want to know—about it.

Experience suggested that we would see Cleo again that day, on her late-afternoon round of deliveries. Maybe she'd show up, at last, with the precious postmark from Portsmouth.

I crossed my fingers, out of sight of my volunteers.

4

LIMPING THROUGH THE DOORWAY INTO MY OFFICE CUM LIVING ROOM, I LOOKED to the right and saw my desk with a pink pile of telephone messages awaiting me, looked to my left toward the front window and got a second surprise.

A visitor, a woman, on one of my facing red loveseats.

So quiet, she'd been invisible during the earlier commotion.

So preoccupied with gazing out the window through her very dark sunglasses that it seemed my own entrance was invisible to her. For a moment, while getting my surprise under control, I stared at her. I thought she must have slipped in from the back parking lot, through the back door, while I'd been in the bathroom. A few years younger than my own thirty-seven years, I guessed, a beautiful woman with red hair cropped short as a boy's and a delicate profile atop a long, lean dancer's body. She wore plain leather sandals without socks, even on this cool day, and rumpled baggy black jeans with a black belt and a black T-shirt, tucked in. All of that black, which looked as if it had been selected for function and only accidently looked like fashion on her, set off her red hair gorgeously. Her hands—with long, thin, elegant fingers—were clasped tightly in her lap. Her skin had that pinkish tone some redheads get instead of freckles; even from where I stood I could see how white her knuckles looked in contrast. Only at the sound of my approaching footsteps on the bare wood plank floor did she finally turn her head. There was a tense whiteness around the corners of her mouth, as well.

"I'm Jenny Cain, are you waiting for me?"

She removed her sunglasses, and I nearly exclaimed in dismay.

The skin around her eyes was dark and bruised. She didn't look as if she'd been struck, so much as if she were haunted. Instantly, I knew who she was, before she even said her name.

"I'm Melissa. Nellie said to come. She said you'd help me."

Melissa Barney, widow. Her voice was low, strained. She spoke in bulletins, as if the only way she could manage to say anything at all was to keep all of her words to the bare minimum: subject, verb, object. It got the job done.

As if to excuse her unexpectedly quick appearance—it had been only an hour since I'd left the Dime Store—she added, "I thought we could make an appointment, if this isn't a good time for you." Obviously, she hoped it was a good time, or she would have telephoned rather than shown up in person.

"No, this is good, this is fine."

I switched the telephone to the answering machine and closed the door to my office all but a crack. I'd know if anyone called or came in, but they wouldn't interrupt us. Then I sat down—carefully testing my knee first before I tried bending it again—on the love seat opposite her, a captain's table between us. The knee seemed okay. I leaned forward, feeling sympathetic. She looked so wounded. I sensed in that moment of stillness—broken only by the muffled noises of talking and movement upstairs and of Cleo coming in the front door—that small talk would torture her.

"Tell me about it," I suggested gently.

She covered her bruised eyes with her sunglasses again and turned her face back to the window, keeping it there even as she spoke to me. I leaned back and neutralized my expression, realizing it was hard for her to face the sympathy in other people's eyes. Maybe we were the ones who ought to wear the sunglasses.

"You know God's Highway?" she asked me, her thin lips barely moving, her profile delicate and stern in the sunlight.

"Where it is and what it is, yes."

"Ben." She stopped, compressed her lips, then opened them to speak again. "My husband." Again she stopped, then started again. Her loss was very, very fresh, Nellie had said, three weeks ago, at most. And if he was anywhere near Melissa's age, he was very, very young to die. "Ben and I loved it. We're both—we were—heavy-duty hikers. We've been using it for years, we supported the idea of it. Signed petitions for it. Voted for anybody who backed it. Gave money to the cause. We were just married, he was twenty-three and I was twenty-four, and it gave us something exciting to do together, to have in common."

She sighed and suddenly her posture softened. Her chest caved in, her shoulders came down, her head bowed forward.

"I wish we hadn't," she said, softly, bitterly. "I wish we'd been on the side of those property owners who opposed it. I wish we'd helped them block it and picket it and fight it in court. I wish it had never been created at all. And Ben—" This time, it was a good thirty seconds before she spoke again, straightening her posture to pull the words up out of her. "And Ben would never have been able to go hiking on that *god-damned* trail, and he wouldn't have been killed by that *stupid* woman . . ."

She whipped her sunglasses off. When she faced me this time, her eyes were blazing in their bruised sockets. "God's Highway." She spat out the words in furious sarcasm. "God's Highway to Hell, is what it is. It was cursed from the beginning, if we'd only realized it. Did you know it was the track of an old railroad line?" I knew all of what she proceeded to tell me, but I sat still and absorbed her version of it, anyway. "Oh, I can tell you all about it, I was so *gung-ho* for it then, it makes me sick to think about it now. It was built in the late 1800s. The railroad leased the right-of-ways from the various property owners, and the land was supposed to revert to them—or to whoever owned the property after them—if the trains ever abandoned it.

"But nature lovers . . . like *me* . . . wanted to have a nature trail. We saw the old railroad track and realized it would be perfect, and so we found a legal loophole in the old contracts, so the property owners all along the trail lost their rights to their land. We were so convincing, it wasn't just the state, but the *feds* who took it over."

That was all true; it was U.S. Park Service land now, which made it subject to federal laws.

"We were jubilant," she said bitterly, "Ben and I. We all thought we'd really pulled a coup, because the feds didn't even have to pay the property owners for the land they lost. The property owners were incensed, of course, that their government would do that to them, just ignore perfectly legal documents as if they didn't have any meaning at all. But we couldn't be bothered with thinking about their rights or their feelings, oh, no. Not righteous us. We had better things on our minds. Hiking. Wildlife. Flora. Fauna. The property owners were also frightened of what the trail could bring to their backyards . . . vandalism, trash, an increase in crime, maybe burglaries, or worse."

She stopped to take a deep, emotional breath.

"Now two people are dead because of that trail, and who knows how many other bad things have happened on it, and now I'm on the other side of the issue, but I'm scared to death it's too late to do anything about it. That trail has to be closed. I know that, Nellie Kennedy knows that, the people who opposed it have always known it. It's got to be shut down, before somebody else gets murdered, like Ben."

I ignored the "murdered," as the hyperbole of grief.

"Two people?" I said. "Do you mean the person who was killed in the snowstorm last winter?"

"No, I mean last Memorial Day weekend. There was a child, a little girl, who was also struck and killed by a car. Hit-and-run driver. She died, too, just like Ben."

"Oh, that's right!" I tended to avoid news stories having anything to do with God's Highway, so unhappy were my own memories of that battle for its creation twelve years earlier, but I certainly remembered that one, and I wondered why Nellie hadn't reminded me of it. "The child wasn't from here, though, was she?"

"No. I don't know where she was from. I don't know anything about her. But I know she was killed in the same way at the exact same intersection where Ben died, down from Nellie's house. Except hers was hit-and-run. The bastard! We *know* who murdered Ben, and she's going to pay for it. But other people are going to die there, too, unless we do something to close that trail."

After a moment, I said, "Would you be satisfied with anything less?"

"What do you mean?" She snapped it, aggressively.

"Improving it, somehow, finding a way to make that intersection safer. Closing down the trail entirely, that's like taking on the legislature and the environmentalists and the legal establishment, all over again. And there's no reason to think they'd lose this time, either. It would affect an awful lot of people, are you sure you want something so drastic?"

She gazed out the window again, her voice trembling now, with a kind of quiet grief that seemed to alternate with her avenging fury. "It's so lovely, on the trail. There are miles and miles of paths now that wind through forests and farms, and there's even that bit of seashore, where the old railroad ran along the coast on top of the bluffs. Ben and I used the trail from the very first day it opened, and we started taking the kids as soon as we could strap them onto our backs . . ."

After a moment, I said, "I'm so sorry."

She nodded, helplessly.

"You have children?"

"Two boys . . ." The grief swung again to anger. "Nellie says you have this new foundation. She says you can move faster than governments can, and you've got money and influence. We need your help to save lives. And we have to do it quickly. My God! Somebody else could die on God's Highway, even today! Right now, as we're sitting here, somebody could be out hiking on that trail, completely unaware of the danger, and he could walk out onto the road and that intersection and get hit and killed, just like—" Her pretty face twisted with grief. "Ben." She leaned back against the love seat, resting her head on the edge of it, closing her eyes. "I'm so tired. I don't sleep anymore, and yet I feel as if I could sleep forever. Maybe I have to close that trail down before I can sleep again. Just shut the fucker down and close it for good."

"Do you know about the festival we're sponsoring?" I asked her.

"Yes." Eyes still closed, head still resting on the love seat.

"I can't do anything for you until that's over."

Her eyes came open. She looked trapped, defeated.

"And maybe not even then," I warned her bluntly. "What I can do, maybe even today, is begin to look the situation over. Talk to my board of directors. Decide if this is something for us to get involved in. I don't know if it is, Melissa. But at least I'll find that out and get back to you with a decision as soon as possible."

"Not this week?"

"Yes, probably this week."

"Really?" She pushed herself up straight, using her palms against the seat. "You'll do that? Nellie said you'd help."

I shook my head. "I don't think it's much."

Her mouth twisted. "You don't know. Compared to what I've run into with other people. Nellie's own daughter, for instance. She won't even approach the town council for me. Or our legislators, they're not interested, they say it's not that big a problem. What do they want, ten people dead? Twenty? How many deaths are a problem? And that other foundation, the one that funded the trail to begin with . . . they won't help, they already said so."

"Did they?"

"You're the only one so far. Because of Nellie, right?"

I chose not to answer that, but shifted in my seat, instead, hinting that I had other things I had to do. She took the hint, gathering herself together and rising to her sandaled feet. With a quick thank-you and a handshake, she was finished and quickly gone through my office door, which I held open for her. I expected her to turn left, to go toward the parking lot, but she turned right toward the front door, instead.

Cleo was just stacking the last box as Melissa left the house.

And then it was good-bye to my delivery woman, as well.

I walked slowly to the door, attempting to manage it without a limp, to watch. I saw Cleo climb into her brown van. And Melissa get into the white Dodge van with the bicycle rack on top.

I frowned at that surprising sight, because it meant she was here, in the house, when I had taken my tumble outside on the street. And if she'd been staring out the window, as she had been when I found her, she'd have certainly seen me. Yet she'd said nothing, hadn't asked if I was hurt—although maybe it was fairly obvious I'd survived—and certainly hadn't jumped to my assistance at the time, as Cleo had. One would have thought, considering her passionate desire to keep people from getting hit by cars . . .

The responses to deep grief were unpredictable, I decided.

I looked at my watch: 12:15. Cleo was slow today; it had taken her an unusually long time to stack those few boxes. To hear her tell it, that meant she was going to get hung by some of the customers on her route. And I was late to lunch with my husband, who was standing just behind me leaning against the foyer wall, silently staring at me, as I turned around to smile at him.

"What?" I demanded.

"It looks good on you, Jenny."

"Yeah? What does?"

He raised his hands, gesturing toward the walls, the ceiling. "All of this. You're very attractive when you're in charge." He smiled, crooking one corner of his mouth up in the way that still made me want to kiss him—right there on that uptilted, sexy corner of his lips—after all our years of being together. "Lead me," he said. "Direct me. Take me to lunch."

He stepped forward for a greeting kiss, and I didn't stop him in time from reaching out to squeeze me in a warm, loving embrace. "Oh," I moaned, which he unfortunately took for ardor, thereupon squeezing me even tighter, so that my breath finally exploded from his boa-hug in a frantic, *"Ouch!"*

5

I LOVED THE MAN, GEOFFREY BUSHFIELD, THE BIG HANDSOME FELLOW I SAT next to in a tight booth at the Buoy Bar & Grill for lunch that day. We'd known of each other as far back as high school—he, four years my senior—and we'd been wed about seven years now, which was his longest running show in three marriages. He was a former near-juvie turned cop. Smart, funny, sexy. My man.

None of which prevented him from driving me crazy now and then.

First, he was furious with Pete Falwell:

"That bastard!"

Geof swore in a string of expletives, truly upset and clearly shaken by my tale, perhaps more than I was, myself. I had tried to lighten the telling of it, so that it wouldn't scare my husband on my behalf. But he, no fool, didn't need a translator to point out to him that Pete could have killed me. One inch more and my head could have been just another lifeless cobblestone. As a longtime cop, Geof had seen his share of bloody encounters between vehicles and pedestrians; he knew who got the worst of them. No doubt, those images fueled his explosive reaction—not to mention that he knew, more than anybody, how very many other ways Pete had hurt my family in the past. This was one more. A near-miss, but still a direct hit.

"That idiot!" Geof pounded the wooden dining table in front of us, causing a few people to glance up from their crab salads. I placed one of my hands over his angry fist, wanting to calm him, to reassure him that I was still here. "That cold-blooded bastard! He should lose his license!

I'll have a tail on Pete Falwell so tight, if he doesn't make a full stop on red before turning right we'll have him in traffic court for reckless endangerment. I'll—"

It upset me, to have upset him.

I wanted him to calm down. He was making me feel jittery, reminding me that I'd come closer than I wanted to admit to possibly serious injury. I'd been taking it lightly up till then, and I wanted to keep it that way. There was nothing to gain, for me, in making more of the accident than it really was. Pete had barely bumped me, that was all. I'd fallen and gotten up.

It took me until our lunches arrived to calm Geof down.

Then I made the mistake of telling him about Mr. Tarantula.

"Call Nellie Kennedy," he said, speaking in a normal voice now, although it was the normal one he used as a lieutenant to direct officers of lower rank. He glanced at me over a crab salad sandwich that was stuffed so fresh and so full it was nearly crawling out between his fingers. "Ask Nellie about it. She'll know."

"Yes," I agreed, over my own lobster version.

"But what about the black plastic spider rings?" he asked, sharply, as he might have asked, *But what about the fingerprints on the kitchen door?* "Why aren't they here yet?"

"I don't know, Geof."

"Haven't you called to check on them?"

"Not today."

"Don't you think you should?"

"I'll give it one more day."

"I wouldn't wait. What about the Portsmouth—"

"No," I said.

"Jenny, you've got to tell those people to get their rears in gear. Tell them this is an emergency, and you have to have those papers—"

"I have done that. Many times. With increasing frequency and volume. This morning, before I went to Nellie's store, in fact."

"Damn, you'd better call them again."

"Geof."

He looked up from his coleslaw, noticed the expression on my face, finally detected the tone of my voice, and said, "I'm doing it again."

I bared my teeth at him, heedless of shreds of lobster.

"Yes," I snarled.

He laughed, at himself, at me. "I'm sorry. It's your festival. You can run it beautifully without me. I know that. Honest, I do."

"Do you want to know what our niece says about boys?"

"I don't think so, do I?"

"She says they always try to tell you what you already know."

"Is that true? Goddamn, what a colossal pain in the ass I must be."

The confession of which greatly endeared him to me.

"Actually," I admitted, "I can't do it without your help. Talk to me about the security arrangements. Fill me with confidence that your guys really can handle ten thousand strangers in one weekend."

He was, as I mentioned, a lieutenant for the Port Frederick Police Department in real time, and I'd dragooned him into recruiting off-duty officers for security work at the festival. He had also called in reinforcements from neighboring communities. Parking, alone, would be a logistical nightmare without them. I felt damned fortune that the cities involved were willing to pay all the extra overtime. They believed, as I did, that the civic benefits would outweigh the cost.

After Geof reviewed for me the numbers and assignments of the constabulary, I said, "You may have one more security problem to watch out for. When I was at Nellie's store today, those Halloween protestors were there, you know the ones I mean?"

Expressively, his mouth full, he rolled his eyes.

"Yeah, well, Ardyth sicced them on me. She practically introduced me as the devil's wife. Insisted on calling it the Halloween Festival, said it was all my idea—"

He swallowed. "Accurate, if not helpful."

"And she got her licks in at the mayor, too."

"You think these people will cause problems?"

"I got the feeling they'll *be* there."

"As nuts go," Geof observed, "they're pretty quiet."

"I guess I'm concerned about what other people might do. With such a huge crowd, the protestors might draw opposition, or even more . . . aggressive . . . versions of themselves. And dammit, I just don't like the idea of anybody trying to take the fun out of it for little kids."

"Like you."

I smiled. "Right." I thought about telling him about the El Greco protestor putting the scratch on my arm. But considering Geof's reaction to the little bit of damage that Pete had done to me . . . I decided I just didn't want to deal with how he might react to somebody who'd threatened me with torture and eternal damnation.

That, I decided, should wait for a calmer day.

He was saying, relaxed and full of stomach and enjoying himself now, "Taking the fun out of things is not against the law, Jenny."

"Ought to be."

He smiled, amused. "Damn right."

"I guess we'd have to build too many new prisons, huh?"

"Probably. Although . . ." He looked thoughtful. "I suppose we could just fry 'em."

"Death penalty for party poopers?"

"Why not? They're already under their own life sentence."

A philosopher, my husband. He was skeptical, though, of my fears about the protestors.

"I know," I said, "it's unlikely. I'm only saying, tell your guys to be aware of these people. That's all. And not to provoke anything. The outside cops won't be aware, as we are, that these are okay folks, unless you tell them so." I looked at him. "You think they're nuts?"

"Sure. You don't?"

"Yeah, I do, but from their point of view there's logic to what they do. Maybe even courage."

"You civil libertarian, you. You should have gone to college in the sixties, Jen." The tough cop was teasing the do-gooder. "You'd have fit right in."

"Nah, I'd look awful in long skirts and granny glasses."

He laughed. "I tried to duplicate the sixties. All those drugs I tried when I was a kid."

"It accounts for a lot," I agreed, the Nice Girl teasing the Bad Boy.

We both laughed. It was great, working downtown, seeing more of him. After a few moments of companionable eating, I said, "Geof? Remember God's Highway?"

"Why, is it gone?"

"Very funny. When it was created, I mean. Ten years ago, more or less. That was before you and I were joined in holy matrimony—"

"Or even unholy bliss."

My smile slid into a lascivious grin of memory. "I'll say. Were you for it, or against it?"

"I was agin it."

He said it with so much force he surprised me. And then he had more to say on the subject: "I hate idealism. I especially hate it when it puts other people in danger and causes more work for me."

"The trail did that?"

"I was afraid it would. I figured, we all did, all of us retrograde old cops, that a hiker's trail like that, with a lot of isolated miles, would attract some people who aren't exactly modeled on Henry David Thoreau or Rachel Carson."

"Gangs? Muggers, you mean? Rapists?"

"That fraternity, yes."

"And has it?"

He looked annoyed. "Not much, no."

I laughed at him.

"You know I hate to be wrong," he said, smiling at me.

"That's because you're an idealist, at heart."

He placed his hand on his chest. "Woman, you wound me."

"All cops are idealists, aren't they? Why else would you do it?"

"For the money," he said and grinned. "Of course."

"I'm as idealistic as anybody you'll ever know."

"No, you're not," he said. "But don't ask me to prove it."

An old joke between us. "I would never do that."

"There have been a few problems," he said, "here and there along the trail, over the years. It's a lot of ground to try to patrol. I don't know how they thought we'd manage that, all these different jurisdictions, for one thing, not enough officers, for another. No way the Park Service can take care of it without our help. All those people who wanted it, they thought only nice people hike, I suppose."

"Who's the 'they' we're speaking of?"

"Everybody who supported it. Your favorite foundation president, Peter Falwell, the people in First Things First—"

That was the name of a national conservancy group that had rallied to our local cause, bringing their considerable clout down on the side of God's Highway. I had surprised myself by detesting them. Normally, me being me, I'd have expected to take up the cudgel of any "good cause," like a nature trail, but I'd been offended by their cavalier attitude toward the rights of the people along the trail, some of whose families had held their property for generations. I hadn't cared if they'd held it since the dawn of time or only a day—no matter how long their tenure, it was theirs, by right of contracts signed in good faith many years before. Dammit.

"Jenny?" Geof waved a French fry in front of my face. "Where'd you go? You were listening, and then I lost you."

"Fond memories of First Things First," I said wryly. Thank God, those people had never come back to town. "I'm sorry. What were you saying?"

"We've actually had an increase in incidents on the trail lately. Minor thefts—backpacks being stolen, fanny packs, that kind of personal thing —and a little vandalism—trees being chopped up and carted away, maybe for firewood, and fence posts disappearing. There's been some breaking and entering in houses along the trail, nothing vicious, nothing very important taken. A little money, some clothes, cupboards rifled. No TVs, or VCRs or jewelry, nothing that amounts to anything, at least from the police point of view. I'm sure it upsets the owners, all the same. However major or minor it is, it's increasing. Sounds to me like a combination of local teenagers on the loose and maybe a few bad apples on the trail, passing through and picking off any visible loot as they go. Not much we can do about them, but the teenagers—if that's what it is—maybe."

I told him then about Melissa Barney.

"You'll never get it closed," he predicted flatly.

"I tried to keep it from opening to begin with," I reminded him.

I had just been hired at the old foundation, a decade earlier, when suddenly Pete was ramming a nature trail down everybody's throat. I had a sense that people weren't being treated fairly. It wasn't just that they weren't being compensated for their property, although that was bad enough, it was that they were *losing* it, even though their own government had promised that would never happen.

"I was idealistic." I smiled at Geof. "I wanted to slow down the process, to try to work things out more fairly for both sides. It wasn't that I didn't think a nature trail was a fine idea; in fact, it was probably a good and logical use for that old railroad line. But it wasn't *available;* it wasn't ours to give away."

I had nearly lost my job over God's Highway, right when I first got hired. Pete had said that if I didn't back off and stop trying to influence the other board members, he would "influence" them to fire me.

My face was warm with shame, all those years later.

"I caved in, Geof. I let Pete and the foundation and the nature lovers and the government walk all over those people. I've always felt ashamed of my part in it."

He looked impatient with me.

"How old were you, Jenny?"

I thought back. "Twenty-four or -five."

"Come on! You couldn't have beaten that crowd!"

"I could have stood up to them."

"Sounds like you did."

"Not enough."

"You were a baby!"

"Boys go to war at eighteen. Joan of Arc was nineteen." I thought of something, a small historical parenthesis seared into my memory. "I'll bet you didn't know that when the church burned her, they hung a sign around her that said 'Relapsed, Heretic, Apostate, Idolator.' "

He gave me a searching look.

"All right." I laughed. "So I'm not Joan of Arc."

"I didn't mean that, I meant—"

"Geof, Melissa Barney told me a child was also killed at that intersection by Nellie's house. She said it was a hit-and-run."

"Still is."

"You never caught him? Or her?"

He shook his head. "I think we're all still looking for him, though, sort of unconsciously all the time. If you ever see an old black VW Beetle in mint condition, get his license and let me know."

"Who saw it?"

"The little girl's mom. They were on bikes, and the kid raced on ahead and got hit just as the mom showed up behind her."

I put down my sandwich, which was suddenly tasteless.

"Yeah," Geof agreed. "Pretty sad."

"How old?"

"Seven, I think."

I didn't say anything.

Geof said, "You see why we still keep looking for the car. What I think, though, is that he was out of state and he just kept driving."

"Would I know the mother?"

He shook his head again. "Tourists. Bennington, I think. Parked her car in town and then got on their bikes to ride the trail."

I fiddled miserably with my half-eaten coleslaw. "If I'd stood up to Pete Falwell—"

"You'd be fired," Geof snapped, though he reached over to cover one of my hands with his. "And that child would still be dead."

We skipped dessert. Geof was trying to lose twenty pounds from his six-foot-two-inch frame, and I didn't have much appetite left. We had walked together from Judy's House, so we parted in front of the restaurant, where he said, "I think the kid's hanging around again."

David Mayer, he meant, his unofficial "adopted" son, our own private juvenile delinquent: eighteen years old, stuck in a year of dead space between high school and (we hoped) college, both parents deceased, other family permanently estranged, semiemployed at a service station, smart and smartass. He had a key, and irregularly we found things like ice cream or beer missing from our refrigerator, usually just when we wanted them most.

I called him "the poltergeist."

When I said as much to Geof, he said, "Maybe David is the Ghost of God's Highway."

"The what?"

"It's got a ghost, didn't I tell you? Jumps out at hikers. Steals things if you leave them lying around on the trail. What I say is teenagers or wandering bad guys, other people claim is a ghost."

I laughed. "Could be Big Foot."

He leaned down, kissed me carefully. "If you ever go out there, watch out for big hairy hands and real bad breath."

"Maybe it *is* David."

Geof looked slightly offended. He really did care about the kid. "He's not that bad, is he? He's clean. I think."

"Well, the dishes aren't, the ones he leaves in our sink."

"Is it okay to hug you? Do you still hurt?"

"Nah," I lied. "I'm fine, so hug away."

My husband, trying nevertheless to be gentle, grabbed me in a public embrace, which, I gathered, was meant to express his gratitude for my putting up with the poltergeist. Smashed into his throat, I said, "I love you, Lieutenant."

"I'll be collecting evidence to support that charge." He released me, and I tried hard not to wince. He added: "Tonight."

"Do I need to bring an attorney?"

"Only if you know one who likes to watch. And I should warn you, everything I have will be held against you."

I punched him in his chest and told him good-bye.

After an hour spent returning phone calls at my office, I made a couple of calls of my own . . .

"A tarantula, Jenny?"

Nellie Kennedy sounded disbelieving, then defensive. "It couldn't have come from here. We don't even sell that kind of thing anymore."

"Not for Halloween, Nellie?"

"Absolutely not."

So what did that mean, I asked her, if nobody on her shipping dock had accidently slipped it into our order?

"Post Haste must have gotten their orders mixed up." She sounded busy, and eager to escape from talking to me. I pictured her, every black hair in place, and a dozen customers at her elbow. "You got somebody else's shipment, that's all."

"But it had our name on it, Nellie."

"It did?" The phone was silent for a moment. "Well, whatever, it was just a mistake. Why is this so important, Jenny?"

Good question. It was such a good question, in fact, that I was taken aback and slightly embarrassed by it. Why was I snagged in this trivial spider's web, when there were so many other, more important, things to do?

"Well, I just wanted you to have it back, if it's yours."

Nellie laughed a little. "Oh, that's okay. You can keep it."

Before she hung up, she apologized for her daughter's behavior toward me that morning. I felt like saying, "Oh, that's okay, Nellie. You can keep her."

Then—speaking of more important matters—I called Portsmouth.

"Where is it?" I wailed at them.

Not today, they said. Not yet. Tomorrow, they felt, for sure.

"Do you know how important this is?" I begged them.

They knew. They sounded defensive. I backed off.

"I know it's not your fault," I said appeasingly, "I know you can't do anything without the signatures from your home office. But we only have a few days left, and the town council says if we don't get the papers by their public meeting on Monday night, they will jerk our festival permits." I tried not to sound as panicked as I felt. "This is Thursday. There's a weekend in between, so we lose one day of delivery service. Please, please, can you hurry them along?"

I felt undignified and desperate.

They understood, they said, they were doing their best.

I knew that. I thanked them. They reassured me again.

I didn't know whether to believe them.

The truth was, they didn't know any more than I did. It wasn't up to me, or to them. It was up to some damned faceless, anonymous insurance supervisor somewhere in a tall building in Boston. At the last minute, our own fire department had demanded more insurance coverage for the festival. None of us could have been more shocked. We thought we'd already answered all their demands: I'd eliminated the fireworks, we'd cancelled our autumn leaf bonfire for the closing ceremonies, our food booths had agreed to do all cooking off the premises and only to warm things using our temporary electrical system. All that, and more, we'd done to keep the fire department happy, and at the last minute, only two weeks ago, they'd declared it wasn't enough. More insurance, more, more. We had no choice but to try to comply, but the insurers didn't like it. They felt it implied much greater risk than they originally anticipated. If our own fire department was this nervous . . .

Damn! It was possible, entirely possible, they would turn us down. Why were they delaying their decision for so long, if not because they had terrible doubts about us? And I, meanwhile, was trying to keep a calm, confident face on the whole situation, with town council members, and the mayor, and the fire department, and the newspaper, and my other board members, and my husband (!)—nervously and constantly bugging me about whether or not the insurance approval had come through. *No,* I wanted to shout at them all, *no, it hasn't,* and short of going to Boston myself and throttling somebody until she coughed it up, I didn't know what to do about it.

I called the mayor, before she could call me.

"Mary? Do you have an hour to spare for a hike in the woods?"

Amazingly, the mayor said she did, but only if we left that minute, at a little after three. I thought it might be good for what ailed me, get my stiffening muscles moving again, shake out the pain of my darkening bruises. I grabbed my camera, a 35mm fully automatic "aim and shoot" gadget for mechanical dummies, like me. I often wished a person could enroll in a course that would teach a person (me) how to work . . . things. Gadgets, gizmos. Computers and I were on fairly good, basic word processing and Internet terms. I was friends with my fax machine and Geof's car phone, but when it came to f-stops and beyond, I was instantly over my pretty little head. It was kind of embarrassing, like being squeamish about spiders, and I wanted to get over it. One day.

City hall lay right on the path of God's Highway.

6

Robert Frost was right: the woods *were* lovely, dark, and deep. Only a few yards from city hall, Mary and I were in a dappled world: shadowy where evergreens predominated, reddish gold where deciduous triumphed. Below our feet, the shuffle of dry leaves, acorns, walnuts, twigs. In the air, a tangy scent—from somewhere—of wood fire. On my fingertips, I felt the dust of a dry autumn season.

In less than five minutes of sturdy walking, I was sweating lightly, but I was feeling better. Or at least I had myself convinced that I was, maybe because I wanted to be. I didn't have time for injuries.

I hadn't even stopped to change clothes again, and neither had our mayor, Mary Eberhardt. Being good little nineties' executive women, we naturally both stashed spare tennis shoes at the rear of our office closets for nights of working late, or to satisfy sudden urges to walk off tension or take a break outdoors. So there we were, tromping God's Highway—Mary in a business suit, and I in my suede skirt and fisherman's sweater, both of us in hose and tennies.

I turned around, said, "Smile, Mayor . . . say 'landslide,' " and snapped her picture. An experienced politician, even on such short notice she managed an ingratiating smile for my camera.

The mayor had brought a late lunch along with her, a disgusting-looking egg-salad thing on white bread out of a machine at city hall. She had offered to split it with me; I had, not very respectfully, declined. Mary was one of my three good black friends in town, the other two being her husband and a social worker on our board. In a town of less than three percent minority population, every time Mary won another term she made *USA Today* and CNN.

"We should do this every day," Mary said behind my back. We'd have been lousy Indian scouts, crackling through the woods as noisily as we were and chattering like squirrels most of the way. "I'd be back to a size 10. Do you know any women over fifty who have *dropped* a dress size?" The mayor was so close to the half-century mark she sometimes told people she was already fifty, "just to hear how it sounds." It looked good on her.

I told her that now.

"Jenny, I want you to know something about menopause," she said unexpectedly, "before you get there."

"Okay." I glanced back over one of my padded shoulders at her. Even hiking, the mayor wore her glasses. "Mom."

She poked me in my back.

"I want you to know that hot flashes can be wonderful."

"What?"

"Really. This is the only time in my life I've ever been warm. I get up to go to the bathroom in the middle of the night, and my feet aren't freezing. It's delicious. Sometimes I lie in bed beside Hardy, and I think, oh, this is so *nice."*

"Only you," I said, a step ahead of her.

She was laughing, anticipating my response. "Only me what?"

"Only Mayor Feelgood, Mrs. Positive Thinking herself, would claim she actually likes hot flashes."

"You wait. You don't know. You're too young. You'll see."

"I'll take your word for it," I laughed.

"Where are we going, Jenny, and why are we here?"

Mayor Forthright.

I told her, and in fifteen minutes of fairly rapid clambering, we were there. The intersection of trail and two-lane state highway where Ben Barney had been fatally injured looked harmless in the midafternoon sunshine. But the trees edged right up to the road on both sides, with only the narrowest of verges separating the dirt trail from the asphalt road. I thought I could see how some unwary hiker might step out too quickly. And if a car were coming too fast . . .

It was quiet now, no traffic, though I had a sense of invisible woodland creatures listening to our conversation.

"I guess he came out of the woods like we are," I told Mary, "and he stepped onto the highway, like this—" I put action to words. Then I pointed to the top of the hill to our left. There were wide-lawned country houses on either side; I guessed one of them was the Kennedys', but

I didn't know which it was. "See the back of that stop sign?" It was right at the top of the hill, outside the fence that surrounded the home on our left.

The mayor said she did.

"The way I understand it," I continued, "is that the driver ran that sign, sped down here, hit Mr. Barney."

"Yes, I recall that accident."

"Do you recall that a child died here, too?"

"Yes, of course."

"That was a hit-and-run. That guy hit her, and then just kept on driving."

Mary and I both turned and looked the other way, to our right. There, the highway curved a few yards beyond us and traveled on toward a dry creek bed. The railroad had originally followed Crowley Creek for part of its way, and the trail followed the railroad, and we had followed the trail. Crowley Creek usually only flowed during and after the spring thaw and rains, and then it regularly washed out local roads to a depth of several feet, making access impossible for a few hours for the residents.

At the same time, we both heard traffic.

"Get off the road, girl," Mary directed me. "We don't want the same thing happening to you. Now what is it that Mrs. Barney wants from us?"

We both watched a blue sedan crest the hill, stop obediently and fully at the sign, and then proceed sedately down the hill, past us, and out of sight around the curve.

"She'd like us to close the trail," I said.

"No can do."

"She might be satisfied with making this crossing safer."

"Possibly can do."

"Pete Falwell has already told me to leave it alone, Mary." I told her then about my literal run-in with him, and she was instantly full of concerned questions about how I was feeling. To get her mind off my health, I had to remind her that it was she who had more to lose, at this point, from being—figuratively—run down by him and his powerful allies. "Your esteemed opponent and her supporters will line up with Pete."

"Against us," she said thoughtfully.

"Against *you,*" I emphasized. With the election less than a month away, which I certainly didn't need to say.

"You're going to study this?" she asked me. "See if it needs fixing?

Find out what we might do to improve it? Make recommendations, either way?"

"I'd like to."

She shrugged, smiled as if nothing were riding on it. "If it needs to be done, we'll do it."

"What if Pete and Ardie paint you as an enemy of nature?"

"What a laugh, coming from them!"

"I know, but they will, Mary."

I had an awful feeling that would be true, even if all we had to do to fix the crossing was to erect simple warning signs. Somehow, because this involved God's Highway and me, Pete would find a way to use it—and me—in the election against Mary.

But she placed her hands on my shoulders and grinned at me. "If your festival succeeds, I will look so good Pete can paint me as an enemy of *babies* and I will still win by a . . ." She smiled photogenically. "Landslide."

I looked into her brown eyes.

"The insurance isn't here yet, Mary."

She squeezed my shoulders, released me, sighed, and said, "I can always go back to being a full-time minister's wife. As I always say, compared to that, being mayor is easy."

While I took photographs of the trail crossing from every angle I thought might help to get a perspective on the problem, Mary wandered off to find a tree stump on which to sit and eat her sandwich. I worked as quickly as possible, knowing mayors never had much time to spare and wanting to be thoughtful of hers.

"Mary?" I called out, when I was nearly finished.

The answer yodeled back from somewhere nearby in the woods. "Over here, Jenny!"

"Could you help me a minute?" I shouted back.

Rustling from the direction of the dry creek bed announced her arrival. "What can I do?"

"Sorry to interrupt your picnic."

"I'm eating so slowly you'd think I had all day." She smiled at me, and I saw gratitude mixed in. "It's so relaxing being out here, much nicer than gobbling something at my desk as I usually do."

"Or eating creamed chicken at a banquet?"

She grimaced in agreement. I told her what I wanted, and she promptly went and stood in the narrow area of grassy verge between the woods and the highway. I wanted to indicate how little space there was for a margin of safety before a hiker or biker stepped or ran or rode out onto the asphalt, and I needed a human body to do that. In the time it took to point and shoot three times from three different angles, I was all finished, and I released Mary to the rest of her sandwich.

She surprised me by coming back before I'd even had time to complete the task of removing the roll of film from my camera and placing it back in its little gray plastic tub.

I looked up. "That was quick."

Mary looked chagrined. "Squirrel stole the other half of my sandwich."

"Oh, no!" But I had to laugh. "I'm sorry."

She, good-natured soul that she always was, laughed, too. "Nobody takes my sandwiches off my desk."

"I should think not." I mock-shuddered, teasing her. "Who'd want them? It looked disgusting. Did you catch the thief in the act?"

She shook her head. "Didn't even leave me the cellophane."

Mary led our way back along the trail to city hall. As I watched her smooth stride, I thought what a graceful woman she was in so many ways. Before we parted—she to attend a water board hearing, and I to head home—she said, "If I'd been mayor then, this trail never would have gone through Port Frederick. It would have stopped at one edge of town and started up again at the other."

I asked her why.

"Because it bothered me then and it still bugs me about how the railroad, the state, the county, the city, we all broke our contracts—legal or moral—with those people who owned land along the trail. It seems to me the very least that people ought to be able to expect from their government is that we'll keep our promises to them. The very *least.*"

Uneasiness rolled through my stomach.

Hearing Mary, I sensed how important it was that she win at least one more term. Ardyth Kennedy, in charge of our hometown? With crooked Pete Falwell as the power behind her? *No.* I only hoped I wouldn't personally cause that nightmare to spring into life.

"It's a wonderful trail," Mary was saying, and we both gazed back where we'd been. We'd had it all to ourselves—except for the egg-salad-loving squirrel. A couple of times I had looked back, thinking I heard the noise of another hiker about to overtake us. But no one had, and so we'd been able to talk in complete, outdoor privacy. "I've nothing against it, *per se.* It's just that it was built on stolen land, that's all."

We eyed one another.

"That's all," I echoed ruefully.

During our hike, the wind had changed direction, coming now from the east, blowing the wood smoke away, bringing a sharp, salty moisture from the sea beyond the city. In another month, it would be snow.

I hugged her in farewell. "Stay warm."

The mayor laughed. "No problem."

From the open door of my car, I yelled one last thing at her: "Hey, Mayor! Ever heard of the Ghost of God's Highway?"

"Hear of him?" she called back. "He steals things all the time from out of our cars! I should have warned you to lock yours! If I ever catch him, he's a dead man!"

"Mary! A ghost already is a dead man!"

She was laughing as she waved me off.

It wasn't that I didn't have any more work to do on the festival that day; only that I could do most of it from home. Ah, the joys of self-employment. One quick stop at the drugstore to leave off my film for overnight development, followed by a race through Judy's House—"Did it get here?" "No, Jenny." "Everybody doing okay?" "Yes, Jenny." "Anybody need anything I can get for you?" "Not right now, Jenny, thanks." "No crises?" "Not a one." "Are you sure there's nothing—" "Good-*bye,* Jenny!"—and off I toodled home in my little white Miata convertible, top up, briefcase full of tasks, body full of aches, head full of worry, heart basically quite happy, soul content.

I looked forward with a shiver of luxurious anticipation to having the house all to myself for a while before Geof got home. I planned to strip, soak, slip into my terry-cloth robe, pour a glass of wine, fix a snack, put Bach—or Bonnie Raitt—on the stereo, and spread out my papers at the kitchen table, with a phone beside me. Maybe, if I got lucky, my husband would take pity on me and offer to do all the cooking this evening.

Insurance notwithstanding, life was good.

If only I could have insured *that.*

We live outside the city limits of Port Frederick, down a dirt and gravel road, in a stone and timber house with chimneys and a slate roof. It has a Germanic, old-world charm in its woody setting on its cliff beside the sea.

I love our house, I am passionate for it.

Geof found it for me, at a time when I desperately needed the shelter of its—and his—arms. Ever since, the property has been our hobby and our refuge.

Tiredly—though I hoped a shower and food would revive me—I stashed the Miata in our detached garage and trudged up our back walk to our kitchen door.

Which was open.

Through the screen, I saw a black ski jacket draped over one of our kitchen chairs.

"Oh, hell," I said and limped in.

The knee had started to throb again when the analgesics began to wear off, and by now it was a full-fledged, if relatively low-toned, drumbeat of pulsing pain. Maybe it was ice I needed, rather than the heat of a tub.

In the kitchen, an empty half-gallon ice cream carton melted the last of my favorite mint-chocolate-chip into the sink where some of it lay congealed in brown puddles. There was a fork stuck down in the carton. For some reason, the poltergeist preferred to eat his ice cream with forks instead of spoons, and he never used a bowl. Maybe that was good —no dish to wash. No dish for *us* to wash.

I put my own stuff down before I rinsed out the ice cream carton, and then put it in the trash. The fork went in the dishwasher. I poured myself a glass of water—instead of wine—to wash down two more pills and slipped off my shoes.

"Ah," I sighed. My calves felt tight from their hike, but it sure hadn't helped much of the rest of me. You wouldn't think—I thought—that a brief tumble to the cobblestones could wrack and ruin a body, but then the body in question wasn't a kid anymore, or an athlete accustomed to being tossed to the ground. I wanted to shrug it all off, felt, in fact, like a baby for even complaining, but dammit, it hurt. I thought about Pete saying to Cleo so coolly, "Oh, she's all right." Well, I was, but it was unforgivable of him to be so much more concerned about the possibility that I would sue him. There were worse things I could have sued him for, if my own family would have let me pursue it.

Tougher than I looked, was I?

At the moment, that seemed in doubt.

I looked across at the black ski jacket.

Maybe I could slip upstairs without seeing the poltergeist, assuming he was still in the house. By the presence of the jacket, I assumed he was, though I wondered why I hadn't seen his battered old BMW motorcycle in our driveway. Maybe he really *wasn't* here. I brightened right up and started to shuffle toward the door that led into the rest of the house.

"Thanks a lot, Jenny!"

The deep, carrying voice of an angry young man came floating down the stairs to me. On repetition, it sounded even closer.

"Thanks a whole hell of a lot!"

I kept quiet. Whatever was bugging David Mayer this time, maybe it would pass before he reached me. But no. Into the kitchen he barged, all six feet of muscle and bone and dark ponytail and teenage skin and furious hazel eyes of him. David slapped a *Port Frederick Times* down on the kitchen table and glared at me as if I'd crashed into his beloved motorcycle.

"Is that this evening's paper?" I inquired.

"You're damn right it is. You've read it, right?"

"Read it? David, I just got home. I haven't even looked at it."

I should have asked, "Why?" but I didn't want to know.

He picked up the newspaper and thrust it at me. Reluctantly, I took it, seeing that it was folded back to reveal something on the editorial page. Even before I saw the headline, my blood began to boil and my heart to sink, if such a thing is physiologically possible.

JUDY, JUDY, JUDY.

That was the headline.

I groaned, slumped.

Remember how Cary Grant made that line famous in the old movie? In print, like that, above an editorial, it looked like a reprimand. As indeed it was, I saw, as I read the damn thing. The *Times* was slapping my hands in print. All about how the insurance hadn't come through for the festival, and about how many "civic and philanthropic hopes and dreams" were riding on said festival, and about how a certain "young foundation director and her all-female board of directors, including our Mayor," appeared to have taken on much more than they could handle. You'd have thought I was seventeen instead of thirty-seven, and they made our board sound like an all-nude review, with Mary in the role of star stripper . . .

And now, "sources suggested," the same women of the Judy Foundation were even thinking of messing with God's Highway, everybody's favorite nature and hiking trail . . .

How unfortunate, they implied, that in this great country of ours *anyone,* even persons with "possibly more money than sense," could start a charitable foundation . . .

And if we weren't careful we would make Port Frederick the laughingstock of New England . . .

"This won't," the paper closed, "be a case in which Port Frederick throws a festival and nobody comes. It could be much, much worse than that: We may find that everybody comes . . . but that we'll have no festival to throw!"

I continued looking down at the paper as I thought about it, rather than looking at David. I could, maybe, have anticipated this print attack, because Peter Falwell had extremely close and long-standing ties to the publisher's family. But I could not have predicted David's reaction to it.

"That's my *Mom's* name."

I looked at him then and saw he was so angry he had tears in his eyes.

"My *Mom!* You said if I let you name your foundation after her it would *honor* her memory. You said it was a *respectful* thing to do. You said—"

I let him rant on about what I'd said, not trying to defend myself. It was true. I had said those things, I'd meant them, I still did. We had, indeed, named the new foundation in honor of David's late mother. Judy Mayer had lived a sad, injured, too short life that wasn't strikingly different from the lives of altogether too many girls and women. I had asked David's permission—asked it over and over to make sure, very sure that he agreed—to allow Judy's name to become our symbol of hope for people who needed help. Under her name, we planned to offer what help we could to people—of either gender—who were suffering her fate of early abuse and early death. It was one of our admittedly lofty aims. He'd been hesitant about the idea at first, then clearly excited and proud.

"Everybody will laugh at her now!" he railed at me.

Actually, outside of Geof and me and David and my board of directors, nobody knew who "Judy" was, a relative anonymity I had suggested to David, even though he had at one point been so enthusiastic about the name idea that he had argued with me that we should call it the Judy Mayer Foundation. Now, although I was glad I'd won that argument, I didn't want to say, "I told you so." If anybody outside of our little group knew the real identity, it would be because David had told them. I wondered if he had—in a moment of pridefulness—and if that was, in part, what was fueling his distress.

He had a right to be upset, I felt.

It *was* his mother's name they were mocking.

Even if I hadn't done anything to deserve the tongue-lashing, I knew David had to let his feelings loose on somebody, since he wasn't quite mature enough yet to know what else to do with them. His longing for his mother—dead almost two years now—was also hidden between the lines of his rage. I could have used logic to stop him, could have said, "David, I double, triple-checked this out with you, and you gave your approval, you thought it was a great idea." But it was my experience that you couldn't apply logic to emotion, as if it were balm to a wound. Logic, for all its appeal, only served to make angry, hurt people feel even more betrayed.

There was also the suddenly worrisome notion that maybe I had misled him. Perhaps he wasn't old enough to make an important decision like that, maybe as the adult of the two of us, I was the one who should have known better.

In my silence, David was getting all wound up to demand the removal of Judy's name from our foundation—a nonpossibility at this juncture, in my view—when we both heard the Jeep crunch over the gravel and roll into the garage.

Geof was home.

Instantly, David was stilled.

He looked confused. Still hurt. Still furious with me. But now, the Man was home. Of all of the welcome miracles that could have occurred in our odd little household, it was increasingly clear to Geof and me that one miracle that really was occurring was that the kid desperately wanted—needed—the lieutenant's respect.

And he wouldn't get that if he were caught verbally abusing the lieutenant's wife.

I could almost see the sequence of thoughts go through David's mind. He shut up. Licked his lips. Sniffed. Touched his ponytail. Shifted his weight. Got his breathing calmed down.

Avoided looking at me.

7

When Geof walked in, I was by the sink, filling a glass with water.

"Hi, boys and girls," he greeted us.

"What are you doing home so early?" I asked him.

He looked tired, I thought, but his smile came easily, for both David and me. He seemed pleased to see both of us, and to see us apparently at ease with one another. He didn't answer my question, but he did come over to tilt my face up so he could kiss it. I returned it with a fervor that made him look into my eyes for a private moment.

"Are you all right?" he asked me, too quietly for David to hear.

For a moment, I thought he'd overheard the kid, after all.

"Sure," I said.

"Those *bastards!*" Geof said, at normal volume, looking as angry as David had earlier. And then I realized he'd seen the paper. That's what he meant by asking me if I was all right. The sweetie. He'd come home because he was worried about me.

"You must have called the office?"

"They said you were here. Do you know that MATV is trying to reach you?"

Our local television station, he meant.

"It'll be on the machine, probably."

"If it rings . . ."

"I don't want to talk to anyone yet, not until I figure out what to do about the editorial."

"How could those bastards do that? It's their town, too. You'd think—"

"That's just it," I said, looking into his eyes. "They do think it's their town."

The kid was being suspiciously quiet through all this.

I glanced over at him.

Geof turned, including David in his attentions. "I've been cheatin' on you, Dave."

"Goddammit," David responded, but this time it was mock outrage. "You've been messin' with my new game without me. You said—"

The cop grinned. "Policemen are not your friends. If it's any consolation to you, I'm already stuck on the first level."

Of a computer game, he meant.

It had become their meeting ground . . . in our dining room . . . at the computer Geof had sacrificed to the cause of connecting with this haunted boy. The computer was now apparently permanently installed there, with all of its attendant wires and modem and printer and discs on our dining room table, with two chairs pulled close together in front of it for Geof and David. Geof had really clicked this time, with a Star Trek Twenty-Fifth Anniversary game. The kid was a fan of the TV series.

Oh, well, it wasn't as if we ever really needed the table for anything else, as we were so happy by ourselves we almost never had company or went anywhere unrelated to business, unless maybe to a movie.

By ourselves . . .

Somewhat wistfully, I watched the two tall, broad male backs disappear from the kitchen. I was tempted to feel a little left out. But then Geof appeared again in the doorway. "Did it arrive this afternoon?"

I shook my head.

David's voice called Geof back into the dining room before he got a chance to start telling me what I should do about my insurance problem. Left out? At that moment, I felt downright grateful to the kid for stealing Geof's attention away from me.

Sure enough, when I checked our telephone answering machine, there it was, along with commiserating, incensed messages from my poor beleaguered board members:

"Jenny? This is Susan Bergalis at MATV. We'd like to get your response to the editorial in tonight's paper. We can do it live tonight at six and run it again on tape for the eleven o'clock. Please call me as soon as possible!" She left her beeper number.

I sighed, craving that hot bath, though my knee felt better.

Susan was a young producer I knew—and liked—at the station. She was smart and fair, and since the festival was a constant source of news bits for her, I knew she thought it was great. We'd always gotten along fine. Which wouldn't, I suspected, keep her from crucifying me if a story required it.

I couldn't do it by "six."

It would take me longer than that to plan a proper defense—a good offense, that is. How to delay Susan, while still getting in a few licks of my own?

After a few minutes of heavy thought, I paged her.

"Susan," I said, when she called back within seconds. "I really appreciate the chance to rebut that editorial." Sarcastically, I added, "I always thought journalists were supposed to try to get both sides of a story before they printed it, didn't you?"

"They didn't interview you?"

She sounded pleased and appalled in almost equal measure to hear of the ineptness or unfairness of the competition. It wasn't such a surprise, really, as the *Times* was a family-owned enterprise, and that family had *opinions,* which they had been stuffing down Port Frederick throats for as many generations as my own family had been living there.

"Never tried to," I said, conveying my own—quite sincere—indignation.

"Well, we'll get you on live at six."

It was already fifteen minutes till six.

I didn't want that. "God, I wish I could, Susan, but I'm already home, and you know how far out I live. I'd barely make it to the end of my driveway by the time you started the news."

"We'll do a phone patch at . . ." She must have consulted a schedule. "Six-oh-three."

Damn, was this their lead story? That was bad news and good news for us. Bad, because it would make it seem just that much more of an emergency and get that many more citizens worried about us; good, because they'd all hear my defense. Assuming I could, in the next seventeen minutes, come up with one that didn't *sound* defensive.

Susan instructed me: "At six sharp, call me back at the number I'm going to give you now." I wrote it down as she dictated it and then read it back to her. "We'll use a file photo of you. One of our anchors will ask you questions—probably Marilyn. Keep it simple if you can, Jenny, we don't have much time. You may only get fifteen seconds out of a three-minute story, because we've got other related interviews, too."

Related interviews? *Shit.*

"Who, Susan?"

"Oh, you know," she sounded harried, but also embarrassed. For herself or for me? "Pete Falwell, the fire chief, Ardie Kennedy, about who you'd expect, and the mayor."

Poor Mary.

"We tried to get somebody from the insurance company, but they won't tell us anything."

You and me both, I thought.

"Call me at six," Susan said, and hung up.

It was by then nearly five minutes until six.

This wasn't how I wanted to do it—my disembodied voice coming from nowhere, unable to look confidently and sincerely into the camera's eye. I hated to think what photo of me they might yank from their files. What if it was one where I looked young—too young—or naively, dumbly enthusiastic, or worried, or angry, or what if it had my eyes at a slant so I looked like a crook—

I made myself stop that.

Two minutes until I was supposed to call back. Three minutes after that to wait to go on the air. Five minutes in all to come up with a brilliant plan.

The phone rang under my hand.

I jumped. Then picked it up and blurted, "Hello? I'm sorry, I can't talk now, can you call back in fifteen minutes?"

"Miss Cain?"

"Yes, listen, I don't mean to be rude—"

"Shut down the highway."

"What?"

I glanced at the caller identification display unit attached to the telephone. The little window there displayed a caller name and number that I didn't recognize.

"Please, I beg you, for God's sake, *close it down forever!"*

And then, thank goodness, the caller hung up. I didn't even have time to react. Anyway, whoever she was, she was now stored in the caller ID system, so I could look her up again later, if I thought of it.

One minute until six.

To prevent the phone from ringing again, I picked up the receiver and put it to my ear . . . and heard, not a dial tone, but electronic noises.

"Oh, no. No." Disbelieving, I held down the button, then released it. "Come on, come on!" Still no dial tone. More weird electronic noises. "I don't believe this!" The phone couldn't go out now, not right now at this moment! What kind of friends would I make in the media if I left them scrambling, live, to fill empty airtime?

And then I knew what the problem was.

I dropped the receiver and hobbled like a one-legged gunny sack racer toward the dining room, shouting, "Get off the phone! Get off the phone! Now!"

I stood—wild-eyed, I'm sure—on one foot in the doorway, while inside the dining room two males stared at me with twin expressions of astonishment. It was Geof, the cop with experienced reflexes, who reacted first. He didn't ask why, just reached up to the keyboard and calmly backed the computer out of whatever telephone modem use they had had it in, thus freeing the phone immediately for me.

"Thank you!" I yelled as I race-hobbled back to the phone in the kitchen and dialed—at three seconds to six. I was dimly aware that the computer freaks had gotten up and followed me in. Great, a home audience.

Susan Bergalis answered.

Told me to hold on.

I looked over at Geof . . . and received strength and confidence from his steady face . . .

Looked at David . . . and all of a sudden felt the *reason* surge through me . . .

Looked out the kitchen window, as Marilyn Stuben asked her first on-air question. Evidently, they had already summarized the story and identified me, because Marilyn started out with a whammy:

"Ms. Cain . . ."

In real life, it was Jenny.

"What if you don't get the insurance?"

"We will. The company assures me we will. They are merely being extra careful, because our own fire department wants all of us to take seriously our responsibility for the safety of so many visitors to Port Frederick. It's not an emergency, Marilyn, it's business as usual."

That is what the insurers had told me, I was actually quoting them.

I wasn't required to say, on air, whether I believed them

"Oh." She sounded a little surprised, and then, bless her sweet heart, she said, "well, that's good news."

I hoped my fifteen seconds were up, but oh, no . . . she had to ask: "But what if they do turn you down?"

Shit. I nearly said it on air, but bit it off in time. "I cannot even imagine that happening, Marilyn. We're going to have the most wonderful weekend this town has ever seen! Are you coming?"

She laughed. "Wouldn't miss it. Thank you, Jennifer Cain, director of the Judy Foundation, organizers of the upcoming Port Frederick Halloween Festival. Now, let's talk to—"

Abruptly, she was gone, and I was talking to air.

Well, she'd phrased it positively—"upcoming"—as if it really would happen, even if she had damned us with the wrong label. Halloween Festival.

Gently, I hung up.

Looked at my men.

"Television," I explained.

David got bug-eyed, then turned and ran off. I heard him slam into the living room, where, I suspected, he would try to see if they were saying anything else about us.

"You done good, kiddo," Geof praised me.

But I shook my head. "I don't know. I can talk all I want, but until the insurance comes through . . ." I smiled at him. "And don't tell me to call them first thing in the morning. I will. You know I will."

He laughed. "Me? Do that?"

In a couple of minutes, David reappeared, looking excited. "I only caught the end of it. The last thing was the mayor saying it would be a great day for Port Frederick . . ."

Sounded like Mary, I thought fondly.

". . . and then some fat broad with black hair saying it could be a black day for Port Frederick. Who's she, anyway?"

"Ardie Kennedy," I said tersely, not wanting to go into it. David was old enough to vote, but he clearly wasn't into learning the identities of the local candidates. I looked at Geof, sharing a thought with him: Damn. What a way to end the news segment. What a thought to leave in the minds of their viewers. Would they remember anything that either Mary or I had said? I wondered what Pete Falwell had said, or the fire chief—whose toes I would personally and gladly have roasted over an open fire.

Well, I'd done what I could for the time being.

I needed to put stage two into action, but . . .

"I'm exhausted," I admitted to them. "Anybody hungry?"

"You go be a lump," Geof said, coming all the way into the kitchen. "Relax. Put your feet up. I'm going to cook."

I glanced at David, bracing myself for an onslaught of complaining about how Geof was abandoning their computer adventures. Instead, he said, "Is there anything I can do to help?"

Geof and I carefully avoided looking at each other.

"Can you tear lettuce?" Geof asked casually.

I walked quietly out of the room, trying to hide my limp so Geof wouldn't have a fit again about Pete, and left the cooking to them. What a shock, David's offer of help! Was it because of Geof, I wondered, or something we said? A wry voice inside my head warned, Don't ask!

I went and was a lump in the living room until suppertime, my right leg propped on a coffee table, the television off, my eyes closed. I was unable to face the stairs at that point, but I prayed food would give me the strength finally to attain the comforts of the second floor.

The phone rang repeatedly, and none of us answered it.

I couldn't nap. Too wired. I'd forgotten something. I just knew I had, but what in the world was it?

After we ate the entire bowl of Geof's best tuna casserole, with David's green salad—he took his supper into the living room to watch the tube—I consulted briefly over the phone with my board of directors. Then, by consensus, I called the one person among my previous employers whom we all felt would be the most likely to rush to our defense.

"Miss Grant?" I said to my former fourth-grade teacher and current member of the board of directors of the Port Frederick Civic Foundation. "Do you agree with that editorial in tonight's paper?"

"My dear," said Lucille Grant, "what a question! I hope you don't take that sort of nonsense seriously?"

Was that a "no"? She was brisk, kind, her voice progressively weaker every year. Over eighty, she had actually taught long enough to have had both Pete Falwell and me as students, thirty years apart. It was a mind-boggling career. I loved her dearly and missed seeing her as often as I had when I was director of the old foundation. Though it pained me to hear her voice sound so weak, I was delighted at the strength of spirit remaining behind it.

"Well, actually, I do take it seriously insofar as it could shake a lot of people's confidence in our ability to get this show up and running. If the insurance doesn't come through on Monday, I'm going to have to persuade the town council to allow more time, and they won't do it if they're scared. Besides, we want people to feel good about this festival, Miss Grant. It's their festival, not ours. As for me, I'm only the go-fer."

"Jenny Lynn Cain, you could have run this festival with your hands tied behind your back in fourth grade!"

I'd been standing, leaning against a kitchen wall. But when she said that, I felt so grateful I had to grab the nearest chair and sit down in it.

"Would you say that? I don't mean that, literally, but something to show your faith in me? On television?"

"I? On TV?" She sounded flustered, then rather tickled at the notion. "Yes, I will, but only if you truly think it's needed."

"I truly do, Miss Grant. And if you think any of the other trustees would—"

"Oh, they will." She chuckled, a lovely sound, because I knew it held equal parts affection for me, determination to do the right thing, and sheer pleasure in the power she still had to intimidate obstreperous boys. "If they want my vote on any of their dreary projects in the future! I'm really quite peeved at you, dear—"

"Really?" Instantly I was alarmed.

"Yes, really. You recruited me for the board of directors, and then we started having fun, you and I, prodding all those stuffy old men to take some philanthropic risks, and then you upped and quit on me! You have left me stranded on a desert island with four old geezers, my dear."

I laughed, enjoying her immensely. The oldest of the geezers was probably a decade younger than she was.

"Sorry," I apologized. "You want to jump ship and join us at the Judy Foundation, Miss Grant?"

"I'd love to, Jenny, but I won't. I fear that would hurt the old boys' feelings." Then she was brisk again. "How do I arrange for myself to become a television star, dear?"

Carefully, down to every detail, I told her. When we hung up, I felt better, but I knew that come Monday, if the insurance still hadn't come through, no quantity of glowing testimonials—not even if they were from the governor, the President of the United States, or the Queen of England—would save us. As for any furor over God's Highway, if I could just keep that tamped down until after the festival . . .

Miss Grant was taking a chance in going public to refute the *Times*. And neither of us could predict at this point whether she was backing a winning horse.

David wandered into the kitchen, empty supper plate in hand. He set it in the sink and then ran water over it. Would wonders never cease? I said nothing aloud, but warned myself silently: *Don't expect this to last.*

"Where's your cycle?" I asked him.

"Behind the garage," he said, pleasantly enough. He was drying his hands, and now he leaned back against the edge of the counter and crossed one long blue-jeaned leg over the other. "My landlady kicked me out, said she needed the space for her granddaughter who's moving to town."

I waited for the other shoe to drop.

"So." He looked briefly at me, then anyplace else. "I thought I'd camp out here for a few days. Just until I find new digs." When I still didn't speak—it's hard to talk when you're in shock—he added, aggressively, "Is that okay with you?"

"Sure," I lied.

"Okay." He unfolded himself. Not thank you, just okay. "I'll check it out with Geof."

There were two nuggets of gold in this vein of heavy lead, I decided after he departed. One was that David might continue to keep Geof occupied after hours, so neither one of them would bug me as much. And the other—and most interesting—was that David had asked me first, before he asked Geof.

Yeah, but what did that mean?

I thought it was probably a good sign, but couldn't have quite articulated why I thought that was so.

On my way upstairs to bed—with my briefcase—I stopped by the living room, where both males were stretched out like great lithe tomcats on the two couches watching a shoot-'em-up HBO movie. The masculine presence in the room was so thick I felt as if I could have moved it around with a wave of my hands, like smoke.

"David?"

He didn't remove his stare from the screen, but he did say, "Huh."

"Would you help me run an experiment tomorrow? For the foundation?"

For the foundation with his mother's name on it, I thought he might perform favors he wouldn't have done for me alone.

"Like what?"

"Watch your movie. I'll explain in the morning. Will you still be here for breakfast?"

He patted the couch he was sprawled on. "I'll be *here.*"

When I was halfway up the stairs, I heard my husband call, "Jenny? Honey? Do we have any chocolate-mint ice cream?"

"No," I called back down, perhaps a shade more brusquely than was absolutely required to answer such a simple question.

8

WHEN GEOF FINALLY CAME UPSTAIRS TO BED, I WAS JUST STEPPING CAREFULLY out of the tub. He came into the steaming bathroom and grabbed a towel and began to dry me off. As the steam cleared, we both exclaimed a bit over the multitude of dark colors decorating my skin, I with clinical interest, he with dismay. Black, blue, and red were the principal colors of the basic design. When Geof's outrage began to heat rapidly from simmer to boil, I leaned against him and pleaded simply. "Don't."

Then I stood limply, like a happy wet rag doll and let him dry me.

After a few blissfully peace-filled moments, he said in a near-whisper, "Can you believe it, Jenny? It was actually kind of nice tonight with him around, don't you think so?"

"One step forward," I agreed, as Geof shifted his efforts from my backside to an even more gentle drying of my front. "And it could be followed by three steps back."

He glanced at my wet face.

My concern probably showed—for him, for his feelings.

"Don't get my hopes up, you mean?" he asked.

I didn't answer, knowing he didn't require me to. I merely groaned anew with lazy, appreciative pleasure.

"I need a shower," he said.

"Not for me, you don't." I was too worn out to wait for him to bathe; by the time he got out, I might be asleep. My hands moved to the top buttons of his shirt. "But we'll have to be quiet, won't we, so we don't wake the baby."

"You're so amusing. Are you sure you want—"

"I want."

We were almost asleep when I mumbled, "Geof? Isn't Lake Dawson a young guy?"

"What?"

I told him at the Dime Store that day Bill Kennedy had said it was amazing that Dawson was still playing football after all these years.

Geof laughed into his pillow. "A joke, Jenny. The Kansas City Chiefs' most famous quarterback—before Joe Montana, of course—was Len Dawson. He's a sportscaster now. Must be in his fifties or sixties."

"Oh. It was sure wasted on me."

Lake Dawson. Len Dawson. The Kennedys. Melissa Barney. God's Highway . . .

"Close the highway!" My eyes opened wide and I stared into the darkness of our bedroom. That's what it was, what I had forgotten! An odd little phone call before my interview. It had been a woman. What had she said to me?

I was asleep before I could remember any of the rest of it. But then I was awakened sometime later by a series of dreams that slipped away before I could remember them. They weren't nightmares.

Fate saved those for the next day.

"David?"

I said it softly, standing above him at the couch where he had spent the night as promised. Geof had supplied him with pillow and blanket, I saw. I also saw that the kid apparently slept nude—unless there were bikini briefs hidden beneath the scant bit of blanket he hadn't tossed off. You always hear how sweet and vulnerable people look when they sleep? Not this kid. He looked tough, guarded, frowning even in slumber. His sleeping fists were clenched as if he could wake up throwing a punch.

"David?"

I hesitated to shake him awake since that meant touching him. *Don't be silly,* I scolded myself, and then shook his bare shoulder. Just as his eyes opened, he moved a knee, and the blanket remaining on top of him fell off. Since David made no move to cover up, I quickly bent down, picked up a handful of yellow wool, and threw it over him.

"What?" he said sleepily, his eyes mere glints.

"What time's your shift today, David?"

At the Amoco gas station where he worked.

"Nine to four," he mumbled.

It was now seven A.M.

"Can you meet me at Judy's House at five o'clock?"

"Humph." He rolled the other way, sticking his face in the back of the couch and leaving part of his ass uncovered again. I didn't know if that was yes or no, or if he'd show up, or if he'd even really heard me. My guess was, the overall answer was no. Well, hell, I'd find somebody else to do me the favor. I didn't care to remain standing there in my living room staring at his bare butt. Especially since it was a better than even chance that he was playing flasher on purpose, to embarrass me.

In the kitchen, I said to Geof, "We could start getting calls from girls. Women."

"For David?" He looked disbelieving.

It was true, the kid was no social lion.

But I thought of the tough young face that was—when we met him—spotted badly by acne. We'd propelled him to a dermatologist, who'd prescribed medicine that was revealing a face that had always been . . . interesting . . . and was now edging damn close to good-looking. I suspected that David—with his intelligence, dark moodiness, motorcycle, wicked wit, and tragic orphan aura—might soon have a certain heart-pulling glamour in some female eyes. And that wasn't even counting his inheritance, which was hefty. And invested. I recalled, too, what I'd seen when the blanket fell away.

"Yes," I said, smiling—I thought—to myself. "David."

"Why are you grinning like that?" My husband's tone was gentle, provocative. "Thinking of last night?"

"That. And how much David reminds me of you, in some ways."

"Really?"

He was pleased.

As well he should be, I thought, this time keeping my smile completely to myself.

It was Friday, an October beauty like the day before, only warmer. Plenty warm enough for me to lower the top on the Miata. As the breeze blew me into town, I felt renewed, if still a little stiff and a lot sore.

Following another impulse—already being pulled along, perhaps, by an invisible thread spun by the weaving spider of fate—I decided to drive by the town common on my way into work.

What I saw there excited me so much I just had to stop and park, facing my car into the common where I could overlook all the activity. I hadn't expected our volunteers to start any construction until the next day, but it appeared that a few eager beavers had jumped the gun, bless their enthusiastic hearts. I saw both men and women out on the green, and they were surrounded by high stacks of lumber, which meant they'd been at it early, picking up the wood—mostly cheap plywood—hauling it, unloading it.

Now they were hoisting their hammers and screwdrivers to build the booths and other temporary structures for the festival.

The ringing music of construction filled the morning.

Church bells to my ears.

Our common was nearly identical to many other old New England towns: basically seven square acres of grassy park and parade ground ringed by restored or reconstructed, historically accurate buildings. The settlers who founded our town set off a common area, then built a church at the edge of it, then a house for the minister, then a school, and then the leading citizens got their pick of the best sites for their homes, facing the green. At the Port Frederick Civic Foundation, I'd had a hand in arranging the financing of the restoration of those original structures.

It was the heart of a modest historical district, nowhere near on the scale of a magnificent place like Williamsburg, but still, our own pride and joy.

The heart of the festival would be there, on the common, but it would also run down the connecting streets and—everybody hoped—profitably bleed its spending money into the stores that would remain open for festival hours all weekend.

A lot of people—not to mention charities—stood to make a lot of money, if all went well. The chamber of commerce was estimating that a half-million dollars could pour into Port Frederick in two days, but then chambers of commerce are *supposed* to exaggerate, everybody knew that. It was their job, I supposed. My own projections, which I'd laid out for the town council months before, were closer to half that figure, but then I may have erred on the conservative side.

That was *my* job, I supposed.

I saw the builders were starting with the first thing we'd need, after the ticket-takers' booths, which was the speaker's platform, dead center. There, at ten A.M. a week from tomorrow, Mayor Eberhardt would officially open the First Annual Autumn Festival. Various sponsors had tried to persuade me to get up there with her and give a speech on behalf of the foundation, but I had demurred, making light of it by saying that the person running the show should remain backstage so no dissatisfied festival-goer could throw brickbats at her. In truth, it was only that I thought the city should be the star that day, with me and my pals (except Mary) merely working as invisible stagehands.

After all the speechifying, our local chapter of the American Civil

Liberties Union would be taking over the platform to sponsor a sort of Hyde Park Corner, where anybody could pay a buck to declaim in public their constitutionally protected views on any subject. Well, what the hell, I'd thought, when they'd first proposed the idea: This is Massachusetts, we're supposed to be inflammatory. But now a wry thought occurred: would Pete Falwell pay a dollar to denounce Judy's House—or the festival—or the mayor—in public?

No, I decided, smiling to myself, Pete would rather see *me* elected mayor than to give a cent to liberal lawyers.

The speaker's platform was only big enough for one person at a time to mount it. I counted four steps leading up about four feet to a rectangle of wood no more than six feet long by four feet wide. As I watched, two carpenters—God only knew what they really did for a living; they could be doctors, lawyers, or even real carpenters—raised a tall wooden stake until it towered over them, and they affixed it to the floor of the platform. And that, I supposed, was where the ACLU would nail their posters.

Vaguely, I was aware of another car driving slowly by.

When its brakes squealed infinitesimally, I glanced in my side mirror. It was a huge, old-fashioned Lincoln, two-tone blue, four doors. I watched the driver lumberingly maneuver the immaculate tank around until he could back it in right beside me.

We were driver to driver, mirror to mirror.

Electronically, he lowered his window.

" 'Morning, Roy."

I knew the car, "Gertrude," and the man, Roy Leland.

"You feel safe in that little bug, Jenny?"

"Safe? From what, Roy?"

He was another of my elderly ex-employers, the retired president of a grocery wholesale conglomerate and an immensely wealthy, former friend of my father. But not our enemy, not like Pete. I used to enjoy big, blustery Roy, irredeemably chauvinistic though he undeniably was. I figured, on this brilliant morning, that I still did. Get a kick out of him, that is. Roy was smoking one of his football-field-length cigars, living proof—so far—that not everybody who smoked died a dreadful death. Roy was too ornery to die that way, I figured, which was fine with me. Fortunately, the breeze blew his fumes back into his own car.

"From getting squashed in traffic by somebody bigger than you are," he rasped. All of my old men trustees had acted paternally toward me when I worked for them—as they acted toward all women—but Roy was the gruff kind of father figure who would bully you in lieu of actually displaying any affection. "I never let my own kids have any convertibles.

Not safe. Muggers. Thieves. Rapists. Slash your top when it's up, slash you when it's down. Not safe."

I smiled at him. "Yeah, but I'm wearing my seat belt, Roy."

Roy never smiled much, merely squinted his small, cunning eyes in his meaty red face.

"Miss Lucille called me last night," he announced.

I nodded, waited, breath held.

"Tried to blackmail me into making some goddamn television appearance." He made it sound as if Miss Grant had asked him to dance naked with her around the common at noon. "Can't help you, Jenny. Wish I could. You know that."

I knew he meant it, but I felt a sinking disappointment for myself and embarrassment for my darling old teacher. Why had I placed her in a position where any of these old guys could say no to her?

"Why can't you, Roy?"

He was blunt. Always. It was liberating, I'd found. So I was always blunt right back at him.

He chomped down on the stogie, speaking through semiclamped lips. "Don't like change, Jenny."

I knew that, knew it of all of them.

"Like things to stay the way they are, way they've always been." He jerked the cigar out of his mouth and used it to point behind him to the activity on the common. "Too much for this town. You know what your problem is, Jenny?"

"Didn't know I had one, Roy."

"You think too big."

I stared at him, startled.

"Too goddamn big," he repeated. "Things get out of control when they get too goddamn big."

I said, matter-of-factly, "Out of control of you and Pete and the other men, you mean."

He squinted at me in what was nearly a wink. But he wasn't joking when he replied, after only the briefest of pauses, "One thing you're not is stupid." He placed a beefy fist around his gearshift. "No hard feelings between you and me."

"No," I said. But what I was really thinking was, *Screw you, and the dinosaur you rode in on.* However, that blunt I wasn't; it wouldn't have helped, and my late mother wouldn't have approved of my being rude to Roy Leland, who only meant to be nice to me.

With a friendly chop of his left arm, which was his version of a goodbye wave, Roy lumbered his old blue boat out of there, his rejection taking some of the glow of the morning with him. Would Miss Grant have any better luck with the other two remaining trustees?

I began to wonder if, in asking her for such a major favor, I had . . . thought too big . . . for my britches.

9

I SANG "OH, WHAT A BEAUTIFUL MORNING," ALL THE WAY INTO THE OFFICE, even if the lyrics weren't quite accurate, since "everything" wasn't "going my way."

There was a man waiting for me at Judy's House, and he barely had on any britches at all. I observed *that* the minute I walked in, seeing him at first only from the, um, rear. It seemed to be a developing theme to my day, I thought, recalling my bare husband in the morning and David, after that.

Not a bad running motif, actually.

Smiling, I quietly crossed my office carpet to within a few feet of the visitor. This fellow, whoever he was, looked about five feet ten inches tall, maybe a hundred and sixty pounds and most of that lean muscle. I knew that, because I could see so much of it. He wore a sleeveless khaki-colored T-shirt and matching short-shorts rolled up to just under his tight ass, and heavy-duty hiking boots with thick heather socks. For those few seconds, I was treated to a great view of tightly muscled calves, knees, and thighs, as well as big shoulders, forearms, and biceps and also whatever those other muscles in the upper arm are called. He had curly black hair cropped very short, and I saw a hint of beard from where I stood behind him. Either this was a true outdoorsman and athlete, or else it was somebody who spent more time at a gym than most people did at their jobs.

I coughed, discreetly.

He turned his face, showing me more tan, the full beard, an accompanying moustache, dark eyes that looked excited to see me, and a wicked grin.

A strangely familiar wicked grin.

"Cain," he said, and held his arms wide as if he expected me to run into them. "I've come back to you. Did you miss me? Of course, you did. Well, everything's all right now. Come to Daddy."

"Oh, my God," I said, and then I matched his grin. "Oh, my God!"

"Greek god," he corrected, and he waggled his fingers as if urging me into the embrace he still held open to me. "Give us a hug, Cain."

Laughing, I did just that, though I quickly stepped away for self-protection: partly, to protect my bruises, but also because I knew better than to get any part of my anatomy too close for too long to Lew Riss, old friend, former reporter for the *Times,* irrepressible and perpetually horny egotist. But this "Greek god" was no Lewis I had ever seen before. The one I remembered was a scrawny, dope-smoking, wise-cracking, feverishly intelligent, and ambitious . . . jerk. Of whom I had always, and against my better judgment, been fond nonetheless.

But that was all years ago, as many as eight or nine.

"Lewis?" I said, from a cautious distance. "Is it really you?"

"I've come back for you," he repeated comically, "just when you had given up all hope that you would ever see me again."

"In your dreams, Lew." I laughed.

He smirked his old lascivious Lewis Riss smirk. "Oh, you've been in many of my dreams, Cain." We'd never been lovers—not a chance—but it was not for lack of effort on Lew's part. "Are you still married to that fascist?"

"Yes, still married to the cop, Lew."

And suddenly I was delighted to see him, this blast from the past, this distraction from my festival, this impossibly annoying man who could make me laugh even when I wanted to wallop him, and I limped back for another careful hug. He didn't appear to notice my careful movements, but then Lew Riss had never been notably observant of other people's feelings.

"You never could resist me, Cain."

Lew smelled, deliciously, of fresh air.

His body gave off a furnace of heat, supplying a reason for his attire apart from sheer exhibitionism alone, which I wouldn't have put past him. He'd always been a show-off, fighting to get his byline into print as often and in as large type as possible during the brief years when he'd worked in Port Frederick. Lew was perhaps the only truly extroverted print reporter I'd ever met, and for that reason—and others having to do with a certain softness in the area of ethics—he'd seemed a bit of a fish out of water in journalism, to me. In fact, he had that in common with Ardyth Kennedy, I suddenly realized: heavy in ambition, light on content. But Lew was a lot more likable, to me at least, than Ardie. His boyish charm could wear on you, but at least he did possess redeeming qualities. Maybe it was his intelligence. No, more likely that plus his sense of humor, always a saving grace.

"I could resist you." I pulled back and made a show of examining him, as ostentatiously as possible. "But that was the other Lew Riss, that skinny, scruffy fellow. This man—" I placed my open right hand against the massive pad of muscle below his left shoulder and pushed in. It gave slightly, as a slab of beef might. "—may be more difficult to resist. Lewis! You're gorgeous! Look at these muscles, look at these legs, get a load of this chest, girls, and look at this hair!"

"My hair?" His hands jumped from me to his own scalp. "What's wrong with it?"

"It's combed. It never was before, that I can recall. I like the beard. I love the moustache. Okay, I'll admit that you used to be kind of cute, in your own degenerate way, but this is the biggest transformation since Beauty kissed the Beast." I walked completely around him, slowly, insultingly, doing my best to accomplish the impossible, which was to embarrass him. "Who got hold of you? A woman? Had to be a woman. She must have been an aerobics teacher. What have you been doing for the last—how many years is it?—besides working out with weights? You've become Sylvester Stallone since I've seen you. Where'd all these muscles come from? Why are you walking around half naked? And what are you doing back in my town? Are you still working for a newspaper? Did you ever win that Pulitzer you wanted? Lewis!" Coming around in front of him, I grabbed hold of his upper arms with both of my hands and shook him until he rocked on his feet. It wasn't easy to do. "You used to be such a wimp, and now you're a bullock! What are you doing here?"

He was preening, not in the least self-conscious.

"Sit," he commanded me. "Uncle Lewis will tell all."

I took him by his meaty hands and led him over to one of the love seats and risked my own virtue by seating myself right next to him. Lord, he radiated warmth like a space heater. He put an arm over the back of the love seat, behind me, and I allowed his hand to drape itself lightly over my shoulder. It felt brotherly. And, besides, I could always punch him, if he tried anything Lew-like.

"I'll get to the personal history," he said, in a voice that was all of a sudden pitched lower and slower than I remembered, more like a man's instead of an overgrown boy's. He smiled, half mocking grin, half sincere. Sincere? Internally, I blinked. Lewis? Even half was half again as much as there used to be. "You probably think I came back only to see you, and God knows normally that would be the only reason to return—"

"Why, thank you." I flapped my eyelids at him.

"—to this one-horse town."

"I guess that makes me the horse?"

He shook his head at me, smiling in a brand-new adult kind of way. Who *was* this stranger, anyway? This guy who only barely resembled Lew Riss, and who now didn't sound like Lew at all?

"You're being silly, but I'm serious, Jenny."

No way, I thought, but I didn't say it, though he must have detected the skepticism in my eyes, because he laughed and said, "No. Really. The only other reason I'm here is that I hear you're thinking of messing with God's Highway."

This time, my blink was visible.

"How do you know that?" I asked him. "And what's it to you?"

"It was in the paper, wasn't it?" he said, explaining nothing, really, for how did he happen to come across last night's *Port Frederick Times?* And then he very clearly answered my second question: "I'm the national director of First Things First."

I felt every muscle in my own body tighten at the sound of those three words, and Lew felt it under his hand, because he got a quizzical look on his face.

"Since when?" I asked.

"A couple of years. Is something the matter with that?"

"What happened to journalism, Lew?"

He squeezed my shoulder, then removed his hand and put it on the back of the love seat. "What I discovered about myself is that I'm an activist, not an observer." Suddenly, the old wired, intense Lew was back, and I realized with a jolt that it made a weird and perfect sense that he would end up as the head of one of the only truly militant conservation groups in the world. Dismissively, as if he hadn't devoted years of his life to it, he said, "Journalism is for people who don't want to get involved, they're not supposed to have opinions, they're supposed to be blank slates on which they write down other people's views of the world."

A harsh judgment, but then Lew had never been what you would call wishy-washy in his opinions. Drugs were good. Sex was good. Laws were a pain in the ass, and cops were fascist assholes. Those were four of the opinions he used to hold. He looked as if he had changed his mind about the first one, not about the second one, and that he'd found a new and dangerous way to express the last two.

First Things First was into staging courtroom scenes straight out of the sixties' peace trials . . . and torching lumberyards to stop deforestation . . . and splashing blood on women wearing fur coats. And there were rumors of other, even more violent methods, approaching true guerrilla warfare, complete with guns and spies. Twelve years before, they'd descended on the little communities involved in the nature trail like dozens of Che Guevaras in dozens of little Havanas. They'd escalated, intimidated, threatened, coerced. Picketed, blockaded, organized, inspired. And won. I had always felt that if FTF had been opposed to abortion, there would have been more dead doctors.

I was beginning to listen to Lew with some dread, thinking: I don't want to fight you, and I don't want you—with your concrete opinions, your inflated view of yourself, and your plastic morality, no matter how sporadically charming you may be—picketing across any line from me. The Lew Riss who would have done anything for a story was not my opponent of choice. Especially not in this new incarnation as a full-grown, purposeful adult male with the physical power to match his considerable mental strengths.

And with the terrorist civilian-soldiers of FTF behind him.

He was still carrying on about the evils of journalism. "It's a crappy way to live. It's like being the wrapper instead of the bread. It's safe, you know?" He put infinite scorn into those words. "Oh, yeah, you can get yourself killed reporting on wars and shit, but you're still not the one who's *doing* the thing that's getting done. You're just looking at what all the real guys are doing. You're the film, instead of the event. Well, I got fucking tired of being film. I wanted to be the event. I wanted to *do,* instead of just report on what other people do. And besides . . ."

His grin had shades of the old Lew in it.

So did his language.

"I was never going to win that Pulitzer, Cain, and I know it and you know it. I'm not that good a reporter. Hell, I hate facts." He laughed. "It's goddamned petty, the way editors insist on them." He grinned at me again. "And balance. Screw balance. A balanced viewpoint? That's for people who live on balance beams, not me. And, besides, I'm such a competitive son of a bitch, after I had figured out all of that about myself, I just lost interest. If I can't be top dog, then I'm getting out of the ring."

"So what are you competing for now, Lew?"

"The life of the planet, Cain. Oxygen to breathe, water to drink, food you can eat without dying of cancer, petty goddamn stuff like that."

He was wry, cynical, hard.

Also arrogant and just ever so slightly insulting.

I chose not to feel insulted.

"Why'd you pick the environment to act on?"

"Because I want to serve nature. Fuck the arts. Fuck medicine. Fuck housing. Fuck business. We don't get the luxury of playing with any of those baubles if we can't breathe, or drink, or eat."

"First Things First."

"Fuckin' A. It's about priorities, Cain."

"Your language hasn't improved any, Lew."

"Like I said, it's about priorities, baby. I'll clean up my language when you clean up the air and the rivers and the ocean and the land. They were here first."

"Me, personally, Lewis?"

"Your own patch of Mother Earth, yeah, that's how it works."

"What *about* my patch of it? The Port Frederick patch of God's Highway? What's your interest in it?"

"We want it pristine. We want it perfect. We want people like you to leave it the fuck alone."

"It's just a hiking trail, Lewis!"

"It's nature, baby. That comes first, always."

"They're not separate."

"What's not?"

"People and the environment."

"Let's forget the semantics, Cain."

"You're relegating people to the category of semantics? Excuse me? People are part of the environment, Lewis, we're not separate from it, and we never have been since we got here. Trying to separate nature from humanity by assigning more importance to either one of them is just nineteenth-century wrong-headed romanticism. Lewis, even quantum theory says that—we're all trading molecules, us and the trees. What's the matter with you, do you hate your own species? Maybe you could take a lesson from nature on that . . . you ever hear of a tree that hated other trees?"

"People!" He snorted. "People fuck."

I wondered what had gone wrong with him to skew him into misanthropy. Or was this only Lewis being melodramatic, for the side of the issue on which his bread was currently buttered?

"Only the lucky ones," I retorted, and smiled at him.

He didn't smile back at me, as he once might have done.

"Lewis, remember what you used to say to me? Loosen up, Cain, you'd say. Well . . . loosen up, Lew!"

"You cannot alter one twig of God's Highway unless we approve it."

"Tell me, please, that you're kidding."

"Lives are at stake, Cain."

"Well, of course, that's why we're looking at whether or not to alter that trail crossing."

"No, I mean birds, insects, flora, fauna."

"How about the mammals called people, Lew? Listen, I know your group, you First Things Firsters. I know how much trouble you love to cause, I *remember.* And I also know that you, personally, may as well have invented Situational Ethics. You make up rules to suit yourself. So I suppose you are perfectly suited to First Things First. Well, I will tell you what rule you may follow in this situation, Lew . . . you may advise us, if you wish. In fact, that would be fine, assuming you have the expertise to do it. But you may not dictate what we do."

"We can make things very hot for you, Jenny."

I looked at him in disbelief. "Lew? You make it sound as if the fate of the world is at stake here. It's just a trail crossing, where a little girl and a father were struck and killed by cars. We may be able to fix it with a few well-placed signs, nobody knows yet. But it's nothing major, Lew, the environment is not riding on it."

"When a butterfly flaps its wings in Russia, the air moves in Mexico," he said, quoting quantum physics right back at me. He suddenly stood, leaving me staring up at him. "You can't touch the trail without our approval, Jenny. There are certain types of trees we won't allow you to touch. There is certain foliage you may not touch, either, and if there are any endangered species in the way—their nests, for instance—you'll back off. I'll be sticking around, me and a few of my guys, to make sure you do it right."

I stood up, too, hanging on to my fury by a wisp of self-control.

"I don't believe this! Lew, it's me! Jenny! We talk to each other, we don't threaten . . . and just what *are* you threatening . . . if we don't do things your way?"

"Bad publicity could kill your festival. There are crowds we can get here on a few hour's notice. For demonstrations. Strikes. Protests."

What did he mean, *kill the festival?*

"We want to know what you plan to do, Cain. Then we'll tell you if it passes muster with us. If it doesn't, we start gathering our troops. If you don't *tell* us your plans, we'll do the same."

So they could put their terrorist tactics into action in order to scare New England clean away from Port Frederick and our festival.

"When was it that you went crazy, Lew?" I inquired bitterly.

He raised his hands and tried to cup my face, but I knocked his hands away, angrily. He shrugged again and grinned the old Lew grin at me. But this time, I didn't fall into it. This time, I merely stared at him.

"I was just going to kiss you good-bye, Jenny," he said. "I wasn't going to rip your head off."

"Will you be at a hotel?"

He looked offended at the very idea. "I live outside, Jenny. In nature. On the move. I don't *observe* anymore, remember? I act."

Yeah, you act like an ass.

Lewis saw himself to the door. Through the front window, I saw a beige van pull up out front and the side door slide open for him. Before he climbed in, I counted five people in the van—a woman driving, a man in the passenger's seat, and three other men in back where Lewis went. They all wore khaki shorts and tops, like Lew, and they all looked terrifyingly healthy and strong and young. There could have been others, but the door slid shut too fast for me to see them. Before she pulled away, the woman who was driving looked up at Judy's House, seeming to stare right into my eyes.

"Good grief, it's just a nature trail!" I said out loud when they were gone. "One little trail crossing! Strictly small-time. Strictly small town. Why does it matter to any of you *what* we do?"

Why did it matter to Pete Falwell, for that matter?

Or to anybody, except one grieving widow, and her sympathetic new friend, and an unknown, but grieving mother of a little girl? And me. Suddenly, it mattered to me, although possibly for the wrong reasons. Threaten me, would they? Tell me what to do and how to do it?

"Like hell!"

"What, Jenny?"

It was our Post Haste delivery woman, Cleo, standing in the doorway of my office with an invoice on a brown clipboard for me to sign.

Hope surged. It overpowered the fury I had been feeling, much like a larger wave overtaking a smaller one.

"Is that *it,* Cleo? Portsmouth?"

But she shook her head, making my rotten morning complete.

Oh, what a beautiful day, my foot.

10

Because of the newspaper editorial, indignation reigned at Judy's House that day. The general view among my festival volunteers seemed to be, "Those dirty rats. How *could* they?"

But there was another attitude lurking in the house, and radiating throughout Port Frederick. I was dismayed to sense it just beneath the fury: doubt. I saw it in glances that slid away from mine, and in the too-swift smiles, and I heard it in the quiet conversations that abruptly ceased when I appeared. I heard it in voices on the phone, as well. Or, thought I did. A hesitation. A stutter over my name. An embarrassed, over-hearty edge to "hello," and a note of relief in the sound of "goodbye."

So they'd accomplished it, Pete and the paper and Ardie and their gang: They'd slipped a wedge of real worry into the final days of preparation. They'd undermined people's faith in us—in me. I began to feel as if I were standing on an earthen bridge with the weather threatening rain, which could erode the whole structure and tumble me into the river below.

The whole thing could collapse.

I fought it the only way I could for the remainder of the day: with hard work. But when Cleo showed up at 3:30 with our final delivery for the day, and there wasn't any insurance approval, I nearly lost it. For a humiliating moment, I was sure I was either going to cry in front of her and my volunteers, or else throw up on her sturdy brown shoes.

I was staring at the floor, fighting for inner control, when I heard Cleo say, "Do you want to know?"

I blinked a couple of times, then looked up. I didn't understand what she meant, but before I could even form the question, she added, "If you're going to get the insurance?"

The question—or rather, the answer—seemed so obvious that I just stared at her.

"I mean, right now, do you want to get an answer about whether or not it's going to come through in time for the festival?"

"Well, sure." I smiled. "Got a crystal ball?"

The deliverywoman put her right hand to her neck and took hold of a thin silvery chain that was nearly hidden by her shirt. She tugged up from inside her clothes a long silver . . . something . . . and held it toward me.

"Sort of," she said. "Crystal, anyway."

The object at the end of her chain looked like a small wand. It was about three inches long, with a crown of amethyst at the top and a faceted crystal attached to the bottom.

"May I?" I asked, and when she nodded, I peered closer. "What's that shape in the middle, Cleo?"

"An Egyptian ankh," she said, "the cross of life. It's kind of a charm representing both the male and female. When the Christians adopted the cross, they removed the feminine part, which is this oval on top." She touched the oval above the crossbar of the little silver cross. "It was probably a goddess symbol way back when, and then it came to represent the sacred marriage of the god and goddess." She grinned, ruefully. "Then they took us off of it."

Cleo peered back at me, quizzically. "Haven't you ever seen a pendulum before, Jenny?"

"I guess maybe not."

She unclasped it, then, and dangled it in the air between us.

"It's a kind of oracle, but it can only reply to questions that can be answered yes or no. If it moves back and forth, that's a yes. Side to side is a no. If it goes in circles, that means it can't—or won't—give you an answer at this time."

Cleo indicated that I should take it from her.

Not wanting to seem rude, I did. The weight of the pretty crystal and silver wand now dangled lightly from my own right hand. My skepticism must have shown in my eyes, because Cleo laughed and said, "It's only your own involuntary muscles that work it, Jenny. I'm not saying it's some disincarnate spirit, or anything." She chuckled. "It's a path into your own subconscious, that's all. It's a way to find out what you really want, or what you really think, deep down." She raised her right eyebrow. "And sometimes it's a way to access information you don't know you know."

"The future, you mean?"

I couldn't tell from her attitude if she was serious.

Cleo shrugged her strong shoulders. "Even science says it's all happening now. The past, the present, the future."

I smiled at her. "The Eternal Now, I presume?"

Her grin broadened. "Yeah. That's the one. Go ahead, Jenny, ask it something!"

I could tell I wasn't going to get out of this, at least not without looking like a prissy little spoilsport. So, hoping nobody came downstairs and saw me doing it, I held the wand in front of me, dangling it from the chain while trying to paralyze my arm movements.

"No, no, not like that, Jen. Go sit down at your desk and prop your elbow up. You want to feel as sure as you can that you're not moving it on purpose."

Once propped, under Cleo's guidance, I still felt supremely silly.

"Do I ask it out loud?" I inquired.

"Doesn't matter."

"Oh, Pendulum," I intoned, with mock sobriety, "tell me if we will get our insurance approval in time for the festival!"

Nothing happened.

And then the damned thing began to swing to and fro, and then to swing harder, higher, in each direction. Away from me, toward me. Away from me, toward me. I felt a real tug on the fingers that held the chain, and I would have sworn to a judge that I wasn't the one who was moving it.

Despite myself, I felt enormous, happy relief.

"Yes!" shouted Cleo. "Hot damn!"

I dropped her necklace onto my desktop.

"How'd it feel to you, Jenny?"

"Strong," I admitted. "I have no idea how that happened. I really concentrated on holding still, Cleo. I guess involuntary muscle movement has to be the answer, doesn't it? But what does *that* mean, except that I really want this to happen? I already knew that."

"Sometimes people think they want something, but their unconscious sabotages them."

I looked at her youthful, tanned face, her halo of brown hair, and I noticed for the first time the intelligence and sensitivity in her gray eyes. This was a most remarkable and interesting delivery person.

"Now you know you don't have to worry about that," she added. "But don't deny the possibility that it also means you really don't have anything to worry about, and the insurance really will come through."

I glanced down at the necklace. Yeah, right.

"Cleo," I said, as she took back her property, "you deliver the most amazing things. And speaking of which, did you check out the source of that spider paperweight we got yesterday?"

"Yeah, and I still say it came from the Dime Store."

"Really? Nellie Kennedy says not."

"Shall we ask the pendulum?"

I was joking, which Cleo must have been able to tell, because she didn't hand it back to me, but just continued to reclasp it around her neck and then to stuff it back down into her blouse.

"I guess there was a time," I said, "when oracles wouldn't have had to hide the tools of their trade." It was funny, but in spite of myself, I felt happier, stronger, more peaceful, thanks to her silly little silver wand. I didn't quite know how to thank her.

"That's okay," she said, "really."

I stared. "Are you a mind reader?"

"It doesn't take a psychic to know what kind of pressure you must be feeling. But . . . I think you ought to remember they're jerks." She flushed, as if she were embarrassed at her own temerity in telling me what to do.

But I was delighted with her advice and laughed out loud when I heard it.

I released a pent-up breath.

"So, Madam Cleo," I said, "how'd you get so smart, so young?"

Her eyes closed, her face drew in, as if she'd felt a spasm of pain.

"Cleo?" I stood up. "What's wrong?"

But she turned away, hiding her face from me, waving away my concern with her hands. "Sinus headache. Comes on sudden like that. No big deal. Gotta go. See ya, Jenny."

She trotted away, out of my office, out our front door.

I felt responsible for making her late on her rounds and sorry if I had contributed extra tension to her headache.

When I stepped to the front window to watch her drive away, I saw an old battered black wasp of a motorcycle parked against the curb. I didn't see its driver.

His voice, however, coming from behind me, made me jump.

"What *kind* of experiment, and why do you need me?"

I turned, disguising how startled I felt by his sudden appearance.

"David," I said.

So he had heard my request. And he'd come. Sounding belligerent, suspicious. Looking like a nerdy Hell's Angel, skinny and tall and dressed all in black, and wearing a black baseball cap with a Star Trek logo. But at least he'd come. Another sign of progress?

With the poltergeist, one never knew.

"Jenny," he echoed, mocking me.

"David, has anybody given you a hard time about that editorial?"

"No." He looked as if I were nuts to ask. "Why should they? I mean, like, nobody knows it's named after her, except you and me and Geof and your board members, right?"

"Right." My wry tone was certainly wasted. "I'll just get my jacket."

The motorcycle ride out to the vicinity of Nellie's house was good therapy for what ailed me. When I told David that, as we alighted from his bike, he said in a mellower voice than he'd used before, "So, what ails you, exactly?"

It was already late afternoon, and getting toward that time of evening when the light is the most beautiful and eerie. As we rode, it had begun to weave a twilight shawl of yellow, pink, violet, and black threads of clouds above us. It was not a warm shawl, however, not on this late October afternoon, and I shivered inside my jacket as I considered David's very good question. We had pulled to a stop at the mouth of the Kennedys' gravel driveway, where I'd run over their discarded Christmas tree the winter before.

A few feet behind us was the big red stop sign.

It looked plainly visible from every direction.

Beyond us, the hill dropped off fairly steeply, and I could just see the beginning of the curve that wound through the deadly intersection with God's Highway. I couldn't see that exact spot from where we stood, nor would any driver have known it was there, unless he was local and familiar with this route.

It seemed to me that was a surmountable problem.

Maybe we could solve it with cheap and simple signage.

I sighed, thinking with half of my mind, *We should be so lucky that it turns out to be so easy,* and with the other half, still pondering David's question.

"Excessive concern about the opinions of other people," was my eventual self-diagnosis, only partially facetious. "I guess." I tore my gaze away from the setting sun and took a chance and smiled at him. There was something about his ancient BMW 1000 motorcycle that softened us toward each other, the way nothing else ever seemed to do. After one of our infrequent joy rides, the kid became almost human. Nearly adult.

Kind of intelligent and likable. Our rides melted me, too, and so I was probably nicer to him than I was at other times.

"Get yourself a motorcycle, that'll cure that problem," he advised. "The only people who approve of cycles are other cycle riders. Everybody else hates us. They think we're stupid or we're foolhardy or we're dangerous and we ought to be illegal. When you're on a motorcycle, you just can't give a fuck about other people's opinions."

My own motorcycle . . .

What an idea . . .

An *idiotic* idea. I shook it off and got down to business, describing the general problem to David. Then I said, "So I want to test the actual safety . . . or relative danger . . . of the trail crossing. I'm going to walk down to the crossing. What I'd like you to do is get back on your bike, far enough up the highway that you can get up to the speed limit. Run the stop sign. Drive on down the hill. Don't exceed the speed limit, just keep going fifty-five. And see how far back you have to start braking in order to come to a full stop at the place where I'm standing."

"Okay, but why my bike? Why not a car? It was cars that killed those people, wasn't it?"

"I will probably repeat this, with cars."

I could see that he was getting interested, even a little eager about this test drive of ours. He waved one of his long arms in the direction of the crossing. "You ought to step out in front of me all of a sudden, Jenny, see if I can stop in a hurry."

"Uh, no, thank you."

"Hell, why not?"

"Because what if you *can't,* David?"

His answering grin was devilish.

Down at the bottom of the curve, I positioned myself right in front of the trees closest to the road, exactly at the place where the trail came out onto the highway. In the mere fifteen minutes or so that David and I had puttered around by the stop sign and the little bit of time it had taken me to stroll down, the sun had declined considerably farther in the west. It was so low on the horizon now that if you were driving west —which the kid would be—it could blind you. I wondered if that was what had happened, if the drivers had been blinded, either to the stop sign or to their victims.

"I'll have to find out what time of day they died," I told myself.

It smelled good down here, fresh and countrified, although there were houses other than the Kennedys' all around, even if they weren't visible precisely from where I stood. Most of them were stuck back away from the highway, behind fences and hedges or rows of long-established trees. This was the far outskirts of Port Frederick, so it wasn't quite city, but it wasn't quite country, either. And yet it didn't feel exactly suburban, either—if you equate the suburbs with newer homes—because most of these places looked as if they'd been around for fifty, seventy, even a hundred years or more. No authentic historical landmarks, maybe, but comfy old farmhouse-type places, all the same. Homes that their owners loved, and homes that had seen more than one generation of a family inhabit them. These were the very property owners whom I felt had been cheated when they lost their private access, their property boundaries, on Crowley Creek when the trail was established.

A roar of a motorcycle engine placed me on red alert.

I heard David approach the stop sign at the top of the hill, and it was obvious from the ensuing noise that he didn't stop there, or slow down at all, but kept on coming at a steady roar. Since I knew he was planning to stop in plenty of time, and since there wasn't any traffic coming from the other direction, I decided to step out into the road, as Ben Barney might have done. Not far, though. Didn't want to place too much temptation in the kid's path, I thought, smiling to myself.

The roar increased.

The car that hit Mr. Barney wouldn't have made that much racket, I reminded myself, might even have been very quiet, so it was possible, I supposed, that he wouldn't have heard it coming. Maybe there was other noise—like a lawn mower, or a tractor in the distance. Or, maybe Melissa's husband was bird-watching, or . . . (I thought, sadly) . . . thinking romantic thoughts about her . . .

I was looking at the curve in the road.

Even so, it startled me to see David zoom around it.

Despite myself, I got scared and jumped back off the highway, losing my balance in the process. While David did just what he said he'd do, sliding to a smooth and steady stop right where he was supposed to, I tripped, flailed about with my arms, and fell backward into the trees, landing on my back in the leaves among their trunks.

From that position, I heard the sound of whistling and applause.

When I caught my breath, I looked up to see David still astride his motorcycle, clapping wildly for my performance. It took him only a couple of moments to pull toward me, switch off his bike, prop it up, and then run over to give me a hand up. He was grinning, damn him, as he pulled me to my feet.

"Didn't trust me, didya?" he accused, but he was laughing.

"You just startled me, that's all."

"Right." Still laughing, he started brushing leaves off me, but I brushed his hands away. "You win the award for Best Imitation of a Tree in a Tornado."

That made me giggle, which made him laugh harder.

"God, you looked funny," he said, grinning at me. "There was this surprised look on your face, like your eyes got real big and your mouth opened like a fish, and then you kind of made this weird rabbit hop, only backwards, and then you did your windmill impersonation, and then you fell down. It was a riot."

"I'm sure," I said sarcastically. "Oh, damn!"

"What?"

"Look, I'm bleeding! I scraped my hand on one of the trees. I'm going to get blood all over my clothes, if I don't do something about it." Besides which, it hurt. It was the back of my left hand, the same arm the Halloween protestor had wounded the day before. "I'm not usually this clumsy!"

"I didn't say you were," David retorted, sounding defensive.

"I know, I know, I was talking to myself. This is the third time I've done something like this in the last couple of days . . ."

I was beginning to feel cursed.

"Come on, Jenny. Just hop on the bike, and I'll ride you back to your office. You can bleed all over me, I don't care."

"No, no, ride me back up to the top, will you? I'll run up to the Kennedys' and see if they're home. Maybe they can doctor me with some soap and water and a couple of Band-Aids." While we walked back over to his bike, I asked him, "What would you do, David, to make this place safer?"

"That's easy," he said confidently. "Put gates up on both sides of the trail—like toll gates, you know?—where you have to stop if you're walking along. And you pay a quarter, maybe, which automatically opens the gates, and it also helps to underwrite the cost of the gates, to defray expenses. If you make people do that, see, then they can't just run out on the road without looking."

Underwrite, I thought? *Defray expenses?* Maybe some of the talks that Geof had been having with David about handling his inheritance were beginning to pay off. They were enlarging his vocabulary, at least. As for David's plan to fix the crossing . . .

"That's inventive," I said, tactfully, I hoped.

"But you gotta consider the qualifiers," he advised me.

I got on the bike behind him again, careful to keep the back of my left hand from touching anything. On our ride out, sitting astraddle hadn't been as easy and comfortable as it usually was, because of the bump on my right knee, from my literal run-in with Pete Falwell the day before.

I said into his right ear, "The what, David?"

He turned his face so I could hear him. "Stuff like time of day, angle of the sun in their eyes, road conditions—like, is it slick because it just rained, or—"

"Snowy," I contributed, remembering.

"Yeah. The amount of traffic. Stuff like that."

There had seemed to be a lot of traffic the night Geof and I had gotten stalled the previous January, but maybe that was only because of the backup. In normal conditions—like now—there wasn't much, surprisingly little, in fact. I recalled two or three vehicles passing us when we stood at the top of the hill in Nellie's driveway. Two cars coming from the direction of town, a van going the other way. Nothing since then. From the standpoint of changing the trail crossing, that wasn't necessarily a good thing. It was tough to persuade governments to install safety equipment, or alter roadways, if you couldn't give them impressive traffic counts.

"I'll keep all that in mind," I assured David, and was glad he couldn't see the smile on my face. He switched on the ignition, and off we roared to the top of the hill, after scattering gravel in a sharp turn at the bottom. For a minute, I thought he was going to leave me there, since I was only holding on with one hand, and when he accelerated up the hill I tilted backward precariously. But I managed to regain my balance and pressed against him until he deposited me on flat ground.

But when I walked up to the Kennedys' house, leaving David back at the mouth of the driveway, it was plain to see that Nellie and Bill weren't home yet. Not that I should have expected them to be, at this relatively early hour. They'd still be doing big business at the Dime Store until nine or ten o'clock, no doubt. I couldn't imagine how they managed to live with such long, hard hours, until I remembered how many hours I'd been devoting to my own favorite cause. *And who is still at work this afternoon?* I teased myself. At one side of their house, I found a spigot, which released enough cold water for me to rinse my hand until the bleeding stopped. The water had another benefit; it was so cold, it anesthetized the scrape, as well. When I was done, holding my hand carefully at my side I walked back to the end of the driveway where I'd left the kid with his engine idling.

No David. No motorcycle.

"Where'd you go?" I asked aloud, and then raised my voice to shout for him. *"David?* David!"

Intuition tugged me toward the crest of the hill, and then on down into the deeping shadows at the bottom of it. The woods still looked lovely, but a good deal darker and deeper than they had just a short time earlier.

"David?" I called out.

I kept carefully to the side of the road, not wishing to become road kill, but nobody passed going either way. I wondered why. Now that I thought about it, we hadn't seen any traffic on that road since shortly after we arrived at Nellie's driveway. How could that be? Particularly at this time of day, when people should have been coming home from work, if they had jobs in town.

It was all oddly quiet, except for the shuffling of my feet through the dead leaves and grass on the shoulder of the highway.

I reached the head of the curve. Walked on, rounding it, until I came out on the other side, facing the way to the river . . .

"David!" I screamed, at the sight awaiting me.

He was down, he and his motorcycle, stretched across the pavement, vulnerable to any passing vehicle. The bike lay on top of him. And the kid . . . David . . . wasn't moving, wasn't making any noise. His battered old helmet was still on his head, but the goggles he wore had broken and been thrown into the street. I stepped over them and ran toward him, shouting his name over and over. When I reached him, I quickly bent to see his face. White against the black pavement. But there was breath flowing in and out of his open mouth. I had to get help for him. He could be horribly injured. But I couldn't leave him lying in the highway while I ran for assistance.

I found out, quickly, just how heavy a 1000cc bike really is.

And how strong I could be when I needed to.

Somehow, straining, intent, desperate to do it, constantly worried about oncoming traffic, I pushed that motorcycle off him without allowing any part of it to fall back down on him. I pushed it into the trees and unceremoniously dumped it, though I knew he wouldn't thank me for being so careless with it. It may have been beaten up with age, but he loved it . . . .

Although I hated to take the chance of moving him, although I was horrified at the possibility of head, or neck, or back injuries, I grabbed hold of the shoulders of his black ski jacket, which was zipped up to his throat, and pulled him off into the trees. I removed my own jacket and covered him with it, fearing shock for him.

Then I left him there and ran toward my memory of one of the nearby houses that had its inside lights on.

It took longer for the ambulance to reach David than it should have, but there was a good—or, at least, an understandable reason for their frightening delay . . .

Somebody had blockaded the state highway above the stop sign and near the bridge.

They'd used actual state highway barricade signs to do it, the ones which were normally used only to block the road when the creek flooded. Drivers, assuming the bridge was out, had taken back roads, like good citizens.

Only the paramedics—inspired by the urgency of my message when I called 911, and then by police lieutenant Geof Bushfield after I reached him—had observed the creek was dry, and so had set aside the barricades.

11

WE TOOK HIM TO PORT FREDERICK MEMORIAL, BECAUSE THAT'S WHERE GEOF had him enrolled in a hospital insurance plan. His beloved BMW we had to leave by the side of the road.

Geof was there ahead of us, already pacing the fluorescent lobby of the emergency room when we pulled into the garage, lights flashing. The two paramedics—one doubling as driver—had with tender care bound David to a board, which they secured to a stretcher. A white neck brace held his head immobile. From the garage, they rolled him into the trauma center and then slickly—keeping him on the board—onto a narrow bed in a curtained cubicle, all within no more than thirty seconds of our arrival. Geof and I were immediately crowded out by people in white, who all looked nearly as young as David.

Geof grabbed my elbow—on my uninjured (as yet) right arm—and pulled me toward the two folding chairs that were placed a yard in front of the cubicle where they were stripping and examining David. I'd heard the paramedics use the words "head injury," and I was badly frightened by that.

Geof pushed me down into one of the chairs and stood right over me. He wasn't trying to intimidate, only to erect a private place for us, using his own body as a shield. He still wore the jeans, plaid shirt, and sport coat he'd worn to work that day, only now the shirt looked wrinkled, its collar open. His face was creased with worry, and he needed a shave.

"What the hell happened, Jenny?"

"That's what he asked me."

"David? He spoke to you? When? What'd he say?"

"He opened his eyes in the ambulance, looked straight at me, and said, 'What the fuck happened?' "

Geof and I both laughed a little.

"Then what?" he demanded.

"Then he closed his eyes and he was out again."

"But that was a good sign. Wasn't it? Isn't that encouraging?"

I clasped one of his big warm hands in mine. "I think so. Sure. It must be. Did you hear about the barricades on the highway? About somebody blocking the road with highway department signs?"

"I'll kill the sons of bitches."

If you find them, I thought.

I told him as exactly as possible what David and I had been doing, and how I had found David lying in the road.

"What was he doing?" Geof asked me, sounding angry, though I knew that he was scared, like me.

"Making another test run," I guessed. "Maybe he tried it too fast. He had wanted to see what would happen if he tried to brake suddenly."

"Moron."

"Excuse me." A doctor, younger than us, bushy-haired, male, had pushed back the white curtain surrounding David's cubicle, and now he was poking his head out at us. "You the parents of this young man?"

Geof and I looked into each other's eyes.

A world of thoughts and emotions passed between us in that second. Of David's loss of his mother and of the man who had raised him as a son. Of Geof's enduring desire for children of his own. Of his acceptance of my reluctance to have any. Of the consequent place that David had won in his heart. I felt tears at the edges of my eyes, and thought, *And mine, too.*

Geof turned toward the doctor and said, "His parents are dead. I guess we're all he's got for now."

"He's concussed," the doctor told us. "And he's awake. Come here."

We went, each of us to stand on opposite sides of David, who was modestly covered by a white sheet. His clothes lay in a pile in a corner. His first words to us were, "I hate this goddamned thing!" Meaning the neck brace, I surmised. His eyes looked dazed, shocky. But his language was clear enough. "Can't you tell them to take it off of me? And get me off this goddamn board, it hurts like hell, and I've got to piss. The fucker only broke my head, for Christ's sake, not my goddamn neck!"

I nearly laughed, he sounded so ribaldly healthy.

He was loud in that little room with fabric walls, while the doctor and a woman in white conferred in much quieter voices.

"What fucker?" Geof said to David.

"His motorcycle," I interjected. "Or maybe the highway."

"Shit, no!" David said, able to shift his vision, looking like an indignant version of one of those dolls whose eyes roll back and forth. "I'm not talking about my damn bike, for Christ's sake. The fucker who hit me!"

I glanced over at Geof, who gave me a look right back.

"What do you mean, hit you?"

My husband's voice—a calm, mellow baritone at the best of times—was so deep with affectionate patience, you'd have thought he had just opened a new vein of the stuff, right then, in his body. I recalled a book by Nancy Thayer, a novel I had dearly loved called *Three Women at the Water's Edge,* in which one of the female characters had remarked—to the best of my memory—that when a baby sucked at her breast, it seemed to open new spaces for love inside of her. Since David's appearance in our lives, new spaces had opened in my husband's heart.

"Were you hit by a car, Dave?" he asked, making it clear.

"Hell no! With a frigging log. Somebody threw a frigging *tree* at me, Geof! Made me break and skid, and I lost it. Damn. How's my bike?"

"Fine," I said quickly.

"Did you see this person?" Geof asked.

"I didn't see zip, except asphalt comin' up at me."

"Then what happened?"

"I don't know." David sounded fretful, anxious. "God, I'm in pain, doesn't anybody fucking care? You've got to get me off of this board. My back is killing me. What have they got my neck in, anyway? I hate this!"

"X rays," the woman in white announced, looking over at us. "To make sure it's only concussion. Check for bones broken, make sure he doesn't have internal injuries. He's badly contused, might have a broken clavicle, or a rib or two, but we don't think he's got internal bleeding. I'm sorry, fellow, but you've got to stay on that board for a while longer. If you have to go to the bathroom, we'll arrange a catheter."

"Shit!" David exclaimed.

The woman smiled slightly. "We can arrange for that, too."

"Let me show you something," the male doctor said, and he started to lift the covering off David's body. But David said, "Stop that! Not with her in here."

Meaning me. Suddenly modest, our David. The doctor withdrew his hand.

I would have left, so they could show Geof whatever it was they wanted to display, but orderlies arrived, and instantly they wheeled David out and away from us.

"Do you always give such prompt service?" I asked the woman.

Her smile returned, lighting her lively young face. "Hey, we're the fast-food restaurant of trauma centers. We're the drive-in window for victims of drive-by shootings. Prompt is our middle name." She winked at Geof. "For relatives of cops, that is."

In other words: No, they'd hustled for David.

"Come by with a stomach ache," she admitted, "and you could sit here for hours. It's the way the system is. The only real health care is not getting sick to begin with. Good luck. Hope he survives."

With that mixed benediction, she was gone to her duties.

The first doctor returned, however.

"You're a cop, right?" he said to Geof.

Geof agreed that he was and gave his name and rank.

"Well, this is weird," the doc said, "but I've got to tell you this." He glanced at me. "I was told that you found him lying on a highway, with his motorcycle on top of him, like he'd wrecked it?"

"Yes," I affirmed.

"He may have crashed," the doc said thoughtfully, "but that's not how he got all of his injuries." Again, he glanced at me, appraisingly, as if he were scanning for a diagnosis. "Tell me exactly *how* he was lying there."

"I don't understand . . ."

"Which side was he lying on?" The young doctor was patient. "His right side? His left? How was the bike lying on him?"

"Oh. David was on his right side, with the bike between his legs, and his left leg still hung over it. I was scared he'd broken the leg underneath."

"No, it's okay." The doc frowned and transferred his attention to Geof. "It's his *left* leg that sustained the worst injuries. In fact, it's his whole left side clear up to his shoulder. I wanted to show you." He smiled at me. "If he'd let me. He's got contusions—they look like horizontal bands going all the way up the side of him, starting at his feet. The kid was beaten, Lieutenant. While he lay there, I'd guess. It looks like somebody took a stick and whaled on him."

I gaped at the physician.

But he hadn't time for our astonishment, or our dismay. He didn't even look especially shocked at his own theory, merely a little surprised. As young as he was, he was probably already nearly unshockable—like my cop husband. At that moment, however, Geof was looking as stunned as I felt.

Other emergency room patients in other cubicles needed help, and like the woman before him, the young man was quickly gone to attend to them.

"Are you thinking of David's relatives?" I asked Geof.

"I frequently do, more often than I'd like to."

"I mean—"

What I meant was that David Mayer came from a background that was rife with physical abuse; it was something of a cherished family tradition, you might say. A religious rite, akin to snake handling or speaking in tongues, only not as much fun. In David's family, the snakes were the grown-ups. Beatings were only part of it. If there was a kid who didn't need another "whaling," I thought he was one. They had been split apart by death and imprisonment; the remaining members of the clan had disappeared from the area, seeming to abandon any claim to David. But for as long as he lived, any mark on his body would probably bring back memories of them.

Were the monsters back?

"They're gone, Jenny, I swear it. Not a trace of any of them anywhere in this state, and they're smart enough to know they'd better keep it that way. They have nothing to gain by coming back for him. I'd stake *your* life on the fact that I'm right about that."

He smiled slightly.

"Thanks," I said wryly. "Would you stake his?"

He narrowed his eyes, but finally said, "Yes."

"Geof," I then said slowly, "Lew Riss is back in town. Remember him? The reporter for the *Times?*"

He looked at me as if *I* were speaking in tongues.

"Lew's not a journalist anymore," I told him. "He's head of First Things First. The national director of it, no less. He paid me a surprise visit today, Geof, to inform me that I can't—according to Lew—touch any part of God's Highway unless FTF says I can. And if I do, he intimated that I will regret it."

Geof absorbed that, his face expressing distaste. "Hyper little bastard, I remember Lew Riss, all right. Had a crush on you, which was his only redeeming quality, as I recall. Always bugging me for insider cop stories. Not a bad writer, but he wouldn't have known the truth if it walked up and kicked him in the nuts."

I smiled. "He told me today that he hates facts."

"Is that right? Well, isn't it a fact that FTF puts up blockades to stop environmental degradation? And isn't it a fact they're known for extreme acts, and suspected of violent ones?"

"I don't know where to tell you to look for him, Geof."

"Not to worry. That's my job."

"The property owners," I said, hesitating, hating to say it, "near the trail crossing . . . twelve years ago, they used blockades, too."

Geof reached for my elbow again. "Jenny. That woman. The one whose husband died. Is she off her rocker? Would she do something like this to close down the trail crossing?"

"Oh, honey, I don't think so—"

"Maybe not even meaning to hurt David, maybe just wanting everyone to think that's a dangerous place that needs to be shut down."

"Geof! He was *beaten,* the doctor said! You can't think that Melissa Barney—"

He snapped his fingers. "That's the name. Thanks. Listen, Babe, I've got to get in on the investigation of that highway barricade. You'll hold down the fort here?"

But the doctor heard that he was rushing past, and he said, "Don't hang around. The kid was in a lot of pain by the time he got to X ray, so we knocked him out. He'll be unconscious all night. Go on home. Call, when you want news. Come back in the morning." He grinned, on the run. "The kid'll be cussing all of us, by then."

Geof and I regarded each other again, a bit helplessly.

"You checked him into the hospital?" I asked.

"Before you got here," he said.

"I don't have my car. It's still at the office. What about the cycle?"

"I'll take you to your car. I'll take care of getting his bike home."

I sighed. "And I'll go sit by the phone, I guess."

He grabbed me in a careful embrace—remembering my injuries from the day before, no doubt—and kissed me and vowed that he loved me. Actually, I would have agreed to sit by the phone anyway, but if he wanted to persuade me with passion, that was fine with me, too.

"What happened to your hand?" he asked, noticing the wounded wing.

I told him, holding it up for both of us to see, as if it were an artifact.

We should have stared at it longer.

The answer to the entire night's disturbance and all of its pain was written—in the thin, bloody script of the abrasion—on the back of my hand. Metaphorically written, I mean. But all I did was ask a nurse for a spritz of antiseptic.

He delivered me to my car, where I sat and thought:

Home? Sit by a phone?

Who was I kidding?

It was only eight-thirty on a Friday night, and I still had errands to run for the festival, which was now only nine days away. And the town council meeting at which they might jerk our festival permits was only three days away. And . . .

I pointed the nose of the Miata toward the Dime Store.

What I really desired at that moment was food, specifically a double cheeseburger with pickles and onions, and fries, and a chocolate malt—comfort food—but my favorite diner would be open all night, while Nellie's store would close at ten. Ten minutes to get there, an hour and twenty minutes to shop and to confer with Nellie about our current orders. Then food. Then home. Then sit by the phone.

Life was easy, when you had priorities.

I had one. An impulse, which was really what was driving me to the Dime Store. A childish one. Utterly silly, undignified in the extreme, and totally unbecoming in a proper young foundation director.

I wanted a Halloween costume.

By God. A particular one, no less. To wear to my fair. We had tons of cotton "First Annual Ever Port Frederick Autumn Festival and Apple Bobbing" T-shirts, which several print shops (with a combined whimsical sense of humor) had donated for us to sell. I could wear one of those. And we'd be selling black and silver half-masks at a buck apiece for charity. But no. I wanted to dress up in my own costume.

There's nothing like indulging a second childhood to take your mind off your troubles. Some people indulged it with motorboats or young lovers. A Halloween costume seemed, by comparison, a modest wish.

I wanted to be a Fairy Godmother.

As I turned into the parking lot across the street from the Dime Store, I had a sudden flash of humorous insight into my own psyche: *This is not,* I realized, *going to come as a surprise to anybody.*

12

NO PROTESTORS CIRCLED IN THE PARKING LOT AS I PULLED IN.

I felt surprisingly relieved in their absence. Maybe, I thought, as I got out of my car, they weren't as benign as I liked to assume they were. If I'd asked the pendulum about them, would my subconscious have told me that, in truth, I was afraid of them, of their flinty-eyed fanaticism?

"Nah," I said, and laughed as I crossed the street.

Sidling in unnoticed among a crowd of shoppers, I edged my way around the perimeter of the wooden floor to the costume section, keeping my head down, eyes averted, not really in the mood to stop and chat with anybody who might recognize me. It's so *damn* hard to go unnoticed anyplace in one's own hometown. That was one reason Geof and I took off for our weekends in Boston periodically—although even there, in the most unlikely places, we ran into people we knew. You know how it is. One time when my sister and I were ten and twelve, respectively, our parents took us on a vacation to the Grand Canyon. And there at the south rim, while we were peering over the sides, up from a hiking trail came an entire family of people we knew from Port Frederick! Unbelievable.

It was cheerful and loud in the Dime Store that night. No new-fangled acoustical ceiling tiles or wall coverings or flooring in this store. Just voices and the noise of lots of movement bouncing off the dusty, scuffed old wood counters, which were stacked with all of the useful and also all of the deliciously useless little gadgets that you could only really find in dime stores. The Kmarts of the world just didn't cut it, when it came to the mystery and fascination of great old stores like this, and we were fortunate still to have one in Port Frederick. Most people younger than I was knew only bright lights and neat, dull merchandise displays, but new generations of our town were still being introduced to the pleasures of a trip to the Dime Store. Many of us worried about what would become of this wonderful tradition when Nellie and Bill Kennedy retired. Nobody expected Ardyth to take it over.

Oh well, I thought, as I had before, it was still here, and the Kennedys would surely operate it for at least a few more years before they retired, if they ever did; in other words, the demise of the Dime Store wasn't anything any of us had to worry about anytime soon.

I weaved among kids, parents, lots of Halloween shoppers.

I was only one of many dozens of customers crowding the narrow, old-fashioned aisles. I saw Nellie standing outside her office talking to an elderly woman, and I caught a glimpse of Bill Kennedy shuffling down an aisle in the toy section, patting the heads of a couple of small children. They each looked up into his face and grinned back at him. Nellie'd said he was good for that, at least, making the kids feel welcome, which made their mothers happy.

After passing the candy and the sewing department, the housewares and the paper goods, I found myself in the costume section, where I took a stand and examined my choices.

Frankenstein's monster was one. He grinned evilly down at me, green face and all, and he was actually one of the tamer, prettier sights to greet my wondering eyes. In addition to the full-length, adult-sized and child-sized costumes that Nellie had hanging on hooks on the wall, there were also whole-head latex masks placed over foam "skulls." She had those positioned in a gruesome long line right above my head—the masks up high enough to keep them out of the reach of little hands. It looked to me like a police lineup of humanity's worst nightmares.

"Were costumes this scary when we were growing up?"

It was my own voice blurting out my thought.

"No way," said a woman's voice to my right. I glanced at her, and we exchanged ironic smiles. She said, "It looks like those pictures of car wrecks they made us watch in driver's ed."

I laughed, and then was absolutely dismayed to see that Melissa Barney stood on the other side of the woman, staring at me. Oh God, what a joke to be making in her presence! My laughter broke off abruptly enough to cause the other woman to cast another look at me. Unfortunately, it also inspired her to make another joke. "Or, maybe they look like people who were in terrible fires, and they didn't get any plastic surgery? If any of these things come to my house on Halloween, I'm slamming my door and calling 911!"

How could I get her to stop, I wondered desperately, to shut *up?*

Melissa was coming toward me, and she'd heard it all. The reminders of terrible traffic accidents, of horrible injuries, even of calling 911.

Her thin, beautiful face was tense, her voice high and strained when she spoke. "You're right. Whatever happened to Daffy Duck, for heaven's sake!" Unlike the other woman, the stranger, Melissa wasn't joking. Her eyes in their bruised sockets burned with real anger. "Or pretty little ballerinas? And Peter Pan and Captain Hook and Tinkerbell?" The intensity in her voice was building, and I thought she looked near tears. "If they're going to be this horrible, why don't they just make Ted Bundy masks and be done with it! We'll just dress our kids up in serial killer costumes, and turn them loose to terrorize the neighborhoods."

I wanted to touch her, to calm her.

The other woman, who was apparently completely insensitive to other people's moods, just laughed delightedly at Melissa's tirade, and babbled her way right back into the conversation. "I guess we shouldn't be so shocked," she said, and then giggled. "I mean, my manicurist told me that she's going to a Halloween party this year dressed as a disgruntled postal worker! She and her boyfriend are going to rent uniforms and carry toy semiautomatic rifles! Little-bitty AK-47s! And I know this other couple, they're going to put those fake meat cleavers over their heads and go as the Cleavers!" She let out a peal of laughter. "You know? Ward and June? From that old television show *Leave It to Beaver?"*

"I know," I said repressively.

Any other time, I'd have laughed at that.

But Melissa Barney's whole body was trembling beside me.

"I still have to buy costumes," she said to me, her voice ragged with what sounded like exhaustion and anger and grief. "For the kids. Life goes on!" A wild laugh suddenly broke out of her, rising in a thin, hysterical syncopation.

Even the clod standing next to us had to notice that behavior.

She stared at Melissa, looked as if she had the thought that this lady was completely wacko, and she quickly backed off a couple of steps, then moved completely away from us, on down the line of costumes.

"Melissa," I said tentatively.

"Mommy?"

A small child saved the situation. His little voice called our attention down to where he stood, grasping Melissa's long cotton skirt. "What's so funny, Mommy?" he asked, looking worried.

He was adorable, no more than three, red-haired as his mother, with a sweet little rosebud mouth and serious brown eyes. My throat closed at the sight of him and my knowledge of his loss. Did he really know? I wondered. Or did he persist in thinking that his father had gone off on a hike, and that he'd be coming home anytime now? Some small children did feel that way, I'd heard, and for years they lived their lives as if they were only waiting for their missing parent to burst through the front door calling, "I'm home! I love you! Did you miss me?"

Melissa knelt down and folded him tightly to her.

In that moment of seeing the child—of staring down at their matching red heads—everything about the trail crossing suddenly got more personal to me. It was odd, really, but more than my own history with God's Highway, more than the power of Melissa's appeal to me, more even than our scare with David, the appearance of this child brought home to me exactly what might be at stake at that quiet, modest intersection of a hiking trail with a highway.

The little boy was staring past his mother's shoulder to a point in back of me. I started to turn around to see what it was, when something furry suddenly brushed against me.

Startled, I jumped as if somebody had touched an electric current to me, and I shrieked. Totally humiliating. If I'd wanted to go unnoticed, that wasn't the way to do it.

There was a small, masked, furry creature standing behind me.

"Oh!" I said to the short creature. It was a "wolfman," complete with a hairy latex mask that covered the whole head, and bloody fangs and gleaming red eyeballs. Below that was a T-shirt, blue jeans, and tennis shoes. "You scared the sh—Schopenhauer out of me."

"Kwool!" breathed Melissa's little boy.

"Growl," said the hideous creature. "Grruph!"

It lunged at the little boy, who screamed in delighted terror.

"Vic!" Melissa said in a sharp, scolding voice. "Stop that!"

She got up from her kneeling position and placed a hand on top of the wolfman's head, and then tugged until she had pulled the mask entirely off of him. Revealed was another redheaded boy, this one more like seven or eight years old, another pint-sized clone of his pretty mother. What had their father looked like, I wondered? Was he a redhead, too, or had he been, physically, the odd man out in this vibrantly colored family?

"Hi, Mom," the wolfman . . . Vic . . . said, calmly.

His little brother reverently touched the furry mask in his mother's hands and murmured "Kwool" again, in an awed voice. He looked up pleadingly, "This one!"

"No, you can't have one like this, Stevie, it's ridiculous, you're far too young, it'll give you nightmares—"

"No, it won't!"

"He already has nightmares, Mom."

"It won't, it won't! I want to be the woofman!"

"Vic," she said to the older one, who seemed to me to be almost too calm, too mature for a kid his age. "Take your brother and make him look at more appropriate costumes. He can have something from *Sesame Street,* or *Barney,* maybe, but no monsters. I won't pay for any monsters!"

"Okay, Mom, okay," he said soothingly.

The older brother took his younger sibling by a reluctant hand. He leaned over and whispered something in the little one's ear, making him giggle. Then Vic clamped a hand over his brother's mouth and quickly moved him away from us, the little one still giggling behind the hand. Melissa didn't appear to notice the byplay between them, but I wondered what they were up to.

My shriek had attracted the attention I didn't want.

"Jenny, is everything all right?" asked Nellie Kennedy, appearing between us. "Melissa, dear, are you finding what you need?"

A few minutes later found the three of us crowded into Nellie's back office, Nellie having quickly intuited that it was her friend Melissa and not I who needed succor. Now the older woman sat behind her desk, Melissa had the other chair in front of it, and I was perched on a corner of it, telling them all about my two-days' worth of investigation into the trail crossing. Nellie, who'd been at the Dime Store all day, hadn't heard about the blockade of the highway near her home until I explained it, and they were both horrified to hear of David's injuries.

"Beaten, Jenny?" asked Nellie, looking disbelieving.

"Well, that's what the doctor thought, but maybe David got dragged a ways by his bike, and it just left odd-looking bruises on him. Or maybe he actually got hit by a car, and he just doesn't remember it."

"You see what I mean now." Melissa had her feelings under a little control now, but still looked awfully shaky and vulnerable to me. Now she turned that intensity once again on the issue of the crossing. "You've almost had a death in your own family—"

"Well, I don't know that—" I started to demur on both counts: death and family, but she wouldn't let me finish.

"Your friend, David, he could have been killed," she insisted.

"Yes," I had to admit to her, "I guess you're right about that, but it's not the same thing as what happened to your husband or to that little girl who died. I mean, this was purposeful, having to do with . . . I don't know what, exactly . . . but it wasn't a case where somebody simply ran a stop sign and hit a pedestrian. It wasn't like that, you see."

"Any way you look at it," she said, shaking her head in disagreement with me, "that intersection is dangerous and deadly. Are you going to help me shut it down, you and your foundation? What have you decided?"

"I'm almost certain we will help you—"

"Yes!"

"Wait," I cautioned her, holding up my hand to make her halt before she ran me down, though I smiled as I did it. "What I started to say is, we'll probably . . . definitely . . . help you find a way to improve it, but I don't know about closing it down, Melissa. And, I'm really sorry, but the truth is we can't do anything more until after the festival. We're swamped, Melissa, I'm sorry to delay you, but it's just going to have to wait until after next weekend." When I saw how distraught she looked, and how prepared to launch into another attempt to get me involved more quickly, I said, "However—"

She and Nellie both looked up, sharply.

Melissa's right hand lay on top of Nellie's desk, on top of the papers there, and Nellie was patting it now and then as though to comfort the younger woman. Although Nellie wasn't saying much—leaving the talking to Melissa and me—her face showed her involvement, her sympathy.

"I've thought of a couple of things you might do in the meantime."

"Tell me!" Melissa commanded.

"First, how about making some warning signs to post on the trees on either side of the trail? You could come over to Judy's House—we have tons of poster board and colored markers, not to mention computerized printing, if you want to make signs that way—and you can work on them there. Our volunteers would probably be glad to pitch in a few minutes here and there. Or bring your boys, let them help you. It might be a cheap, easy, temporary fix."

"Okay," she said, nodding. "Okay. What else?"

"Would you like to have a booth at our festival?"

She looked surprised, puzzled, as well she might be.

"What I mean is, I could arrange for you to have a booth, like any of the charities who will be there. If you could think of a special . . . something, I don't know what . . . to sell or to display, some gimmick, in other words, you could use the booth to promote your cause. Educate people about the need for safety at the trail crossing. Get them to sign a petition, if you want to. Gather ideas. Any money you collect, you'll get to keep for your cause. Would you be interested in doing that?"

"Yes, absolutely, I want to," she said.

"But what would you *do* at a booth, Melissa?" asked Nellie.

Her boys had come in quietly while we were talking. The little one had crawled up in his mother's lap, and the older one—Vic—now sat cross-legged on the floor near her. He said, "You could do your pumpkins, Mom."

"I could, couldn't I?" she said, looking thoughtfully at him.

"Oh, yeah," chimed in her youngest. "Your punkins are really kwool!"

Melissa explained for Nellie and me: "I'm a sculptor, you know. And it just happens that I am something of a Michelangelo of the pumpkin-carving world." For the first time since I had met her, a real smile touched her face, and I saw it mirrored in the faces of her sons, especially in Vic's sad and worried eyes. "Aren't I, boys?" Vigorously, they nodded their agreement with that assessment. "In fact, I probably carve the world's best jack-o'-lanterns. I think they really are good enough that I could charge money for them. But where will I get the money to pay for them, before I carve them and sell them? And how many would I need? And—"

We spent the next few minutes happily ironing all that out, with Nellie generously offering to sponsor the booth, which meant forking out enough money for dozens of pumpkins, for which Melissa would pay her back out of the proceeds. The point of this booth wasn't necessarily going to be the amount of money it earned, as it was the number of people it enlisted to Melissa's pet cause. Or, maybe the real point of it was to give her something meaningful to do, to bridge her anguish, even if the bridge only held up for a week of preparation and the weekend of the fair. I didn't try to organize it for her—the volunteer assistants she'd need for decorating the booth and for taking money and for cleaning up, and so forth—preferring to leave her with a lot to do, to keep her occupied. Besides, I had a big enough load of responsibility of my own, without adding her booth to it.

"Gotta go," I announced, edging off Nellie's desk.

"Will David be all right?" she asked.

"Yes, I think so, thank you."

"What will the police do about it?"

"Right now they're looking into First Things First—"

Melissa's face turned swiftly toward me, registering shock. "What did you say?"

Hungry and worn out by then, and sore from all of my many scrapes and tumbles, I really didn't want to explain about Lewis Riss and FTF to her and Nellie right at that moment, though of course I did.

They reacted quite strangely, I thought.

I expected both women to be dismayed at the news that the militants were back to support the cause of a pristine trail. Instead, Nellie looked downright happy, but then maybe she hadn't been one of the property owners who opposed God's Highway. I didn't know; we'd never talked about it. And I was much too tired to ask right then.

Melissa looked dismayed, all right, but it was an unhappiness that exceeded any bounds I might have anticipated. She looked literally sick at the news; I even thought, for a moment, that she might actually throw up, the way she got so white, and the way one hand flew to cover her mouth and the other to clasp her abdomen.

"Mom?" her oldest son asked her, jumping to his feet.

Both Nellie and I said, "Melissa?"

She put her left arm around Vic, drawing him close to her, and she bent her head to her youngest boy, Stevie, so that her face was hidden in his hair. At that worst of all possible moments, the poor little kid chose to announce: "Mommy! Vic bought me the woofman costume out of his own allowance money! I'm gonna be a woofman!"

So *that's* what they were up to, I thought, and I held my breath for them, hoping she'd let them get away with it.

"No!" Their mother's head snapped up. "I said, no!"

"Mommy!" Stevie's face screwed up, but it wasn't clear—possibly not even to him yet—if he was going to cry or throw a tantrum. "Vic bought it for me! It's mine! I'm gonna be woofman for Halloween!"

"Mom, he really wants it—"

"And I really don't want him to—"

"Daddy will let me!" the little one said, furiously.

There was a deathly sad silence in the small office.

"I'm sorry, Mom," Vic started to say, in a tiny voice.

"No, it's okay," she said, blinking hard, and her words came out ragged with emotion. Still, she hugged both boys, each with a separate arm. My heart ached for her valiant effort. "Vic's right. Daddy would let you. And Daddy would be proud of Vic for being so generous to his little brother. I'm being . . . I don't know what I'm being, boys. Crazy. Over-protective, maybe."

Her older son continued to look devastated, stricken.

Which was how I felt—and Nellie, too, no doubt—just looking at them. I decided that *nobody* else was going to die at the intersection of God's Highway and the state road, not if I could help it. And maybe that was also the moment when I dived into a deeper understanding of "our"

David, who had lost not just his father, but also his mother before he was even seventeen years old. I thought I'd had sympathy, empathy, whatever you want to call it . . . but whatever it was I'd thought I'd felt before, I felt it stronger now.

Oddly enough, it was Bill Kennedy who saved the day.

In his shuffling way, big Bill ambled into the doorway of the office, grinning in a way that seemed like a physical non sequitur to the atmosphere within. Then he brought out from behind his back two orange plastic pumpkins filled to their brims with candies and toys of all sorts.

"Merry Christmas!" said Bill. "Ho, ho, ho!"

The children's faces lifted instantly from gloom to glee.

Which brought smiles to the three of us women, as well.

As I left, a few minutes later, I gave Bill a kiss on the cheek and murmured, "Thank you, Santa."

13

Aching everywhere I had muscle or skin, I eased my tired old body into a black vinyl booth at the Beantown Diner, which was fatteningly located right on my path home. I still didn't have a Halloween costume. I hadn't been able to do any business with Nellie. The only way to redeem that Friday night would be to ingest every greasy bit of a double cheeseburger, fries, and malted and, what the hell, maybe hot cherry pie à la mode, too. I'd gained weight while working on the festival, because I'd loaded up on too many of those comfort plates from the diner, and too often late at night.

"There will be time for vegetables," I said to the waitress.

"You're working too hard, Jenny," she said, pad in hand. "I can always tell when you're working too hard, because you say things that make absolutely no sense whatsoever.

"What *you* do is hard work," I retorted. "By comparison, what I do is play."

She thought about that, tapping her pencil on the pad. Finally, she said, "Now you're making sense, so maybe you're not working too hard."

"Anybody ever hears us, they'll think we're both nuts."

"That makes sense."

We both burst out laughing at the same time, and then she went to put in my order. A television was playing over in the corner by the cashier, who was, I couldn't help but notice, avoiding my eyes. It reminded me of how some of my volunteers had acted that day at Judy's

House, in the wake of the previous night's newspaper. Evidently the cashier, a woman who ordinarily greeted me by name and often dropped by my table to gossip, had read it, too. Her behavior made me kind of glad there was nobody else I knew in the diner at that time. I do so hate to embarrass people when they're eating.

While I waited for my burger to cook, I went to the pay phone outside the rest rooms, and called Port Frederick Memorial to check on David's condition. Asleep, they told me, but they wouldn't tell me the confirmed nature of his injuries. I'd have to wait to talk to the doctor about that, they said, especially since I wasn't a relative. I returned to my table feeling only partly reassured. Why couldn't they just say, "broken clavicle, concussion, contusions?"

The waitress came over to pour me a cup of coffee.

"Hear about that weird thing out on the highway?"

"What thing?" I asked her, playing dumb.

"Some damn fools put up barricades on both sides of the highway over there at Crowley's Creek. Not just highway barricades, either, mind you, but big fat tree limbs, so nobody could get around. It was all over the TV news tonight. Somebody got hurt because of it, some teenager, but they wouldn't give out his name on the air. Maybe his family didn't know about it yet, or something. And they had an interview with this good-looking environmentalist guy, who said his group didn't have anything to do with it." The corners of her mouth turned down. "Like that doesn't tell you right away that they did it, right? I mean why would he bother to go on television and deny it, unless they really did it?"

"Well, maybe because they really didn't?"

"You think? He was cute. Muscles out to here."

"He used to live here," I told her. "His name's Lewis Riss, at least I suppose that's who it was—"

"Yeah, yeah, that was his name. You know him?"

"He was a reporter here in town." I smiled up at her. "Want me to bring him by for a cup of coffee sometime?"

"Yeah, do that," she said. I happened to know that she was long married and the mother of twins, a substitute grade-school teacher during the week, and a part-time waitress at the diner on weekends. "Like I've got time for a lover, right?"

"Was there any news about the festival?"

She pulled several little white plastic buckets of cream out of her skirt pocket and handed them to me for my coffee. "Yeah, but you don't want to hear it."

"You're right. I don't."

When she came back with my food, I had to ask, however, "On the news, did they mention my name?"

"Well, you little swell-headed thing, you." She grinned, but it was sympathetic. "Yes, but like I said, you don't want to know."

I stared glumly at the food that was supposed to cheer me up.

When she returned at the right time with my cherry pie, I asked, "Did you happen to notice if there was an interview with Miss Lucille Grant on the news?"

I didn't have to explain to her whom I meant; Miss Grant was legendary in town, both among her former students and among all the teachers, past and present.

"I don't believe so, although I didn't pay much attention to the sportscast. Any chance she'd have been on that?"

We smiled at each other, knowing the obvious answer to that one.

And then I stared glumly at the pie, because if Miss Grant hadn't been on the news that evening, it meant that the plan in which I had enlisted her must have failed to work. I was going to have to call her over the weekend and apologize for putting her to the trouble of attempting it.

I left the Beantown feeling heavier, in all ways.

You'd have thought I'd have a car phone.

Considering how many details and events and people I had to be coordinating at any one time in my job, it would have seemed sensible. But I didn't. A lot of people, including my husband, thought I ought to. They claimed I'd be safer, for one thing, and more efficient, for another. I didn't deny they could be right, but I still wanted an island of space and time in which I could travel about alone with my thoughts. And I wanted to discourage any false sense of urgency in myself. I don't have anything against car phones; actually, I think they're fun. But, personally, I figure there are very few things that can't wait long enough for me to get to a grounded phone. And in the meantime, I would have time to think things over, learn patience, calm down . . .

My big greasy supper left me sleepy. If I'd had a phone in my car, I might have settled for calling the hospital again to insist that they define David's condition for me, so that I could go home without that to worry about it. Instead, I drove back into town, back to the hospital, to see him for myself. And if I hadn't done that, I might not have realized how uneasy I had been feeling, all along, about the fact that neither of us had stayed behind to watch over him, to make sure that they gently transferred him into his bed, and to let him know—somewhere in the sleeping, unconscious part of him—that somebody cared enough to stay with him.

He was sleeping in the darkened room.

His face looked relaxed, and as a result, the handsome man he would soon become was more than just a hint in the strong lines of his face, in the long eyelashes, the good nose, and the fine, strong chin.

I left him a note, promising to come back in the morning with Geof, a promise David wouldn't necessarily appreciate, of course, and I knew that. But somebody, besides Geof, had to start saying she cared, and saying it more directly. If, indeed, she did care?

Yes, I did.

I signed it, "Love, Jenny."

What in the world would he think of that?"

One of the night nurses turned out to be someone I knew, and he didn't hesitate to confirm: "Cracked clavicle, contusions." David didn't even have a concussion, it turned out, although the impact had knocked him silly. He ought to be able to leave the hospital the next day, my nurse friend told me.

I looked forward to it.

"Unless you've arrested somebody," I said to Geof, when he tiptoed into our bedroom around midnight, "I'm too tired to listen until morning." I was in bed, under the covers, my eyes open only just enough to see him in the soft glow of the light I'd left on for him in the hall.

"Great," he said, as he started to get undressed. "Because we haven't, and I'm too tired to talk about it tonight."

"I saw David."

"I know, I saw your note."

"You were there?"

"Yeah, I just missed you."

We smiled at one another. Shook our heads. Laughed a little at ourselves. Managed, barely, to discuss the kid's condition.

Then there was silence, while he finished stripping.

While he was removing his last sock, I said, "Have I ever told you that this is one of my favorite parts of the day? That I really love watching you get undressed?"

He looked up. "Really?"

"Oh, yes."

"That is a very sexy thing to say, and if I weren't a hundred and thirty-two years old, I might do something about it."

"Well, you know what they say," I commented, as he lifted his side of the covers and climbed in, my own personal big, naked man, "when couples have a good thing together, they have sex like crazy for the first few years, because the excitement of falling in love gets their adrenaline going. But then things calm down, and the endorphins take over, so they feel more warm and peaceful and loving, and they have less sex, but what they do have is very intimate and sweet."

"How do you know that?"

"I heard somebody say it on TV."

"Well, it must be true then."

He positioned his left arm so that I could lay my head on his shoulder. I dropped my right hand onto his chest, and then he curved both of his arms lightly around me. We lay there like that, quietly, for awhile. Then he said, with a smile I could hear in the dark, "Plenty of endorphins around here."

"I should say so."

"But I'm expecting a fresh shipment of adrenaline first thing in the morning."

I smiled into the soft hair in his chest, kissed him, yawned, and fell asleep, feeling a sense of comfort that no cheeseburger could ever give me.

In the morning—postadrenaline rush—we posed naked together in front of the full-length mirror on our closet door.

"Look at this one," I bragged, pointing to the bruise on the outside of my right knee, and then to my thigh and shoulder on the same side, all evidence of what happened when a human body got sandwiched between a Jaguar and a street full of cobblestones. "And these."

"Pretty impressive," Geof conceded, "but don't forget these," and he turned around so that certain scars on his back were visible in the glass.

"Not fair," I protested. "You always win with those."

"What else have you got?" he offered generously.

I held the newly abraded back of my hand to the glass, and I offered him a view of a spreading bruise on my rump, which I had earned by falling among the trees in the woods the day before. "Oh," I said, "and there's still this." The long, healing red stripe on my left arm, I meant. "And this." I pointed to an old wound, from a battle in a lobster pound, of all places.

"It's a good thing we had sex under the covers this morning," Geof observed, "because if I'd seen you in the light, I would have been afraid to touch you. So, okay, I guess I'll have to concede the honors for this week," he admitted, "but overall . . ."

"Oh, yes," I cooed, reassuringly, "overall, you're much the worse for wear, darling. As any self-respecting police officer ought to be. Why, if I had all the scars you do, I'd want to be paid for the job, too."

"That's more like it," he harrumphed, with a mock braggadocio that made us both break into laughter. I gently stroked his poor, scarred back; he sweetly kissed all my new bruises. On the way to the shower, I limped a bit more dramatically than I needed to, just to remind him whose pains were fresher.

But when the soap stung the back of my hand, I was sorry I had won the contest.

"Yes, you can go home with us, as soon as the doctor releases you," Geof said, for at least the second time, to David later that morning at the hospital. The kid was groggy, stiff, alternately cranky and docile. He complained that every time he moved, his shoulder hurt, and his head ached, and both sides of his body felt like . . .

". . . somebody beat on me with a two-by-four."

Geof and I exchanged looks, I from my post in a green vinyl armchair in a corner by the window, and Geof by the other side of David's bed, where my husband stood, looking endearingly awkward and ill at ease. We seemed to be exchanging glances a lot lately, he and I, but then we often did where David Mayer was concerned. Those glances struck me as being disconcertingly parental.

If David had been alert and feeling up to par, he'd have caught that glance and demanded an explanation of it. As it was, he was frowning down at the sheet on top of him, unhappily plucking at it with his fingers, and so he missed the latest glance.

"David," Geof said, "I can tell you some things about what happened last night, and I will, but first I need for you to tell me everything you remember—"

"I was born—"

"From the point when Jenny got off your motorcycle and she walked up to the Kennedys' house to get a Band-Aid. Start there, would you?"

Surprisingly, he cooperated with little fuss, and he told a simple, straightforward tale: of deciding to test a sudden stop at the bottom of the hill, of revving up his engine, roaring down—"

"How fast were you going?" Geof asked.

"Not very, I wasn't even up to the speed limit, there wasn't enough space for that." He looked at Geof. "I'm not crazy, you know. I wasn't out to kill myself. I knew I'd better keep it at a low speed, or when I braked, I might go over the handlebars. I just wanted to see . . . what if somebody did stop at the sign . . . and then they were accelerating at a normal speed down the hill . . . and suddenly somebody stepped off the trail onto the road in front of them . . . could they stop in time? So I probably wasn't going over twenty, twenty-five miles an hour, if that much."

"So, you got to the bottom, you braked—"

"No, I didn't even get to the bottom, and it all happened before I could do what I planned to do. It was like out of nowhere! Suddenly there was this *log* flying into me. I mean, I saw it! It, like, practically landed in my fucking lap! And it wasn't like it hurt me or anything, but it startled the shit out of me, and I just . . . lost it."

"Anybody would," I offered.

He gave me a sardonic look. "Thanks, Mom."

"You mean, you lost control of the bike? What did you do, brake? Lose control of the steering, what?"

"Like, everything!" David exclaimed, turning his indignation from me to Geof. "I don't know what I did, I just did everything wrong, that's all I know, and the bike's suddenly rolling out from under me, and my hands are flying off the handlebars, and my legs are flying out like I'm on a horse and I've lost my stirrups, and I'm eating air, and I'm thinking, oh shit, oh shit."

"And then—"

"And then I wake up in a fucking ambulance." He started to turn his neck toward me, but the movement cost him. "Ouch! Dammit!" He settled for merely swiveling his eyes in their sockets again. "And the only thing I see is her looking down on me like I'm in a casket and she's all worried-looking and pretending she'd, like, miss me."

"I'm such a good little actress," I said dryly.

"Do you recall seeing any people, David?"

"No."

"Any cars, another motorcycle, any kind of vehicle?"

"No, I've been thinking about it. No."

"Could you hear anything, over the noise of the bike?"

"Are you kidding? I couldn't hear a train behind me if I was running on the tracks and it was gaining on me. Now you know everything I know. But I don't know everything you know, right?"

Geof gingerly sat down on the edge of the bed. "No, you don't. There are two things you don't know. The first one is that while this was happening to you, the highway was blocked off, barricaded from both directions, so no traffic could get through."

"What does that mean?" David asked.

"Well, one thing it means is that whoever did this to you was able to get away with doing it without being seen."

David absorbed that for a moment, then looked up again. "Do you mean somebody planned this, just to wreck me?"

Geof shook his head. "Probably not, David. We think the blockade was related to the issue of the changes that Jenny's involved in making at the trail crossing. There are people, maybe she told you, who don't want anything done to it. They may have wrecked you as a warning. Sort of, 'Don't mess with the trail, or you'll get hurt,' that sort of craziness. That's one possibility. Although, I'll admit that we haven't heard from any protest group, which would ordinarily be the way they'd operate. Of course, they may have backed off from taking any responsibility, once you got hurt. Maybe, from the point of view of their leaders, that wasn't supposed to happen."

"I hate these people," David said with feeling.

"But there's another theory, which is that it might have been done by people who want to prove the trail crossing *is* dangerous, and that it *should* be fixed."

"I hate those people, too," he said with equal fervor.

"Got any other theories?" I piped up.

Geof smiled over at me. "No. You?"

I shook my head. He had asked me to let him put off explaining the status of the investigation until he could tell both David and me at the same time. So the kid and I were hearing it first together. "Did you locate Lew Riss or any of the other folks from First Things First?" I asked him.

"Who's that?" David wanted to know. "What's that?"

"Ecoterrorists," Geof informed him. "And their leader, who just happens to be an old pal of Jenny's."

"I guess any friend of hers," the kid said, "is not necessarily a friend of mine."

"I hope that's not true."

"What?" both men asked, not having heard me.

"Never mind."

Geof continued with his explanation of First Things First: "They were heavily involved in establishing God's Highway to begin with, and now they're back, because they've heard some people want to change it."

"Some people," David said darkly. "You said there were two things I didn't know—"

"Right." Geof took a breath. "The second one is that one of the doctors here—the guy who saw you in the emergency room—doesn't think you got that line of bruises from the wreck. He thinks you got them from being beaten up. He thinks somebody came up, while you were knocked out on the pavement, and—in his words—whaled on you with some object, a branch off a tree, maybe."

David blinked several times and didn't speak.

"Do you remember anything like that?" I asked him gently.

He pressed his lips together, closed his eyes, then opened them and stared out the window.

Geof pressed: "Do you, Dave?"

He shook his head, evidently answering us.

But still, he wouldn't speak.

14

We all sat in silence for quite a long time.

A nurse came in and checked the bindings that held David's left arm clamped to his side, to help keep his broken bone temporarily immobilized. Another nurse came in and offered him pain medication, which he refused with a stubborn set to his jaw and a careful shake of his head.

The phone in his room rang, and Geof picked it up.

"Wrong room," he said, setting it back again.

An orderly came whistling in with David's lunch tray, cheerfully set it up on the silver tray that wheeled into place over the bed, said, "How're you, folks?" and whistled out again.

David ignored the food, which, even under silver covers, smelled like broccoli. I was hungry and wished I could eat it if he wasn't going to. And still, the doctor hadn't arrived to release him. And still, the kid didn't respond to Geof's explanation of the doctor's theory about what had happened to him.

We didn't rush him.

He had a lot of fears and memories to filter through.

Geof got up and went into the bathroom, closing the door behind him. In a few minutes, I heard the toilet flush, then the water run, and then he came back out and this time came over by me, turned his back on David, and commenced to stare out the window.

David spoke, in a small voice that was trying to sound cynical.

"Has anybody seen my uncles?"

I let out my breath.

Geof turned around again and said, "Your uncles are still in jail, Dave."

For murdering David's stepfather.

David had testified against them.

"Are you sure?"

"Yes. Actually, I checked, last night."

"What about my grandfather?"

Who had probably ordered the murder, and other crimes, and who could not be charged, much less convicted, for a number of frustrating reasons.

"The rest of the family is gone, David, still gone."

"How can you be sure?"

"We'll find out who did this, and it will turn out not to be personal, Dave. It won't be about you. It will turn out that you just happened to be there, at the wrong time. Believe me, it will all turn out to have nothing to do with you."

I believed him, but there was no reason for David to.

At which moment, the doctor finally appeared.

We took a subdued teenager home an hour later.

Once there, he took the pain pills and went to sleep on one of our living room couches. But only after he had made us close and lock all of our doors and windows, and only after the last thing he saw before he dozed off was Geof sitting opposite him, holding his favorite Colt .45-caliber semiautomatic pistol under his hand on an end table. When Geof was sure David slept, he quietly got up, put the gun away in his hiding place on top of the refrigerator, and joined me in the kitchen for lunch.

Before he put the gun up, though, he showed me the open window in the top of it: no magazine. No ammunition. It had been only for show, for David, to make him feel safe enough to go to sleep.

"What am I going to do about him?" Geof asked me, over take-out gyro sandwiches I heated in the microwave, and potato chips and beers for each of us. "I can't stay here and play bodyguard for him until he gets his nerve back."

"Just do it today and tonight," I suggested. "By tomorrow, he'll begin to feel stupid, and he'll start accusing you of babying him. You weren't planning on going anywhere today anyway, were you?"

"No, although I thought I might help look for some answers."

"It looks like you can be the most help right here."

"What are you going to do this afternoon, Jen?"

I smiled at him. "Escape from this prison, warden. I'm gonna go build me an autumn festival right smack-dab in the middle of the town common."

Exactly one week to go.

"Oh, may next Saturday be a twin to this one," was my prayer as I nosed the Miata into one of the few remaining parking slots that slanted into the north curb at the commons. Today, everything was perfect: sunshine, temperature in the fifties, only a hint of wind, a mere lilting lift to the spirits and the hemline. Perfection.

My heart was full as I observed the activity that filled the broad swath of community property. To each volunteer carpenter, architect, painter, and pounder, I sang a silent hymn of praise and gratitude. I felt, in fact, overwhelmed at that moment. Not, for once, by responsibility. Rather, by the *reality* of all of it.

"You," I told myself, "are privileged today to watch a dream coming true."

How could I ever say to anyone how marvelous if felt to realize that all of those people, all of that activity, had coalesced around an idea in my head? I probably couldn't utter it, at least not without sounding as if my ego had inflated with helium.

Which, in figurative fact, it had.

I felt lightheaded as I got out of my car and walked toward an afternoon of physical labor. I practically floated, a few inches off the grass, over to pick up a hammer and pitch in.

There's nothing like hearing people talk about you to bring you back down to earth.

The volunteers were singing, whistling, laughing, cussing, complaining. In my oldest jeans and one of Geof's old flannel shirts, I got to be one of the crowd for most of the day, and I didn't have to supervise anybody, didn't organize anything. I just carried lumber, unloaded cars, twisted screws, and picked up trash with everybody else. It was a nice place to visit, though I wouldn't have wanted to live in that position. I did so enjoy being in charge, God help me!

Some of the volunteers—quite a few—didn't know who I was, so I got to hear, firsthand, the local gossip.

"Do you think there's any point doing this?"

"Doing what? What d'ya mean?"

"All this work. Today. Building these booths. You read the paper? You think this thing's really going to happen?"

"The festival, you mean? Hell, it better. I could be home watching football this weekend."

"Why don't you bring that little portable set of yours tomorrow? Hell, we've got electricity here, we could plug it in and watch the Pats tomorrow."

The New England Patriots, they meant, they who had lost ignominiously to Kansas City last week. I thought of Bill Kennedy's dumb joke and vowed to dig up a better conversational gambit than football for the next time I saw him. I was listening to the two women football fans, while unobtrusively—I hoped—holding up one end of a plywood sheet for them to nail into the booth frame that would become a demonstration quilting bee for the ladies from our local Salvation Army. I just did my job and kept my ears open.

It wasn't only the future of the festival that I overheard being dished that day in lively discourse. God's Highway, the trail crossing, the previous night's incident, and yours truly all came up for debate, too.

"You watch, they're going to spend our tax money fixing that intersection, all because a couple of damn fools couldn't remember to look both ways before they crossed a street. It just burns me up—"

"I don't think that's what happened. One of them was just a child, anyway. And what I heard is, those drivers were drunk—"

"Huh?" I thought.

"No, they were speeding—"

"Whatever anybody was doing," said the first speaker, "you can bet it's going to cost *us* money."

Then, a little later, over by the booth for the used book sale by the Brandeis University women, I heard two of them, college age, talking:

"Can you imagine being in charge of all this?"

"God! I know who is, it's a woman, I just can't remember her name. My mom doesn't know her, but she knows her sister real well, and Mom says the sister is a major volunteer in town, like she's in charge of the docents over at the museum, and she ran the symphony benefit last year, and she's some big deal with the Episcopal church women. And the sister's not having anything to do with this festival. And Mom says, what does *that* tell you?"

It told me that Sherry had grown understandably fed up after a lifetime of having a big sister who was always getting her name or picture in the newspaper (for better or for worse). It told me she still felt as if she were always walking in my shadow, and that she still hated it. I never had known what to do about that, so I still did nothing. Sherry Cain Guthrie cast a pretty impressive shadow, herself, it seemed to me, just hearing that partial list of her recent accomplishments. But it was hard to know if she did all those things because she really wanted to, or if she was still competing with me. It was a competition I'd never felt and that she fought alone, but then older siblings never had to engage in that nasty battle, by and large. It was one of the advantages of being born first, I supposed. Unlike Sherry, I'd had a couple of years to feel like the center of the universe, with everybody doting on me all by myself. When you think you're the sun, you don't pay much attention to shadows, which can be a problem of its own, of course, but one that would not have reaped any sympathy from a younger sister. Poor Sherry. I didn't know how to detach my shadow from the soles of my feet, so I could only hope that she would eventually step boldly away from me, in the direction of something she really loved to do, where nothing I had ever done would make any difference to her, or to anybody else. I hoped that, someday, she would get to see my shadow shrink to a mere wisp of fog in her path.

It was while I was dumping trash into a bin that I heard the patronizing tone of my own thoughts about my sister, and I grimaced. *Yuck,* I thought.

"You hear what happened out to the east edge of town last night?"

I shamelessly eavesdropped on two burly fellows waiting in line at the port-a-potty next to the ones the women were using.

"Something about the highway being shut down? Some car wreck down on the bridge?"

"No, some kids on motorcycles, they blocked off the whole damn road, just so they could race their bikes up and down the hills. Can you believe that?"

"No shit? How'd they do it?"

"Parked their cars across the whole damn road, is what I heard, so nobody could pass in either direction."

"Damn kids. They get caught?"

"Cops nabbed one of them."

"Good. I hope they get all of them. They ought to string them all up, pulling a stunt like that."

"That's no stunt, that's criminal behavior. Rush hour, too."

"Damn kids."

I boggled at their version and decided that I just couldn't let it pass. The men were nice about it, when I gave them the right story—leaving myself and David's name out of it—but just before one of them stepped into the tall blue cubicle he said, "Probably turn out to be teenagers, anyway."

"No doubt," said his buddy.

I gave up the good fight.

Anyway, they could be right, I supposed, it could have been a kid's "prank."

But it was as I lay on my back in the dark in the dirt, underneath the elevated platform for the clog dancers and square dancers, that I overheard the most interesting—and disturbing—bit of gossip.

It seemed to be three voices whispering.

"Meeting tonight."

"What time?"

"Eleven-thirty. On the trail, this side of the bridge."

"Who's gonna be there?"

"Central committee and some outta-towners, bunch of folks from national."

"No kidding?"

That whisper sounded impressed, excited.

"Yeah, did you know the national director's here? Things are going to get hot, man."

"Hot damn! It's about time we saw some action around here!"

"The cops think we shut down the highway yesterday."

I heard quiet laughter.

"Are we admitting anything?"

"Are you kidding? FTF doesn't talk to the gestapo, ever."

I was trying to see them through cracks in the wood flooring of the stage, but all I glimpsed were shoe soles and flashes of sunlight. I wanted to crawl out from under, to identify the whisperers, but my job at the moment was to steady a perpendicular post that served as a major support for the whole structure. I was stuck, and the whispering voices moved away from my hearing. When I emerged from down under, I stared around, searching for whispering trios, but I didn't succeed in recognizing any such groups of conspirators.

There was political talk that day, too, some of it favorable to my friend the mayor, and some of it decidedly not. Taking my own internal poll of what I heard, I still put Mary ahead of Ardyth by about 51 percent to 49 percent, which was worse than it sounded, because Mary had been a shoo-in in her last election. From what I was overhearing, everything rode on this festival, which she had backed with all of her clout and reputation. Folks who thought we'd pull it off tended to favor Mary; the doubters were coming down increasingly on Ardyth's side.

"Still," I reminded one of Mary's other supporters, quietly, "even the doubters are here. Every nail they drive is actually a nail in Ardyth's political coffin, whether they know it or not. And, at the same time, they're nailing Mary's flag to the wall."

"May the best woman win," she responded, smiling at the pleasure of hearing those words that would have been so improbable only a couple of decades before.

"That," I remarked dryly, "*should* leave very little choice."

Along toward the end of the afternoon, the Halloween protestors straggled onto the common, carrying their familiar posters. When they'd all come together in a group, they hoisted their posters on high and began their familiar, peaceful circling.

"Damn" slipped out of my mouth.

"Who *are* those people?" inquired one of the volunteers, a woman who was obviously new to town.

I waited to see how somebody else would answer that.

"Oh, they're just our local fruitcakes," came the quick response, and I heard both condescension and irritation in the words. "They've been around Port Frederick for years. They're fundamentalists from some little nobody-ever-heard-of-it church in town. They've never done any harm, that I know of, but they always show up in October, I guess to try to stop us poor foolish heathens from giving any candy to children. They don't *approve* of Halloween, they don't *approve* of trick-or-treat, they do not *approve* of goblins or ghosts. I think the idea is that we're not supposed to *do* anything *they* don't *approve* of."

The sarcasm was blistering, but fortunately it was being voiced too far away from the protestors for them to hear it.

The first questioner said, "What's the matter with them? Haven't they ever heard of the Holy Ghost?"

Everybody around her broke up in laughter, and then we all got back to work. Unfortunately, that last joke gave one of the volunteers an idea. About fifteen minutes later, hearing exclamations around me, I looked up from sweeping sawdust off the dancer's platform to witness a strange spectacle: A tall man had thrown a painter's drop cloth over his body, covering himself down to his shins, and he'd nailed together a couple of crossbars and was advancing toward the little circle of protestors, the cross held out in front of him.

Dropping my broom, I jumped off the platform and started running.

One by one, the protestors noticed the apparition advancing toward them, and they each abruptly stopped moving, causing the one behind them to run into them, backing up the circle almost comically.

I was not laughing as I raced their way.

Breathless, I pulled up beside the joker in the drop cloth, grabbed his arm through the thick material and, pulling at him roughly, said, "What the hell are you supposed to be?"

A sepulchral chuckle sounded under the cloth. I could see where he'd poked holes for vision. "I am the Holy Ghost!"

He shouted the words, loud enough for all of us to hear.

"Oh, no, you're not!" I grabbed his shoulders and swung him around, which made him stagger. "If you go over there and insult those people, you're definitely a dead man—because I promise I will personally kill you—but you are *not* a ghost. Please do not offend those people. Please save your costumes for Halloween."

"Goddammit!" yelled the Holy Ghost. He struggled with the drop cloth and me, pushing me backward by pressing the cross against me. Then he threw it to the ground and pulled the material off over his head. He was a young guy, I saw, but certainly old enough to know better. When his mouth was clear of the fabric, so was the smell of beer on his breath. My chest hurt, where a corner of the cross had dug into me.

With his face contorted, he shouted at me.

"You bitch! You ruined my joke!"

He started toward me, and I saw that the general idea was to bowl me over and keep marching toward the protestors. God only knew what he would do or say when he got there. Or, how they would respond. I had no choice but to stand my ground as he advanced. He lowered his head and bunched his arms in front of him. I put my own arms up to protect myself and propped my legs wide apart. But I was no match for his size or his drunkenness. He just bulldozed me, scooping me off the ground and dumping me on my side. From down there, I rolled out of the way of his big feet and looked back at the protestors. With stiff backs and injured expressions on their faces, they were staring at the two of us, and then, to my dismay, I realized they were disbanding and heading back to their cars. Not that I blamed them; it was a mighty intelligent move on their parts to avoid contact with the drunk who'd upended me. I tried to scramble to my feet, but I was having trouble getting my breath. It wasn't that I wanted them to continue their protest, necessarily, it was just that I wished they would stick around long enough for me to offer apologies.

And meanwhile, the drunken idiot kept on charging.

He didn't get more than a few feet beyond me, however, because other volunteers arrived en masse to tackle him. A couple of men who were even bigger than he was, grabbed him and then marched him smartly away, putting up with no verbal guff in the process.

"Tyler, you're drunk," I heard one of them yell at him, "so just shut up!"

Hands reached down to help me to my feet, voices clucked over me in concern for me and indignation at him.

By that time, only the gaunt, handsome man who looked like an El Greco painting was left standing in the circle, staring directly into my eyes when I looked at him. With my shoulders, my hands, my face, my entire body, I tried to signal apology to him. But when I moved in his direction, he turned and hurried away from all of us.

I got plenty of help and sympathy brushing myself off.

"That's okay," I joked, "I'm getting used to it."

Not that anybody knew what I meant by that.

Maybe I'd have new battle wounds to show off to Geof tonight, I thought, which even I realized was a hilariously extreme case of making lemonade out of the proverbial lemons of life. When nobody was looking, I peeked at my skin under the flannel shirt I was wearing. It was with a feeling of absolutely perverse satisfaction that I took in the sight of fresh blood where the corner of the cross had torn both my shirt and my flesh.

Another day, another Band-Aid, I thought, a shade hysterically.

Facetiously, I wondered what the morrow would bring.

But I wasn't going to have to wait that long for the next call for medical supplies; by evening, our town would be calling for more serious healing than any mere bandages could ever give to us.

15

When I told Geof and David the story and got to the part about the Holy Ghost advancing on the fundamentalists, they laughed until Geof cried and David begged for mercy on behalf of his broken clavicle. But Geof sobered up quickly when I related the next part, the one where I ended up on the ground.

"Did he hurt you?"

"Not really."

"He did." Geof stood up. "What did he do? Where are you hurt?"

We were all in the living room, because that's where David was still hunkered under blankets. Geof had cooked hamburgers and soup for the two of them before I got home. I was inhaling a take-out tenderloin that I'd picked up from the diner on my way home. It was pork, of course, pounded to perfection, crunchy and greasy in a garlic-laced breading, and huge—hanging over the edges of the giant buttered and toasted bun, with pickles, onions, lettuce, tomato, and mayo spilling over the rim, too. Eating like this, it was no wonder I'd put on a few pounds during the busy months of preparation for the festival, not to mention that I had probably already turned my arteries to wallpaper paste. I licked mayo from my upper lip and attempted to make light of the incident. "He only hurt my dignity." I pointed, vaguely, toward my chest. "And a little scratch, is all."

"I wondered how you tore your shirt," David said, which went a little way toward proving what I often suspected—that he noticed us, even though he liked to act sometimes as if we were invisible.

Geof, looking as angry as a father whose daughter has just been groped on a first date, came over to where I sat hunched over a TV tray dripping grease onto my plate. The television was silently tuned to a cops and robbers show they'd been watching. Shielding me from David's view, Geof delicately peeled back the torn edges of the rip in the shirt I'd lifted from his closet and swore at what he saw. I was surprised, myself, to see that what had originally looked like a deepish scratch was now a large, swollen red welt above the left side of my bra. He'd gouged me pretty good, I saw. No wonder it stung every time I lifted the pork tenderloin to my mouth! When I had arrived home, I had been far too hungry to worry about doctoring my latest injury.

"The mark of the cross," I intoned, trying for humor as I patted the shirt fragment back into place.

"What's this jerk's name, Jenny?"

I flapped a hand at him. "Sit down, honey, please."

He obeyed, though he leaned toward me, looking intense.

"His *name,* Jen?"

"I heard somebody call him Tyler."

"Jenny, you realize I can arrest the SOB, bring some fairly serious charges against him?"

"He'll just say I tackled him first, which is kind of true."

"And how many witnesses do you have to tell the judge how it really played out?" The lieutenant was gently sarcastic with me, reserving his anger for the drunken joker. "Who else saw him do this? Give me names, so I can locate him."

"Yeah," David chimed in from the couch, "sue the bastard."

"Wait, guys." I held up my greasy hands. "Wait. If you go looking for him, Geof . . . if I were to sue him, David . . . then we bring this Tyler person into our lives in a big way. I don't want anything more to do with him. Okay? I don't want to have to identify him, or charge him, or talk to prosecutors about him, or be deposed by defense attorneys, or spend a single second of my life or a single penny of our money in any sort of effort to get revenge on him. I don't want him knowing who I am, much less have him directing any personal animosity at any of us."

"But, sweetheart—"

"Aw, come on, Jenny, you're no fun—"

"He was just a dumb drunk, that's all." I smiled at them and said lightly, "I have spoken."

They could tell I meant it, though. David didn't appear to care one way or another, and there was no reason he should, he was just egging me on for the entertainment of it. But Geof was not looking convinced by my arguments.

"Please," I said, just to him, "forget it. I'll heal. I'm alive, a status which was never in doubt anyway. This is no big deal. Running backs go through much worse a hundred times a season, and they don't try to have the defensive linemen arrested for assault, do they?"

"They're in training for it."

"Yeah, well, I'm getting there," I said dryly, alluding to my week of pratfalls. "Next time something like this happens, I may be able to break tackle and run downfield." Because Geof still didn't look satisfied, I tried a diversion. "Come into the kitchen with me, will you? There's a funny thing I've remembered, and it's stored in the phone in there."

He insisted on moving the TV tray out of my way and on carrying my empty plate for me—as if I hadn't already managed both of those lightweight tasks on my own already that night. It was a sweet gesture, however, and I wasn't about to object to my husband's show of concern for me.

It was dark outside by then, the time when our home often felt the most cozy to me—our cottage on its isolated curve of rocky ground and tall old trees, with the ocean little more than a stone's throw away from our front door. We had once flown down the coast at night in a friend's single-engine private plane, and we picked out our house from up there. We'd purposely left lights on, just so we might be able to spot it along the dark coast, and there it was—our small, warm, golden point of light in the deep black landscape of the Atlantic night.

As Geof and I left David behind in the living room, I heard the sound come back on the television.

"Is he feeling better?" I asked in the hallway.

"Oh, yeah. He slept all afternoon and woke up complaining, so I figure he's almost back to normal. What is it I'm supposed to see?"

"Remember when I did that phone interview for the TV station?"

Walking in front of me, he nodded.

"Well, in the middle of all that chaos, I got a call, a quick one. I had to get off the phone, because of the interview. But it was some woman who said I should shut down the highway."

He held open the kitchen door for me, looking mildly intrigued.

"She sounded extremely upset," I told him, as he crossed in front of me again, carrying my dishes. "It seemed as if she was pleading with me." I smiled in deprecation of my own words. "Understand, I'm reading all of this into about ten seconds' worth of conversation. Anyway, I've got her name and number stored, and I thought you might want it, since you're looking for people who could have strong feelings about that trail crossing. I realize this is probably no big deal—"

"Let's have a look at her."

While he ran water over the dirty dishes, I punched up the stored information from the caller identification feature of our telephone. Geof came up and looked over my shoulder, wiping his hands on a towel.

I wrote it all down for him, saying the number out loud.

"Wilheim, Dorothy," I read off the little window. "Never heard of her, have you?"

"I think maybe I have." Geof stuck the note into his shirt pocket. "I'll check it out Monday."

"Who is she?"

"Oh, that I don't know. She just sounds familiar."

I erased Dorothy Wilheim, whoever she was, from the memory of our telephone. She had, bless her, served my purpose of distracting my husband from his desire for vengeance on the drunk. Now, if I could just quietly disappear upstairs, I would get out of the ruined shirt that still posed a clear and present red flag to him.

"Hey, you guys in there!"

It was David, paging us from the front of the house. When we entered the living room, he pointed at the television screen.

"Look at this," he commanded us.

What we saw was a special local news bulletin.

There was Marilyn Stuben, the anchorwoman who had interviewed me, standing with her microphone in hand, talking to our local fire chief, Roy Stabaugh, he who had caused me no end of grief with his excessive (in my opinion) fire prevention and insurance worries.

Marilyn was saying, "Are we looking at an act of arson here, Chief Stabaugh?"

Geof said sharply, "Arson, where?"

"Wait!" David shushed him.

"Oh, we won't know that for some time, Marilyn," the fire chief was saying. "Not until we get this thing put out, and our investigators are able to get in there."

"What a tragedy!" the anchorwoman said.

"Dave," Geof began again, but again an upturned young hand stopped him, so we could listen.

"Yes, it is," responded Chief Stabaugh, who, in my embittered opinion, looked as if he could have stood there all night being interviewed while his men risked their lives trying to extinguish whatever it was that was burning offscreen.

Finally, a camera showed us our first glimpse of the actual flames.

Something large was being utterly consumed by a true inferno, from the looks of it, even while we watched as fascinated voyeurs.

Geof recognized what it was before I did.

"Jenny, it's the Dime Store."

"Oh, my God!" My hands flew to my mouth in shock. "Oh, no!"

"Man," said David, with delighted relish, "look at that sucker burn."

I stood there only long enough to hear the anchorwoman say in a voice-over, "Chief, would you say this tragic fire points up the importance of the city having adequate fire protection and insurance coverage for the festival that's coming up next weekend?"

Guess what the fire chief said?

"Yes, Marilyn, I would say that it certainly does."

I raced upstairs then, to slip on a different shirt. When I got back downstairs, Geof was already wearing a jacket, waiting at the bottom of the stairway, and he was holding out a jacket for me. I stuffed my arms into it, hiding my winces.

"You guys can't leave me!"

It was an indignant shout from the living room.

"You'll be all right!" Geof called back, without pity. "Just don't get scared and shoot yourself!"

I expected an outburst of profanity in response to that, but there was only silence from the front room. I walked to the doorway and looked in on him. There he was, still a hump of teenager under blankets.

"The owners of the store are friends of mine," I told him. "We want to offer any help we can. Will you really be okay, if we leave you here by yourself?"

My attention seemed to surprise him, even disarm him. I had the feeling that his next words slipped out before he had time to censor them. "Hey, listen, I understand. Don't worry about it. You guys go on and do what you gotta do. I'm fine."

I smiled my appreciation at him, but he had already turned back to the television. They were still showing the burning of the Dime Store. It was big, big news on a Saturday night in our town, and from what I could see, the firemen weren't having much luck in putting out the fire.

Only on the way into town did I finally remember to tell Geof about the whispered conversation I had overheard while I was underneath the speaker's platform that day.

"With this fire, we'll be lucky if we can spare anybody to go out there," he said, but he got on his car phone to talk to the dispatcher. When he hung up, he looked frustrated. "She'll try. I suppose I could do it. But I'd rather send somebody they won't recognize."

I asked him why.

"Because if our guy gets detected, as a last ditch he can claim he's a local nature lover who heard about the meeting and wants to join in. If Lew saw me, that would be the end of it right there." He shook his head. "No, I can't be the one. We'll have to hope she comes up with somebody else."

All that wood. It burned like a bonfire. The modest and old-fashioned retail store that had been a beloved institution in Port Frederick was half gone to ashes by the time we got there.

It was amazing, how people reacted to that fire.

They walked, drove, wandered over from miles around—pulled to the sight of the end of a tradition in so many of their—our—families for generations. The fire blocked traffic, snarling it completely, but that didn't seem to matter to any of us. All of the fire-fighting equipment was already in place, along with most of our police force, both the on-duty cops and the ones who were supposed to be off-duty at that time. Like everybody else, they came streaming in, leaving their own cars parked wherever they found space, then threading their way into the heart of things to take on assignments in crowd control, or in helping the firemen however they could.

It wasn't one of those avid crowds, where people are just there to ogle and there's laughter and, eventually, hot dog stands.

No, this was family, this crowd.

They were shocked, saddened—there were many tears shed over childhood memories of visits to the Dime Store for Halloween costumes and birthday party favors and Valentine's cards and Christmas ornaments and Hanukkah candles and school supplies. Rulers and pencils and water colors and Big Chief notebooks, we'd bought them all at the Dime Store, along with licorice whips and our first pairs of earrings and sets of plastic dishes for our dolls and toy guns and colored construction paper and . . . and it was all drifting away in the smoke.

After Geof went off to lend a hand, I ran into many, many friends and acquaintances. To a person, they seemed to feel the fire as a personal loss, a blow, even.

Nellie Kennedy I located among a circle of concerned customers who included Melissa Barney and her two boys. Bringing them there—after so much grief of their own—wasn't what I would have done, I thought, as I watched the three red heads glow in the flickering light. Too much morbid excitement, I'd have decided, which probably only went to show that it was a good thing I wasn't a mom. And, what did I know from baby-sitters, anyway? If Melissa wanted to rush to the moral support of the Kennedys—as Nellie had come to hers—she couldn't very well leave a three-year-old and an eight-year-old home alone.

The Barneys didn't notice me.

Like so many others, they only had eyes for the flames.

Nellie was sobbing. Bill was staring at their store, looking stunned and bewildered. You could almost read his thoughts in his face: *How could this happen to us?*

Everyone else looked helpless to help them, and that's how I felt. But Nellie saw me standing near and reached out for one of my hands.

"Your festival," she said through her tears. "All the things you still need . . ."

I'm human. I couldn't deny that thought had also crossed my mind, but I didn't want her to worry about it now.

"Oh, please, Nellie," I said, "don't give it a thought! Heck, it's less than a week away now, and we've got almost everything we need. We'll sort it all out, don't you worry."

I wasn't going to ask her, "What happened?"

I figured that she and Bill had already been asked that question too many times already. I'd find out, like everyone else, sooner or later.

But Nellie told me anyway.

Or, rather, she told me that she didn't know.

"There were just suddenly flames, Jenny. Some customers smelled smoke, and they told Bill, and he came looking for me. We didn't have time for anything except getting everybody out."

My God. My own knees weakened at the thought I hadn't thought before: Of course, the store had still been open for business, probably packed on the last Saturday night before Halloween. Suddenly, I realized how terrible it could have been. Again, I didn't even have to ask Nellie the question that was in my mind. She offered the answer.

"We got everybody out, Jenny. Oh, thank God. The children—"

I put my arms around her as she started to sob. Bill heard her and came toward us, and I turned Nellie around and literally placed her in his arms. Slowly, sweetly, without saying anything, Bill patted Nellie's back as they held each other, the short, sturdy woman in her sensible dark dress enveloped by the tall, lanky frame of her husband.

Their daughter, I saw, was wasting no opportunity to make political hay out of her own family's tragedy.

Illuminated by television lights, interviewed by the omnipresent anchorwoman, Ardyth cut a memorable figure standing beside the fire chief—he in full battle regalia—and both of them visible to everyone—most of whom were registered voters—from everywhere.

"Jenny," I muttered to myself, as I stepped over cables to try to hear what Ardyth and Chief Stabaugh were saying, "you are such a cynic."

What mayoral candidate Ardyth Kennedy was saying so sincerely to the camera was this: "And when I am elected, I will bring into office with me my memories of this night's loss, so personal to me, along with a strengthened conviction to protect the citizens of this city. This terrible night will not be without meaning, not if I can help it. I will wrest from the ashes of my family's sad loss an utter devotion to the cause of protecting the families of our city from the depredations of fire, crime . . ."

War? I thought. Famine? Plague?

At the end, many onlookers burst into applause, which I could only hope was specific to the sympathy they felt for her on this night. I was heartened to overhear a woman whisper to another, "That phony bitch! If she's so sad for her family, why isn't she over there helping her poor mother and father?"

Good question, I thought, but I knew the answer as well as they and Ardyth did: Opportunist to the end, she had political fish to fry in this fire.

And whom *wasn't* I surprised to glimpse in the background of the interview? None other than Ardie's de facto prime minister, Peter Falwell himself. He was looking gimlet-eyed and evilly Machiavellian, I thought, but maybe it was the flickering light playing tricks with my eyes.

"Speak of the devil," I said, as Lewis Riss appeared beside me.

"Hey, Cain, got any marshmallows?"

He reached under my hair and tugged on my left earlobe. Lew always had taken personal liberties that the degree of our friendship had never supported. He was dressed macho again, this time in a snug black body-builder T-shirt over equally snug black jeans that displayed every bulge of his, uh, thighs. Most of the rest of us in the crowd were snuggled into warm jackets and sweaters, but not Lew—he had his new muscles to keep him warm. Man, I thought, catching the catty drift of my own thoughts, this supposed old pal was pissing me off even more than Ardie Kennedy did. The very small part of my brain that was managing to remain emotionally detached, wondered: Why?

I ignored his tasteless joke.

"Almost makes me pine to be a reporter again," he said, grinning at the fire and then at me. "I'm a sensation junkie."

"Where were you," I demanded of him, beating around no bushes, "around five-thirty to six o'clock yesterday afternoon?"

His maddening grin reappeared. "You mean the highway blockade? Kinda looks like our work, doesn't it?"

"And what about throwing logs at motorcycle riders, Lew?" I was infuriated by his bad-boy attitude. "Is that kinda like your work, too? The kid who got hurt, Lew? He's like a son to us."

He is? I thought, startled by my own dramatic license. If it hadn't been such a serious matter, I might have laughed at myself.

"Hey," Lew protested, raising his arms in mock defense against me. "Lighten up, Cain. Would I hurt you or yours?" He pointed a forefinger at me like a pistol and lifted one eyebrow in an expression of outraged innocence. "Think it over!"

Maybe I owed him an apology, but since he hadn't even answered my original question, I wasn't feeling any remorse about it.

"Okay then, where were you when it happened?"

"With my friends." Emphasis on the last word.

"Where were they?"

"With me."

"And where was that?"

"What is this, Cain? Do I need to call my lawyer? You gonna read me my rights? Aren't you a little confused? Isn't your husband the one who's the cop?"

A crashing sound behind us caused me to turn away from him—just in time to see part of the roof on the adjoining building to the south go crashing in. A collective gasp surged through the crowd as new flames and sparks flew high into the smokey sky.

When I turned back around, Lew was gone.

To a mysterious eleven-o'clock meeting by the bridge? I wondered.

And what would they do there, celebrate a successful fire?

No. I couldn't believe it of Lew. I couldn't. And besides, why would I even think they would do this, when there wasn't any reason to connect First Things First either to the Kennedys or to their Dime Store?

I shook off the odd, irrational, unwelcome notion.

The crowd remained for hours, long into the night, and some of us even into the first minutes or hours of the next morning. I saw Nellie and Bill Kennedy leave, and who could blame them, as there was nothing they could do, and this was heartbreaking for them to watch.

By midnight, we all had speckles of soot on us and our cars, gritty souvenirs of an unforgettable night in our town. I stood for a long time with the mayor and her husband, who was a minister. They were magnets, drawing citizens over to them to share reminiscences, to criticize, to opine. I came in for some of that myself, mostly to do with the festival. It was fascinating—the whole thing—like watching a huge living organism, which happened to be our community, move and shift and feel its collective emotions and think its collective thoughts. The only people who seemed out of it were the strangers and the newcomers. I saw the Post Haste delivery woman wandering in and out among the parked cars, as if she didn't know what to do with herself, compared to the focus of longtime residents. They—we—knew why we were there—to witness the passing of an era, and to be able to say years later, "I was there the night the Dime Store burned."

The only others whose appearance jarred with the natives that night were the Halloween protestors. I looked for the El Greco man, but didn't see him among them. By now, I could recognize several of the others, however. They stood in a tight little huddle in the crowd, forming their own private island in the sea of spectators. The expressions on their faces as they stared at the conflagration were so smug, so self-righteously "I told you so," that I couldn't stand to look at them for very long. What were they thinking? I wondered. That this fire paid the wages of sin? That this is what you got for selling Halloween costumes? At that moment, they looked about as attractive to me as the Frankenstein monster mask that was probably a melted puddle of latex by then.

The buildings on either side of the store were total losses, too. The fire department heroically limited the devastation to those three structures, however, although businesses for blocks around would be dusting ashy residue off their premises for months to come.

Geof found me a little after midnight and said, "They can get along without me. Let's go home." On the way back, he called the police dispatcher.

"Nobody made Lew's meeting," he told me.

A few minutes later, he slammed the palm of his right hand against the steering wheel. "Damn! I made a mistake about that, Jenny. After this fire . . . I should have done the surveillance on that meeting, myself."

"Geof, there's no reason to think FTF set it. Is there?"

He shook his head, looking thoughtful. "No. But they're in town. You saw Lew at the fire. And you know how it is with groups like that, Jenny, sometimes they have reasons that don't necessarily make any sense to the rest of us. Damn! I should have been there."

We were only able to sleep for a couple of hours, before the phone rang on his side of the bed.

"Bushfield," he snapped into the receiver, the cop in him coming awake first.

I heard the babble of an excited, high voice.

"Mrs. Kennedy," he said, in a calm, firm, steadying tone, and I immediately sat up in bed, alert, listening. "Mrs. Kennedy, have you called 911? That's good. How are you, right now? How is your husband?"

He listened and again I heard high threads of hysteria from the phone. *Nellie?* I thought. *What more? What now?*

"Mrs. Kennedy." He kept saying her name, focusing her on the fact of her identity. "Do you feel safe now? Have you relocked all the doors? Do you think you'll be all right until officers and the paramedics arrive?"

"What?" I whispered, not expecting an answer.

"You could call neighbors to come over to be with you," he said next. "Yes, all right, we can do that. Yes, Jenny, too. We'll leave for your house as soon as you and I get off the phone. Mrs. Kennedy? It's over. Hang on to that thought, will you? And remember that the cavalry's on its way." He smiled a little, and I felt the reassurance emanating out from him over the telephone wires to her. "Hang in there."

I was already out of bed and pulling on jeans and sweatshirt.

"What happened, Geof?"

He tossed the covers off and stepped naked out of bed. "Some thugs were waiting at Nellie and Bill Kennedy's house when they got home from the fire. Beat Nellie up—"

I gasped, but there was more.

"Beat up on Bill, tore up their house."

I was too shocked for speech, but my thoughts were clear enough: *How could anyone do such a thing? And why? And were they the same people who hurt David?*

We finished dressing and left a note for the kid.

The first time I found speech, it was to ask, "Why'd she call us?"

"You."

"Okay, me. She had to know we're a package deal, though. Order one foundation director—"

"And get one cop thrown in, for free."

I laughed a little as I pulled a brush through my hair. "We're doing each other's punch lines now."

"That's probably just as well, sweetheart." He was standing in the bedroom doorway, waiting for me to put away the brush and hurry down the stairs with him. "Since you can never remember the punch lines to jokes."

I had to laugh again, in agreement.

And it was thus that we happened to distract ourselves from my original question, which was: Why *did* Nellie call us—me—when she surely had a town-full of other, older, better friends to call? If she wanted the presence, the comfort, of a friend . . . why me?

* * *

We made it out to the Kennedys' in just under twenty minutes.

On the way out, Geof called in to headquarters to ask who had been sent out ahead of us and to let them know he was coming, too. That's when we found out what the rest of Port Frederick wouldn't know until morning . . .

Firemen had found a body under the stockroom rubble of the Dime Store. So far, unidentified and unidentifiable.

"The fire was so hot," Geof told me, "that it charred a silver cross the victim was wearing."

And that's how I came to be the first person to know the identity of the single human casualty of the fire.

"It's the El Greco man," I said.

Of course, I didn't know his name.

I remembered that handsome, dramatic face, and I felt very disturbed. He, not I, had walked into the fires of hell.

But had he also set them?

16

THERE WAS STILL A LOT OF SMOKE IN THE AIR.

We couldn't see it, but we could smell it—a pungent woodiness—especially in low places in the road where it gathered in aromatic pools, like invisible, fragrant fog. I began to feel that were coated in it, our clothes, skin hair, even the car. It was odd to think that our entire hometown was now similarly perfumed, as if we had all bathed the previous evening in a scent called *Nostalgia.* Or, been hung in a woodshed, to soak the smokey flavor of the fire into our pores.

We paused at the large red stop sign that was becoming very familiar to me, before turning into the Kennedys' driveway. Two police cars. An emergency medical van. A dark Oldsmobile Cutlass sedan parked behind the cop cars, arrogantly angled in behind them, blocking their way out. That was obviously somebody who'd arrived after the cops had, I thought, and I could guess who it was, just from the way the car was parked. At least she hadn't blocked the med van.

Geof pulled the Jeep onto the grass, out of the way.

It looked like every light in the house was on.

Nellie and Bill had raised Ardyth in this modest house. In the daylight, what you saw when you looked at it was white siding, shake shingle roof, a sort of farmhouse-looking structure, with spare parts added on—an upstairs dormer bedroom that stuck out in an architecturally ungainly fashion above the original first floor, an enlarged kitchen in back, and a clump of a room stuck onto the west side, where one of the original bedrooms had been expanded to provide a television den.

It was clunky, ugly, and oddly inviting, from the outside.

Inside, everytime I'd seen it, it was messy in the way houses can get when both the husband and wife work (as I ought to know), with papers strewn around, along with enough paraphernalia to make it look like an annex to their store: boxes of unsold this and that and marvelous, colorful, useless cast-off bric-a-brac.

And yet, there was still living, walking, sitting space within, and there was something about the old, unfashionable slip-covered furniture that made a person want to take off his shoes and sit down and stay awhile.

That's how it had appeared to me, anyway, on the few occasions I was there when I was growing up. I recalled a birthday party, possibly two of them, for Ardyth, when her mother had probably forced her to invite all the girls in our class. And there'd been a couple of committee meetings in high school. And then there was my midnight visit in January, of course.

It was a perfect house for a politician to come from, I thought—modest, unassuming, kind of populist-looking. And it looked a great place to live or to visit, for a child, because of all those *things* from their store. Can you imagine, having as your best girlfriend when you were, say, eight, a kid who had never-ending, free access to unlimited arts and crafts supplies, and toys and candy and doll clothes and doll furniture? I had always wished I liked Ardyth—or, failing that, that at least she liked me—so I could dive into that cornucopia of doodads! But, no such luck. Bad chemistry had kept us apart, all the way back to kindergarten.

The lie she told about me then—by the way—the first one I remember, was that I didn't wear any underpants. *"Jenny, Jenny, doesn't wear panties!"* I'd had to show a few girls that I did, just to prove Ardie wrong. And, of course, she'd made hay with that, too. *"Jenny, Jenny, shows her panties!"*

Mortifying, at five.

A grown-up would have forgiven her, by now.

Bitch, I thought, the minute I suspected that was her car blocking the police cars in her parents' driveway. If only I'd had such a useful vocabulary back then, in kindergarten!

"What are you doing here?"

She wanted to know, when she answered our knock at her parents' front door and then blocked our access to the inside of the house.

"Your mother asked us to come," I told her.

"I don't believe that for a minute. You're always pushing in where you don't belong, Jenny. You're here to pick up any scandal you can use against me in the election, aren't you? You're here for Mary."

I nearly voiced the only rational response that came to my mind: "Liar, liar, pants on fire." But I didn't.

"I don't know about my wife," Geof said, in a voice so dry it could have passed for British. He had reached into one of his back pockets and pulled out his wallet, and now he flipped his police identification at Ardyth's pugnacious face. "But I'm here on police business, Miss Kennedy."

Ardyth made a frequent public point of distancing herself from "Ms." God forbid she should be linked in the voters' minds with those dangerous feminists!

Her face turned slightly red at his multilayered gibe.

"Knock it off, Bushfield."

Looking as reluctant to let us in as if we were the people who'd assaulted her parents, Ardyth opened the front door a little wider. Wide enough, it turned out, to admit only one person at a time. Geof was closest, so he stepped through first.

I moved one foot—and found the door closed in my face.

"Ardyth!" I protested to the door.

I knew what to expect next. Geof would use the opportunity to get Nellie's permission to let me in, and Ardyth could scream and yell all she wanted, it wouldn't make any difference, not if Nellie said, "I invited her." I did, for a moment however, recall the way Nellie had seemed to cave in to her daughter the other morning in front of the Dime Store, the way, in fact, Nellie had always caved in, rather than stand up to her willful, spoiled offspring. *Oh, dear,* I thought, *am I going to be left standing out here in the dark, on the front stoop?*

It took about a minute, while I grew nervous.

But then the door opened to the sight of my husband, shaking his head at whatever had transpired within. He was alone.

"Where's the twit?" I whispered to him, as he let me in.

"Arguing with her mother."

"About?"

"You."

"Now? She's arguing with poor Nellie about me, *now?* Miss Sensitivity, isn't she? If I had a daughter like that, I wouldn't be satisfied with merely disowning her. I'd hire a hit man."

Geof hid his laughter by disguising it as a cough.

I took my attention off the multiple character flaws of the daughter long enough to register what had happened to the home of the parents. What I saw made me reach for Geof and whisper an exclamation of surprise and dismay.

It looked like a broken dollhouse.

Lamps, knocked off tables, shattered on the carpet.

Ashtrays, statuettes, much of the accumulated and displayed mementos of their lives, thrown about, most of them broken.

It looked as if somebody had taken something like a pool cue or a cane and swept everything off every surface in the living room and—when I looked beyond—the dining room. In there, I saw about a dozen shipping boxes upended on the floor. When we walked past, I saw they looked as if somebody with big feet had stomped on them, probably smashing whatever they held.

I began to feel more afraid for Nellie.

"Geof?" I whispered. "Is she badly hurt?"

"I don't know, but I think maybe not."

There wasn't time for us to sightsee any further, or to talk about the mess around us, because there was too much else going on to demand our—particularly his—attention.

In the kitchen we found, not Ardyth arguing with her mother, but Nellie, Bill, three uniformed police officers, and two paramedics. It wasn't a very large kitchen, and now it seemed as crowded as a utensil drawer, with brawny people and starched uniforms.

I recognized all three of the cops, but the medical technicians were not the same pair who had rescued David less than twenty-four hours earlier. These were a different couple of lifesavers, a man and a woman, on a different shift. The cops and I nodded in a friendly way to one another, but I didn't speak to them, since this was all business, and they were concentrating on it.

Two of the cops, both of them men, had been talking to Nellie and Bill as we walked in. It looked as if they'd just started their interview; the shorter of the two cops was still uncapping his pen. The third cop—a woman—was loading film into a camera. She'd have a lot of pictures to take, I thought, not envying her the task. Cops had to be so exacting about such things, photographing everything that looked as if it could possibly be evidence, and notating everything, down to the f-stop of the film and the precise time they took the picture. With the mess we'd seen in the living and dining rooms, she'd be lucky to finish that job by noon.

"Lieutenant?" The cop who had been speaking to Nellie when we walked in looked over at us. "You want to take over here?"

Nellie saw me and said, "Jenny!"

I rushed to her and dropped to my knees in front of her, taking her hands and gently squeezing them as I looked into her face.

Behind me, Geof said, "Sure, I'll do that. If I talk to the Kennedys, it would set you free to help collect evidence." He shook his head again. "There's enough of it out there."

The woman cop looked up from her camera and rolled her eyes in passionate agreement with that assessment.

"Yes, sir," said the short cop, "that would sure help."

If they wondered why we were there, they didn't ask; if they asked Geof later, he could tell them that he didn't really know.

The three uniformed officers quickly shifted to the front rooms, leaving us alone with the Kennedys and the paramedics. Geof pulled an empty chair out from under the kitchen table and sat down in it. He took his own notepad out of his inside coat pocket and his own capped pen that came from the same supply storeroom.

I lowered my behind to the floor and curled my legs in.

Bill sat in the third chair, his hands on top of the table, his face looking as pale and blank as a brand-new bulletin board. He was looking straight ahead, ignoring us, ignoring the uniforms, paying no attention to anything except whatever shocking images were playing themselves out in his mind's eye. He never turned his head, seeming deaf and blind to all of us.

I didn't know where dear Ardyth was.

But I had a sudden mental image of her upstairs in her old bedroom, frilly white bedspread and all, using her old pink Princess phone to call her mentor, Peter Falwell. But then I thought, more charitably, maybe she was using the bathroom.

The paramedics hovered, looking hurried and worried.

"Lieutenant," said one of them, a stocky, good-looking woman with hair dyed so yellow that her head looked like a spring crocus, "we want to take these people to a hospital. No bleeding, no bones broken, or anything like that, but he looks like he could go into shock any minute now, and we think they both need to be checked for internal stuff, you know what I mean? She looks like she got hit pretty hard, and all we've got is bruising and swelling so far, but it could be worse, you know? So can you make this fast, or better yet, can you interview them in the hospital?"

"No hospital!" Nellie said loudly.

I couldn't actually see anything wrong with her—until I noticed a long red welt swelling up near her jawline. And then I noticed another red raised mark under her right eye. Nellie was wearing her usual work clothes—a dark, long-sleeved dress and hose—so she was pretty well covered up, and I wondered if other vicious marks lay hidden beneath her clothes. She smelled of smoke, as did they all. The whole kitchen reeked of it, and I guessed that all of the cops and medics had been working the fire, as well. Geof and I were probably the only ones who'd had a chance to change clothes, much less to shower or rest. I hadn't been doing anything heroic—as they all had—but I knew we must all have been a pretty exhausted-looking bunch of people, even given the two hours of sleep that Geof and I had grabbed. I felt selfish about that sleep, as I saw the bags under the medic's eyes as she spoke to him.

I touched my fingers to the air just above Nellie's jaw.

"Where else did they hurt you?"

Tears sprang to her eyes, as she pointed, rather than telling me. Both arms. Her back. Legs, chest. Hips.

"Bruises," the other paramedic explained, shoving the word out in an indignant, staccato explosion. "They hit her with, like, a stick, or something."

I flinched at the awful image.

"But we're okay," Nellie said, still speaking in a louder voice than normal, almost as if she were gathering strength from the sound of her own voice. "We can take care of ourselves now. We're not leaving home." She looked up at Geof. "I want to stay home!"

He glanced over at the medics.

Both of them shrugged, and the woman said, "Can't force 'em. They're not dying, or anywhere close to it. Should we hit the road then, Lieutenant? It's a long way back here, if they should happen to change their minds . . ."

"We won't!" Nellie said, her voice growing ever firmer. "Will we, Bill?"

Her husband didn't turn his head, didn't answer.

"See what I mean?" the woman paramedic said to Geof.

But Nellie called him sharply out of his funk. "Bill!"

He jerked, as if coming awake, and began talking, as if she'd pulled a cord in his back. "A gang," Bill said, as if talking only to the wall straight in front of him. He looked older, weaker, vulnerable, which made me feel sad for both of them. He looked so frightened, as he said, "What did they want here? That fellow, he hit her. He kept hitting her. I couldn't stop him. Who were they? Where did they come from? What did they want with us? Do you think they'll come back?"

"Oh, Bill," Nellie said, in a much softer voice. She reached for one of his hands and squeezed it, though he didn't respond to her. "Honey, don't worry, it was some kind of mistake, I'm sure it was. They got the wrong house. They'll never come back to bother us again. You tried hard to fight them, Bill." Her voice broke, and she bowed her head, and began to sob. Through her tears, we heard her say, "He did. He really did. He tried so hard to fight them. He was so frightened, and I was, too, and he tried so hard to make them go away. Bill was so brave." Through her tears she looked at him, and she took her hand and turned his chin around until he faced her. "Honey, it isn't your fault that they hit me. You were brave. You stood up to them like a giant. You were a hero. My hero. Please, don't be so upset, Bill! It's over now."

I thought Bill didn't look convinced; he looked shamed.

Damn this society's macho crap! I thought, unhappy that Bill should have to feel humiliated because he wasn't "man" enough to stand up to an entire gang of hoodlums all by himself. He might have actually saved Nellie's life, and his own, I suddenly thought, and so I said it out loud.

Nellie looked down at me, gratitude in her eyes.

"He did save my life," she said, and then to him: "You did, Bill."

"That fellow," he said, looking very much as if he might start crying, too. "He hit you. I can't believe he hit you. I wanted to make him stop, I wanted to . . ."

"You did," Nellie said, in that sharp voice I'd heard her use so often with Bill. Only now I thought I understood it better. It was sharp the way a mother's voice is sharp: *Stop that!* And this time, at least, she was only trying to get him to snap out of his shock, his shame, his sorrow. His reaction, more than the devastation in the front rooms, even more than Nellie's bruises, made me realize what a terrifying ordeal they had just survived—and on top of the destruction of their entire life's work. It was almost beyond ordinary comprehension, their loss in so few hours. If Bill looked like the shell-shocked victim of a war, well, no wonder. And if Nellie acted toward him like a cross between a battlefield nurse and a sergeant, well, that was nothing to wonder about, either.

And where was their only child, to comfort them?

Now that *was* something to wonder about.

Finally, it was just the four of us left in the kitchen.

Geof started them off with some gentle, mundane types of questions, to help them relax a little, to ease everybody's tension. How they spelled their full names. Their ages. Their occupations, as if he didn't know. Their address, their phone number, *et* calming *cetera.* Geof tried to encourage Bill to answer the questions regarding himself, but Nellie kept interrupting, answering everything for him, until finally Geof said, "Mrs. Kennedy—"

"Nellie. You make me feel so old!"

"I'm sorry." He smiled. "You're certainly not that, although this night you've had would have aged me about a hundred years, I think. Are you holding up all right? I'll try to make this as quick as possible, so you can get to bed—"

"We'll never sleep tonight."

"Well, we can always do this again tomorrow—"

"I'd rather be here, doing it now," she assured him. "If we do this, then I don't have to think about everything that has happened to us tonight."

He tried again. "I was just going to say, perhaps you would let Bill answer for himself?" He was exceedingly tactful. But when she did keep quiet, some of Bill's answers seemed those of a man still in a state of profound shock.

"What time'd you get home, Bill?"

"Time to go home," Bill said, looking at Nellie.

She said, "It was one-fifteen, I saw it on the clock in the car."

"Both of you come home together, Bill?"

Bill shook his head, but Nellie said, "Yes, sure, in my car, we always just take one car to work, no need for both of us to drive. I always drive, I like to, actually . . ." She laughed a little. "I'm a better driver than he is, he's a little absentminded about his driving, like he is about most things. Right, Bill?"

Geof gave up the valiant effort to get Bill Kennedy to talk. He looked at Nellie, smiled encouragingly, and said, "Well, why don't you just tell me what happened, what you saw, everything you can remember, from the time you left the fire—"

She told about leaving, heartsick, being helped through the maze of traffic by the police, coming out onto the open highway, and driving slowly home, so tired and upset she was afraid of having an accident. She didn't recall seeing anything, or even paying attention to anything, on the way home.

"I don't even remember driving home," she said. "It was one of those drives you have when you just drive by instinct, because you're thinking about other things. I was thinking about the fire. I pulled into our driveway, I guess, not that I exactly remember doing it, and . . . I don't know, there wasn't anything unusual or special. We just parked the car in the garage like we always do, and we came into the house like we always do."

"Was it locked, Nellie?"

"No." She looked embarrassed, then defensive. "We don't lock our houses out here, so I can't claim it's like they had to break in. I guess they just walked in. And they all had on gloves, Lieutenant—Geof—all of them, so there's absolutely no point in your looking for fingerprints, because you're not going to find a single one. Not one."

"What kind of gloves, Nellie?"

She blinked and looked at Bill. "Do you remember, Bill?"

"I don't remember gloves," he said. "I don't think they had on any gloves, Nellie, did they?"

"Yes, they did, Bill! Yellow sorts of gloves, you know, those soft leathery things like farmers wear sometimes."

Suddenly Bill broke in, as if a verbal dam had broken in him, releasing the words he'd been too shocked to give us before now. "I came in the front door, and there was this fellow standing over in the corner. I'd never seen him before. I said, what are you doing here? And I knew he was up to no good, and I wanted to grab something, but this fellow, he had these other people with him, these two women and these other two men, and they were out in the kitchen, out here where we are, and they all came in, and they started tearing things up!" Bill glanced at his wife, and the look they shared was one of horror remembered.

She said, "I came in behind Bill."

"And that fellow," Bill said, "he had something in his hands and he was hitting things—"

"And I started screaming," Nellie interjected, "and the man saw me, and he ran over and started hitting me."

"With what?" Geof asked quickly.

"With a lamp," Nellie said, leaning forward, her breathing coming quick, as if she were panicked and under attack all over again. "With one of our lamps, is what it was, the green one with the ivory shade on it." She made an hourglass shape with her hands, to show what it looked like. "It didn't break." Her eyes were wide, round, as we all shared the wonder of the lucky fact that the attacker hadn't broken it on her body, and that she hadn't been cut with the edges of a broken lamp.

"What did he look like, Nellie, this man?"

But she shook her head, tears filling her eyes again.

"Short, tall? Skinny, fat?"

"I don't know, I don't know."

"It's okay, it may come back to you. Do you remember the color of his skin?"

"I don't know!" Nellie said, crying again.

"He was a white man, but some of them were black people," Bill said, suddenly. "The women, they were black women." He frowned with the effort of recalling their appearances through the fog of his own terrific shock. "One of the other men, he may have been black, too. I don't understand it at all! Why did they come here? What do they want with us?"

Geof couldn't get any better descriptions out of either Nellie or Bill, not descriptions of hair, faces, nothing more. She said the group of people had all been wearing lots of clothing, outerwear, coats and hats, that covered their weight, their bodily features.

"I don't know how you know they were black people or white people," she said, in an exasperated, worn-out tone of voice to her husband. "They were all covered up! I know I couldn't tell if they were Asian or white . . . or Martian!"

But Bill stubbornly insisted on his version.

They'd all worn masks, she told us, making his certitude about the color of their skin—or even their gender—seem even more unlikely. Gloves. Heavily clothed. Masks. Nothing showing. And nothing left to identify them, at least nothing from their own bodies, no fingerprints, no hair, no blood, nothing at all to scrape up and bag and take to a crime lab.

"No," Bill said, objecting to her version. "Masks?"

"Oh, Bill." She laughed a little. "Our masks. Like we sell, honey. Those ones that look like real people. Jimmy Carter. Bill Clinton. Hillary Clinton, you know, those kinds of masks. Did you think we were being attacked by the National Democratic Party?" Nellie started to giggle through her tears, which made me start to laugh, too, and Geof had to smile, through his official demeanor. Even Bill smiled a little.

"I guess not," he said. "I don't remember masks."

"What did they say?" Geof asked.

"They were talking in the kitchen," Bill said, "when I came in. I could hear them. I don't know what they were saying, but I heard one of them—one of the men—say to one of the women, 'He doesn't want us to be here.' "

Geof and I glanced at each other. Very strange.

"Are you sure?" Geof asked, because he had to.

Bill nodded and said, "But that fellow, the one who attacked Nellie, he never said anything."

"That's right," Nellie agreed. "Not one word."

"Did he hit you, Bill?"

Although Bill shook his head, Nellie said, "Oh, yes, he did! Bill, you just don't remember, you were so busy trying to stop him! Where do you think you got those bruises! He hurt you, all right!" She looked at me, her eyes showing as much shock now as her husband's. "I've never been so . . ." Her voice dropped. "Frightened."

Bill said, "Why was that fellow so angry? Did we do something to make those people mad at us?"

I hoped some of this was making sense to the lieutenant, because I couldn't make heads or tails out of it; it was turning out to be one of the strangest stories, and one of the most disturbing, that I'd ever heard. A gang of masked attackers. Furious. Destroying everything in their path. And for what possible reason?

But then why, too, would anyone beat a boy lying in the road?

The rampage had halted the minute Nellie got to a phone and managed to tap out 911.

"He just stopped," she said, looking amazed. "I yelled at him, I said, I'm calling the police! And he dropped the lamp, and he stopped hitting me and . . . he just stopped."

"And then what did he do?" Geof prodded her.

"He was gone," she said. "Just like that. One minute he was there, and crazy, a crazy man, and then he left, they all left, and everything was quiet again, and we were safe. Although we didn't know if we were safe. We didn't know if they'd come back, but we didn't think they would, not with the police coming. And then I called you, Jenny, because . . . because I just needed to have a friend to be with us."

I put my arms around her, gently, and hugged her.

"Do you think," she asked, "it was the same people who set fire to our store?"

"What," Geof asked, speaking slowly, "makes you think somebody set fire to it, Nellie?"

She blinked and looked as startled as an owl.

"Why," she said, "I don't know why I think that, I just . . . do. Maybe, maybe it's because I've always been so careful about our wiring, for one thing. Our store was so old, with all that wood, and I always felt so responsible for the safety of our staff and our customers. I guess I just can't believe it was anything accidental, like an electrical fire. And we know it wasn't lightning, don't we? And we never allow anyone to smoke in the store. Never. There weren't any space heaters. There wasn't anything that might cause a fire, not one single thing that I know of. So, it had to be that somebody set it." She looked from one to the other of us, sadly. "Doesn't it?"

"That fellow set it," Bill said. "I don't know why."

"Oh, no, Bill!" Nellie's hands flew to her mouth.

"You saw him, Bill?" Geof asked, and I could hear excitement under his calm tone. "Are you saying you saw the same man at your store, the one who attacked the two of you here in your home tonight?" It always tickled me, a little, to hear him talk like a cop; it seemed they so often had to state things that seemed obvious, but that was only because so often things weren't. Obvious. What things were, usually, was muddled, and it was his job to make them clear. I, too, felt the excitement of thinking that Bill had just given us the major lead to the first of the major crimes of the night.

But that wasn't what he had meant, it turned out.

"I didn't see him, but I know it was him."

Not good enough, I thought, with an inner sigh.

And then Geof pressed Bill to tell us how he "knew," that was all.

"But who is he?" I broke in, having kept silent throughout. "And why would he do either of these terrible things to you?"

"He'll get caught," Bill predicted. "He'll get punished."

"Let's hope," Geof said, flipping his notebook shut.

"No," Nellie murmured, and when I looked at her quizzically, she said, "You'll never find him. They don't get caught, these criminals. We'll never know why."

"Nellie," Geof chided her in gentle remonstrance. "Have a little faith."

But Nellie looked as if she had lost faith that long night in everything that she had ever believed in. And who was going to tell her to trust a universe in which such things could occur to such sweet and innocent people? And that Nellie and Bill Kennedy were the innocents in all of this I knew to the core of my soul. She was, clearly, wounded by these events, and Bill—though he had often annoyed me with his stupid jokes and clichés—was a sweet and gentle fellow, there could be no doubt. Of the two of them, even though her bruises were worse, I was very much afraid that Bill was the more dreadfully injured, with blows to his sense of security and self-esteem that might be permanent, for all that they were invisible.

When we left the house, we found Ardyth.

She was outside, where at first we thought all the light we were seeing outside was coming from the sun rising.

Nope. It was television cameras, filming the latest chapter in the heartrending drama of the mayoral candidate. She stood on the same stoop where earlier she had shut me out, this time with a courageous lift to her chin and her right hand held to her heart.

"My parents are inside at this moment," we heard her say, through the door, while we stood on the other side debating whether to open it or to slip out the back way. The uniformed officers were still putting objects into bags in the two devastated rooms. "I can only take this short instant—"

To Geof, I whispered, "There are other kinds of instants?"

"—to assure all of our dear friends and the concerned citizens of this wonderful town, whose heart has gone out so generously to my family in this hour of our greatest tragedies—"

Geof whispered, "What was the beginning of this sentence?"

"—that we will survive, as this city has survived through all the generations we have lived here, serving the mothers and fathers, the boys and girls, the grandparents—"

I whispered, "The first cousins twice removed."

"—who came to the legendary store that is no more. Uh."

Geof snickered. "I think she lost it, too."

"Uh. And not just survive, but continue to thrive—"

I snapped my fingers. "Oh, man, such jive!"

"—just as our city will do under my leadership, because it is through the fires of adversity that one emerges, stronger, braver, more sensitive to the needs of other people, and—"

Geof said, "Able to leap tall buildings in a single bound."

I grinned at him—and opened the door.

We were blinded by the light.

"Oh, what is this?" I exclaimed, flinging my hands to my face in my utter surprise. "Ardyth?"

"Goddammit!" came a shout from beyond the lights. "We'll have to do that last part again. Get those people out of there, Ardyth! Wait a minute . . . is that Lieutenant Bushfield? Geof? Hey, man, stand there! No, don't move, stay right where you are! Hey, Jenny! Is that you? Get that cute little rear over here, outta my lights! Miss Kennedy, move over, will you, so we can talk to the top cop on the scene? Hey, man, talk to the camera about what's going down inside. We're not live, it's only tape. What happened in there? And what's this about some guy's body they found in the rubble of the Dime Store? And how about First Things First, you think they had anything to do with any of this? I heard you're lookin' for Lew Riss about what happened out here on the highway yesterday. Jesus! Was it only yesterday? What day is this, anyway. Say, Miss Kennedy? Dear? Councilwoman, ma'am? How about we do you tomorrow, maybe at your office? Thanks, babe. I mean, sir. Ma'am. Thank you! Okay! Go, Lieutenant, talk to us!"

Like the mayoral candidate, Geof was also accomplished at moving his mouth without really saying anything. I did feel, however—observing him from my vantage point among the TV crew—that his completely phony act was much more sincere and charming than hers.

"We are pursuing our investigations," he summarized.

"No shit," said the voice off-camera, and everybody laughed.

"Well," Geof said, smiling, looking relaxed and handsome, "we are."

"And people call this news?" asked the voice, to more laughter.

If the dashing lieutenant had been running for mayor, my friend Mary wouldn't have had a chance after his calm and reassuring appearance. He practically oozed authority and confidence.

The man sure had my vote, anyway.

It was unseemly and insensitive, all of us standing out in the Kennedys' front yard, giggling like that, and if anybody there had liked or respected Ardyth in the least, nobody would have behaved like that. We all must have been giddy by then, from too much stimulation and sleep deprivation. I hardly even noticed when she went back into her parents' home, slamming the front door behind her.

In the Jeep, going home again, with the sun appearing in the rearview mirror, I said to Geof, "May I tell you something that you'll swear you'll never tell anyone I said? All these things that have happened to the Kennedys? One good thing is, they'll distract the media from our insurance problems with the festival."

"Why don't you want me to say you said that?"

"Because it's so self-serving, that's why."

"The heat of the fire takes the heat off you?"

I closed my eyes and leaned my head back against the seat. "Something like that. At least until the town council meeting two days from now."

"One day."

My eyes opened again. "What?"

"It's Sunday already, Jenny. They meet tomorrow night."

There was really only one thing to say to that: "Oh, shit, that's right!" My chest felt as if my heart had suddenly seized up, paralyzing the flow of blood to my brain. I couldn't even think for a moment, I was so frightened by the possibility that the insurance wouldn't come through. What would I do? What would I *do?*

"Geof," I whispered, "what will I do if—"

"It's going to be okay, Jenny."

What else could he say?

Neither of us knew.

It had been such an impossibly long night that when he asked me to drop him off at the police station, and then suggested that I go on home without him, I never expected him to stay in town and work all day.

But he did, devoted public servant that he was.

As for me, I took the phone off the hook and slept into the afternoon, after leaving a note that threatened David with dismemberment if he made any noise that disturbed me. When I looked in on him, I saw that he was still asleep on the couch, and our first note looked untouched. Evidently, he'd slept straight through our absence. I climbed back up the stairs to our bedroom, hauling myself up by the bannister and shedding my clothes as soon as I closed the door behind me.

As I got back into bed, I prayed that I, too, would sleep like a teenager—which, as everybody knows, is as close to the sleep of death as any living person can get without drugs.

17

I DREAMED OF STANDING UNDER A HUGE GATE.

Actually, it looked a lot like McDonald's golden arches, and I stood right under the midpoint of the M. That's all I remembered about it when I woke up, to find sunshine covering the bed as warmly as if it were an extra blanket.

What day was this?

I lay in deep comfort and figured it out: still Sunday.

I was barely awake—at two o'clock that afternoon—and just into my second cup of coffee, having a leisurely read in the Sunday paper about how some legislators in Washington wanted to lease more off-shore land for oil exploration, when the phone rang. It had probably been ringing all day, but I'd unplugged it in the bedroom.

As I was in the kitchen by then, barefoot and naked under my favorite robe, I reached for the receiver there.

"Ms. Cain? Jenny?"

"Um," I agreed, sleepily.

"Uh, this is Polly? You know, Polly Eppel? I'm the one you talk to all the time when you call us in Portsmouth?"

It was a young, female voice, sounding timid, nervous. Polly. Portsmouth. All the alliteration would have tickled me, if they hadn't been such p-p-p-problems. Suddenly, I was awake, or struggling to be. Polly! She was—what was she?—the office manager, supervisor, receptionist, what?

"I'm the secretary, you know?"

"Oh! Sure, Polly, how are you? Isn't it a gorgeous day? How are you?" Nonsensical. I was babbling. My heart was hammering. Was she trying to be the first to get to me to tell me the good news? I tried to settle myself down into something approach sanity. "Do we know anything new, Polly?"

"That's—that's why I called. They were going to wait until Monday to tell you." She sounded a little babbly, too. She was talking faster and faster, like an overwound talking toy, in her light, breathy voice. "They knew on Friday. At the end of the day, the word came down. But they didn't want to call you then, they're planning on . . . well, what they're doing is leaving you a message on your answering machine, for you to find when you go into your office in the morning—"

I wasn't aware of breathing any longer.

"And I didn't think that was right." She stuttered on the last word. "It's awful, is what it is, chicken, and just . . . cowardly. So I stewed about it all yesterday, and then I went to church this morning with my husband and our three kids, and our minister, he gave this sermon about moral steadfastness, that's what he called it, and I prayed—because I can't afford to have my bosses mad at me, and this is really none of my business, I suppose—and it seemed like God said—"

"Polly," I pleaded.

"He said I should go ahead and tell you that you're not going to get the insurance. That's the final decision from the home office. I'm so sorry. I'm really, really sorry. I know this is, like, disaster for you. What they said is, they'll still underwrite the festival, I mean, they'll indemnify you for the original amount you applied for, but not for the extra risk coverage. And I guess they came real close to canceling the whole policy, altogether."

"Amounts to the same thing," I said, so softly that she had to ask me to repeat myself. I cleared my throat. "I said, the original plan is useless to us now. Our town council will cancel our permits and remove their sanction of the festival if we don't get the exact coverage the fire department recommends."

If? It was no longer "if."

"That's what I was afraid of," Polly said sadly. "I really don't understand how this could happen, Ms. Cain. Jenny. You'd think any insurance company would jump at the chance to sell you all the coverage you wanted. Wouldn't you?"

"Unless the risk is too great, I suppose."

"But it's not, is it? I mean, maybe I'm just a secretary, and I don't understand these things, but don't they hold festivals and fairs like this all over the country? So why can't you get insurance?"

I had asked myself that so many times the question no longer made any sense to me.

"I don't know. Is there any recourse for appeal, Polly?"

"No. They're going to tell you that, too. I think they really don't want to hear from any of you ever again about this, it's like they want to wash their hands of the whole thing. I can't believe that they strung you along like this until practically the very last minute. I just feel awful for you, and I feel kind of embarrassed for my own company. Kind of ashamed of us, if you really want to know."

"Oh, Polly, it's not your fault—"

"Still. What can you do now?"

"Kill myself," I joked.

"Oh!" I heard her shocked intake of breath, so I hastened to tell her I didn't really mean it. I thanked her for her kindness. I told her she had done me a favor (although I wasn't sure what it was). And then I disengaged myself gently from her sympathetic, chattering, well-meaning clutches.

I was alone in the house.

David had been up and gone by the time I had wandered downstairs and looked in on a scene of rumpled, empty sheets and potato chip and corn chip bags and beer and pop cans. You'd have thought he'd had a party. But I had learned, over the months we'd known him, that one American teenage boy could easily consume in one day enough junk food and drink to keep an entire third-world nation alive for a month.

When Geof would come home was anybody's guess.

I had planned on driving in to the town common to pitch in again on the manual labor for the festival. That was pointless now. Instead, I just stood for a long time in the kitchen, not knowing what to do next. The tidal wave that I had glimpsed in the distance—and that I had hoped would turn out to be only a figment of the fears of my imagination—had finally reached me, and it was real. It was so deep, higher than I had even imagined, so much heavier than I could have guessed, and as it washed over me it felt like a million tons of lead crashing down upon my spirit.

The worst had happened.

I tried saying it out loud.

"Okay, the worst has happened."

I tried reminding myself that I was alive. That I still had my arms and legs. That it wasn't World War III. And still, the tidal wave kept crashing and crashing, until I simply sank from the burden of it and fell to my knees on the kitchen floor, stunned.

I'd already "done" anger.

Hell, I'd spent every other hour for the past couple of weeks feeling furious, and cussing and stomping around in helpless rage.

I'd done panic, too.

From the first moment that Mary told me her council was backing the fire chief's request, through every delay that came down from the insurance company, I'd felt the quiverings of panic.

Tears? Been there, done those.

I'd cried them in private moments of frustration and fury, like an actress rehearsing for the role of Medea. She'd killed her kids; now I had to kill my brainchild.

And ways of escape?

We'd investigated all of them, as far as we knew. My board and I . . . Geof and I . . . the mayor and her supporters and I . . . my volunteers . . . we'd all brainstormed ways around the problem. Try another insurance company? Too late. Attempt to change the fire chief's mind? Too impossible. Eliminate other fire hazards? There weren't any more. All good ideas. None of them—for many different reasons—worked.

We hadn't been able to get out of the path of the tidal wave.

Like Japanese villagers on an island with no ferry, we had sat tight and crossed our fingers.

Crash.

I had to tell people. Had to halt the construction. Must send the volunteers home. Pay our debts.

Cancel the festival.

I had to do those things.

"No. I have to think."

Sitting there on the kitchen floor, I was like the Little Engine That Could, only I was sliding back down the mountain, inwardly screaming, like metal wheels on the rails,"I can't. I can't. I can't."

I was still there on the kitchen floor—studying the crumbs between the refrigerator and the sink cabinet, where a broom would never fit—and still doing my imitation of a tree felled by a lumberjack, when a surprise visitor arrived.

"Hello?" a light voice called.

Maybe she'll go away, I thought.

"Knock, knock?" said the voice.

Still, I didn't budge or speak.

The back door was actually open, leaving only the screen to block me from whoever it was who was out there. I heard the screen door creak as the visitor opened it like somebody who knows you're home, but who feels shy about walking in.

"Hello? Jenny? Anybody?"

I turned my head and saw her the instant she spotted me. "Cleo?"

"Jenny! Did you fall down? Are you all right?"

It was our Post Haste delivery woman, whose last name I could never remember. What the hell was she doing here? I wondered. I felt confused, seeing her out of context. The tan uniform and sensible shoes were gone, replaced by a snug violet T-shirt under a loose and pretty sundress, over bare legs and beaded sandals. She'd pulled her flyaway hair back behind her ears with a skinny violet ribbon, and beaded, dangly earrings swung from her lobes. This was a new, completely feminine Cleo I would hardly have suspected was hiding beneath her work clothes and sturdy muscles. The colors she was wearing made her eyes look lavender-blue.

I thought about getting up.

"Come on in. I'm fine."

She didn't look convinced, but she let the door slam behind her anyway, and then she walked over to me. She bent down toward me, placing her strong tanned hands on her knees. "I didn't see a Jag in your driveway."

"What?" Then I laughed. "Oh. No, Pete didn't run me down this time. I have had the wind knocked out of me, though. They turned us down for the insurance, Cleo."

"No!" She squatted, her dress falling down around her to the floor. "I don't believe it!"

"So much for the pendulum's prediction, huh?"

"Well." She smiled sympathetically. There was something about her, some depth of emotional perception, that seemed older than her chronological age. "I only promised it would tell you what *you* wanted at an unconscious level. Anyway, the future isn't set in stone. We always have choice, things can always change."

"Oh." I sighed and gave some more thought to getting up, maybe even getting dressed. "That would be nice."

"What'd they say, Jenny?"

"They said no. I don't know the details or their reasons." I laughed a little. "I think I'd better pack up and leave town, Cleo, before they find a rail to ride me out on."

She bit her lower lip, then said, "Perspective."

"I beg your pardon?"

"What you need in this situation—what we all need in a crisis—is some perspective. Got a mountain we could climb this afternoon?"

"Nope, no mountains round here."

"That's okay." She grunted and let herself down to sit cross-legged on the floor with me. "I've got something that'll do just as well." She reached into the big brown suede purse she had carried in with her and pulled out of it a much smaller gray pouch that was tied with a satiny ribbon. She also brought out a small, thin gray book with gold lettering on it. Something clattered inside the pouch when she put it on the floor. I couldn't read the book's title upside down.

"How'd you find us out here, Cleo?"

"I spend my days searching for addresses, Jen. If there's anything I'm getting good at, it's finding somebody. I suppose you're thinking, what am I doing here, bothering you at home and on a Sunday? I realize it's not as if I'm one of your real friends, I'm just the girl who delivers the spiders." Her lavender-blue eyes had a mischievous laugh in them. "I don't really know anybody in town yet, except my customers. I just moved here last summer, you know—"

Her eyes were exceptionally expressive, I thought, and I could have sworn what they were expressing at that moment was loneliness.

"No, I didn't. From where, Cleo?"

"Vermont." She shrugged, causing one of the straps on her sundress to fall off her shoulder. With a casual hand, she pushed it back up again. "I guess I haven't had time to make friends. I've been so obsessed with my job. But after the fire last night . . . were you there?"

"Yes, I saw you."

"You did? Where?"

"In the street. You didn't see me, you were just walking around."

"Yeah, I do that a lot. But last night, I felt like such an outsider. Everybody seemed to know everybody else, and to care about each other. And nobody knew me."

"Or cared about you?"

She made a face, as if to disparage her own words. "Feeling sorry for myself, I guess. The funny thing is, I didn't even know I was lonely. Not until the fire."

I listened, keeping quiet.

"So, this morning I thought, nobody really needs you, Cleo, kid, 'cause they've already got their own established lives and friends. So don't be expecting any invitations to tea anytime soon. If you want to have friends, you're going to have to take the first step, kid."

She blushed, which made me smile.

"I'll bet you don't have time for a new friend," she ventured.

"Why, Cleo, we've been becoming friends for the last few months, didn't you know? In fact, you probably know more about my bad habits and peculiarities than many people who've known me all my life, just because you see me twice a day five days a week. Usually when I'm pissed, too." I offered her a lopsided grin. A chagrined grin, you might say. Building friendships took time? Well, I had lots of time now. "What've you got in the bag?"

"Runes."

She dumped it out. A bunch of whitish oval stones with strange markings on them clattered down.

"Scandinavian," she explained to me. "Another form of oracle, like the pendulum, only more talkative. Really ancient, often used by women. I use them to explain the past, reveal the underlying issues of the present, and connect it all to the future. It's more than just yes or no this time. You bring up an issue, a situation, a hope, a dream, a problem, a relationship, whatever, and you ask the runes to give you some wisdom about it, which you can choose to use—or not—to guide your actions. Like the pendulum, it puts you in touch with your higher self, the one that knows more than you think you do."

I looked at the stones with their mysterious brown marks and said, "Help."

"That's good enough," Cleo said, and she began to gather the runes and put them back into the gray pouch. "We can work with that."

"Just, help?"

"Um." She held the bag out to me. "I think we'll do a one-rune reading, since you're a beginner. Some other time, we could do a more elaborate spread, up to six runes at a time, for a more complete picture of your question. But for now . . . just pick one. Reach in, don't look, and let one of them stick to your fingers."

I didn't much like the chalky texture of them. But I let them slip through my fingers, like rough pebbles on a beach, and then it did feel as if there was one left that wanted to stick to my palm.

"I've got it," I told her.

"Bring it out, and lay it down, vertically."

I did. We both stared at it. It was blank.

"Turn it over," she instructed.

It showed an odd marking that looked like a straight line with a triangle sticking out from the right side of it.

"Gateway," said Cleo immediately, and then she began to page through the little gray book with the gold lettering.

"What did you say?"

She looked up. "The rune is called Gateway."

I stared at her. "Well, that's kind of funny. You'll love this. I had a dream just before I woke up, where I was standing under a gate, right in the middle of it."

"You're right, I love it."

"So what does it mean?"

"Pretty simple, really. It suggests you are at some sort of gateway, Jenny, but it's an important one, merely the gate between heaven and earth, that's all."

"Oh, is that all?"

"Um. It's a point in your life at which you can begin to join your earthly and spiritual natures. It might take the form of a spiritual crisis, I don't know exactly how this will happen. But it suggests you are standing at a place where you can't, and shouldn't try to, do anything. It's a lesson in nonaction. You're supposed to contemplate, meditate on everything in your life so far that has brought you to this fix, and then . . . let it all go."

"Let it go?" My heart sank beneath the kitchen floor.

"Yes. Then you will find your power. Which you must share! That's important, too. Reflect. Release. Accept your good fortune. Share it. Okay?"

Four easy steps to inner peace. Right.

"What good fortune?" I asked bitterly. "I can let it all go, all right, because I have no choice. But then there will be nothing to share anymore. Good-bye festival."

She cocked her head, so one of her earrings brushed her violet shoulder. The pendulum hid in its silver chain, inside the T-shirt. "No, not that way. You have to *really* let go. Emotionally. Without resentment."

"Oh, sure!"

"I'm telling you, nothing else works, Jenny. You've got to empty your heart, before it can fill up again."

I grabbed hold of the edge of the counter and began to hoist myself to my feet. "Bah, humbug," I grumbled.

Cleo never seemed to take offense at my skeptical reactions; once again, she just laughed and then said a cheerful "yes" to my offer of a cup of tea.

We talked about her job. My job. The festival and everything I'd have to do to shut it down. Her previous life in Vermont, although she seemed shy about talking too much about herself. And when she left, an hour later, I didn't really know much more about her, but I liked her even more than I had before.

At the door, she turned back and said, "That gateway you saw in your dream? What did it look like?"

I laughed. "Like McDonald's golden arches."

Her eyebrows lifted, and then she fumbled through her brown suede purse, looking for the gray rune book again. This time, she showed me a page with a picture of a rune that looked exactly like a capital M, rather like my dream.

"It's the rune that means Movement, Jen. It means that things are going to get better, and it specifically refers to business. It says that as you change yourself, inside, everything on the outside must change around you. And, Jenny . . . it says you're safe." Her eyes searched mine. "I think everything's going to turn out all right for you."

"I hope you're right, Cleo."

But as I waved good-bye to her, I thought, "Yeah, and maybe it means I'm going to drive into town for a quarter pounder with fries and a large Coke."

She drove away in a little blue Honda Civic.

At that moment, I did have an insight, but it wasn't into my own future. I thought maybe I knew why Nellie Kennedy had called me last night, instead of her closer friends. What my visit with Cleo had reminded me was that when things were closing in too tight, sometimes you didn't want around you the people who knew you best, because their powerful desire to *help* you could make you feel claustrophobic and, ironically, helpless. Sometimes it was easier to pick yourself up and dust yourself off in the presence of people who didn't know you so well.

I'd already picked myself up—off the floor—thanks to Cleo.

Now I moved into the house to "dust myself off," by showering, and by putting on real clothes. It was six o'clock when I finished putting on lipstick, and I felt ready to go . . .

. . . to bed again.

18

PERSPECTIVE, HUH?

I didn't know what to do with myself. Some awful restlessness inside of me was driving me, so I took that as a (Cleo) sign, and got in the Miata and drove.

Into town. Past the Dime Store—a smoldering hulk. Then past the common, where the volunteer builders were packing up for the night. It was a skeleton town of flimsy booths and phony facades and homemade signs.

Soon it would be a ghost town.

Then torn down.

I kept driving, and ended up parked back near the Dime Store. There was a line of sightseers in cars, though soon it would be too dark for them to see anything. Two fire trucks were still on hand, a few cops, the usual yellow crime scene ribbons, whether or not there'd actually been a crime.

I parked, not because of all the traffic, but because of a little band of people who weren't in their cars. They stood in their familiar ragged circle, carrying their familiar signs, moving slowly. Only, this time their signs had different messages:

God Bless God's Martyrs
Martyr to the Devil
Not Even the Fires of Hell Can Burn the Cross!

It wasn't just the sight of them that drew me. It was also the fact that standing right there with them was my husband.

Geof looked renewed, when I had expected to see exhaustion etched upon his face in lines as dark as those on Cleo's runes. As I walked slowly toward him, I saw him notice me, but he didn't signal any other recognition. I took that as my signal to proceed tactfully, as he was probably engaged right at that moment in police business. Rather than march up to him and say "Hi, Honey," I angled my approach away from him and the protesters, as if I were there to see the fire damage. In that way, I drew near, while seeming to move closer only to the yellow tape.

Out of the corner of my eyes, I saw that one of the protestors, a man I did not recognize, had stepped out of the moving circle to talk to Geof. I walked sideways again, imitating a crab, until I could hear them talking. Geof had his hands in his pockets, no notebook in sight, which told me these people were edgy, unwilling to talk to him if he came on too much like a cop.

The man was speaking, and Geof was looking bland.

"We are all willing to die for the Lord, Officer. Brother Anthony only did what any of us must be willing at any time to do."

Anthony. Was that the first or last name of the El Greco man?

"I was under the impression," Geof said, "that you folks wouldn't enter any place you felt was contaminated by Satan's work. Is that true?"

"Yes, it is."

"Then why did Mr. Phillips go into the Dime Store last night?"

His name: Anthony Phillips.

The answer was prompt, perhaps too prompt. "He went on a rescue mission. He dove into the flames of hell to try to save the sinners from the doom they had brought down upon themselves."

After a quiet moment, Geof's matter-of-fact questioning continued. "Are you saying the fire was already burning when Mr. Phillips went into the Dime Store?"

"Brother Anthony said he saw flames in the rear of the store, Officer. Or, maybe he said smoke."

"Where were you, and he, and the others at that time?"

"In front of the building next door." He pointed to the west, to one of the two other stores that had been destroyed.

"Then how did he see flames in the back?"

I sneaked a look. The man appeared embarrassed. "Officer, nature calls, even when one is doing the Lord's work."

"You mean he had to take a leak?"

I turned my face away, so I could smile unseen.

"Yes." The man sounded offended, as if the Lord had slipped up, somehow. "We are as sadly human as you are, Officer."

I grinned, unobserved, and wondered if Geof would be able to resist that opening.

"I'm pretty happily human," he said, and I had my answer. "So Mr. Phillips went down the alley between the stores to piss, and he—what? Came back and said he saw fire?"

"Or smoke. I can't remember. And he said he was going to check on it. And we never saw Brother Anthony after that."

"What did you think, when he didn't come back?"

"I, myself, didn't think much about it, not until the fire all of a sudden burst out in a big way. Then we moved across the street, and we kept thinking he would come back at any moment. When he didn't, we prayed for his safe return."

"Didn't any of you run down the alley to check on him?"

There was a—possibly shamed—silence. Then the man said, "We knew he was safe in the hands of the Lord. We do not interfere. We merely try to influence by our presence. We advertise, so to speak, the word of the Lord. But we do not take actions which might interfere with the Lord's will."

"Do you know anything else about this fire?" Geof inquired.

"No."

"About his death?"

"No, sir, I do not."

"We will want to talk to each of you who were present last night. Will you agree to be interviewed down at the station?"

"Do we have any choice, Officer?"

"Do you believe in free will?"

"No, we believe in predestination."

"Well," Geof drawled, "then I guess you don't have a choice, do you?"

I listened as he told the man that another officer would be setting up appointments for them. "Thank you for your time. I'm sorry about the death of your friend."

"There's nothing to be sorry about," the man said crisply. "He is alive in the Lord forever, and we celebrate his freedom and his everlasting joy today."

"Ah," Geof said.

I glanced over and saw the man slip back into the circle. He had anything but a joyful expression on his face; his mouth was set in a grim, straight line. As one of the women in the circle approached the point closest to me, I saw tears flowing steadily from her wide open eyes. She looked young enough to be Anthony Phillip's daughter, and her handsome face had a bit of that long, soulful, Spanish look to it. Whatever their faith said they were supposed to be feeling, what she was apparently really feeling was profound grief.

I angled back to my car, from where I watched Geof speak to a uniformed officer, who then walked toward the moving circle of fundamentalists.

Geof looked over at me.

Then he got in his Jeep, did U-turn in the traffic, and slowed down as he pulled alongside me and then in front of me. I took the hint—I was getting good at reading signs—and pulled out behind him. I followed him to his destination, which turned out to be: home.

"Have you eaten dinner?" he asked me.

"No, but I'm not hungry. What about you?"

"The same."

"You must be ready to drop."

"I am. Did you get some sleep?"

"I did. I got a call—sort of a saboteur one—from the secretary of the insurer's office, Geof. They're turning us down."

The look on his face said it all: shock, dismay, sympathy, anger, helplessness.

"You don't have to say anything," I said.

So he said the right thing: "How are you?"

"Paralyzed."

"Have you told—"

"Only you." And Cleo.

He did the right thing then, too. Didn't condemn me for failing to notify everybody, didn't offer suggestions, didn't press. Just stared at me, with his eyes saying exactly what I was thinking: *One disaster too many. Don't anybody ask me to cope, not anymore today.*

I said, "Are you going to bed now?"

It was not quite eight o'clock.

"I'd like to, but I need to unwind before I can sleep. Where's Dave?"

I shrugged.

"On his bike? How can he drive, with that shoulder?"

Another shrug from me.

"Would you come upstairs with me, Jenny? I think I need to talk. You want to hear what's been going on?"

No shrug this time, although I felt like it. Instead, I smiled at him and just said, "Sure."

* * *

"Anthony Frederick Phillips."

We were lying on top of our bedspread, both of us trying to work up the energy to get undressed and get officially ready for bed.

"The victim," I said.

"Fifty-six years old, widowed, a daughter, two sons, conscientious objector during the Vietnam War, moved around a lot, became a lay preacher the year his wife died—of cancer—and seems to have supported himself, barely, on the contributions of the various small congregations where he preached. Tended to gravitate toward causes and movements. Antiabortion. Pro-death penalty. Anti-sex education in the schools. Pro-prayer in the schools. The Halloween thing was the latest."

"Who told you all this?"

"One of our guys, actually. You never know who'll turn out to be a Bible thumper." Geof named a sergeant, a spic-and-span officer with a stern, reserved personality and a paradoxically sweet smile. "They were fairly good friends, and our guy's pretty upset about it. Says Phillips was a real moral guy, a straight shooter."

"That's how he struck me, too."

He turned his head. "You met him?"

"I told you that! Last night. Remember? How else would I have identified him from that cross?" Clearly, Geof felt the effects of exhaustion, too. "I met him in front of the Dime Store last Thursday. He gave me a lecture about the evils of Halloween, and he seemed quite concerned for my immortal soul. He also gave me this." I pulled back the arm of my cotton shirt to display the long, thin, scabbed scratch. "Accidentally, I think. The end of his signpost brushed against me. I don't think he even realized it happened."

"I thought you got that when Pete ran you down."

"No, it's definitely the mark of—"

"Cain," he said, and his grin reappeared for the first time that day. We talked a while longer about my encounter with Phillips and my impressions of the man.

"Fearless," I assessed him, finally.

"You think he was the type who'd run into a fire?"

"In a minute."

"The type to set one?"

"That, I can't tell you."

I rolled over and pressed against him for warmth and comfort. "Was it arson?"

"Apparently. It was set with candles."

"Is that a method that professional arsonists use?"

"I wouldn't think so."

"Could it have been an accident then? A Halloween prank?"

"Well, it was purposeful, wouldn't you say? You don't light candles by accident."

"But, I mean, candles can catch fire by accident. Do Nellie and Bill know?"

"Yeah, and I'd swear they were both shocked by the news. Nellie says they always had boxes of candles back there, because they sold them by the gross practically."

"Are they suspects, Geof?"

The question saddened me.

"Owners are always suspects, Jenny, until proven otherwise."

"But the beatings, the break-in!"

"Neighbors were unhelpful. They were all either asleep or down at the fire, themselves. It's a hard kind of thing to investigate. Planned—look at the gloves they all wore—but senseless, on the face of it. They took nothing, said practically nothing, they came out of nowhere and disappeared back into it. Who the hell are they?"

"First Things First?"

"But why? We still haven't located Lew Riss and his gang. Got any ideas?"

"Well, no. Why can't you find him?"

"You sound annoyed."

I laughed. "Do I? I always sound annoyed when I talk to or about Lew Riss."

"We can't find him, because there's too much fucking else going on in this town, and we're fucking running out of cops who are still awake on their feet."

"Sorry I asked."

"You want to take a shower?"

"First, before you do, you mean?"

"No, I mean together, with me."

"You devil, you."

"Maybe that's why I still smell like smoke."

We were still awake when it was time for the last local newscast of the day, so we watched it from bed.

There was Marilyn Stuben. Did the woman never sleep?

"Police report no real progress yet in their investigation of the highway blockade on Friday evening . . .

". . . of the destruction by fire of three downtown businesses.

". . . in the death of Anthony Frederick Phillips, a local man, in that fire.

". . . or in the assault early this morning of the owners of the Dime Store, where the fatal fire originated."

By the time Marilyn had finished her discouraging litany, Geof had sunk far down into the covers.

But I had already beat him there, because the lead story that night was about, "the rumors now confirmed by impeccable sources that the Judy Foundation, organizers of the Autumn Festival that was scheduled to draw up to fifteen thousand people to Port Frederick next weekend, have been turned down in their request for additional insurance. Does this mean the biggest event in Port Frederick history will have to be canceled? Tune in tomorrow for our full report."

After the news, I popped out of bed long enough to call Susan Bergalis, the MATV producer, at home.

"Who's your impeccable source, Susan?"

"I can't tell you that, Jenny! Is it true? Did you get turned down? We called you, but you weren't there."

"Tit for tat, Susan."

She chuckled. "Ardyth Kennedy. But you didn't hear it here."

"Yes, it's true, but you can't say you heard it from me until I call you officially in the morning."

I had to protect my source, too.

"Will you really call me?"

"Of course."

"Shit, Jenny, is it over?"

"There's still the council meeting tomorrow night."

"They'll never go against the fire guys, not after the fire last night."

"I'll threaten to shoot myself."

"Jenny. You won't have to threaten, 'cause they're going to request you to do it."

Damn, I thought.

"Good night, Susan."

"You who are about to be crucified, I salute you," she said, and hung up.

Geof was watching me.

I told him what she'd said.

"Nice to know who your friends are," he observed wryly.

"Even better to know who my enemies are." I lay back down. "And I wonder . . . Geof? How did Ardyth know?"

* * *

Maybe because I'd slept that day, maybe . . . who knows why . . . I woke up around three o'clock with an attack of the three-o'clock deep, black, heart-palpitating, cold-sweating, think-I'm-gonna-die terrors. Anxiety—no, hell, call it what it was—fear, lay like a monster on me. Cop in the bed beside me or no, I woke up feeling as if my worst nightmares were crawling into bed with me.

To escape them, I fled.

The bed. The room. The house.

I dressed. And, driven by my demons of public failure and humiliation and . . . failure, I drove. Faster than I should have. Harder. Faster. Streaking toward I didn't know what.

"What" turned out to be the common.

I parked, got out.

There it was, the nearly finished construction of my ambitious dream. "You know what your problem is, Jenny? You think too big."

Too big. Too big.

The bigger they are, the harder they . . .

The road to hell is paved with . . .

Too big for my . . .

Fall. Good intentions. Breeches.

Something was burning.

A light, flickering in the middle of the common. A flash. A small glow.

I started running.

It was at the "Hyde Park Corner," the ACLU's platform for free speech. Something on the platform was burning.

I ran over the fall grass, the uneven ground, the leaves I couldn't see under my feet in the dark.

Flames, higher.

Brighter.

I pulled up a few yards from the platform, staring.

What was it?

Something attached to the tall post in the middle, something with shape, fabric, not a person.

Closer, close enough to see flames lick black fabric. A dress? No, a robe. A mask with a grotesque pointed, warty nose. Pointed black hat. A witch. A costume, Halloween costume, nailed to the post.

A witch.

They were burning a witch at the stake on the common.

In the distance, sirens.

I walked back the distance to my car and sat there, feeling the burns on my own skin, fingering the ends of my hair as if they were singed.

I knew who they were burning in effigy. Which witch. Feeling burned to my soul, I turned the key on my little white convertible broomstick and flew away.

I found a stretch of beach, rocky night ocean beach, and a huddle of boulders where the sand wasn't wet in among them, and I hunkered down against the night.

Sometime between then and sunrise, I surrendered. It wasn't a giving up, it was a letting go. And then I slept. And when the dawn woke me gently, I faced it with a strange peace in my heart, and I said, "All right. I accept everything. This is the way it is. I surrender. You may have me."

I stayed and watched her rise, my big, red, shining sister. There were shells to turn over, too, to exclaim over, and then to abandon to their destinies upon the shore. I took only a small souvenir, a spiral shell, ivory, a bit broken with a hole on one side in its middle, and I put it carefully in my pocket.

The ocean was very cold when I waded in it, so I didn't do that for very long.

Like the shore after the tide pulled out, I was emptied, washed clean and full of the knowledge that the waves would return. Again and again. Bringing detritus to decorate the expanse of my life, and most of that—no matter how ugly or beautiful, how benign or dangerous—would wash away, leaving me alone and scraped clean again.

19

I GOT HOME BEFORE GEOF WOKE UP. IN TIME TO MAKE COFFEE, TO PUT BACON IN the pan. David had returned while I was gone. The aroma of the bacon pulled him in from the living room, grousing about the early hour. It dragged Geof down from the bedroom, happily hungry for what he was smelling. I put in eggs and toast. I decided that when it's too difficult to "seize the day," one could always serve it, instead. So that's what I would do. I would not ask this day to save me or my festival. I would serve this day, and everybody in it.

"Sit down, Jenny," David said, "I'll bring your plate to you."

"Thank you," I said, with a heart full of surprise.

"When are you going to tell your board?" Geof asked me.

"Board?" I stared at him. "Board? *Board?* Oh, my God! Oh, Geof!" I leaped at him, kissed him gratefully. "Thank you!"

"What did I say?" he asked David.

It was a gift from the gods, on a day when I wasn't going to ask for anything. But what to do with this gift? At only seven o'clock, it was too early by at least an hour to call Polly from Portsmouth to check out my brainstorm of an idea. Suddenly, my nerves were ajangle again, only this time with excitement. I tried to remain calm, tried not to hope. Told myself it was only an idea, merely a last desperate wisp of a theory. But my heart lifted anyway, no matter that I warned myself against it.

"What did I say, Jenny?"

Geof wanted to know why I was jumping about the room like a crazy woman. Immediately, I settled back down in my chair at the table with them. I clutched the edge, breathed deeply—and smiled with such an enormous grin at him that it was a wonder he didn't throw up an arm to shield his eyes.

"I can't tell you," I said, meaning that I didn't want to say it in front of David. "I'm afraid I might jinx it. In an hour—" I looked up at the clock above the sink. "—maybe a little later than that, I'll know something. Then I can tell you."

"Is it about your festival?"

"I can't tell you."

David said, "Is it about me?"

I laughed and shook my head.

"I'm sorry, guys, but I'm too scared to tell anybody. Yet. We have to change the subject. Geof?"

"What?" He frowned at me. "Why won't you tell me?"

"She's got a lover," David said.

"Right." I smiled at both of them. "But I won't know for sure if he's leaving his wife until I call him at his office at eight o'clock, because he told me never to call him at home."

"Board," Geof muttered, staring across at David. "I said board, isn't that what I said? Did I say anything else?"

"I went out last night," I told them, a little desperately. But even then, they wouldn't let me finish.

"I did, too," David said. He looked awful—dirty hair and face, dusty jeans and T-shirt—as if he'd been for a ride on his motorcycle and hadn't cleaned up before sacking out on our couch again. I knew that underneath our table, his big feet were bare, but I chose not to look at them to determine their state of hygiene. "You want to know where?"

"Yes!" I clung to any change of topic.

Geof said, "How'd you manage, with that shoulder?"

David didn't shrug, as he normally might have, probably because shrugging would have hurt too much. Now *there* was an unexpected benefit to derive from his mishap, I thought: We'd get a shrugless teenager around for a while. He bragged, "I can hold 'er up with one hand. You want to know, or not?"

"Yeah, where?" Geof obliged.

"I went looking for the fuckers that did this to me."

He got Geof's full attention with that statement, all right, and the cop's attention deepened right along with the story.

"How'd you know," I asked him, "who to look for?"

"Your friend," he answered, accusingly. "That Lew Riss jerk, those First Things First assholes."

My initial reaction was to think, astounded: He *listens* to us. But that was followed quickly by, *Oh, God, what kind of trouble have I got him into now?*

"David, we don't know—" I started to say.

"Any luck?" Geof asked him.

The kid nodded, looking superior. "Leave it to me to do what the cops can't manage." (Geof forebore comment.) "Found 'em down by the riverside. But not until nearly daybreak. They've got a camp down by Crowley Creek."

"Out by the trail crossing?" I asked. "Where you got hurt?"

"No, maybe five miles on downstream. There's no real campground. They just parked and put up a couple of tents."

"How do you know it was them?" I asked.

He gave me a look. "That was real difficult to figure out, Jenny. But my first clue was the letters FTF on the side of their van."

"What'd you do?" Geof asked him, looking worried.

"I did nothing. Are you kidding? There was all of them and only one of me, and I'm not what you could call in fighting form, thanks to those bastards."

"We don't know that," I repeated.

"Will you cut that out, Jenny?" He was angry. "We *know* that. Who the hell else could it have been?"

"Tell me everything you saw," the cop commanded.

David mock-saluted, but then he complied. "Not much. It was night, may I remind you? Nobody was moving, except for one guy who got out of the tent and walked into the trees. Scared the shit out of me, because he came straight at me. I thought he knew I was there, and then when he unzipped his fly, he was so close I was afraid he would whiz on my toes."

"You saw just the one person?"

"Yeah. Big guy. Not tall, but a muscleman."

I looked over at Geof and said, "Lew."

"Okay, what else?" Geof asked. "One van, two tents—"

"Yeah, those rounded kinds, like igloos."

"Was there a campfire?" I asked him.

"No." He laughed. "There was a barbeque grill. You're behind the times. Campfire! Who do you think these people are, boy scouts?"

"You didn't see any women?" Geof asked.

"I *told* you, only the guy."

"How'd you find them, Dave?"

The kid looked a little befuddled at that question. "I don't know how I did it, exactly. I was just riding, you know?"

We nodded.

"And I got to thinking, how I got hurt near the creek. And how the creek's lined with trees, all woody, and how that might be good for hiding in, and how maybe whoever did it, they must have come out of the woods, so they probably went back to the woods afterwards. So I cut off the highway and rode the trail—"

My eyes widened. "God's Highway?"

Geof bowed his head and laughed out loud.

I said, "David, you rode God's Highway—through all those residential sections, practically in people's backyards, on federal property—on your motorcycle?"

"Jesus, Cain," he said, "you think I was gonna *hike* it?"

I imagined the roar of the engine breaking the night silence, and I shook my head and grinned.

"Am I an investigator, or what? Think you'd better hire me, Geof?"

"But David," I said, "didn't the FTF people hear you?"

"They may have," he conceded. "Because I was just beboppin' along in first gear, when I saw them through the trees. Really startled me. Hell! But man, I was thinking fast, and so I just kept on riding. I'll bet I rode another three miles before I thought it was safe to cut my engine. Then I left the bike, and I tiptoed back."

I smiled at the image. But three miles? I doubted it.

"Good work, Dave," Geof said.

"Thanks. When will you arrest them? Man, I want to be there."

Geof was getting to his feet. "I'm on my way. Whether there will be any arrest, I don't know. And I do want you to come along, so you can tell me where I'm going." He looked over at me. "But if we leave now, when will we find out what's got Jenny so excited?"

While we talked about David's adventure, I'd been keeping tabs on the passage of time: Still twenty minutes to go, before I could make the necessary call to Polly in the Portsmouth insurance broker's office. "Looks like you'll have to wait," I told him.

I walked them to the door.

"David?" I said. "Shoes?"

"Oh." He looked down. "Yeah, I guess so."

While he was racing back into the house for his socks and sneakers, I took Geof's left arm and strolled outside with him. "Geof, when you said the word *board,* that made me think of my board of directors, and that made me think of my old board." At the Port Frederick Civic Foundation, I meant. "Which made me think of Pete Falwell, which made me think of how he loves to look important by sitting on lots of boards. I think Pete must be a director of half the corporations in Massachusetts. And that made me think of the boards of directors of insurance companies."

Geof stopped abruptly on our path, and I saw a dawning understanding and a hope in his eyes that mirrored my own feelings exactly.

"You think?" he asked me.

"I don't know. But, Geof, that day Pete nearly killed me? I made some crack about insurance, and then I was afraid he'd nail me with a sarcastic comment, but he didn't say a single word about it. I thought it was odd at the time. Pete *always* takes every chance to dig me. Why didn't he do it then? And now I also wonder, why was his grandson out of school that morning? He and his grandfather were going somewhere together."

"Boston?"

"Maybe. I'm so afraid to think . . . maybe. But, Geof, it's really, really possible—"

"That Pete is on the board of directors of the insurance company that turned you down."

"And that if that's true, it is also really, really probable that he has secretly, personally sabotaged us."

"You and the whole town, if it's true. Would he do that?"

"Pete? Are you kidding?"

"Just to make you look bad, Jenny?"

Put that way, my theory did sound a shade solipsistic. Fear began once again to seep into all of the clean and empty spaces where calmness had resided for a short while in my soul.

"Somebody burned a witch on the common last night." I told him about it. "She had on a blonde wing. Guess who?"

He folded me into a comforting embrace. "My witchy woman."

David burst out of the kitchen, letting the screen door bang shut behind him. "Cut that out. We've got felons to apprehend."

By the time the Jeep had disappeared down our driveway, the clock showed dead-on eight o'clock. I decided to give Polly five more minutes to put down her purse, pour herself a cup of coffee, and get settled at her desk.

Then, I'd call.

I spent five of the tensest minutes of my life putting breakfast stuff away. But then I thought I'd better stop and compose myself for any eventuality. Yes, no. Pete was, he wasn't. He did, he didn't. The spider of fate was weaving a tight and intricate web around that man and me. Which of us would she trap? Which would she mercilessly devour?

Our October day was sunny, crisp, another harbinger of perfect festival weather, if only . . .

I didn't know what the weather was in Portsmouth that morning.

I didn't care.

At five minutes past eight, I placed the call.

"Good Morning. Evan Quilt Insurance Agency, representing business and homeowners statewide. This is Polly speaking, may I help you?"

"Hi, Polly, it's Jenny Cain. Don't say anything, Polly. I don't want to get you in trouble. Just answer me one question: Do you recognize the name Peter Falwell?"

"No."

Even that simple word sounded breathless, scared.

"Would you know—or be able to find out—if he is on the board of directors of the company that turned us down?"

"One moment, please."

Her nervous singsong segued into telephone music. When I heard the selection, I had to laugh: "Wouldn't It Be Loverly," from *My Fair Lady.*

Oh, yes, it would be so loverly.

"Ma'am?"

"Yes, Polly?"

"The answer to your query is most certainly yes. Would you like to speak to one of our agents?"

"You're sure, positive, absolutely certain?"

"Yes, Ma'am!"

"Oh, Polly, you have saved my life."

"Really?" There was a happy little squeak to her voice. "I'm so happy I was able to assist you. Is there anything else we may help you with today?"

"Yes, may you live long and prosper, and all your children's children after you. 'Bye, Polly. Come to our festival!"

"You're kidding?"

"I don't think so."

"Hooray! Ma'am."

She hung up, before she could betray herself.

I hung up and danced.

I danced, danced, danced around the kitchen, looping out into the dining room, and then dancing up the stairs and into my closet, where I put on an electric blue silk suit, which was the very color of the heart of fire.

"Have you ever heard the old Bill Cosby routine about the football team in the locker room?"

Three hours later, I was at my office, leaving a message in Geof's voice mailbox at the cop shop.

I continued: "It's the one where it's the big game day, and they're all suited up in the locker room, and the coach is exhorting them to get out there and kill the other guys, and he gets them all worked up, and they're so ravenous for the kill they're practically drooling, and the coach finally releases them, and they rush the door like madmen, and—it's locked. I laughed hysterically when Bill Cosby told that. Now I know how the coach felt.

"Geof, the answer to this morning's questions is yes! Yes! But can I find the man to confront him with this information? The answer is no." I closed my message with: "How'd it go with you and David?"

Pete Falwell wasn't at the office, his secretary said, every time I called, never giving my name. He wasn't at the office of the Port Frederick Civic Foundation. Or at Ardyth Kennedy's campaign headquarters. Or at home, where they gave me his car phone number when I told them I was a reporter calling. Nor did he answer that traveling telephone.

"Maybe he's dead," I thought, but that idea, which ordinarily might have delighted me, failed to satisfy. "Don't you dare die, Falwell, not before I get to you."

I didn't want to kill him.

I didn't want to flog him in public, gratifying though that might have felt.

I only wanted to make him sell his soul to the devil, the small corner of it that remained from all that he'd already traded away, that is, and the devil I wanted him to sell it to was the one with the blue dress on.

We had a history, Peter Falwell and I. There was a time when he and my dad ran in the same golf-playing circle of Port Frederick tycoons. They had a lot in common: Both of them were Port Frederick natives, both of them were the heads of family-owned seafood canning businesses that went back generations. For Jimmy Cain, it was Cain Clams, which was once the largest employer in the area. For Pete, it was the "friendly" competition, Port Frederick Fisheries. Of the two men, Pete was the better businessman, by far.

He was smart and ruthless.

In an earlier chapter in my family's life, he had connived, through the use of industrial sabotage, to lure my dad into commencing a building spree that doomed our company. Then, when Cain Clams was bankrupt and under court-appointed management, Pete stepped in to purchase it at rock-bottom prices.

I'd proved it happened that way.

I knew how he did it, even who he did it with, and I could have helped a team of attorneys make a case out of it.

But the rest of my family turned their faces away from that prospect.

My dad? He didn't even believe me; he wouldn't hear my evidence against his old "friend." My mother was dead, having been emotionally eviscerated by that and other disasters. My sister said she'd already had enough infamy to last her a lifetime, and she refused to let her life be turned into a public courtroom drama. They didn't need the money; our company failure didn't pinch the family's personal assets.

I was the only one who wanted to go after Pete, but I was a pit bull straining against my family's short leash.

He knew—Pete did—that I knew.

And he knew that in spite of my knowledge, he'd gotten clean away with it.

Maybe my family was right to just move silently past it.

The statute of limitations made it all moot by now, anyway.

But the statute hadn't run out on my loathing for the man. Oh, yes, we had a history. He had won every single battle up to this point, but this time I had a fighting chance to alter the course of that juggernaut.

20

It was hard, at work, to answer the one question everybody asked: "Jenny, is it true?" There wasn't, in fact, much time for any other activity than answering the phone, and every caller wanted to know the same thing.

"Jenny, should I even bother coming over to work on the festival today?"

"Oh, yes, absolutely, please come."

"But is it true, about the insurance?"

"We are having a festival."

"It's not over?"

"Not on your life."

"You mean we did get the insurance?"

"Could we hold a festival without it?"

"Oh! But where'd the TV station ever get the idea that—"

"They were probably misinformed."

That's what I told the television producer, Susan Bergalis, when she called, and said, "But Jenny, I talked to a vice president of the insurance company, and she said you didn't get it."

"I haven't heard any such thing from them, Susan."

That was true, but only because I had not listened to the messages on our office answering machine.

"But Jenny, our source said that you definitely didn't—"

"Ardyth? Come to the town council meeting tonight, Susan. Bring a crew. You'll get your 'definitely' then."

"You swear?"

"On the lives of my children."

She must have forgotten I'm childless, because she hung up sounding satisfied with my promise. It was an incredible strain, trying to be truthful without being candid, and I was obviously beginning to fail at it. It was proving so difficult, in fact, that I finally just gave up and fled from Judy's House.

Right into the arms of the law.

"I want you to come with me, Jenny. Can they spare you from the festival for a little while?"

Geof was just getting out of his Jeep when I left Judy's House by the back door.

"Perfect," I replied, without saying why. "What happened with you guys this morning? Where's the poltergeist?" Suddenly that didn't sound right anymore. "David."

"They were already gone when we got there. I dropped Dave off at his bike, and he was going on from there to his job. He's going to have a time of it, pumping gas and washing windows with that bum shoulder."

"He didn't complain this morning."

"He doesn't, you know?"

"Doesn't complain?" I asked incredulously.

"Not about real stuff, haven't you noticed that, Jenny? He makes an initial fuss, then he bears up under it, whatever it is."

I smiled a little. "You're not suggesting he has character?"

He smiled, too. "You will agree that he *is* a character."

"I will stipulate to that. Did you get my message? I still haven't located Pete. It's very difficult to beard a lion when you can't catch him in any of his dens." I cocked my head. "What do you want with me, my dearest?"

He waggled his eyebrows.

I laughed. "Besides that?"

"We'll take my car," was his only answer. "Hop in."

Ten minutes later we were parked in front of a crab shack, which was literally a shack of a tiny take-out restaurant that sold simple seafood fare to go. Fried clam baskets. Boiled whole lobsters. Crab salad. Potato chips, slaw, soda pop, and coffee. The entire menu fit on a board above the window, and all the cooking was done on the premises. These little shacks had some of the best food around, and the owners could make a small subsidiary living out of them—hardly ever enough to support a family, but enough to buy VCRs and second cars, and maybe even college educations, over time.

"Is it lunchtime already?" I asked, in amazement. "And if it isn't, who cares? Let's go. This is a great idea, Lieutenant, honey."

But he held me back, literally, by placing one large hand on my arm. "Sorry, we're not eating, just looking."

"What?"

"Take a good look at the cook, Jen."

I peered out the open window of the Jeep and squinted through the sunlight at the dark figure moving inside the shack. A man, it appeared. Big—tall and beefy. Wearing a white baseball cap turned backward and a white uniform.

"Who is he?" I asked. "I can't see his face."

"Wait until you can."

That didn't take long, not with a carload of dock workers pulling up and getting out. But those guys were all so burly, themselves, that it was still hard to get a decent glimpse of the cook's face, behind them.

Then the customers shifted. At the same moment, the cook stuck his head out of the window of the shack and yelled to a man who had just walked off, "Hey! You want chips with that?"

I got an excellent view of him and quickly pulled myself back into the car. "It's him!" I said, feeling completely and unpleasantly taken by surprise by my husband. "The Holy Ghost. That guy, Tyler, who threw me to the ground! Geof, what are you doing? How did you find him? You know I said I don't want anything to do with him!"

"He was easy to find," Geof said calmly. "How many big guys named Tyler would have been working at the common last Saturday? I figured he'd be memorable, considering what he did there. People might know him, or at least who he is. Turns out Tyler is his last name. Meryl Tyler. Only had to ask three people. The third one said, 'Oh, you mean that stupid son of a bitch, Meryl Tyler.' "

I started to speak, but he held up his hand.

"What if I were to tell you that Meryl Tyler has hammer and nails and an empty can of gasoline in the bed of that pickup truck back of the shack?"

I stared at him.

"Our boy Meryl is into burning witches, Jenny, especially pretty blonde ones who stand up to him."

I blinked and stared back at the shack, suddenly feeling considerably different about the man inside of it.

"Jenny?"

I turned back, to find an extremely sober police lieutenant staring at me. "Where would a man get a witch costume, do you suppose?"

I brought my hand to my mouth and whispered through my fingers, "Oh, my God, the Dime Store."

"Our boy Meryl was in the store Saturday night before it burned. A sales clerk remembers a man of Meryl's description buying a wig and a witch's costume. She remembers him because he was rude to her." Geof glanced over my shoulder and smiled coldly. "Our boy Meryl is not very bright."

"Geof? Why did you think of him?"

He reached over to stroke my hair—the very tresses that had gone up in figurative smoke. "You were clearly the witch being burned. The list of people who hate you is very short, maybe even nonexistent, but I knew you did have one very recent, very public enemy."

"Thank goodness you made me tell you his name."

I sighed, as we pulled away from the curb. "I guess this means fried clams are out?"

That afternoon, the Port Frederick police arrested Meryl Tyler on suspicion of torching the Dime Store, and on the considerably lesser charge (to them) of burning "me." He confessed to the lesser charge—they had him on everything from an eye witness I.D. by the clerk from whom he bought the costume, to bits of black lint and yellow wig hair in his truck. But he wouldn't cop to the far more serious charges of arson and homicide. On the other hand, nobody expected him to, because such situations are what defense lawyers are for.

As for Lew Riss and his merry band of ecoterrorists?

Definitely flown from their campsite and nowhere to be found. As Geof said so accurately of his morning: win some, lose some.

Afternoon found me still avoiding the office, while continuing my search (and destroy) mission for Peter Falwell.

I spotted Cleo in her truck and waved her down, stopping her on her route long enough to enlist her assistance.

"You said you're good at finding people, Cleo?"

Her affirmative answer and her smile were reminders of the odd but pleasant hour we'd spent the day before on my kitchen floor.

"Well," I said, "remember the man who hit me, and his car, the Jag?"

"I could forget?"

"I really need to find him."

"But then how will I find you?"

"I don't know," I admitted. "You've got me stumped there, Cleo."

She laughed down at me from where she sat perched behind a steering wheel that looked a size too large for her. "Leave it to me, Jen."

"Oh, and Cleo? Don't say anything to anybody about the festival insurance, okay? Things have changed since last we met."

"Told you," she said. "Didn't the pendulum say you'd get it, and the runes say you'd be safe?"

"Well, I won't count my tourists until the gate opens on Saturday morning." I waved her off. "Thank you!"

Sometimes it seems as if when fate finally opens the door, it lets in a big wind that blows everything your way for a while. Cleo did find Pete, and she did find me, and the amazing thing was that both events happened at the same time.

I was chowing down on a bowl of lobster bisque at the diner about half an hour after seeing her, when I heard a heavy honking outside. Looking up, I saw her Post Haste truck right on the tail of a Jaguar convertible. Cleo was honking like mad to get my attention.

"How'd she know I was here . . . ?" I said aloud.

The Miata. She'd seen it parked in front.

I dropped my spoon, threw money onto the table, and raced for my car. Soon I was following a silver-haired city father at the sedate pace at which he liked to cruise the town he thought of as his own. Cleo had already turned off, with a jaunty, triumphant thumbs-up for me.

I saw Pete notice me in his mirrors.

I also saw the little smile he gave himself, which goaded me into pulling my car out and around until I paralleled him in traffic. Both of us had the tops of our cars down. "Pete! Pull over! I want to talk to you!"

With a self-satisfied smirk that he didn't even try to hide, Pete did as I asked, turning into the first available parking lot, which turned out to belong to a grocery store. Why shouldn't he smile, I thought, as I parked and got out of my car to walk over to him; as far as he knew, he had nothing to fear from me.

He surprised me by getting out.

Then I realized that enabled him to look down on me, no doubt putting him more at his ease. We stood there beside his car, facing one another.

"What do you want, Jennifer?"

Nothing about insurance, I noticed, no gibe about the news and the rumors.

"Don't you want to make some joke at my expense about the insurance, Pete?"

Something like humor glinted in his eyes, but he put on a sober mien for me. "It isn't an amusing situation, Jennifer. When you build the hopes of an entire city, only to tear them down after so much work, and so much expense, you cannot expect people to laugh it off."

"I'd think you'd be glad, Pete. You never approved of my festival. You know that if it doesn't come off, Ardyth's chances to be elected will rise astronomically."

"I would never think of myself and my own interests at a time like this, Jennifer."

"Pete? When you talk to me, why do you end nearly every sentence with my full name?"

He looked startled, then disgusted.

I was having way too much fun, I warned myself.

"If this is why you stopped me—"

"I don't want to stop you. I want to get you started."

"I beg your pardon?"

"Yes. I want to get you started moving to your car phone to call our insurance company in Boston."

"I? I can't save you, Jennifer."

"Really? You're helpless? A member of their board of directors?"

He opened his mouth, then shut it. Fury glared out of his eyes, until he lowered his lids so that I could barely read any expression. He was caught. And he knew it. And he didn't know what I was going to do about it. Would I spread it all over the news that one of our very own most powerful city fathers, one of Ardyth Kennedy's most influential backers, sat on the board of directors of the insurance company that scuttled our festival?

"You've been a bad boy, Pete. You've been telling them stories and frightening them with your opinions about what a risk this festival would be, and what an irresponsible person is running it, haven't you? You scared them off, and they turned us down. I won't even ask why, Pete. Maybe it's just because you hate me and my family. Is that all it is? No? Maybe it was solely to advance Ardie's candidacy, to give you the power behind her throne. I don't think I care why. But here's the what of it: You will get on your car phone and call the powers that be, the ones you convinced to reject us, and you will change their minds. You can plead, you can threaten, you could even try telling them you made a mistake about me, but you can and will do it." I looked him square in the eye, toe to toe. "Won't you," I said, not asked.

He was a very intelligent man, Pete Falwell was, canny as the clam plant he stole from the Cains. A good, ruthless general always knows when he's licked, and he never risks a further hair on his head after that point. He knew what I would do, because it was exactly what he would have done, in my place.

"If I don't," he said, brisk as if we were conducting business, "you'll announce my affiliation with the insurers at the council meeting tonight?"

"Of course."

"Yes." He nodded, as if seeing the wisdom of that move. "All right. But if this gets out, Jenny, I'm dead in this town, so I'll have nothing to lose."

"And you'll reverse field again. I understand. You get me my insurance, Pete, and I'll never mention that you ever heard of that company."

He turned to his car, got in, and picked up the receiver. As he started to dial, he looked up at me. "Go away. I don't want you to listen to this. And keep your mouth shut until the meeting tonight. I will tell you then."

"I want to know now."

His smile was sudden, oddly charming, and deeply ironic. Until that moment, I hadn't known Pete had any irony in him. It was kind of a shock to see a more interesting element of his personality revealed. "You may take it for granted that your faith in me is not misplaced."

I was so surprised that I laughed.

And then I acceded to his request and walked away, thinking of my victory: Pete hadn't ended the sentence with "Jennifer." Whether he knew it or not, the patriarch of Port Frederick had just acknowledged my coming of age.

So did the other four trustees of the Port Frederick Civic Foundation when they appeared—led by Miss Lucille Grant—on the news that evening to vent their collective and individual outrage at the burning of the "witch" on the common, and to voice their confidence in their former employee: me.

Even Roy Leland was shown among them.

When I called each one of them afterward to thank them, Roy said, "That witch burning, that was too much for any of us to take, Jenny. We think the world of you, no matter what Pete says, and we decided it was high time to say so to the rest of the world. No matter whether you hold that damn festival or not, you've done your damnedest, and we want you to know you have the support of all of us, er, almost all of us." *All of them but Pete,* he meant, without knowing that now I even had that "support." They may have been a shade late in coming forth, my old bosses, but I found it no less heartwarming, for being beside the point.

But Pete got the last laugh after all, at the town council meeting that night.

* * *

In a packed hall, with the fire coverage for the festival the first item on the agenda, with Mayor Mary Eberhardt looking worried and sick at heart every time she glanced at me, and with local journalists abounding, Pete grabbed the spotlight and danced with it.

He nodded to me across the room when he first entered it. True to my word to him, I'd continued to avoid everyone and managed to say virtually nothing about insurance to anybody.

Then the mayor gaveled the meeting to order.

"Under old business," Mary said, looking grave, "our first issue is the insurance for the festival. I will ask Jenny Cain—"

"Madame Mayor!"

It was Pete, stepping forward, looking authoritative.

"If you please, Mayor, I hold the key to our insurance problem."

Her eyebrows climbing nearly to her hairline, Mary threw Robert's Rules of Order clean out the window and said merely, "What are you talking about, Pete?"

For my part, I had started to stand up, but now I didn't know what to do. I sat. My heart rate hit light speed as my life, with Pete at the helm of it, flashed by me.

He strode forward, looking so distinguished that no doubt every citizen in that room considered him a source of civic pride. He employed quite a few of them, which no doubt helped their attitude. In the spotlight of television cameras, he stopped dramatically, turned around, and smiled like Santa at all of us.

"I bring you," he said, "tidings of great joy."

Christ! I thought, but anticipatory gasps went up all around me.

"Few people know that I am a member of the board of directors of the company to whom we have made application for fire coverage."

Now a murmuring arose, to accompany the gasps.

I stared. The man was a marvel of nerve and wit and cunning, a veritable fox. I could see precisely where he was going, and I nearly grinned in sheer admiration at the gall and brilliance of it.

Pete told his spellbound audience: "I have not wished to make much of my position before this, because I felt humbled by the task before me, which was to convince a great, cold corporation—in a city where our hopes and plans mean little to them, and against all of their inclinations —to insure us to the full measure of our needs."

He paused, looking radiant.

The crowd leaned toward him, as did the council members. Mary glanced over at me. I wanted to put my face in my hands and either laugh until I cried, or cry until I laughed, I couldn't decide which. How could I have failed to anticipate this maneuver of Pete's?

"I will admit to you tonight," he said, looking brave, "that I thought I had failed. As late as yesterday, I confided in your fine council member, Ardyth Kennedy—"

Ardie was at her seat, three down from Mary, looking electable.

"—that I feared all was lost. Many of you knew that she and I—and many others—have had our doubts about this festival—" He glanced at me and quickly changed his tack. "We could never, however, fail to support it fully, once it was so well established as a dream in the hearts of so many of you and your friends. And so tonight, just before I left home, when I was feeling more discouraged than perhaps I have ever felt before in my long life . . . just then, I decided to make one last attempt to change their minds. I called the chairman of the board. I must admit to you that I *pleaded* our case . . ."

One beat, two beats of silence.

"He gave his approval. We will have our insurance!"

The room exploded with relief. Cheers. Clapping. Huzzahs.

And Pete, like the good and ruthless lying son-of-a-bitch general that he was, marched out of the room, before anybody could be so rude as to inquire as to any details. We were getting it. That was all we knew, and all we would ever need to know.

My own subsequent progress report on the festival seemed downright mundane after that performance.

"Never mind," I whispered to Mary after the meeting. "The main thing is we're insured. The show goes on. And when it goes on perfectly, no one will think of any name but yours on the ballot. You will float in to victory on a tide of goodwill."

She gave me a sourly amused look. "You sound just like Pete."

"Mary, you really know how to hurt a girl."

It was a great night in Port Frederick. Not only because of the insurance and the festival, but also because the good citizens thought we could sleep safe in our homes that night, with the homicidal arsonist in jail.

A few considerations got forgotten in that rosy celebratory mood. For one thing, the cops could not place Meryl Tyler at the Kennedys' house when they were attacked, or at the scene of David's injuries. For another, there were still four days between now and the festival opening, and in that length of time, anything could still happen. We forgot something else, too, those few of us who knew about it: the dead tarantula. Nobody pursued the provenance of that repulsive spider of fate. It was so creepy I didn't want to think about it, and besides, it seemed so unimportant.

I should have repressed my shudders and followed that spider back to its dark nest.

21

AMAZING, HOW SIMPLE LIFE SEEMED IMMEDIATELY AFTER THAT.

That night, I slept one of those delicious deep sleeps that feel as good as chocolate tastes. And the next morning, while David slept in, Geof and I talked quietly over the most relaxed breakfast we'd had together in weeks.

Between bites of scrambled egg and toasted bagel, I told him: "I don't think it was Meryl Tyler who burned down the Dime Store."

"Why?"

"Well, it seems to me that Meryl is a man who has an instinct for striking sensitive spots. Turning me into a witch was a real nasty antiwoman sort of . . . statement." I smiled at my own bland word. I also noted how Geof and I had developed the habit of calling Tyler "Meryl," contemptuously, as if he weren't a person to take seriously. Was that a mistake? I wondered. "And when he made fun of the Holy Ghost, he really hit those fundamentalists below the belt, too. So Meryl's got natural talent, all right, I'll grant him that much."

"But?"

"How'd you know there was a but?"

"Because you're taking so long to get to the point."

I slapped his arm; he laughed and said, "I didn't mean it."

"You did, too, and just for that I'm going to say the rest of this very slowly."

"I will hang on your every syllable."

I shook my head at him and smiled. "But . . . Meryl's a prankster, I think. A drunk. And while I wouldn't advise you to turn your back on him, if you did, he might only tape a 'Kick Me' sign to your shirt."

"So you don't think Meryl's up to arson?"

"I don't know what Meryl's up to, but the fire seems so much more . . . serious than what he did to me, for instance."

"He halfway beat you up."

"He was drunk, and I was in his path."

"Maybe he was drunk Saturday night at the Dime Store. And doesn't lighting candles sound more like a drunken prank than it does arson?"

"Oh," I said. "That's true."

"If I were arguing against him as our arsonist . . . ," Geof began.

"Yes?"

"I would tend to think that a man who was drunk enough to do something as stupid as burn down a store at nine o'clock would either be too drunk or too passed out to organize himself into a witch burning at three o'clock."

I thought he had a good point there.

"Can you keep him in jail through the weekend, Geof?"

"I don't know if we can. Even assholes have constitutional rights."

"Damn, there ought to be an amendment against that."

"Are you worried, Jenny?"

"I don't relish the notion of his being loose in town over this weekend, no."

"I don't either."

"So?"

"So you'll have to hope we either definitely pin the arson death on him, or else he hires himself a really bad lawyer."

"That's possible, isn't it?"

"Given our boy Meryl's level of intelligence, I'd say so, yes."

On that perverted note of "hope," we finished breakfast.

At the office, work flew by so smoothly you'd have thought our festival had never been bothered by so much as a ripple of a problem. Everyone, everywhere seemed so *happy.* Our volunteers were released from the understandable worry that they'd been working in vain for a festival that wouldn't happen. As one of them said to me that Tuesday, the morning after the council meeting, "I didn't realize how much pressure we were all under until it was over. I'm so excited now, I can't wait for this weekend to come."

Probably because everybody felt as sprung as pebbles in a slingshot, they sprang to work with an efficiency that left me with little to do. I congratulated myself on good delegation and decided I could spare the time on the following day for two unrelated chores—checking on the condition of the Kennedys, and completing my evaluation of Melissa Barney's project. When, with a single phone call, I made an appointment with the Kennedys at their house, I figured it was going to be a two-birds-with-one-stone kind of day. Or, as a vegetarian friend of mine prefers to say, "Maybe I can feed two birds with one thistle."

On Wednesday, my drive out to the Kennedys' house seemed blissfully peaceful—almost humorously so compared to some of my other treks along that road. First, there'd been the January drive that turned into a snowstorm. Then there'd been the harrowing ride to the hospital with an unconscious David, and finally, our high-speed chase in response to Nellie's urgent telephone summons the night of the fire. But now, after everything that had happened, nothing at all was happening. "And thank God," I said to that.

Top down, with an Indian summer breeze ruffling my hair, I could take this latest drive at the speed limit, enjoying the scenery. No hurry. No siren. No snow.

We'd picked our timing just right for our festival. All along the city streets and into the suburbs, I drove under canopies of trees glowing with the luminous colors of a Massachusetts autumn. So rich were the reds of the maple leaves that my skin on top of my hands looked pink, when I drove under those trees. And when the yellow leaves of the oak trees shimmered above me, the white Miata turned golden, and I felt as if I were driving through clarified butter. The sun warmed the crown of my scalp, the back of my neck, and my shoulders and arms. I kept inhaling deeply, as if I could breathe all of that sweet scented beauty into my cells and carry it with me forever.

I stopped at the sign just before Nellie's home and gazed down the hill for as long as the traffic behind me would allow me to sit there. Below, I could see the tops of the trees that spread out from the creek, forming the band of woods that ran for miles. It was a palette today—Renoir's, I decided—with dots and daubs of color everywhere. The sky was a swath of a watercolorist's cerulean, and the houses were romantic dabs of oil paint, not real at all.

"So this is what peace feels like," I said to myself.

The Kennedys' home seemed peaceful, too, and rather unexpectedly so, given the circumstances for their being here, rather than at work. I suppose I had been imagining the two of them—and their house—in the same shattered state in which we'd last seen them. But the Nellie who answered my knock was smiling, and the rooms behind her were all cleared up.

"Jenny, come in," she said warmly. "The coffee's ready, and you'd better not say you're not hungry, because I made my famous orange peel muffins, and they're still warm from the oven." She bustled me inside, talking all the while. This was a verbose, relaxed, off-work Nellie I'd never seen before. She was even wearing a pink sweat suit and tennis shoes, a far cry from the business attire I was used to seeing on her. "How's that teenage friend of yours and Geof's, the boy who got hurt? We weren't here when that happened, you know. I felt so bad that we weren't here when you needed us, but Bill and I were both still at the store."

"David's doing great," I told her, and thanked her for asking. "If you're thinking there might have been something you could have done to prevent it, believe me, there wasn't. The only people who could have kept it from happening are the people who did it. Or the person."

"No . . ." She hesitated. "Leads?"

I laughed. "You've been seeing too much of the police lately, haven't you, Nellie? No, no real leads, as they say." Impulsively, given that she was acting like a new woman, I did something different, too: I gave her a quick, gentle hug—being careful of both her wounds and mine—and I told her how glad I was to see her look and sound so well.

She made a rueful face and said, "I'm as colorful as the trees, though, if you could see my other bruises." I saw then that she'd very effectively hidden the one on her jaw, but it did look a bit oak yellow and maple red under her makeup. "Nothing really hurts, though, at least not with a couple of aspirin to see me through."

"Your living and dining rooms look almost back to normal," I commented, as we walked through them on our way to the kitchen.

"I've been working hard, and Bill has tried to help, too."

Tried to help? I thought. Why didn't he just *help,* or better yet, just do his share? I had a husband who didn't even think in terms like "try" or "help." Geof did what he and I both considered to be his share; neither of us thought of it as helping me. But then, the Kennedys were a generation older, and what a difference that could make in the division of marital tasks. It occurred to me that the relationship between Nellie and Bill, which I had always interpreted one way, could be seen another way: Maybe she was one of those people who call themselves perfectionists, when what they really mean is, nothing's right until everybody does it their way, and that's why they end up doing so much themselves.

I stared speculatively at the back of her head.

A few minutes later, I hauled myself up out of those ungracious thoughts and thanked my hostess when she handed me coffee in a mug and a muffin on a plate.

Bill wandered in, dressed in jeans and a plaid workshirt that was buttoned wrong, and he looked at us vaguely as if he couldn't quite place what the two of us were doing there in his kitchen. I wondered how he managed to find his socks of a morning. Nellie probably had to hand them to him. *Stop that,* I commanded myself, and said, "Morning, Bill."

"Is it?" he asked, and then wandered over to the counter, took the muffin that Nellie had placed on a plate for herself, and ambled back out of the room again. "Have a nice day."

I laughed, assuming a joke.

"Does he ever sit still, Nellie?"

"Oh, he's just like a toddler, always on the move. He picks things up and puts them down places, and I never know where I'll find them. It just drives me crazy, sometimes. I thought he'd stop that at home, but now I think maybe he was better off with all those aisles at the store, so he could wander up and down to his heart's content."

"What are you guys going to do now, Nellie?"

She sat down at the table with me, with a substitute muffin and her own mug. "Insurance will pay for us to rebuild . . . or retire, Jenny. We don't have to rebuild, although we could even do that, and then sell it. Hardly seems worth the effort though, when we could just take the money and sit things out. It may be better this way, to quit now because the fire forces us to. Otherwise, we might dither about it for years, until we're both half in the grave. The fire may have done us a favor and made up my mind for me."

"A young retirement." I smiled at her. "And well earned, everybody would say. What will you *do,* though?"

"Oh. I imagine we'll just stay put. Together. Here."

"No grand travel plans? No cruises, no Airstream trailer?"

She smiled and shook her head. "Jenny, what will we do about your remaining orders? I'm afraid the office is gone, and all of the papers that were in it."

"I have my copies," I reminded her, and so we spent the next hour going over them, with Nellie frequently picking up the phone to talk to her suppliers for me. When we finished, we were both satisfied with our work.

"Only two days left to get all this stuff," she reminded me.

"If it arrives, it does . . . if it doesn't, it doesn't."

"Things are going to turn out all right," she observed.

"I guess they are. I get my festival. You get to retire, if you really want to. And the police get their man."

"Oh, they'll never convict him, I told you that."

"No? He confessed to setting that effigy on fire, Nellie. And he was in your store that night."

"But they'll never manage to connect him to our fire, Jenny."

"Why not?"

"Because the man didn't have any reason to do it!"

"I don't think arsonists need a reason beyond their own pleasure, do they?"

"Well, you'll see that I'm right."

"Don't you want it to be him?"

"Heavens, Jenny, not if the poor man is innocent!"

"Well, no . . . but if he did it . . ." I trailed off and then said, "I met the man who died in the fire, did I tell you?"

"Please." She put up her hands. "Please don't talk about that. I can't stand to think about him."

"I'm sorry, Nellie."

Bill shuffled through just at that moment when I needed something else to talk about, so I asked them both where they'd stood originally on the issue of God's Highway.

"Our property doesn't go down that far," Nellie told me, but she looked depressed now, with the thought of the victim of the fire on her mind, thanks to me. "Besides, we were always too busy at the store to get involved in politics."

Unlike some daughters I could mention, I thought. But what I said was, "Bill? How about you? Were you in favor of the nature trail, or opposed to it?"

"Oh, Bill didn't know any more about it than I did. If you want to know who really fought that trail, it was the family to the north side of the bridge. The Solbergs. They practically lay down on the railroad tracks to stop it."

I smiled. "Not much danger there, no train had run in years."

"I wish we still had the train," Nellie said wistfully, and I really thought she might cry. "I get tired of driving. It would be nice just to hop on a commuter train and go to town."

Bill stirred himself to utter a lone but—I thought—pertinent and happy word. "Muffins." He was eyeing the ones remaining in the tin. He shuffled over and began to dig one out with a knife that was lying on the counter. By the time he got it into his hand, it was almost all crumbs, and he'd made a mess on the countertop.

"Oh, Bill!" Nellie got up and began to clean up after him. "First you take my muffin, then you get crumbs all over everything! Can't you be more careful? You should have let me do that."

"I've got to go," I announced, and stood up. "I'll tell you, Nellie, those muffins are wonderful, no matter how many pieces they're in, right, Bill?"

That seemed to mollify her, to judge by her smile. Still, I knew I was leaving a less happy and relaxed woman than the one who had met me at the door, and that it wasn't Bill's fault if that were so. It was mine, for my thoughtless talk of the fire. I should have realized how bleak that could make her feel. Her face, as she said good-bye to me from her front doorway, showed the strain that hadn't been there only an hour previously. She opened the door for me without unlocking anything.

"You're not locking your doors?" I asked her, surprised.

"Oh!" The shadow across her face deepened, and I thought: *Nice going, Jenny, first you make her sad, then you scare her.* "Did I forget to do that when you came in? It's hard to remember after all these years of never having to lock anything."

I finally departed, not exactly leaving cheer and sunshine in my wake.

I remembered the Solberg family, and as it turned out, they remembered me.

"Of course you may have a word with us," Appy Solberg, the octogenarian patriarch of their large and opinionated brood said to me when I appeared on their doorstep, having crossed the bridge and all of their "No Trespassing" signs, as well. "I remember you, Jenny. That's *why* you may have a word with us. You tried to help us, that's what I recall about you. Brave girl, that's what Tressa and I called you then, and I don't expect you've changed, ten years or no. Come in, come in, right this minute."

Tressa Solberg was his equal in force of personality, if not quite in age. Like Appy, she was—to use Polly's preacher's term—morally steadfast. She appeared, wiping her hands on a towel and smiling from ear to ear. They had a reputation for fearsome cantankerousness, but they never directed it at their friends, who were legion.

Tressa pressed food and coffee on me, and I really had to be firm to get out of there quickly without getting stuffed with her cooking like a Christmas turkey.

"You know the fatalities at the trail crossing?" I asked them. "The young man and the little girl before him? Well, the widow of the man who died wants my foundation to come up with a scheme to make that crossing safer for people on the trail."

"I have the perfect scheme for you," Appy said.

"Yes, close the whole darn trail." Tressa finished his thought for him. It was an entirely different sort of interruption, though, than the kind that Nellie inflicted on Bill Kennedy. This was more like two halves of the same brain. "If they hadn't opened it, nobody would have gotten hurt."

I made a regretful face. "Too late. But really, what if I wanted to hold a hearing—nothing formal, more like a meeting of interested parties—to get everybody's ideas about how to save the most lives for the least expense. Or the most expense, I suppose, if that's what it takes. What do you think the reaction would be from the folks around here?"

"They might say go to hell," Appy warned me. "Except that it's you calling the meeting—"

"And," Tressa added, "there was a child died down there, and nobody wants that to happen again."

"You're giving me too much credit," I told Appy, "but . . . you'd come, both of you?"

"Jenny," said Tressa, "did you ever hear of a Solberg who didn't express his or her opinion any chance they got?"

I smiled at them. "Never did."

"Never will," Appy declared, and he grinned, spreading wrinkles across his face like ripples in a pond. Before I left their house, he admonished me to "give that police hubby of yours a piece of my mind about all the trouble we've had because of that darned trail. Things just up and disappear from our patios, and we don't dare leave anything outside overnight. Firewood disappears like snow on a sunny day. I'll wager I've lost a cord of it, all total. It's just the sort of trouble we predicted ten years ago."

"We have to lock things up now," Tressa chimed in, "especially after that horrible thing that happened to Nellie and Bill Kennedy. I offered to help her clean up afterwards, but she wouldn't hear of it, said she could take care of it all by herself. I think she was feeling bad, myself, just feeling too bad to want anybody else around. Sometimes people just want to lock themselves away from everybody when they've been violently invaded, like that." She looked thoughtful. "We never used to have to 'lock up,' either figuratively or literally. If it weren't for the trail, we still wouldn't have to."

"Appy," I said, a few minutes later, as he showed me courteously to the door, "what's your latest crusade?"

"Gun ownership," was his prompt reply, and he looked every bit a stouthearted man of the Massachusetts militia—the original one. "If a man can't have a right to defend his property and family, I don't know what this country's coming to. And you know who we have to be ready to defend ourselves against, ultimately, don't you?"

"Tell me."

"Our own government!" He nodded, looking outraged and sage. Appy Solberg never cared if his causes were popular or fashionable; once he formed an opinion, it remained solid. Some people dismissed him and Tressa as right-wing fanatics, but I'd never thought of them as nuts, just as having strong ideas which, unlike many citizens, they actually acted on. "Never trust a government that wants to disarm an honest citizen. Gotta keep your eyes and your sights pinned on those bastards at all times."

"Apner!" came a sharp reproof from inside the house. "The price of freedom may be eternal vigilance, but not at the cost of your language, sir!"

Appy, having cocked an ear to his wife's admonition, leaned close to me, so she couldn't overhear. "I'm not sure that made much sense, do you think it did? You think maybe the old girl's getting feeble, maybe getting Alzheimer's?" A wink told me he didn't mean it.

"You're both too contrary to age," I retorted. "You and Tressa will refuse to get old, if it denies your constitutional right to the pursuit of happiness."

Appy laughed loud at that. "That was a good one, Jenny!"

That wink went a long way toward reassuring me that we might be able to help Melissa Barney without causing controversy among the neighbors. The Solbergs were always the most confrontational and oppositional folks around; if *they* cooperated, the rest of the neighborhood was sure to go along, too.

Dorothy Wilheim's address, as taken off our telephone caller identification system, was 3223 W. 63rd St. Circle, which put her in the corner unit of a block of two-story condominiums on a bluff overlooking the ocean. It was prize real estate, because such high ocean views are rare in our area, where most of the terrain marches flatly to the sea. We're not marshy, like the Cape, and neither are we the Berkshires. Our land is straightforward, much like our citizens, I suppose.

These condos were easily in the quarter- to half-million-dollar class, with terrific views—if you actually like watching hurricanes come to get you.

I had dithered about calling Wilheim first, but decided not to, on the grounds that if there is one thing an anonymous caller is clear about, it's that she doesn't want you to call her back. A surprise visit was my tactic, therefore, and I hoped I had more than a macabre reason for staging it.

If I were a hurricane approaching her door, she wasn't going to see me coming.

"Let this not be an exercise in ghoulish curiosity, Jenny," I warned myself. "You'd better be here only because this woman can tell you firsthand exactly what's wrong with that trail crossing."

She was home—or somebody was, judging from the quick clatter of footsteps down a stairway inside the condo. It sounded for all the world like tap shoes on marble.

The woman who opened the door said immediately, "How did you find me?"

22

"CALLER I.D.," I TOLD HER, FEELING PRETTY SURPRISED, MYSELF.

She was small, thin, with a stylish cap of short silver hair and the most beautiful complexion I'd seen in a long time on any woman of any age. I guessed her to be around sixty. She was wearing a black leotard, black tights, and black tap shoes.

"You are Jenny Cain?" she asked, as if making sure.

"Yes, but how—"

"Your picture's in the paper a lot, and you've been on the news, because of that festival. I don't think I would have called you, if I hadn't seen you. You have a sympathetic face. I never expected this, though. I guess you'd like to come in?" A strange expression crossed her rather pixieish face. "Or maybe you don't. But I guess you must, or you wouldn't be here, would you?"

A fellow ditherer, I could tell.

When she opened the door wide, I accepted the invitation and stepped inside. There was white marble on the foyer floor, and going up the stairs. The rooms I saw from where I stood were light, mostly white, an individualistic blend of luxury and space. Oil paintings—which I somehow had a feeling she had painted—were explosions of emotional color on the white walls.

"I mostly live upstairs," she said, leading me into a pristine white living room with a wall full of spectacular blue ocean view. Her tap shoes clicked pleasantly across the floor, then were muffled by a thick pile carpet with a design woven in different shades of ivory. Her thin arms swung at her sides, like a tin soldier's. "It's just one room up there. I use it as my bedroom and my do-everything studio. It's where I dance and paint and play my flute and hide."

"This is beautiful." I sat down on a soft ivory sofa, facing the sea. Everything in the room faced that view, including Dorothy Wilheim and me. She sat two cushions away, creating just the right aesthetic and psychological distance between us. I thought about what she had just said and murmured, "Hide?"

"Look," she said, in a frank way, "you're here because I did that stupid thing of calling you. And the only reason I did that was because sometimes I drink too much, and when I do I feel sorry for myself, and I do dumb things. I wasn't," she said quickly, "drinking the day of the . . . accident."

"You told me to close the highway."

She flushed, so her face looked very rosy against the white wall and sofa. "Like I said, dumb. I know you can't do that. That was just me being melodramatic. But if you take the idea down to a more logical level, do you think that trail crossing—just the crossing—could be closed?"

"Well, people—hikers, and the like—would still have to get from one side of the path to the other. I wonder . . . could you tell me . . . what *is* wrong with that place? Is it the stop sign? Is it the hill, or the curve in the road, or the way the trees are so close to the street?"

"In other words, you want to know what happened."

"I guess I do. I hope it's not just prurient curiosity."

"Is there any other kind?"

She took some time unfastening and slipping off her shoes, then tucking her feet up under her. Finally, she looked out to sea, while I looked at her, and then she started talking.

"I don't—still don't—know exactly what happened, Jenny. May I call you that? I'd been out for a drive, looking for something, some fresh something, to paint. And I was heading west and it was around seven in the evening on that Sunday, when suddenly I saw my painting. There it was! It was the sunset right in front of my windshield. I was enchanted by the colors. So I was just kind of driving along on automatic pilot, I guess, and drinking up all of that purple and gold and rose and blue and seeing it transferred, just like it was, into oils."

She paused, and while she was quiet, I looked at the view to which her face was turned. What I saw was blue, blue, blue; but to an artist, how many other hues, or even shapes and movements and designs were visible, that were not apparent to me?

"Do you know," she said, as if reading my mind, "that you can look through polarized sunglasses at twilight and see a latticework of Celtic crosses in the sky? One bar of each cross will be yellow and one will be blue. What you're actually seeing is the electromagnetic field of the earth. The blue band is the electric field, the yellow band is the magnetic field. If you do that enough, eventually you can detect it with your naked eye, and then you can't even look at a blue sky without seeing those crosses. I was wearing really dark polarized sunglasses that evening, because I was driving into the sun, and I saw the crosses in the sky. That was my painting: that skyful of ancient symbols. I was staring at the crosses when I hit that man."

I waited a beat, then asked her, "Had you stopped at the sign at the top of the hill?"

"Stopped?" She laughed bitterly. "I didn't even see the damn sign! I just drove right through it."

"Were you speeding?"

"I don't honestly know, Jenny." She shrugged. "They say I was, by maybe five miles an hour, because I guess they can judge by the force of the . . . impact." She bit her lower lip. "There weren't any skid marks, I understand. That's because I never saw him before I hit him, so I wasn't even trying to put my brakes on. When I hit him, I was so shocked, I let my foot off the pedal, and the car just died and rolled . . . Oh, God . . ." She lowered her head onto one hand. "Over him. It rolled into the trees then, and just stopped dead. I ran out and I saw him, and I was hysterical. Big help, huh? I just couldn't believe I had done that!" She shuddered so heavily I could see it, and she clenched both of her hands into fists and began to beat them against her forehead as if she could beat the memories out of her brain. "I still can't believe it! I can't have done that! I can't! I can't have killed somebody!"

She jumped up, as if somebody had pushed her off the couch, and she walked over to the wall of glass. "He was still alive. In such pain. Oh, God. I didn't know what to do. Should I move him off the road? Call for help? Run to a nearby house? People, other drivers, stopped right away, and they kept asking, what happened, what happened? It was like I couldn't even hear them, not really, as if the only two people in the world were that poor man and me.

"I ran over and touched him—I think I may have even kissed him, on his forehead, isn't that odd?—and I said, please, please, hang on. I'm so —God! Sorry! And I have a phone in my car, so then I ran back to it—when I knew other people were there to watch him—and I called 911. And then I ran back to him, and when people asked what happened, I just kept saying, I did it, it's my fault."

She pressed her forehead and her hands against the glass.

"What's going to happen to you?" I asked her.

She turned to face me, so that she was now pressed backward against the window. "I was charged with a whole bunch of terrible things. There's been a hearing, and I was declared guilty of everything except World War II. There will be a sentencing in a few weeks. I could go to prison. I could pay a lot of money in fines. I could get some kind of probation, even something really lenient. There's no way to know until the sentencing. Mrs. Barney will probably sue me. A lot depends. I've never even had a speeding ticket before. Lots of parking tickets, I'm bad about those, because I'm always leaving my car someplace too long while I'm off painting in the sand dunes, or some crazy place like that. But no wrecks, at least none that were my fault, and no moving violations. Not one, and I'm sixty-five years old." She smiled, painfully. "My lawyer says I'm a model citizen—except that I killed a man.

"The system's really cynical and biased, he tells me. He says that if I'd hit a white child and I was a poor black man without much education, they'd probably throw the book at me, but since I'm this respectable, senior citizen white lady, I could get off easy, even though I killed a young man with two children. He says the courts are starting to get tough with older drivers who cause accidents, but that it's not like I'm eighty-four years old, and half-blind and feeble. He's trying to decide whether I should dye my hair, to look younger, but he says I can probably get more sympathy looking like this, and besides, the judge has already seen me with white hair. It's not too good that I'm rich, and an artist, he says; it would be better if I were a struggling widow or a retired schoolteacher. Isn't that terrible? Don't you hate it?"

She said all that in a hard, biting tone of voice, but it was obvious that the hardness was all directed toward herself.

I said the only thing that came to my lips, "I'm really sorry."

"Don't be, be sorry for him. I was careless. Negligent, as the law says. And he's dead."

"But it sounds like something that almost anybody could do if the circumstances were right," I said. "Or wrong. Everybody's driven on autopilot, as you described it. Everybody gets distracted from the road, at least for a second or two, now and then."

"You don't have to try to make me feel better."

"I'm not really, I wouldn't presume to think I could. It's just that it's so scary, it's so there-but-for-the-grace-of-God . . ."

"Well, I called you," she said, "because I can't bear the thought of anybody else on the face of the earth ever feeling like this, like I do. And, of course, as bad as it is for me, it must be immeasurably worse for Melissa Barney and her children. My husband was never much of a father, but that doesn't mean our children wouldn't have missed him horribly, if he'd died when they were as young as those boys." She squared her thin shoulders and faced me. "Can you put up a real stoplight, instead of just a sign that idiots like me can drive right on by without seeing?"

"That's a real possibility," I hedged, not wanting to promise.

She nodded. "Good."

I stood up, unable to think of any reason to justify my further presence in her life. I wasn't even sure I'd had a good one to begin with, although she had certainly pounded one more nail in my determination to take on the project.

"Pardon me for asking," I said, "but you're not from here?"

"You hear the South in my accent?"

I smiled. "Just a touch, yes."

"New Orleans. But my three children grew up, and my second husband found my new hobby of tap dancing to be incredibly annoying." Suddenly Dorothy Wilheim smiled at me, the first glint of humor and warmth that I'd seen on her face. She was instantly likable, and I felt just as immediately sorry for her. "And who can blame him? Maybe I took up tap to drive him out of the house."

We both laughed a little, at that.

She continued: "But I'd always wanted to paint the Atlantic. This kind of light is different from Gulf light, which is moist and heavy and warm and glowing. This is hard, clear, rational light, I call it. Gulf light is emotional light. So, anyway, I found this place to rent with an option to buy if I really want to move here permanently."

"You won't stay, probably?"

Her glance at me was bleak. "I don't know. The question is: Will I have a choice?"

"Are you happy with your legal team?"

" 'Team' is right," she said wincing, "and by the time this is over, I'll think I could have bought a football franchise for what these guys are costing me. But, yes, I think I'm happy with them, although how will I know until the sentencing? I had to rely on somebody else's advice in order to find them at all, since I'm new here. There was a woman at the accident—she's one of the neighbors—who has been extraordinarily kind to me. She gave me the name of several excellent local defense attorneys. I don't know where I'd be without her, or them. Jail, maybe."

That sounded like Tressa Solberg to me: Tressa and Appy knew every lawyer in town, and the Solbergs always weighed in on the side of the underdog. I asked Dorothy Wilheim if that's who it was.

"No, her name is Nellie Kennedy. She's been my own personal saint. Why, do you know her?"

I was so surprised, I could barely get out, "Yes."

"She was so kind to both of us—Mr. Barney and me—at the accident. In fact, I think she even rode in the ambulance with him. But she also said to me that she felt terrible for me, and that she knew I hadn't meant for it to happen." Her voice quivered at the mere mention of sympathy and understanding from another person. "She gave me some lawyers' names, and she has called here a couple of times since then, just to see how I'm doing, and to tell me to keep the faith."

"Bless her heart," I said.

"Amen," responded Dorothy Wilheim, with feeling.

As I drove away, putting the ocean behind me, I thought that it really was wonderful of Nellie to help Wilheim, but wasn't it also a little weird? Or, if not weird, at least it was a difficult balancing act, helping Melissa Barney on the one hand, and also offering moral support to the very person whom Melissa hated for killing Ben.

"You're a strong woman, Nellie Kennedy," I said to her image in my mind. "When I'm in trouble, I definitely want you on *my* side."

After those conversations—with the Kennedys, the Solbergs, and Wilheim—I returned to the office and phoned Melissa Barney to tell her I could definitely recommend to my board that we take on her project.

"Maybe we'll solve it with signs," I said, feeling hopeful.

"Small children can't read," was her sharp retort. "That little girl who was killed by that hit-and-run driver was only six years old. She probably barely knew her alphabet! No sign is going to keep a child like that from running out into the street, Jenny."

I was taken aback, both by the truth of what she said and also by the anger with which she said it. Her voice was shaking with it, and she cracked out the words as if they were twigs she was breaking: *snap, snap, snap!*

I couldn't say, "Melissa, is everything all right?" because obviously everything was never all right for a newly widowed young mother with two sad children. So I disengaged from the conversation as quickly and tactfully as I could. I'd wanted to ask her not to mention my decision to anybody else—at least not until the festival was over—because I thought that way we might avoid any problems with Lew Riss and his First Things First gang. But then, who was she going to tell who would tell Lew?

I hung up—gently—feeling sure the secret was safe with her.

It had been a revelation, that visit to Dorothy Wilheim, as I told Geof later. I'd thought there were only four principal victims when Ben Barney was killed: him, his wife, and their children. Now I felt there were five, including his "killer." Depending on how the legal system disposed of her case, and on how she responded to this black hole in her life, I might have to extend that number of victims to include her family, too.

"You hear about victimless crimes," I said that night, "but now I wonder if there aren't also some—for lack of a better word—villainless crimes."

"She ran the sign, Jen."

"Hasn't everybody, once?"

"She wasn't paying attention to her driving."

"Do you, every single moment?"

"He's dead."

"Yes," I agreed, with heavy and accepting irony. "There is that."

But I couldn't help it: As bad as I felt for Melissa Barney and her sweet boys, I also couldn't help but feel dreadfully sorry for Dorothy Wilheim.

Geof had brought home with him the accident reports on both the Barney fatality and the fatal hit-and-run involving the child six months earlier.

They were straightforward police reports, written in proper officialese, but easy enough to comprehend. The first accident happened on Memorial Day weekend on a rainy day when the police and medics were delayed in reaching the scene because the bridge was temporarily closed due to flash flooding. (I remembered that weekend, the last wet one of that seemingly endless rainy spring.) The child's death was not blamed on that delay, however. She had died instantly, upon impact, I read. That accident—just like the one Dorothy Wilheim was involved in —happened on a Sunday.

I flipped back to the first file to see what time of day that was: seven-thirty P.M., it said, and the reporting officer had noted the weather and pavement conditions. "Highway was rain-slick," she reported, because of storms for several hours previously, but the rain had stopped approximately one hour before the child was struck. At the time of the accident, the sky was clear, with only a few clouds remaining. But, the officer noted, visibility may have been poor because the setting sun might have been directly in the driver's eyes.

I perused the reports of the subsequent investigation into the accident and the search for the black VW Beetle. As opposed to the Barney/Wilheim case, this hit-and-run file was still open. I wondered whether, if

I ever met that driver, he—or she—could possibly arouse in me any of the sympathy I felt for Wilheim.

All of that was simple, not very helpful or suggestive information in regard to improving the safety of the crossing. But there was one item in the reports that shot me out of my chair like a ball out of a cannon: The child who died was named Elena Patricia Talbot. The report said there was "no father." Certainly an impossible biological event, but possible in practical terms. The mother's last name was also Talbot. Her first name was:

Cleo.

Mother and child were from Bennington, Vermont.

"What should I do?" I asked Geof, even later that day, in bed. "Should I say something to her, or should I pretend I don't know?"

"I think you'll know what to do," he replied, "the next time you see her."

"But that would be awful, Geof, to say something to her at Judy's House with so many people around. If it has to be, I think it has to be private." I swallowed, dreading it. "In case she starts crying, or something." I stared at the ceiling of our room. "God. They do say it's the worst thing that can happen to you."

"Jenny, don't you think it's a little unusual that she'd come live here where her little girl—what was her name?"

"Elena Patricia."

"Where she died? If you had a child who was killed, would you go live in that town?"

"Maybe," I said slowly, an idea just then forming in my mind, "if I was looking for the car that hit her."

23

Thursday before the festival, Cleo Talbot came and went, and I didn't say anything to her. But I caught myself staring at her, transfixed by a deeper interest and sympathy and—yes—curiosity about her.

"Hi, Jenny," she said, as usual, each time.

"Hi, Cleo," I responded, as always, although now I felt self-conscious about adding, "How you doin'?"

She appeared so calm, so efficient, so ordinary—in her unordinary way—that I had a hard time reconciling the woman carrying the boxes with the mother in the accident report. Watching her, while I fielded phone calls and volunteers in our happy last-minute flurry of stuff-to-do, I thought back on our brief history with Cleo, looking for clues to her other, darker life that she had not chosen to reveal to us.

There wasn't much to recall; I couldn't give myself much credit, either, for seeing through her cheerful facade to what was surely churning below the surface. Yes, I'd thought she had an aura of an emotional maturity beyond her age, and yes, I had thought I glimpsed loneliness in her eyes, and there had been a movement or two when she had seemed to blink back tears and to retreat into herself. But beyond those few hints, no clues.

Friday morning, Cleo arrived a half hour earlier than usual with her first delivery. She walked up, smiling, to where I sat on one of the love seats as I was going over my notes, and she sat herself down on the facing love seat and plunked three shiny quarters down on the captain's table between us. She had two books with her: One was a fat hardback with a gray and yellow cover and the other was a trade paperback edition with a black cover.

"What's this?" I asked her, laying my notes aside. "You making a contribution to the festival, Cleo?"

She laughed. "No. Well, maybe, in a way. You want a reading, before it happens? I think you're ready for the *I Ching.* I thought you might like to see the big picture of what to expect from this weekend, and how it all fits into your own psyche."

"Wow," I said, at the ambition of it. "E what?"

"I Ching." She pronounced it carefully for me, and it sounded like a long *e* followed by the word *jing* as in jingle bells. "Most Westerners say it incorrectly, but you're going to learn it the right way."

I tried the words, tasting their foreign flavor.

"That's right," she approved. "Ever heard of it?"

"Yeah, but without ever really knowing what it is."

"It's an ancient Chinese source of wisdom and divination. Another kind of oracle, like the pendulum or runes, but more talkative, by far. Confucius used and explicated it, but its source goes far back, even before him. For the person who has ears to hear and eyes to see, it can be a spiritual guide, like an invisible guru."

"Exactly what will it guide me *to?"* I was feeling nervous around her, not quite sure who it was I was dealing with; finally I just fell back into being myself—regardless of who she might be, either mysterious oracle, brisk delivery woman, or grieving mom.

"It will guide you to integrity," she said solemnly. "It guides me toward discovering the integrity—that is, the wholeness—of my self, and it helps me to live a life of ever greater integrity in the world." She made a face, mocking her own self-importance. "But if it can't give me the right numbers to win the lottery, what good is it, right?"

I laughed. She was such a funny little mystic, a good witch delivering the wisdom of the ages, along with boxes of orange plastic pumpkins. *How do you do it?* I wondered. *How do you walk smiling through the day, while grief is alive, inside of you?*

"What's the matter?" Cleo asked me.

Lord, I was close to tears and couldn't let her see it.

I blinked, fumbled for a tissue, as if I had a runny nose, and behind it, said, "So how do we get this reading?"

She told me that I could ask "the Ching," as she called it, a specific question, although she said that really wasn't necessary, because it would automatically either address the question that was uppermost in my mind, or it would talk to me about the question that *should* be uppermost in my mind! Then she demonstrated to me how I was to "throw" the three coins six times, which I did, choosing not to ask a question, just to see what it would come up with on its own. Each throw seemed to tell her something, which she transcribed into chicken scratches on the back of a Post Haste envelope. When I had completed my six throws, I said, "So what have we got?"

"Goodness," she responded. "What we have is six changing lines, which means that you are involved in a very volatile situation, indeed." Upon seeing my reaction to the word *volatile,* Cleo hastened to say, "Well, maybe volatile is too strong a description, so let's just say that this is a situation that's in a very pronounced state of flux."

"Yeah," I agreed, laughing a little, "let's say that."

She proceeded to refer to the book with the yellow and gray cover.

"It says that recently you had a problem which was solved, and now you feel peaceful about it."

"Yes! The insurance!" I exclaimed.

"Okay. It says that the problem was in your public life, and was caused by sly foxes. But you had enough inner strength to combat them and to win."

"Wow," I said, impressed with her "reading" already.

"But here's a warning, Jenny, against being insolent or careless. There could be a theft."

I shrugged, since that didn't sound too dire.

"It seems to be saying that some people around you will not be true friends, and you must get away from them."

I didn't have any idea what that meant, or how it related to the festival.

"Ooh," Cleo said. "It says there is an enemy! A really wicked one, and you must shoot him down."

Cleo looked at me and suddenly grinned like a teenager.

"Cool," she said and laughed.

She had the most charming way, I thought, of smoothing sharp edges.

"Did any of that," she asked, "say anything meaningful to you?"

"The first thing you read certainly did—about the peace that comes after problems have been overcome. That's exactly how I've felt all week, after I first thought we wouldn't get the insurance, and then we did." I thought a moment. "And that bit about the foxes in public life?" I laughed. "That's Pete and Ardyth and their group, as I live and breathe."

"Well," Cleo said, "that's all in the past, anyway, although you are probably still dealing with the consequences of it. I do think you'd be well advised—if I do say so myself—to hang on to your valuables, with that warning about theft. Sometimes the Ching is talking metaphorically, but a lot of times when it says something like 'the nest burns up,' it really does mean that you'd better check to see if you turned off the iron before you left the house!"

I confessed to her that I hadn't understood a word of any of the rest of the reading, and that I couldn't see what it could possibly have to do with the festival, which was what had been uppermost in my mind when I threw the coins.

Cleo replied, her face utterly serious once again, "I think it means that you'd better stay alert, Jenny, because there's still . . ." She gave me a tentative, rather apologetic smile. ". . . there's still an enemy out there which you have to, metaphorically I hope, kill."

I felt chilled by her warning, and suddenly, also a little resentful of it. *Just what I needed, a dire warning from a gypsy!*

Cleo seemed to sense my feelings, because she laughed and said, "Can ten billion Chinese be wrong?" She was amazing, the way she could absorb skepticism without getting defensive on behalf of her own beliefs. Nor was she insensitive to my feelings, which must have been plain on my face: "Hang on, though, there's good news. My other source book—" She pulled the black one toward her. "—says this situation is upward, which is to say, away from danger. It also says that, ultimately, you'll be tested in your capacity to pardon and forgive."

I must have gotten a give-me-a-break look on my face, because she laughed and said then, "One more thing, Jenny. The coins you threw made a pattern that is called Deliverance, or Liberation. But in this particular reading, that pattern changes into another one called Family."

"Family?"

She made an embarrassed face. "I don't get it, either. Maybe it will all seem clear to you later, when it's all over. Look, maybe this was a bad idea. If I had thrown the I Ching for myself this morning, it probably would have told me not to offer help unless somebody specifically asks for it."

"That's one of my life lessons, Cleo."

She glanced at her wristwatch. "Shoot! I've got to get going. Hope I haven't spoiled your day, Jenny."

"No way. Cleo, why don't you be a fortune-teller at our festival? I could arrange to set up a booth, and you could raise money for your favorite charity, how about it?"

"No, thanks!" She held up both hands to ward me off like an evil spell. "I think I'd better stick to predicting my own future."

Without thinking, caught up in the fresh conviviality of the moment, I said, "What *do* you see for yourself?"

I could have kicked myself.

Especially when I saw her face tighten, and when she turned away as she had done before.

She murmured four words like an incantation: *"Thurisa reversed, Fehu, Inguz."*

When she faced me again, there was a coldness in her eyes. "The runes say that my past was . . . suffering at the gate of heaven. My present is . . . ambition satisfied. And for my immediate future . . . I must be prepared. I must be calm. I must complete a task and make that my first priority out of all others."

I nearly said something to her then. Came close to grabbing one of her hands and confiding the tragic information that I had—without intending to—learned about her. But she was in a hurry to leave. And two volunteers walked into the room. The phone rang.

The chance dissolved.

I still didn't have a fairy godmother costume. If it had actually ever existed, it had burned up in the Dime Store fire.

"Just as well, I guess," was my conclusion, voiced to Geof and David that night at supper. The kid had heated frozen pizza for all of us, and it tasted awful, but who was complaining? Not Geof, who appeared intensely satisfied with freezer-burned cheese; not David, who looked proud of himself, and not I, who had never actually wanted to experience Canadian bacon, pepperoni, hamburger, and Italian sausage all at the same time.

"Why?" Geof asked me.

"I'd look ridiculous."

"You'd look adorable."

I blew him a kiss, but David gave him a look. "She'd look ridiculous." To me, he said, "Uncool."

"Yeah. Darn. And here I wanted to go flitting around, cooing like Glenda the Good Witch, and flicking my wand at people and making all of their dreams come true."

Geof laughed.

David rolled his eyes. The kid had rarely complained all week of his aches and pains—in fact, he'd been something of an inspiration to me, so that I complained less about *my* aches and pains. Geof and I winced every time David did, even if he didn't say anything about it. What he did complain about, though, was how nobody had been called to account for his injuries.

That evening, I talked out loud about the little jobs I still had left to do before tomorrow, and Geof told us about their continuing investigations on many fronts. The fundamentalist Halloween protestors were now demonstrating in front of the jail, he said, where Meryl Tyler was being held. Although he had allegedly killed their "brother," they seemed inclined to think of that as a death in the line of duty, Geof said. Where they might have considered Tyler the devil incarnate, they seemed instead to believe that Meryl had actually been *trying* to burn the minion of evil—the Dime Store and the witch—and so they didn't seem to have their hearts behind their pickets this time.

"I can see where they'd feel ambivalent," I said, a shade bitterly.

David said, "You've got the guy who burned Jenny, Jenny's got her fucking festival, but what are any of you people doing about catching the jerk-offs who tried to kill me? Isn't anybody thinking about me?"

When he wasn't looking, Geof and I smiled across the table at each other. It was almost reassuring to know that although David might be stoic about pain and although he might cook a pizza once in a while, he hadn't by any means turned into a saint.

Geof and I took a late-night drive in Port Frederick to wander hand in hand around the ghostly structures on the common. The town was already crowded—the motels were showing "No Vacancy," and there were more cars on the streets than I'd ever seen before. Tomorrow, the cash registers in Port Frederick would be jingling. Once we'd nicknamed ourselves "Poor Fred," part in ironic truth, part in affection. That hadn't accurately described my hometown for several years, but this weekend—and, I hoped, all of the annual ones to follow—would help to bury that pitiful title forever.

A crew had rebuilt the speaker's platform where the witch had burned. The singed grass didn't show up in the dark under our feet, but we could feel the hard crunch of it, and a smokey smell still lingered around the spot.

"Tomorrow." I leaned against my husband, who put his arms around me and pressed the side of his face against my hair. "I can almost believe it's going to happen."

He kissed the top of my head.

We just stood there a while, with me reminiscing about putting it all together, and he just listening and keeping me warm.

When we drove home, I felt rested, and I knew I'd sleep well . . .

. . . until five o'clock the next morning, when I woke up a minute before the alarm blasted. Quickly, I shut it down, dressed in my festival T-shirt, jeans, and sneakers, gathered everything I would need for the day, and—heart pounding with anticipation and happy nervousness—slipped out of the house, leaving the two men still sleeping.

24

I WAS THE FIRST HUMAN TO PARK AT THE COMMON THAT SATURDAY, SO NATURALLY I got the best parking spot. Out on the grounds, the autumn colors of the trees were dimmed at this early hour, but they'd soon be aflame—God's arson, not Meryl's. They would cast a leafy glow onto the ground, where thousands of visitors would be shuffling along from booth to booth.

The gates were to open at ten A.M.

My mind filled with imaginary sounds and colors—and cash for good causes—as a second car pulled in to park, and then a third, fourth, and fifth. My board members were here for our picnic breakfast in the leaves, just as we'd promised one another we would do, months earlier.

Mayor Mary Eberhardt and I stood together, off to the side of the speaker's platform, where, in about fifteen minutes, she would officially open the festival and welcome all comers.

"But *why* would Peter Falwell risk so much in order to sabotage this festival?" Mary had been antsy, so to speak, all through our board picnic, giving me urgent looks, until finally I let her pull me off for this private confab. "Haven't you thought about that, Jenny? It's all I *can* think about. Why did he want the nature trail so much to begin with, why has he thrown his clout and money behind a female candidate, why is it Ardyth? Why is he so opposed to making any changes to the trail? Why would he risk his reputation in this town in order to secretly block the insurance, and thereby ruin this festival that everybody else wants?"

Our imperturbable mayor was perturbed.

"Mary, if you've been obsessed with those questions," I said to her, "have you thought of any answers?"

"Maybe." She pointed to a spot just behind the permanent, reconstructed historical buildings. "You know what runs right behind there, Jenny?"

"The trail?"

"That's right." This was not news; the trail ran unobtrusively through most of the heart of Port Frederick, everybody knew that, but nobody thought about it very much. I certainly didn't. But Mary said, insistently, "I've been trying to see any connection between this festival and God's Highway, and that's the only one I can find. Proximity."

"So?"

"So, Jenny, when does Peter Falwell ever do anything that does not in some way benefit himself and line his pockets?"

I shook my head. "Don't know of any time that hasn't been true. What are you getting at, Mary, that there's something in the trail for him?"

"It would be characteristic of the man," she pointed out.

"Yes, but—"

"I know. A decade has passed since the trail opened. But what if whatever it is that Pete wants to do requires an exceptionally strong political base in town? What if, in order to do it—whatever it is—Pete thinks he needs his thumb on the mayor and the majority of the town council? What if the time has to be just right?"

"God, Mary, it's a long time to wait!"

"How long did he wait and plot to steal Cain Clams from your family, girl?"

"Okay. But if you're right, Mary, what the hell does he *want?*"

"I don't know." She seemed, for her, frazzled, worried, a mayoral dog with a community bone. "But I have to go be mayor now, and give my speech, and smile big. You think about it, Jenny, and think about it hard, because the election is very much upon us, and Pete could have untold tricks up his sleeve, couldn't he?"

Damn, I thought. *He could, indeed.*

While Mary mayored, I ambled among the populace, whose (mostly) smiling faces were turned up toward her. Port Frederick was proud of themselves for having a black mayor, and a woman, at that. It pleased the citizens to see her carry off this ceremonial duty with her customary grace and dignity, and to know she made them look good to all the tourists on this day. But then, when didn't Mary look good? Maybe she slept gracelessly.

"Bitch."

It was a growled whisper, near me. I whirled in the direction of the voice, in time to see the hateful expression on Meryl Tyler's face before he pulled a silver Halloween mask down over his eyes, and disappeared into the crowd. He hadn't meant Mary; he'd been staring straight at me. I went searching—on the run—for the head of festival security, who happened to be my husband.

"Why couldn't you hold him just two more days!" I said. "And if you can't do that, can't he be prohibited from being here, considering what he did?"

"He has been warned off, Jenny." Geof took hold of my right arm and tugged me to where David Mayer stood watching kids try to climb a Jacob's ladder. "But that can't stop him from slipping in, not with a crowd this size for him to hide in. You say he's wearing a silver half-mask?"

"Yeah, but who isn't!" I protested bitterly. "We're selling the damned things, and there's no telling how many hundreds of people are already wearing them. Why couldn't he stay in jail, just for one measly weekend!"

"Because we don't have the evidence to hold him on the arson homicide, and unfortunately, Tyler didn't hire a lousy lawyer. A good one showed up this morning and sprang him."

"What's happening?" David asked, when we reached him.

"You want a job?" Geof asked him. "You'll even get paid."

"Maybe. What?"

"Be Jenny's bodyguard—"

"Geof!" I exclaimed.

"—for the rest of the day and tomorrow, too, if we need you. I'll pay you the same as the extra security personnel are getting."

But David objected. "How am I supposed to guard her body when my own body is still screwed up?" He pointed toward his broken collarbone; and, indeed, he was still noticeably holding that side of his body, and his head, quite carefully.

"If you can hold yourself upright on a motorcycle," Geof said, "you can carry a walkie-talkie, right?"

"I guess so, but what if somebody jumps her bones, and I have to jump their bones?"

"You're not to *do* anything," Geof said in his lieutenant voice. "That's why I want you for this job, so you can't harm anybody by mistake. If anybody misbehaves, you get hold of me, immediately. I'll do what needs doing." He looked at me. "And your job is to scream and run."

"I can do that," I assured him, and smiled a little.

He leveled his lieutenant's stare back at the kid again. I actually thought this was quite a good idea, which might also give David a sense of involvement with the day, so he wouldn't just stand around all the time looking bored and superior—or, worse, depressed at the sight of so many all-American families coming together for the kind of day he'd probably never known with his own parents. The kid looked at me, doubtfully, as if the prospect of my company for so long didn't appeal to him. But then, he allowed us to see a small grin.

"Yeah," he said, "okay, but you'll have to pay me, to spend a whole day with her."

Geof looked to me for my approval, which I gave with a nod.

To David, he said, "You'll have to watch her. She's slippery."

"What am I watching for?"

"Go," I commanded him, "get your walkie-talkie with Geof, then come back here, and I'll tell you."

My bodyguard and I strolled over to where the opening-hours crowd was dispersing from around the speaker's platform. Mary came down the steps and grinned at us.

"How'd I do?"

"Brilliant," I told her, knowing it was true, even if I hadn't actually been there the whole time to hear her.

"You were totally, awesomely mayoral," David assured her. "I mean, I didn't actually see you do your thing, but I know you were." He liked her, and the feeling was mutual. She patted his cheek affectionately, something I could never have gotten away with, and thanked him.

I thought of her questions to me earlier and, on impulse, said, "David, if you knew of an old railroad line that had been torn up and converted into a hiking path, but you wanted to put that long, narrow strip of land to some other use—something that might be controversial, but which might make some people a lot of money—what would that be?"

"The obvious," he said promptly.

Mary and I gaped at him.

"Which is?" she prodded.

"Another railroad, of course," he said, as if we were both idiots for not having thought of it. Which we were, all of us.

"Pete's tie tacks!" I cried. "His passion for trains!"

"Light rail!" Mary exclaimed. "Ardyth Kennedy's been going on and on about the 'connections' linking every town from here to Boston!"

"Mary, it's federal land. They can lease it or give it away or sell it anytime they want to, to anybody they want to, for any use they like. If the feds can hand over national forests and Indian burial grounds to the lumber companies, and if they can hand over off-shore property to oil exploration companies, and if the deficit is as big as we think it is, and if the park service is as broke as it says it is—there is nothing stopping them from selling, or leasing, or giving away our insignificant little strip of federal parkland, just to be rid of the expense of maintaining and administering it."

"Great idea," David said. "A train into Boston?"

Mary and I stared at him again, and then she laughed. "I kind of like the idea, myself, but then I'm no hiker. And I still don't like to think about the way Pete helped finagle all that land away from those owners ten years ago."

"Pete would say that was just smart business," I told them, knowing that from my family's bitter experience with his cutthroat methods. "But I wonder what *those* people will have to say about his plans, if indeed David has hit on the truth?" I pointed to a large and noisy group of men and women who were purposely making a commotion as they gathered around our ticket booths.

They were carrying signs.

But these weren't fundamentalists, not fundamentalist Christians, anyway—they were Lewis Riss and a much, much larger group of First Things Firsters.

Pulling David with me—and telling Mary to head for the far opposite corner of the common, so that she wouldn't alienate any voters—I started trotting toward the ecoterrorists, who thought they were saving God's Highway for the squirrels. I wondered, as we hurried there, just how many squirrels died every day under the tracks of railroads, no matter how "light" they were!

By the time we got there, I had ecoterrorists to the left of me and religious fanatics to the right of me. The Halloween protesters had arrived, dressed in baby blue choir robes. The members of both groups were carrying signs and staring suspiciously at each other, all of them milling about and blocking the entrance from our paying visitors.

"Could you folks please make your circle a little more over that way?" I requested of the blue-robed protesters. "Thank you so much!" As they moved off, rather sweetly obedient even to my dubious authority, I moved in on the First Things Firsters, aiming for the First among equals.

"Lewis?"

"Hey, babe, I warned you, don't say I didn't!" He was sleek as a seal in black lycra tank top and bicycle pants. "You mess with parkland without checking with us first, we're going to let the world know you don't give a damn about spotted baby tree toads."

As if you do, Lewis, I thought.

"Lew, honey?" I took hold of his biceptual right arm and began to tug him off to the side. His cohorts were busy hoisting signs and warming up their vocal chords, so they didn't try to intercept us. "There is one thing I have to tell you before you carry on today."

But then I realized I was making a tactical error:

I *wanted* Lew's gang to hear this.

So I tugged him back into the heart of them and made sure I talked loud enough to be heard by all of them, and everybody else in the vicinity. Lew was telling me, self-importantly, how I couldn't stop them, when I said, "Oh, I'm not trying to, Lew. I think you have every right to protest any little old issue you care about so deeply. I just thought you might want to know that I've heard that the nature trail may be turned back into a railway, for light rail this time. It's federal land, as you know, and I've heard that some of our local bigwigs are lobbying to get the government to turn over all those miles for a little old commuter railroad to run between here and just about everywhere else."

"What?"

It was a single strangled cry from a dozen throats at once.

Lew's face was turning a deeper shade of tan, perhaps mixed with purple. "Are you saying that we're busting our butts to protect that trail so somebody can put a *railroad* through there again?"

His gang went crazy, gesticulating, shouting at me, at Lew, at each other, while I just kept discreetly murmuring disclaimers like, "Now, it's only a rumor, Lew. It's what some people think, it might not even be true. Although, it makes a certain kind of sense, doesn't it? It's really the perfect use for that land if you don't use it for a nature trail . . . but I don't know if any of this is actually *true* . . ."

A woman yelled, "No rail on the trail!"

Immediately, the others took it up, until the air vibrated with their new battle cry. As for Lew, in the midst of the mutiny, he suddenly put his hands on his hips and gave me a long look.

I leveled one right back at him.

He shrugged. "What the hell. I love action, whatever it is."

Ever the man of principle, I thought.

It was then that David's good arm shot out, and the fist at the end of it hit Lew in the nose, knocking him to the ground. Then David stood over him, making threatening gestures and noises.

Damn, I had totally forgotten that David was convinced that the First Things Firsters had wrecked him and beat him. In fact we still didn't know that they hadn't done it.

Lew scrambled like a boxer to his feet, blood pouring from his nose, fury on his face. "What the hell did you do that for?" All of his new muscles tensed in preparation for launching a counterattack against David, who was, I was frightened to realize, in absolutely no shape to defend himself.

Lew dived toward us.

I grabbed David's T-shirt and pulled the back of it for all I was worth, jerking him off-balance so he nearly fell, but also ruining Lew's aim, so that he stumbled to the ground again, this time landing on his hands and knees.

Not waiting for Lew to recover a second time, or for his pals to wake up and jump in to support him, I yelled, "Come on!" to the kid, following that up with, "David, come on, he's got a gun!"

Even David Mayer was smart enough to get scared at the sound of those words, and off we ran—me hanging on to his shirt and he clutching his left arm to his side to keep the jarring down on his broken bone, which must have hurt like hell, nonetheless.

We burst past the ticket booths and ran into the crowd until I felt sure we were inconspicuous there. I guided David to a booth where people were selling tie-dyed vests to benefit something or other, and I bought him one and made him slip it on, even though it clearly hurt him to do it. Then I followed that up with a white baseball cap, which I bought at another booth to take the place of his usual black Star Trek hat, and then I made him put on a full-face Halloween mask of Jason the movie madman. Finally, I declared him unrecognizable, except for the fact that he was still hanging out with me.

Through the mask, he mumbled, "Did he really have a gun?"

"Uh, no."

David was indignant, and the mask came whipping up off his head. "He *didn't?*"

"I lied about that."

"I could have beat the shit out of him, I could have dragged him over to the cops, I could have made a citizen's arrest—"

"You could have gotten badly hurt, and then you could have gotten arrested for assaulting him, and then you could have gotten sued because they may not be the people who hurt you!"

"Shit!"

I took a deep breath. "David." I took another breath, observed how many people were now staring at us, and lowered the volume of my voice. "David. I'm sorry. I keep getting you into bad situations. I think maybe this was a bad idea, you staying with me. I'm fine. I can take care of myself. And, frankly, I have things to do, and I want to enjoy my festival. So let's split. You go back and find Geof and make sure he knows that Lew Riss is here, and I'll go off on my own again."

"No," he said, looking angry and stubborn. "I have a job to do." David eyed me grimly. "And I will protect you if it kills me. Or, I kill you first."

I had to smile and then to laugh.

He didn't, which worried me.

25

"HI, JENNY! COULD YOU HAVE ORDERED A MORE PERFECT DAY?"

"We're having a great time, Jenny!"

"Fabulous day, Jenny."

Over and over again, wherever I strolled, that was the happy refrain I heard. People were having fun! Money was being spent. Every time I ran into one of my busy board members, she was beaming. All around, Port Frederickans wore their volunteer T-shirts proudly. My heart felt full as a beer barrel, and I was as intoxicated by my own success as if I'd drunk it all. Luckily, I had my own personal teenager beside me to keep me humble. David, still steamed at me for removing him from the scene of battle, kept up a running commentary of sarcasm, most of it along the lines of, "What are they making such a big fuss over you for? Running a festival? Big deal, any android could do it."

I soon ran nearly out of cash, just buying food to keep his mouth occupied. While David was still gnawing on a huge roasted turkey leg, I made him stop with me at the booth where Melissa Barney had set up her pumpkin-carving demonstration.

I was fascinated to see that she was carving caricatures out of pumpkins that had been earlier scooped out and that were now capped and empty shells, awaiting her artist's knife to give them personality.

We watched her talking to a little boy who told her, when she asked, that he would be "eleven in a couple of months." He was surrounded by several other boys of a similar age, who were obviously egging him on to be the guinea pig of the group, before they committed their own three dollars apiece to immortalizing themselves in pumpkin.

"What's your name, sweetie?" Melissa asked him.

I didn't see her own boys; they must have scampered off to roam the festival grounds while their mom worked. She was wearing her black jeans and black T-shirt and sandals, and her red hair showed orange highlights to rival the pumpkins.

"Chapman," the kid said.

I looked more closely at him and suddenly recognized him as Pete Falwell's grandson, the nice kid I'd met the week before.

"Is that what your friends call you, Chap?"

"No," said one of them, who crowded close, "we call him dumbbutt!"

The whole little gang of ten-year-olds broke into giggles at that, while Chappie, as his grandpa had called him, turned red and vainly attempted to hush them.

"Chappie," he said, valiantly answering Melissa's question.

First, she took his head gently in her hands, pushing his brown bangs off his forehead, getting a good look at him while she made faces at him that made all of the other boys laugh. They seemed a sweet bunch, no more scatological than your average group of ten-year-old boys, and good-natured in their fun. It looked to me as if Melissa was tactfully feeling the shape of his head, as if she were blind, but with her eyes open.

"Nice head," she said to him, which set his pals off in a fit of teasing giggling. Several times they poked him and repeated, "Nice head, Chappie's got a nice head!" One of them swaggered like an adult man and said in a mock-deep voice, "That young man's got a good head on his shoulders!"

While they had their fun, Melissa sorted through her pumpkin shell pile, eliminating perfect round ones and lopsided ones, and finally picking up one that was shaped uncannily like the child's own skull: longish, with a high forehead (if a pumpkin could be said to have a forehead), and concave indentations at the "temples," curving out into long "cheeks," and then rounded off in a dimpled chin.

"Okay, sit on the ground, sweetie," she instructed him, and she sat, too, in her chair beside a card table.

Her "model" plunked down cross-legged on the ground at her feet, close to her sandals, while his friends hurried around to stand behind Melissa so they could both see what she was doing and point and make fun of Chappie, as well. She asked him to put his hands between his legs and then to raise his chin and look up at her: instantly, you could see why she did it that way—it gave his face a sweet roundness, despite the hourglass shape of his head; suddenly, he looked all cheeks and eyes and mouth.

"Now don't bother us for a minute," she chided his friends, but she didn't shoo them away from where they crowded at her back. This was the first I had ever seen her appear relaxed, and even close to enjoying herself. You could see she was used to having boys around, and she liked them. "And don't make him laugh, okay?"

Quickly, Melissa set to work, pulling the empty pumpkin shell into her lap, holding it between her legs and tilting the shell so its "face" was looking up at her, just as the child was.

Hardly looking at the pumpkin, keeping her eyes on the child, her right hand flew over the orange face, sketching a portrait in black ink. In only two or three minutes, I saw the child's face magically, or so it seemed, transferred from his own body to the pumpkin.

The boys behind her were noisily impressed.

"You oughta see this, Chapman, it looks just like you!"

"Yeah, like a pumpkin head!"

Giggle, giggle, giggle.

"You can move now, sweetheart," she told him.

"Thanks!" he exclaimed. "I was gettin' stiff!"

"Bet your nose itched, too, didn't it?" she said, as she picked up her carving knife.

"Oh, boy, did it, how'd you know that?"

He was on his feet by then, and he came around behind her to butt his way into the center of his friends, and to stare as his own face appeared out of the pumpkin, more of it appearing with every quick, confident slice of her knife.

"It's a law," Melissa informed the boys while, quick as a slasher, she sliced and diced and carved. "When you sit real still, your nose has to itch. Also, you have to want to sneeze. And usually at least one of your elbows will itch, too, so bad you think you'll go crazy if you can't scratch it."

"Oh, yeah!" he agreed, and wildly scratched at his left elbow with his right fingers. "How do you *do* that?"

"I inherited the ability," she said, as her knife poised above the pumpkin's left eye. "My father was Peter, Peter, the Pumpkin Eater, and my mother was the wife he couldn't keep, not until he put her in a pumpkin shell, and there he kept her very well."

"Oh, gross," one of the boys exclaimed. "She's cutting your eye open, Chappie!"

Melissa responded in a sepulchral voice, accompanying word to deed: "And plucking it out!" She handed the chunk of pumpkin back over her shoulder for one of the boys to grab. They had a field day after that, turning every twist of her knife into a bloody surgical procedure.

"She's slicing your nose!"

"Stabbing your other eye!"

"Drilling your teeth without any anesthetic!"

Gross, gross, gross was the operative adjective in the short five minutes it took Melissa to complete her pumpkin bust of Chappie the almost-eleven-year-old. When she was finished, and had neatly wiped out his "eyes, mouth, and nose," with a wet rag, she turned and handed it to him, placing it in his hands, its face looking up toward his face, which was staring down, open-mouthed, at it.

"Awesome," was all he could manage to say.

"Me, next!" cried one of his pals.

They jostled to be next in line for the privilege of being turned into a pumpkin like Cinderella's coach.

But a grown-up swaggered among them and asserted his prerogative.

Thank God, I saw him coming in time to get David out of there.

Quickly, I dug into my pockets until I came up with my last two dollars in change. "Cranberry fritters," I said to David, knowing food was the only bait I could dangle to lure him away. I also knew the cranberry fritter booth was clear across the field on the other side, and that it was so popular it had one of the longest lines of customers at the festival. "For both of us, please."

Still gnawing on his turkey leg, with the walkie-talkie hung on his belt, David ambled off, and I breathed more easily again. I stepped behind a tall man and peeked around him.

"Sorry, boys," said Lew Riss to the ten-year-olds. "I'm next in line."

"No, you're not!" one of them bravely asserted.

Lew ignored the children, who didn't have much choice but to back away from him. I was surprised that none of the adults who were watching objected to his pushiness, but there was certainly something about him now, with all those muscles, that would have made almost anybody hesitant to mess with him. The boys looked terribly resentful, as well they should, and I badly wanted to stand up for their rights, but I didn't think they would benefit from witnessing what Lew might do if he noticed me—and then came looking for David again. They had probably heard worse language and seen worse violence that very morning on television, but still . . .

Lew pulled a chair close to Melissa's chair, smiled knowingly, slouched down in it with his knees wide apart in front of her, and said, "Do me."

She was already picking out a pumpkin, without first examining Lew's head by sight or feel, but I saw her pluck a perfect shape from her pile: angular, aggressive about the "chin" and "brow." Without a word to him, and with a hard line to the set of her mouth, Melissa picked up her knife and quietly began to carve, so that soon an amazing likeness of Lew began to appear in mocking orange. She was capturing something besides the lines of his face: a sly narrowing of the eyes she carved in the pumpkin's face, an arching of the eyebrows that gave Lew's replica just the ugly contemptuous expression he really did have on his face at that moment. A twisting slice imparted the sensuousness of his mouth, and a gouging in of the "cheeks" produced an eerie likeness of his newly-prominent cheekbones. She even captured something of his muscularity of ego and will.

Melissa turned it in her hands until it faced him.

Lew didn't even look at it. He just winked at Melissa, took three dollars out of his wallet, and threw the cash in her money box. "Keep it, honey," he said, clearly enough for anyone to hear. "To remember me by." Then he pushed himself to his feet, turned cockily on the heel of one of his black running shoes, and strutted away, leaving the pumpkin in her lap. It was a shockingly rude act, seeming to come out of nowhere, directed at a total stranger.

Melissa gently placed the sculpted pumpkin on top of her card table so that the shell was facing her. She raised her knife and brought it down violently into Lew's "face."

"Melissa," I whispered, as bits of pumpkin flew. I stepped out from behind the tall man and started toward her. "Melissa, take it easy."

She slashed at the pumpkin, holding the knife, not like an artist but like a soldier, her fist wrapped around the handle, with the strength of her entire arm, of her whole body, behind her blows to the helpless vegetable.

Slash. There went Lew's left eye and part of his cheek.

Slash. There went his nose, sliced in two, and the right side of his sneering mouth.

In the crowd, people were backing away from her. Parents were shielding their children and turning them quickly in the other direction. The boys, Chappie and his friends, were open-mouthed, looking both horrified and fascinated.

I got as close to her as I dared and said her name very clearly and calmly. "Melissa." I said it again. And then one more time.

Finally, she turned a jack-o'-lantern grin on me.

I suppressed a shudder of real fear—at the grin, at the knife grasped high—and took a chance and held out my right hand to her. "Come take a walk with me." When she looked stubborn, I said, "Now." And then, when she did get up from the table, but she still had the weapon clenched tightly in her hand, I added, "Without the knife, please."

We sat on the ground on the back side of the reconstructed schoolhouse, away from the movement of people on the common.

"What happened back there, Melissa?"

She was still trembling, but now tears were flowing, too, and she dabbed at them with the hem of her T-shirt. I offered her a clean tissue, and she took it, murmuring, "Thanks."

She said, "It's what happened a long time ago." For a moment, she just cried, and when they tapered off, she continued: "When there was the original battle over God's Highway? Remember I told you that Ben and I got involved with it?"

"Yes, you told me."

"Lew was a reporter then—"

"Lew! You know him?"

"Know him?" She shuddered, laughed, sobbed. "Oh, yeah, I know him all the ways you can think of. He was the reporter the *Times* sent to cover all the God's Highway battles, and we kept running into him. At protests, at meetings. Sometimes Ben was there. But a lot of the time—"

"He wasn't."

She nodded, looking miserable.

Once I had recovered from the initial surprise of hearing about her connection to Lew, I wasn't shocked so much at her behavior as I was at her execrable taste. I wanted to say to her, "And you call yourself an artist?"

"Lew was cute," she said, "and sexy and he had this vitality and charisma—"

To each her own, I thought, wryly.

"And Ben was quiet and nice and stable and—"

"Boring?"

Again, she nodded. "It sounds so awful to say, I mean, I loved him, I really grew to love him."

Kiss of death, I thought then, to marry somebody you have to "grow to love."

"I think I really did it because all my friends were doing it—"

She told a familiar, depressing story that ended in a confession of the year-long affair she had ten years earlier with Lew Riss.

"He was such an *ass* about it when I told him we had to stop," she said violently. "He claimed he never cared about me, he only did it for the sex, and the thrill of seeing a married woman, and he said he felt sorry for me, because I'd never be able to forget him."

Tactlessly, I laughed. It was so Lew.

Melissa looked up, clearly offended by my reaction.

"Lew is memorable," I conceded, attempting to sound apologetic.

She looked as if she were about to get angry, when she suddenly started to laugh and cry at the same time. "He is, isn't he? I guess he was right about that, in a way. He's just so unforgettably awful."

I thought I understood better now why Melissa's response to Ben's death had been to launch a passionate crusade against the trail crossing where he was killed. And then, sitting there in the calming, comforting shade, she herself confirmed my speculations.

"It was so terrible that Ben died on the trail," she told me, in an emotion-filled voice. "I could hardly believe it. I felt—I feel—like I've been slapped in the face by God. The truth is Ben thought the trail was a nice idea, but he didn't care one way or another about it. We had a good time going to a few protests together, or at least, I did. It was really Lew and I who got behind the trail . . . together. And when that controversy died down, so did we, I guess."

She looked like she could drown in self-pity.

"Sometimes I think Lew and I killed Ben. I mean, if we hadn't used the trail as an excuse to get together, we wouldn't have fought so hard for it, and maybe it would never have been created, and then Ben wouldn't have gone hiking that day, and he wouldn't have died."

Oh, please, I thought unkindly. If God was going to slap her, I thought this was a good time to do it.

"You and Lew didn't create the trail, Melissa. Believe me, there were forces much more powerful than the two of you behind the creation of God's Highway. There'd still be a trail, even if you had never heard of it, or of Lew Riss."

For just the briefest of moments, she looked disillusioned, disappointed. Then relief began to dawn, and I thought I could almost see her shoulders lift from a lightening of the false load of guilt.

"Melissa, have you talked to Lew any other time since he came back to town?"

She nodded. "In fact, you called, right in the middle of his visit. He had the nerve to knock on my door, supposedly to tell me how sorry he felt about Ben's death. Guess what he really wanted?"

"Is that why you sounded so angry when I talked to you?"

She confirmed that it was, and now I also knew, without even having to ask her to confirm it, how Lew had gotten the news so fast that we were going to work on changing that trail crossing. He'd been at her place when I called to tell her! And then he'd gathered his troops for today's protest. Some things, I thought, half-amused, are so easy to understand . . . when you understand them.

She didn't go back to carving pumpkins that day. She also never went back to the cause of improving the trail crossing. Melissa Barney left that in our laps, from that day onward. And I left her, there behind the schoolhouse, after giving her an encouraging pat on her shoulder.

When I got to her abandoned booth, I found disaster brewing.

Lew Riss and Pete Falwell were squared off and glaring at each other, the little boys were gathered around them like an audience at a prize fight, and David was pacing the perimeter like a young lion who can't get in for the kill.

26

My first response was to run for David's walkie-talkie, and when he resisted, I just turned it on and spoke into it at about the level of his hipbone.

"Geof! Bushfield. This is Jenny, come in! Come to the far south end at the pumpkin-carving booth! Do you read, over?"

From the device came an unrecognizable voice. "I'm on my way, Jenny. What's going on? Over."

I yelled at David: "Hold still, dammit!"

"I'll take the damned thing off, if you'll just stop talking to my dick!" he yelled back at me.

"David!"

Eventually, after he managed to remove the walkie-talkie with one hand and gave it to me, I depressed the "talk" button and said in a much quieter tone of voice, "It's not about Tyler, Geof, it's a standoff between Lew Riss and Pete Falwell. They're yelling at each other so loud they can't even hear me. David is also here, waiting to beat Lew to a pulp, and altogether, I'd say we need help. Over."

"Tell David to chill. Over."

I looked at the kid. "Geof says—"

"I heard, I heard."

From across the common trotted the Mounties in the guise of my husband and two of his off-duty cops, both of them women, and all three of them dressed in the casual clothes we'd agreed upon, to make security less obvious, less threatening to the good folks. What they were equipped with in their backpacks, purses, or fanny packs was another story, however: pepper spray, mace, maybe even a gun or two, for all I knew, or wanted to know. We had anticipated no real problems and certainly no violence, mostly because we weren't selling beer or any other inflammatory agents.

Just short of where David and I were, Geof and his all-girl crew slowed to a walk, approaching the two arguing men from an oblique angle. I didn't even have to listen to Lew and Pete to know what their problem was, but as it happened, when they finally spotted me in the crowd, Pete brought the fight directly to my face.

"Jenny Cain! This meathead says you told him we're going to put a light rail line through on the nature trail! Where'd you hear such goddamned nonsense as that?"

Pete advanced on me, his face florid, his body stiff with outrage. Lew stalked right behind him. Beside me, David stiffened. And Geof picked up his pace as he tacked in my direction. I felt like the lone hen at a rooster convention.

I stood my ground and decided to enjoy this.

"In the first place," I said loudly to Pete, "I never mentioned your name, Peter Falwell, in conjunction with light rail on God's Highway. I can't imagine why Lew would think of you in the same context as an avaricious, cunning scheme like that. And in the second place, how can I tell you where I heard it? It's the rumor, Pete, it's the story that's going around. Are you denying it?"

"If I deny it, I will give it more power!" he said, which was a clever dodge, if the idea were true. With that single equivocation, Pete went a long way toward convincing me that it was. "This rumor has to stop."

"Rumor, hell!" Lew said—and then he saw David. But he had to finish his attack on Pete first. "It's true, Falwell. Everything I know about you tells me it's perfect logic. And it won't be hard to find out, either, not for an ex-reporter. I'll just make some calls to the top light rail experts in the country, and find out what sorts of inquiries they've been receiving from around here."

"All right." Pete looked as if he'd like to bite somebody. "So it's true, so it's a damned fine idea, and you and your eco-nuts are not going to keep it from happening!"

"True?" I said.

"True?" echoed David and Lew.

"True?" murmured many others who were listening. "Light rail? On God's Highway?"

As usual, Pete had known instantly when he had lost a battle. Now, I could see from Lew's face that Lew thought the old man had caved in easily; Lew didn't recognize Pete's genius for tactical retreat. Somehow, I knew that Pete Falwell would turn this loss of public face into a public relations—and probably monetary—victory for himself.

I hadn't a single doubt about that.

It was getting harder all the time to continue hating him: He was just so damned interesting an enemy! Superficial and conventional on the outside, but the "fox" of Cleo's I Ching reading on the inside. It wasn't always his goals I hated, anyway, but his means for obtaining them. I suddenly realized I would never really "beat" Pete Falwell at anything, but it didn't really matter anymore. Besides, there was always this: He was old; didn't he have to die, someday?

I wondered if I would miss him.

Nah.

Geof was nudging David out of the scene of combat, and I decided to follow them.

"But—" David protested.

"Lew didn't attack you at the crossroads, Dave," Geof said in a low voice. "They were all down at the Cape picketing a marsh drainage, saving an endangered butterfly."

"Well, shit," David said, but he allowed himself to be moved right along. "If they didn't do it, who did, Geof? Are you sure my uncles—"

"Yes." Geof put an arm around David, taking care not to put pressure where it would hurt. "I am still sure. Listen. Calm down." He glanced at me. "Advice for all of us, all right? Calm down. Those two back there—Pete and Lew—deserve each other. They can take care of their own business. I doubt they'll kill each other, at least not today. So how's about the three of us going to get corn dogs? Let's take it easy for a while."

I smiled at him. "The two of you can. I'm going to see if anybody needs anything I can help with."

But then I changed my mind and went with them. It was time to be nobody but another masked face at the festival. I couldn't think of a better way to spend an hour than to eat a corn dog and to cruise the common with my guys. David didn't even seem to be mad at me anymore; most of the steam had gone out of him when Geof imparted the news that Lew was not guilty of the attack on David.

So we walked. At some point, I started to laugh.

"What?" they asked, as one.

"David," I said, "I was just thinking about how I had to talk to your belt buckle to use the walkie-talkie."

"Geez," he said, and actually blushed.

Geof noticed the blush, with amazement, and he turned to look at me, and he asked, "How'd you do that?"

27

THE SECURITY WAS GOING GREAT, GEOF TOLD US, WHEN WE ALL THREE FOUND empty seats at a picnic table. There had been a few minor fender benders in parking lots, a number of outside drunks, one or two cases of shoplifting.

"But overall, it's a nice crowd," he said. "The weather's helping us. It's not hot enough to fry people's dispositions. It's not cold, which would make them cranky, and it's not rainy, which would complicate traffic."

Neither Geof nor I felt urgently needed anywhere at that moment, so we sat with David, watching the festival-goers. Many folks spoke to us, and several of them delighted in surprising us from behind their masks. "Guess who?" they'd demand, and when we couldn't they happily revealed themselves.

"Everybody's a kid today," I happily observed. Our kid seemed content again to have his mother's name adorn the foundation that sponsored the festival. I hoped he felt proud.

"I wish something would happen," David complained, while I was having those sentimental ideas. "Like somebody would shoot off a gun, or something."

"Why would you wish for that?" I asked him, appalled.

"So then I could say, 'Who *was* that masked man'?"

We all laughed at that memory of the Lone Ranger.

About a half hour into our sojourn, I pointed out Nellie Kennedy in the crowd to Geof. He looked, then did a double take.

"Oh, no," he said softly.

He stood up, looking unhappy.

When I asked him what was wrong, he looked down sadly at me and said, "You know how I told you that Meryl Tyler hired himself a damn fine attorney? That's the guy. Talking to Nellie."

Shocked, I turned to stare.

They weren't just chatting as strangers might. No, Nellie and the attorney were standing close together, deep in apparently serious conversation. To my dismay, she touched the man's arm, patting it in a way that looked friendly, even encouraging.

The owner of the burned Dime Store . . . talking to, encouraging, the defense lawyer for the man suspected of that same act of arson and homicide?

"Oh, my God, Geof." I looked up at him. "She can't have had anything to do with it! If she did, surely she wouldn't be seen talking to the arsonist's lawyer in public!"

"Jenny." He looked loath to move. "We couldn't figure out where the money came from to hire his guy, or to spring Tyler. Meryl hasn't got that kind of dough, or those kinds of friends. Somebody hired this guy for him."

I put my head in my hands.

"Well," Geof sighed. "I guess I've got to take Nellie in and ask her some questions." One more sigh, and he was gone to his nasty duty. David wanted to know—right then, that instant—what the trouble was, but I was feeling too much inner turmoil to tell him.

"Too many people around," I hedged. "I'll tell you when I can. David, look, I know you're supposed to stick with me, but I have to go to the toilet."

He held up his hands. "You're on your own."

"I'll be right back."

I meant it, too, but I didn't count on seeing Cleo Talbot wandering among the cars in a parking lot near the facilities. When I saw her, I felt pulled in her direction and forgot all about my promise to David.

"Cleo?"

She glanced up. Her face wasn't flushed, like almost everyone else's was from the sun and the excitement. Hers looked pale, her eyes looked weary. She wore a T-shirt, jeans, and sneakers, like me.

"Hi, Jenny," she said, sounding as tired as she looked.

I felt at a loss as to what to say next to her. But—as the extraordinary sensitive she was—Cleo noticed my confusion. Her face changed, sagged somehow, and everything I had looked for, but hadn't seen in her before—the terrible sadness, the pain—was all there, visible at last.

"You know?" she asked me.

I stepped toward her. "Yes. Cleo—"

"Don't say it."

She looked away, squinting at the setting sun. It was late, getting on toward twilight. Then she pointed, but I didn't understand what she was pointing at, at first. "In an impact," Cleo said, "between a car and a human body, imprints can be left in some fabrics. Like leather. Or vinyl. An entire license plate can be imprinted into the clothes the person is wearing."

Now I understood: She was pointing at a license plate on a car.

"It had been raining," she said. "Elena had on her favorite raincoat. It was a yellow vinyl slicker. When it stopped raining, she didn't want to take it off.

"So when he hit her, the license plate number was pressed into Elena's slicker."

I said, "Cleo, there is no license plate number in the police report."

"No." Cleo looked carefully at the backs of cars as they drove past us. "I took her slicker off her, before anybody got there. Because I couldn't hold her properly while she had it on. I wanted to feel her close to me.

"I still had it with me—the slicker—when they took me back to my car. We had driven in that day, just to bike the trail together. We thought it would be fun in the rain, God knows why. It was harder to do, for her, than I realized it would be. I had thought it was a paved trail, but of course it's dirt, which made it harder for her to pedal.

"I think that's why she rode out on the highway without stopping. She'd finally gotten up a good speed, and she was too excited to stop. Or, maybe she didn't even see the road. I didn't see it, myself, in time to stop her.

"So then, afterwards, I was back in my car, and my daughter's body was in a mortuary in a town I'd never been to before, and it was so strange. There she'd been with me in the other seat of our car that morning, just a few hours before, and now I was alone in the car, and my daughter was dead.

"And there was this slicker on my lap. When I turned it over, I saw the number imprinted. I knew, right then, I knew I'd never give it to the police. I knew it was my task to search for him, and then it would be my responsibility to decide what to do about him.

"I never went back home at all, Jenny. I never did. I called." She laughed, an odd, strangled sound. "And I told my parents what had happened, and I said, I can't drive back without her. I just can't. And they were unbelievably understanding, and they didn't ask me to do what I couldn't do. They said, we'll take care of everything. Elena and I lived with them. They said, we'll come to you. They said, stay there, we're coming down there to be with both of you.

"So they did, my wonderful mom and dad, and other friends have also come to see me, but nobody can convince me to go back without her."

After a moment, when I was sure she was finished talking, I said, "You got the job as delivery woman—"

"Yes, so I could have a good reason to drive everywhere looking for that license plate. I got a private investigator to look it up in the motor vehicle registry, and I know his name, Jenny, and lots of other things about him."

"Tell me?"

"His name is Johnny Vaught, and he's forty-nine years old. He's an alcoholic, and he's got a criminal record for a whole bunch of stuff. He's not married, never has been married, no children of his own. At the time he killed Elena, he didn't have a job, and he was on probation."

"If you know who he is—"

"And I know his address."

"Then why—"

She looked over at me, with an unreadable expression. "Why haven't I confronted him? Or turned him in? Because nobody has seen him since the accident. Nobody's heard from John Vaught since the day he killed my daughter."

That surprised me so much that for a moment I couldn't even think. But then I said, "Cleo, doesn't that probably mean he just kept on driving, that he left this town, and probably even left this part of the country?"

She shook her head. "My private investigator is good at finding people. My parents helped me get enough money together to hire the best one we could find—we saw him profiled on television, he's so famous. He's *good,* and he swears Vaught has never surfaced anywhere."

"Then he could be dead, couldn't he?"

"Where's his body? Where's the car? Why doesn't anybody who knows him know that he's dead? Our investigator believes he's still alive. I think he hid the car. If I keep searching, eventually I'll find it."

With those words, I was suddenly not only distressed, but also frightened for her. This was an impossible, possibly insane obsession. The investigator should have discouraged her. Her parents should have stopped her. But then, I realized: Who could? There'd been a terrible time in my own life after my mother died, when I had been similarly obsessed with finding "truth." And, I had to admit, I had found it, against all odds. Maybe Cleo could, too.

I didn't know anything to say, except, "Can I help you?"

She smiled that wise, compassionate smile that belonged on the face of a much older woman, not on one who was still so young. "Actually, you have, all of you. You've treated me like a normal person. You've let me think I could have a life with friends in it someday. Just . . ." Her smile faded. "Not yet."

"I didn't have any idea," I admitted.

"Don't feel bad, nobody ever does. I work really hard at accepting it all, and you'd be surprised how often I actually feel a little peace. First, it was only maybe one second out of an entire week, but now it's sometimes several minutes at a time, maybe even half an hour, usually on a day when I've been really busy and people have been really sweet. This is a nice town, you know? People are really nice. Without even knowing the truth about me, you're all so patient and friendly to me."

"But that's you, Cleo. You're kind of a remarkable person."

"Oh, no, I'm not."

There wasn't any point in arguing that, but I was right: If people were unusually sweet to her, it was because she inspired that kind of response.

"Sometimes lately, I feel comforted," she said, "as if Elena is still here, somehow. And sometimes—quite a lot of the time—I just feel, well, this is the way my life is, and I have to accept that. But that's only sometimes. Most of the time, I miss her so much, and it just about killed my parents, and it's so awful—"

She stopped talking and just looked at passing cars.

"But one thing I can't surrender," she finally said, "is my need to find him. It's my job. I have to do that, and I'm not even sure exactly why anymore, because it's not as if it would bring her back to me."

Dimly, I'd been hearing the loudspeaker from the festival. Now it sunk in that it was saying my name.

Cleo and I both heard it at the same time.

"Jenny Cain! Come to the front gate immediately! Jenny Cain, please come to—"

We weren't very far away from the gate.

I was surprised when Cleo kept me company as I turned and walked that way. I was glad she did, though, because that meant I didn't have to abandon her when what I really wanted to do was to take her hands and hold them. I stepped in close to her and put my arm around her shoulders as we strode together toward the "witches."

"Jenny!" It was an elderly "witch," one of the volunteer ticket takers, who ran up to us. I took my arm away from Cleo, but she stayed close to me. "The most awful thing just happened. My ticket bag fell off my belt someplace between here and the portable toilets, and I've looked and looked, but I can't find it!"

What she was referring to was a big black cotton drawstring pouch that was issued to every ticket-dispensing witch at the entrance gate. Inside each pouch was a precounted roll of entrance tickets—they were orange and looked just like old movie theater tickets—that the witches threaded out one at a time through the opening in the pouch. It had been a clever idea cooked up by our volunteers, who'd also sewn the bags and stuffed them.

If a pouch went missing, it meant we'd be vulnerable to scalpers who might sell the tickets—at six bucks per adult—to tourists who wouldn't know the tickets were worthless unless they were punched at the time of sale. Tourists also might not know that children were supposed to get in free. It wasn't the worst thing that could happen, but it wasn't great, either.

"Did you notify security?" I asked her.

"We thought we should tell you first, Jenny."

Too bad, I thought, since Geof's security guards might already have spotted the pouch, if they'd only been told to look for it.

"I'm so sorry!" She seemed upset out of all proportion to the problem.

"Don't worry," I tried to reassure her. "Obviously, our foolproof system of tying the bags to your belts wasn't really foolproof. It's not your fault."

"But Jenny!" Tears came to her eyes. "I put my belongings in there. My billfold, with some cash, and my driver's license and my credit cards are all there—"

I began to comprehend her dismay.

"And my wedding rings," she said, topping off the bad news. And then she burst into tears. "They were snagging on my costume, so I took them off. I never dreamed—oh, Jenny, I have to have them back! They were my late husband's grandmother's rings, and they mean everything to me." Through her tears, she added, "I'd better tell you that they're worth a lot of money. There's forty-thousand-dollars' worth of diamond rings in that bag!"

I could have happily hung that witch, right there on the common.

Instead, I asked her to jot down for me a rough estimate of the number of tickets she'd already torn off, and to go around and warn the other witches to double-check the security of their ticket pouches. Then I asked her to walk me along the path she'd taken when it disappeared. Cleo came along with us, and I alerted every security guard I saw to be on the watch for somebody carrying it.

"Maybe," Cleo suggested, "it just got buried over with leaves."

It wasn't going to be easy to see, if it was still on the ground, especially with evening coming on. After we three had carefully shuffled and kicked our way back to the toilets, I picked my way around back of them, because the lightweight bag could have gotten kicked back there by a succession of unwary feet. With my head bent to the task, I wouldn't even have noticed the boys, if one of them hadn't made the mistake of yelling, "Oh, geez, it's her!"

I looked up.

There was the little band of ten-year-olds, all masked, now surrounding a boy on a bicycle. I heard one of them yell, "Go! Go! Before she catches you! Go, Chappie!" The little gang broke apart, and there was the lone bike rider—Chappie, in a silver half-mask—and I saw something black and weighted hanging from his handlebars. He took off pedaling as if demons were chasing him.

"Wait!" I shouted, as I started running. "Chappie, wait! It's okay, just . . . wait!" When I reached the other kids, they were already scattering away from me, but one of them didn't move fast enough. I nabbed him by the back of his T-shirt.

"Whoa, big fella. What's the deal?"

He looked more defiant than scared.

"You messed things up for Chappie's grandpa!" he said, glaring at me in spite of his fear. "Chappie says his grandpa says you'll be the ruin of this town. Chappie says his grandpa says everything you do costs him money, and causes trouble, and somebody ought to stop you! So we grabbed that lady's tickets when they fell off, and Chappie says he's going to throw them away, so it'll hurt this festival, 'cause you hurt his grandpa!"

"What's he planning to do with the bag?"

"He's going to throw it in the river!"

"River? There wasn't any real river around here, but then I thought: *Crowley Creek.*

I released the boy, who ran after his friends.

Cleo, who'd come trotting up and heard the whole thing, said, "Jenny, the kid's on God's Highway. I'm going to stop him."

The other boys had abandoned their bikes, which were more or less propped against the back of the reconstructed church. Cleo grabbed one of them and hopped onto it. It was only after she rode off that I realized something she didn't seem to know: Chappie wouldn't be aware that she was chasing him to try to help him; he'd think she was coming to get him—to arrest him, no doubt, to his kid's mind—so he'd only pedal faster and faster to try to get away from her.

"Cleo!" I shouted futilely at her back.

I faced the inevitable: I, who had not mounted a bicycle since I was thirteen years old, was going to have to get on one, and a stolen one at that. I plucked a green one out of the pile and swung a leg over. I wobbled a lot at first, but then it was fairly easy to ride. Since the bike was a little too small for me, I felt more in control of it than I would have on a full-sized adult bike. When I had last ridden a bike, it had one gear and foot brakes; this thing had sprockets galore and slender silver handbrakes, and I could only hope I wouldn't end up going ass over handlebars.

28

GOD'S HIGHWAY WAS NOT, AS CLEO HERSELF HAD EARLIER POINTED OUT, paved. It was hard, packed, somewhat rocky earth. It was regularly used as a bike path, however, so it wasn't all that difficult to navigate—except that bikers usually didn't have to pedal at top speed, didn't have to dodge festival patrons, and also had probably actually been *on* a bike sometime in their previous twenty-five years of life.

There was actually no speeding for me until I got the full hang of it and I ran out of crowds. By the time that happened, I was on my way out of town, with no sight of either of the bikers ahead of me. No Cleo, no Chappie.

Dammit, Pete, I thought, *why'd you have to do that? Why couldn't you keep your mouth shut around the child?*

The trail took me through gentle glide slopes and around wide turns —nothing challenging to somebody accustomed to it. But my breath was already coming hard, and my legs were sending up notice that they weren't going to be good for twenty miles of this.

Crowley Creek wound along near the old railroad bed for much of its route in Port Frederick, but there were only a few places where there was easy biking access from the trail to the water. All but one of those places lay behind us, in the direction the boy had not taken. The only other good spot to stop, bike down to a bridge, and toss something into the water, was at the trail crossing near Nellie's house.

At that precise moment, with that realization, an irrational fear—at least, I hoped it was irrational—began to seize me. The farther I pedaled—my lungs and my legs protesting more and more—the greater became the fear, until I felt nearly sick from it.

No. Nothing bad was going to happen. I said that and other reassurances to myself in time to the wheels.

"Oh, Chappie," I cried to the wind, "Please, please stop."

He didn't stop.

But he must have tired and slowed, because about a mile from the trail crossing—when the only thing keeping my legs moving was dread—I could see the back of Cleo's T-shirt.

Somehow, I pedaled faster. And then I saw the back of Chappie's shirt. He was bent over his handlebars, pumping like mad, his ten-year-old legs probably used to soccer and basketball and baseball and probably not even tired.

The crossing was a half mile away. Or less.

"Cleo!" The shout wouldn't leave my lungs. "Cleo!" It was only a faint cry. "Stop! Don't force him into the crossing!"

She never heard me.

There was a child ahead of her, and she was going to "save" him.

I started praying, even as I pedaled. "Please, please, don't let him get hurt. Nobody hit him! Oh, please." I thought of the sweet face looking hesitantly up at me from inside his grandfather's car . . . of how he had made a funny face when I said there would be arts and crafts at the fair . . . of how he laughed when I joked that we'd have to get in lots more food to feed him and his friends . . . of how scared and upset he was when Pete had knocked me over.

The three of us came flying around the last bend before the crossing, flying through the warm and dark gold and purple light cast through the leaves by the setting sun. The shadows were long now, and it was hard to see the bumps and rocks in our path. I prayed for a rock to spring up in Chappie's path, for his bike tires to bend askew and send him sprawling. A broken arm, even a bump on his head, was preferable to—

"Stop!" Faintly, Cleo's cry floated back to me. I heard desperation in it. She'd finally recognized the real danger. By trying to catch him and to save him from getting into big trouble, she could—we could—drive him pell-mell, heedless, into the highway, into the path of anything that was coming down the hill from Nellie's house.

Cleo screamed and screamed.

The boy rode on.

Toward the opening in the trees, he flew. And then, when he was almost on top of it, he seemed to see or to sense danger, because his bike suddenly began a sideways slip. Sliding, sliding, he was going down, down toward the highway pavement.

And then I saw that Chappie hadn't braked because of the highway. He was trying to stop because there was a person lying across the trail, right at the highway's edge.

Chappie's bike struck a *person* lying there.

I saw the boy fly off his bike and land on top of the person, whose body lay in the way. He—a small, raggedly dressed, filthy-looking man—put up his arms to shield his face from the boy and the bike, but they hit him hard.

Chappie tumbled off, then quickly picked himself up and started to run.

"My God! Stop!" I screamed it.

Cleo was off her bike already and racing toward him.

But it was the man—the stranger—who flung himself toward the boy and the highway first. He grabbed Chappie, lifted him off his feet, and threw him back onto the trail, practically into Cleo's arms. Then the man, stumbling from the force of his own efforts, fell into a crouched position in the road.

Chappie lay in the dirt and started to cry.

Cleo was crying, too, as she knelt beside him.

So I was the only one left to witness the accident.

Dumping the bike I'd been on, I trotted up to Cleo and the boy, and then started to step toward the stranger to see if he needed help. But just as I neared the asphalt, I heard an engine. I looked up to the top of the hill. A pickup truck was cresting it, right where the stop sign should have been visible, but I couldn't see the sign. Something long and brown covered it from the top down. And so the truck drove on, never stopping, picking up speed as it came on down the hill toward us.

When I looked back, the man who had seized Chappie was still in the middle of the road, still down on his knees and his hands, as if he were hurt or winded, or both.

I screamed at him to move.

When he didn't, I stepped into the road to wave down the truck.

I could see the driver clearly, but I realized the setting sun was directly in his eyes. When he didn't slow down, I knew he couldn't see us. Suddenly, I felt hands on me, and—like Chappie—I was shoved violently out of the way.

Even as I rolled to safety, I saw it happen:

The grill of the pickup truck struck the stranger full on his chest, pushing him forward and then down, and then rolling horribly over his body.

The truck driver, realizing he'd hit something, pulled to a stop, opened his door, and let out an anguished cry when he saw what he'd done. In the road, the stranger pulled himself up, and dragged himself like a mortally wounded creature to the side of the road, and plunged into the trees. We all heard him crashing through the brush.

None of us could seem to move to help him.

Cleo was still hovering over the boy.

I was stunned and hurting, and the truck driver looked paralyzed with shock. He said to me in a horrified voice, "I didn't see anybody! The sun was in my eyes! I didn't see anything in the road!"

Cleo was the first of us to get up and to go after the man.

For a few moments, I still couldn't seem to move, and even then I felt compelled to go to Chappie first. "Honey . . ." I crawled into the leaves near him. "I'm so sorry this happened to you. Listen, you're not in any trouble with me, or anybody else. I know you were only trying to help your grandpa, and I don't blame you at all. And everything's going to be all right, really it is."

"I made that man get hit!" he exclaimed.

"No, no! It wasn't you! It was the sun in the driver's eyes."

"Really, it was?" Chappie's face crumpled up, and he started to cry again. "I'm really sorry. I was just—"

I put my arms around him and held him and stroked away the bits of leaves that clung to his face. "I know, it's okay, you just wanted to help your grandpa, because you thought I was mean to him, right?"

He looked up at my face. "Were you?"

I smiled a little. "Let's say that your grandpa and I are not best friends. But I know you love him, and I would never want to hurt a boy's grandpa. Besides, he's a big guy. Don't you think he can probably take care of himself?"

He nodded, with more tears. But he also said, "I really knew you were okay. I did. I just saw the bag—"

"Never mind." I crooned. "We can talk about it later, if you want to, or we can forget it. Now, stay right here and wait for us, okay? I want to go check on that man, okay? Promise me you'll stay here?"

"Yeah. My bike's broken anyway," he said sadly.

When I stepped back onto the highway, I saw that the driver had not been helpless. He had parked off the road, then used a telephone in his vehicle.

"I called 911," he informed me. "Goddamn, you think I killed him? What was he doing in the middle of the road, anyway? What's the matter with the boy? What the hell's going on here?"

"Let's go look for him and my friend," I said. "And I'll tell you."

We scrambled about a quarter mile through thick brush, with him leading the way and pushing branches back out of the way for me. In the very thickest of the woods, in between the trail and the creek bed, we followed a faint path down a slope and came upon a strange sight.

There, in the dark recess of the trees and earth, was a junk pile, with Cleo and the injured stranger in the middle of it. The man lay huddled into himself, on his side. Cleo sat cross-legged about five feet away from him, watching him. She looked up, acknowledged our arrival with a nod of her head, but then went back to watching him.

Then I realized it was not a junk pile that surrounded us—it was a kind of camp, artfully constructed to look like nothing more than junk and litter mostly covered by leaves and dirt. I saw fresh food—one whole grocery bag of it, in fact—and various plates and cups and pots and pans that looked as if they had come from many different kitchens. It looked to me as if we had found the Ghost of God's Highway. But then I saw that we had found much more than that.

Stuck back in the farthest recess of the earth, nearly invisible in the growing darkness of the twilight hour, there was a black Volkswagen Beetle car.

Cleo saw me staring at it.

The truck driver, who had run directly to the stranger's side, looked up now and said, in a stunned, emotional voice, "He's dead. He's dead." The driver stood up slowly, wiped his nose with the back of his hand, and told us he would go back up to the highway to wait with the boy for the arrival of the emergency vehicles.

"It wasn't your fault," I said as he trudged past me. "We'll tell them so."

Cleo was silent until he was gone back up through the brush.

Then she said, "He told me he got caught in the flooding that day. The water came up over the bridge and washed him downstream, and the car lodged up there. And he stayed here. He knew what he'd done. He knew he didn't have anyplace to run to, and he figured he'd hide here, until they found him. Only, they never did.

"He must have gone a little crazy, because he got the idea that he should save people from getting killed on the highway. He would make voices at the edge of the trail to startle them, so they'd stop and notice the highway. One time he saw a teenager on a motorcycle try to hit a woman on the road, so he blocked the highway to trap the motorcycle rider, and then he beat him up."

My God, I thought, and I stared at the healing abrasion on the back of my hand. *That woman was me, that teen was David.*

Cleo's voice was quiet, calm. She looked at me, and I came and joined her there on the ground. "He wanted to atone," she said.

"He told you that?"

"Not that. The rest of it. I just think that's what he wanted."

There were questions I wanted to ask her. In the near distance, I heard sirens. It was now quite dark in Johnny Vaught's junky campground by the creek.

"You probably want to know," she said, "if I could have saved him."

"Cleo—"

"I let him tell me. That's what I did. He asked me who I was."

"Did you tell him?"

"Yes. He asked for forgiveness."

I waited for her to tell me if she gave it to him, but she never did say. Before the police came down, however, she reached into the fanny pack she had on at her waist and pulled out her rune bag. She reached into it and pulled one out and looked at it. When she saw that side was blank, she turned it over, but the other side was empty, too. Cleo walked over to the stranger and slipped the rune into one of the pockets of his dirty jacket.

After the police had taken over the camp and the body . . . after I had used the truck driver's car phone to locate Chappie's mom and dad to tell them he was on his way home . . . after Cleo and I had bundled the boy into a police car (very thrilled and not at all intimidated) and she got in with him . . . after I had told all that I had seen and heard . . . after I'd asked them to hide the bikes someplace safe until we could come back for them . . . and after they'd taken custody of the valuable black pouch . . . after all that, I gratefully accepted a ride, but only as far as Nellie and Bill Kennedy's house.

As we crested the hill, I saw Nellie pulling into her driveway, with a Jeep right behind her.

"You can let me out here," I told the cops.

I walked up the driveway, past Bill Kennedy, who—wearing house slippers and a cardigan buttoned wrong over a white shirt and Bermuda shorts—was raking leaves onto a large brown tarp that was spread flat on the ground.

I didn't say anything to him, and he didn't look up.

Most of the leaves he was raking were flying away in the breeze. It was a strange time to be raking, because twilight had already surrendered completely to the night.

I left him there, raking in the dark.

At the Jeep, Geof was waiting, and he said, "I was just about to put out an all-points bulletin on you. David thinks you've been kidnapped."

As we walked together up to Nellie's back door, I told him all that had happened on the trail, and then I asked, "What about Nellie?"

We went into her kitchen before he could tell me.

I wanted to tell Nellie about the "Ghost," and his death, but she was sitting at the kitchen table, quietly crying. I was, myself, too tired and hurting to do much more than sit down beside her and cover one of her hands with one of mine. I looked up at Geof, waiting for him to explain, but all he did was sit down there with us, until finally he said, "Bill set the fire, Jenny."

Nellie looked at me out of eyes as anguished as those of the driver of the pickup truck. "Bill's been getting sick. His thinking, his talking, even the way he walks. It's all gotten . . . sick. Ardyth told me I was imagining it, she won't believe me when I try to tell her how strange he's become. The way he doesn't make any sense in what he says. He can't even dress himself right." Tears fell down her cheeks. "Did you see him outside? The way he's dressed? Raking leaves in the dark?"

I nodded, filled with sadness for them all.

"I knew it was Bill who set the fire, because I caught him with a candle and matches in his hands. But Ardyth wouldn't believe her dad could do that. She said it would ruin her election chances if her dad got arrested for arson."

Nellie paused to wipe her eyes on her sleeve.

The gesture reminded me of the truck driver, who had also wiped his eyes, and who would forever be haunted by the ghost he had killed—because Nellie didn't have the courage to face the terrible truth about Bill, not any more than their daughter did. If Ardyth had denied it, so, too, had her mother.

"I couldn't tell anybody that Bill did it, but I couldn't let that innocent man go to jail, either," she said.

"Meryl Tyler, you mean?" I asked her. When she nodded, I said, "Nellie, does Bill have Alzheimer's?"

"He's only fifty-seven years old!" she cried, as if that were an answer. "I'm only fifty-six! It can't be that, it can't!"

Geof and I glanced at each other, knowing it could be, or if not Alzheimer's, then some other dreadful, similar form of dementia. Geof said quietly to me, "Bill hallucinated the intruders. He thought people were in the house, and that Nellie was one of them, and he started hitting her."

"He didn't know who I was," she said, sobbing. "And then when I convinced him, he tried so hard to be sane. He was so frightened and so brave, and he's been trying so hard to hold himself together for me and for Ardie. I'm tough on him, I shouldn't be. I know I snap at him sometimes. But he does the craziest things, like order things we don't even sell, or ship the wrong things off to customers, like that hideous tarantula you got. I always tried to keep him out of the way of the shipping clerks, but sometimes he'd get in their way. I get so frustrated, and I keep thinking if he'd just try harder . . . but he does try, he does."

That was when I had to tell them both what I thought I had learned that evening.

"Nellie," I began, "when there was that wreck last winter and I stopped here while Geof went down the hill to help, your Christmas tree was lying across your driveway and I drove over it. I thought Bill had dragged it there for the garbage collectors to pick up, but that wasn't it, was it? Bill had propped that tree in front of the stop sign, hadn't he? And so a driver missed seeing it, and ran the sign, and that's what caused the wreck . . ."

I looked at Geof.

That death was the first, and it was a death we had all practically forgotten about—an anonymous somebody, whether a driver or a passenger in one of the cars that crashed that snowy night—and whose name probably none of us even knew.

"No!" Nellie shook her head violently.

Geof was watching, carefully.

"Well, that's only my guess, Nellie," I admitted. "But I know that Bill's tarp was draped over the stop sign tonight when a pickup truck ran it—"

She gasped and uttered a little scream. "Oh, no!"

"Nellie," I said, "what really happened when the little Talbot girl died and when Ben Barney was killed?"

The kitchen clock ticked and ticked until she gave up entirely.

"When the child died . . . that evening . . . it was a Sunday, and we were home," she said, completely defeated. "Bill was out mowing the yard. When I heard a woman screaming, and I ran outside, I saw at once that he had draped his jacket over the stop sign, while he was mowing. I took it down before I even went down the hill, and I never told him what he had done. I thought he never had to know, that no one did, because it was a hit-and-run, and because it would have killed him to know he had hurt a child."

Geof said, "And Ben Barney?"

She took a tremulous breath. "I'd been so careful with Bill. I suspected about the Christmas tree—" She looked at me, and I saw the shock of truth in her eyes. "I thought maybe he had propped it against the sign, and then it had fallen over, but I only knew for sure about the child. I didn't think anything so horrible could ever happen again, but I watched him anyway. Except that day. I was sick, I don't know what it was, the flu, and I told him to stay in the house, but he always wants to be helpful." Her face collapsed in grief, and she struggled to go on. "While I was asleep, he went outside to dig out the ditches along the side of our driveway. And only God will ever know what there was in his poor confused mind that made him do it, but he took one of the black leaf bags and he put it over the stop sign."

And Dorothy Wilheim—the sun in her eyes, entranced by the view—had driven on through to a fatal collision with Benjamin Barney.

"That driver faces serious charges," Geof commented, and for the first time I heard undertones of anger in his voice.

"You tried to help her, too," I said, thinking of how Dorothy Wilheim had told me that it was Nellie who provided her lawyer's name. But I knew that nothing could alter the fact that Nellie had allowed Wilheim to suffer in order to protect Bill and her own family, and that she had caused terrible suffering for Melissa Barney, her boys, poor Cleo, even the "Ghost" and the man who hit and killed him. David, too. Even Meryl Tyler.

"Forgive Bill," Nellie sobbed. "God forgive me."

There wasn't much doubt about God, I thought, as I put my hand over hers again, but what about the law?

Epilogue

"THE LAW WILL NOT BE SO FORGIVING," WAS GEOF'S PREDICTION.

Ardyth had come out to the Kennedys' house to be with her parents; lawyers and prosecutors were notified, and soon they would begin the long, terrible process of legal unraveling. As for us, we drove into town and parked in front of the common, to watch my cleanup crews prepare the grounds for the final day of the festival.

"It's really sad, Geof."

"For a lot of people besides the Kennedys," he reminded me, but of course I knew that. After a moment, he touched my shoulder. "Still think you'll do a second annual?"

"Festival? You bet."

"Will it be anything like this one?"

"I certainly hope not," I said, and he laughed.

We couldn't sit close together, so we settled for holding hands over the gearshift, while we watched the moon rise.

"How did our ghost manage to blockade the highway?" I wondered, marveling at the seemingly impossible feat of timing.

"He had time," Geof observed. "The highway signs were already there, off the road and ready to use. I'd guess he put up the one by the bridge first—"

"While I was talking to David."

"—because that was the direction he thought David would go."

"So then when David gave me a ride back up the hill, instead—"

"Our ghost only had to run up there behind the cover of the woods and pull out the other highway signs."

"He just wanted to halt David long enough to attack him, I guess. We really had him running."

"Guilt's a hard driver."

Cleo Talbot gave me a set of runes for Christmas that year.

I looked up, in the book that came with them, the name and explanation of the blank rune that she had slipped into Johnny Vaught's jacket pocket before his body was removed from his camp. Its name was: *Odin: the divine.* It was a talisman and a meditation for the spiritual warrior who steps alone into the unknown. After the festival, I finally remembered to pick up those photos I had taken at the crossing the day Mary and I went for our walk. In one of them I thought I saw the back of a ragged man as he slipped off into the woods with a cellophane-wrapped egg salad sandwich in his hand.